Christmas Delights

Also by Heather Hiestand

The Marquess of Cake

One Taste of Scandal

His Wicked Smile

The Kidnapped Bride
(novella)

Christmas Delights

THE REDCAKES

HEATHER HIESTAND

KENSINGTON BOOKS
KENSINGTON PUBLISHING CORP.
www.kensingtonbooks.com

KENSINGTON BOOKS are published by

Kensington Publishing Corp.
119 West 40th Street
New York, NY 10018

All Kensington titles, imprints, and distributed lines are available at special quantity discounts for bulk purchases for sales promotion, premiums, fund-raising, educational, or institutional use.

Special book excerpts or customized printings can also be created to fit specific needs. For details, write or phone the office of the Kensington Special Sales Manager: Kensington Publishing Corp., 119 West 40th Street, New York, NY 10018. Attn. Special Sales Department. Phone: 1-800-221-2647.

First Electronic Edition: November 2014
eISBN-13: 978-1-60183-258-0
eISBN-10: 1-60183-258-3

First Print Edition: November 2014
ISBN-13: 978-1-60183-259-7
ISBN-10: 1-60183-259-1

Printed in the United States of America

In memory of my grandmother Mildred Ruhoff and her Christmas fudge which always helped make the holidays special for our family.

Acknowledgments

Thank you to Eilis Flynn, Mary Jo Hiestand, Delle Jacobs, Judy Laik, and Jacquie Rogers for your critique assistance and support. Thank you to my boys for making Christmas a time of wonder and excitement.

CHAPTER 1

December 22, 1889

"I'll tell you a story while we wait for the carriage," said Victoria, Lady Allen-Hill. "Once upon a time, long ago, in the south of England, a princess was left behind to guard the family castle while her father was at war in France."

"Is this the castle where we're spending Christmas?" Penelope Courtnay asked from her seat against the wall in Redcake's tearoom. Cutouts of Father Christmas dangled on green ribbons above her head, dancing against the wall as waitresses called cakies walked around briskly, serving customers.

"Yes. Though it was in sorry shape in those days." Victoria had to bend over the table to be heard through the din of patrons clattering teacups against saucers and talking excitedly about holiday plans.

"Continue," said Penelope.

Victoria thought her nine-year-old cousin sounded very grown-up, but then, she had little experience with children. "Very well. This princess, Everilda by name, had spent the beginning of winter stuffing herself with all sorts of game, every bird that could be slaughtered, bread, and frumenty. She'd made herself so ill that when a strange old serving woman approached the dais of her father's great hall on Christmas Day, with the first mince pie of the Twelve Days, she refused to eat any of it.

"Her retainers looked nervous. The chamberlain bent over her shoulder and whispered, 'Princess Everilda, it is bad luck to refuse mince pie.'

"'Oh good heavens,' the princess said. 'Here, serving wench, bring me your pie.'

"The woman approached, offering her enormous pie with trembling arms. Princess Everilda stuck in her spoon and pulled out a steaming mass of liberally spiced shredded meat and apple. While she had never heard of the chamberlain's superstition before, she did know you were supposed to make a wish with your first bite of Christmas mince pie. So she closed her eyes and wished for a husband to take all the cares of running the castle away from her. Thankfully, this was a reasonable wish, as she was betrothed to none other than her beloved, after overcoming a number of obstacles.

"No sooner had she swallowed her first bite when the old woman dropped the mince pie on the long table in front of the princess. She seemed to grow before the princess's very eyes, until she stood upright, much younger than she had seemed, and now dressed regally.

"'Queen Avice!' the princess shouted in horror. It was her stepmama, returned from the grave."

"Ewww," Penelope said, then coughed as her soup went down the wrong way.

Victoria stood and patted her on the back. "You have to expect ghosts in fairy tales."

"And wishes," her cousin added with another cough.

"Exactly." She reseated herself.

Penelope took a sip of milk. "I'm fine. Go on. We still have lots of time before we have to go to the train station."

Victoria nodded. "The shade cackled and pointed her finger at the princess. 'Twelve times shall the clock turn round and round before you find your love. Strife and spice, mummery and magic, ghosts and goblins, quests and questions shall fill your days and nights.'"

"My goodness, what a stirring tale!" exclaimed Penelope. "Are you just making this up as you go?"

"I'm glad you like it," Victoria said. She was enjoying her story spinning. "Yes, it is my own creation."

"Will you tell me more? I'll try to be quiet."

"Finish your soup," Victoria told her young cousin. "Redcake's makes the most delicious cream of broccoli."

"Why didn't you want any?" Penelope asked, spooning up a glistening green-speckled spoonful.

"I'm reducing," Victoria said mournfully.

"Haven't you reduced enough? Why, you are entirely a different shape than you were on your wedding day."

"From the mouths of babes," Victoria said, raising an eyebrow. Was her cousin correct? Had she beaten her unruly curves into submission?

"I could never say no to a bun," her cousin said.

"Not at Redcake's, certainly," Victoria murmured. "They make the best in London." She sighed and looked down at the crumbs of her abstemious plate of clear chicken soup and single slice of gingerbread.

"I expect, now that's it's been almost a year and a half since Sir Humphrey died, you'll want to find another husband. Is that why you're reducing? You didn't have trouble finding your first husband."

"My father found him for me," she said. A cakie leaned over their table and lifted the lid of their teapot, then poured in more steaming water.

"Didn't you like him?" Penelope's forehead wrinkled. She was much too young to understand the complicated getting of titled husbands.

"I hardly had the time to discover whether I did or not. He died so soon after the wedding." Victoria smiled her thanks to the cakie.

"You didn't even know if you liked being married or not," Penelope stated.

"Exactly." Sir Humphrey had been red-faced and sniffling on their wedding day. By the next night, he'd had a fever. A week later, his cold had gone into his chest. Bronchitis followed, then pneumonia. He'd left her, his still-virgin bride, for a permanent home in Highgate Cemetery less than a month after their wedding. She'd always wondered if she'd been more physically appealing, would he have managed to consummate the thing on that first night, before he'd become too ill. As it was, she'd been denied the mysteries of physical love.

Penelope spooned up her last bite of soup, then cut her scone in half and layered it thickly with strawberry jam. Saliva pooled in Victoria's mouth. To distract herself, she spun more of her tale.

"Princess Everilda knew her betrothed was meant to arrive at the castle that very evening. What could possibly happen to keep him away for another twelve days?

"'What have you done?' she shouted at the dead queen's shade. 'Prince Hugh is supposed to ride in at any moment.'

"The ghost's eyes were nothing but dark pits as they stared into the princess's very soul. 'You have treated him badly.'

"'He was your stepson,' the princess hissed. 'I assumed he was as wicked as you are. But I've learned he has a heart of gold. What must I do to save him?'

"'I'll make you a bargain,' said the shade, its voice as caressing as shards of ice."

"No bargains," Penelope said around a mouthful of scone. The jam had stained the corners of her mouth red. "Bargains are always bad."

"Tell that to the princess," Victoria said smartly. "Now, back to the story.

"'What must I do?' Princess Everilda gasped. Her stomach grumbled and she dearly wished for a bowl of frumenty.

"The shade smirked, as much as shades can smirk with their faces going in and out of focus. 'Save the merman in the sea, visit two croaking ravens, let three bells stay unrung, allow four jars to be unopened, notice five melting coins cold, see six tarts untasted, bring seven swans their lives untaken.'

"'That's only seven,' said the princess sharply, for she was no fool," Victoria said.

Penelope giggled and thrust out her foot, kicking over an overflowing bagful of Redcake's Tea and cookie tins that belonged to patrons at the next table.

"Oh, dear. Terribly sorry," Victoria murmured without looking up. Penelope added her apologies.

" 'You'll give up long before that,' said the shade, with a hint of the black humor the dead queen had possessed in life. 'You never had much sticking power.'

" 'How dare you!' Princess Everilda cried. 'This is Prince Hugh's life at stake!' " Victoria said.

Someone at the next table tittered, and Victoria glanced over to see one of the Redcake sisters, the youngest one the same age as she, staring at her with amusement.

"What?" Victoria asked. Had she been too loud or overly dramatic? Her story was carrying her away.

"That isn't a very Christmassy story," the blonde Redcake said with a cough. "It sounds like something for All Hallow's Eve."

"Dickens used ghosts in a Christmas story," said Victoria, defensive.

"Very well," said Miss Redcake. "But it needs refinement. Why is the princess so obsessed with food? Aren't princesses all perfect?"

"Not my princess," Victoria snapped.

Miss Redcake tilted her head. "You can't ever have been terribly concerned with food. You have a dashing figure."

Victoria blinked. "You must never have seen me before today. I used to be as plump as a Christmas goose."

"Actually, I thought we were acquainted," Miss Redcake said. "Or I wouldn't have spoken. I'm in London so rarely that I simply thought I'd forgotten your name."

"I'm Lady Allen-Hill, but I was Victoria Courtnay before I married Sir Humphrey."

"Oh, your name does sound familiar. I'm Rose Redcake," she said.

"I've met your brother-in-law and his brother," Victoria said. "The Marquess of Hatbrook and Lord Judah? I've seen the rest of you at parties and things, ages ago."

"You haven't been to London recently?" Miss Redcake inquired.

"No. I was in mourning, you see. My husband died." Victoria picked at the jet mourning ring she still wore on her left hand.

"How dreadful. One goes to such trouble to find a husband, you don't want to lose him."

"Exactly," Victoria murmured. "Found one for yourself yet?"

"No, I'm buried in the country, thanks to my lung problems," Miss Redcake said. "I can't come into Town without becoming ill, you see."

"You're here now," Penelope interjected.

"Just to run errands, really. I only spent one night here, but I had some new dresses ordered. Then it's back to Sussex on the train."

"We're leaving for Sussex soon, too," Penelope said. The high pitch of her voice told Victoria her cousin was eager to join in the adult conversation. "We're going to Pevensey."

Miss Redcake smiled. "We live near Polegate, only about four miles from Pevensey. Are you going to the house party at Pevensey-Sur-Mer Fort? Some friends of ours are going, and we've been invited for dinners and balls and such."

"Speaking of the Fort, we should leave for Victoria Station soon," Victoria said.

Miss Redcake looked up at the clock on the wall, which had been wrapped in red ribbon for the season. "So should I."

"Let's share a carriage," Penelope said eagerly. "Then we can hear more of my cousin's story."

"I'm sure Miss Redcake doesn't want to hear that," Victoria protested.

"But she was listening to every word," Penelope insisted. "I saw her."

"It's not polite to watch people," Victoria said, her cheeks flaming.

Miss Redcake looked amused. Then her expression shifted and she lifted her handkerchief and coughed, a phlegmy, rattling sound. "I would be happy to join you. I didn't expect to travel alone, but my sister was delayed in Bristol."

"Uncle Rupert was delayed in Liverpool. We weren't supposed to travel alone either," Penelope said.

"I'm sure three ladies together will be perfectly safe," Victoria said, pulling out her reticule and putting coins on the table. Miss Redcake hoisted her rattling bag, which made her cough again. This time, a wheeze came with it.

Victoria reached out her hand and grasped the bag. "I'll take that, shall I? We sent our baggage on ahead."

"Oh, thank you," said Miss Redcake, flustered. "I just have this small valise." She hefted a heavy-looking leather case that had been resting under her table.

Victoria looked at the case, then at Penelope. The girl was too small to carry it. She handed the shopping bag to her cousin and took the valise herself, thankful her new slimness and less cumbersome second-stage mourning attire gave her the energy to haul heavy luggage.

Thankfully, her carriage was only a couple of paces away from the front entrance of Redcake's, and the luggage was soon stowed away for the trip to the station. An hour later, they were seated in a first-class compartment heading to Sussex. Victoria found the gentle jostling rather restful, but she could tell the train fumes made Miss Redcake increasingly ill.

"I have a flask of cognac. Would it help?"

"No," said Miss Redcake, pulling out a vial. "But I shall apply my smelling salts." She opened the vial and breathed deeply. A hint of color returned to her pale cheeks.

The scent of lavender oil filled the cabin. Penelope wrinkled her nose, but Victoria found the scent soothing.

"You know," said Miss Redcake, "ghost stories go very well with Sussex. We've been told Roman and Norman soldiers haunt ruins near our house. There are shell keep remains on the grounds."

"Can you tell us a story?" Penelope asked.

"I think Miss Redcake should rest," Victoria said. She hoped this part of her holiday didn't foreshadow how the house party would go. She was hoping for some good old-fashioned fun of the sort that had doors opening onto corridors and tiptoeing around late at night, not tea with children and ghost stories. By Twelfth Night, she wanted all the mysteries she'd been denied exploring to be completely open to her.

"I know a story about birds," Miss Redcake said dreamily. "I particularly remember it because my cousin Lewis used to make automaton birds. They spoke in the eeriest voices. When I hear the story I think of his creations."

"Oh, do tell," Penelope urged. "You can stop any time you feel out of breath."

Miss Redcake nodded and began to tell her story, intermixed with pauses to sniff her salts.

"My goodness," murmured Victoria, barely listening. Another tale of spurned lovers. She'd rather hear one about a lover catching the girl. The tale enthralled her young cousin, though.

"Lucky her," Victoria said sarcastically, as her companion wrapped up her poetic tale with the heroine's virtue untouched.

Miss Redcake giggle-coughed. "Lady Allen-Hill," she chided.

"Victoria, please," she interjected. "And I must call you Rose."

"And me, Penelope," the child said, eager to be included in this gesture of friendship when Rose nodded assent. "Where did you hear that story?"

"It's the sort of thing my mother likes," Rose said. "She's a painter. I expect she told me the story while sketching out the scene."

Penelope stilled. Was she thinking about her own mother? Victoria didn't know why her father had taken on guardianship of their cousin. She had found it an irritation without considering too deeply the reasons for it. Penelope had stayed with them the summer before she'd married as well. She'd been much more withdrawn and child-like then. Victoria had heard her crying out in her sleep every night, though it didn't wake the girl. Now she was just angry and overly active.

"Has your cousin designed a sedge warbler automaton?" Victoria asked, mentioning a bird she knew was common near their destination.

"No, he makes larger, prettier birds. Or so he did, when he had the leisure to do so."

"It does sound like a fascinating hobby." She liked the idea of a man who knew how to use his hands. And physical labor tended to build up the muscles. Very attractive.

"Very dirty." Rose scrunched up her nose. "All those machine parts and greasy substances. But the end results were either interesting or useful."

"I want to hear about the Romans and the Normans," Penelope said.

"They wouldn't be the same story," Rose told her. "Romans and Normans were more than a thousand years apart, I believe."

"Then why are Romans haunting a Norman shell keep?"

"I expect there was a Roman structure there before the keep. Defensive features are often reused."

"You sound very well educated," Victoria murmured. "Do any of those doughty ghosts take corporeal form?"

Rose giggled. "Lady Allen-Hill! I mean, Victoria. How racy of you."

The train lurched, and Penelope fell against Victoria.

Penelope righted herself. "I want a Christmas story. Do you know any Roman ones, Rose?"

"The Romans didn't celebrate Christmas, you know. They were pagans," Victoria said.

"They did have Saturnalia," Rose said thoughtfully. "It's a pagan festival in December, celebrating the Roman god Saturn."

"Do you know any ghost stories from your neighborhood about that?"

"I do actually. 'The Ghost Lights.' "

"That sounds promising," Penelope said, resting her head against Victoria's arm as the train jerked again.

"Ice on the tracks?" Victoria asked.

Rose wiped a spot clear on the window and peered out. "It's snowing."

A conductor opened the door and poked his head into the compartment. "We're getting word of trouble with the branch lines. I believe the end of the road tonight will be Brighton." He shut the door.

"That's twenty miles from Polegate," Rose said.

"We'll have to cable to get a carriage," Victoria said. "Unless we can hire something at the station."

"My father's driver, Robbie, will have it all arranged," Rose said with an air of confidence. "He will have discovered the line to Polegate is closed and will drive to Brighton. We can take you to the Fort."

"Are you sure? It will be a cold drive."

"They will keep us for the night, if it is too late to return to Redcake Manor." Rose hid a yawn behind her gloved hand.

"'The Ghost Lights?'" Penelope probed with a childish disinterest in their travel arrangements.

Rose sat back. "Oh yes. On the mound, every December eighteenth. That's when Saturnalia began, so we're told. It was a festival of lights, you know, to make the human sacrifices more visible."

Victoria's brows lifted. "They had human sacrifice?"

Rose nodded cheerfully and continued her tale. "Of the local Christians."

"How Christmassy," Victoria said, remembering Rose's earlier complaint about her story.

Rose threw up her hands. "But the lights are pretty."

"They're real?" Penelope's eyes widened.

"Yes. Probably gases or bugs or something."

"Or the ghosts of a hundred Roman soldiers, protesting the death of a good Christian," Penelope said reverently, fingering the cross around her neck, one her mother had given her for her seventh birthday.

Christian zeal irritated Victoria, and Penelope's mother had been something of a fanatic, following her vicar's wife around Liverpool like an acolyte, aping her good deeds. Victoria had never liked the desperate light in her aunt's eyes. Why had her child been removed from her? Because of religious fervor?

They continued trading stories until their train pulled in at Brighton Station. The wind buffeted them when they reached Trafalgar Street, but Rose recognized her family's carriage.

"How did it get here so quickly?" Victoria asked, battling with her hat against a gust.

"They must have known hours ago." The sound of Rose's cough was hidden by the wind.

The driver jumped down from the seat to help the porter they had acquired with Victoria and Penelope's considerable baggage.

"We've warm blankets," Robbie said. Rose allowed him to help her into the carriage as the porter wrestled with the bags.

With a sigh, Victoria took Penelope's arm and followed Rose. She hoped they could reach Polegate in two hours, but that speed was unlikely with hired horses and their baggage weighing down the carriage. At this time of year, it was already dark. Inside the carriage, a lantern swung dizzily, creating a kaleidoscope of her companions' faces.

The driver had been able to supply thick sandwiches and jars of water. Victoria refused it all; she could see that whoever had prepared it had not been expecting to feed three people. Penelope was growing fast, and in a spindly stage. She needed the food far more than Victoria.

A good three hours passed before the horses slowed as they approached Polegate. "I'm sure we can find accommodation for you at the Manor," Rose suggested with a yawn.

Victoria blinked, startled out of a half sleep by her words. "How much farther to Pevensey?"

"Another seven miles," Rose told her.

"Then we shall accept your kind invitation," she said, looking at her cousin, fast asleep with her head on Victoria's lap. Once again, she remembered the bawdy fun she'd dreamed of when she'd first accepted this invitation for a holiday house party on the coast. Nothing was working out as she had imagined.

CHAPTER 2

They had a late start the next morning, since Lady Redcake, Rose's mother, had insisted they allow Robbie a full night's rest. Victoria and Penelope ate breakfast with the family in the formal dining room. The two fireplaces, one on either end of the room, were covered in holly and evergreen boughs, and two small trees on tables near one of the fireplaces had cheerful red ribbons tied to many of their branches, along with an assortment of German ornaments. When Victoria had two steaming cups of black tea in her, she realized that the next day was Christmas Eve.

"How nice to have a house full of family," she said politely to Lady Redcake, hoping to distract herself from the plate of fried apple dumplings that had been placed in the middle of the table after everyone had served themselves from savory dishes on the sideboard. The scent of cinnamon had her mouth watering.

"This is not everyone, of course," Lady Redcake said, her flowing sleeve drifting into her bowl of porridge. "Just our youngest daughters and one grandchild. We will see Alys and her family tomorrow afternoon, and Sir Gawain and his family for Epiphany."

"I didn't realize you'd married, or been widowed, Lady Allen-Hill," Matilda, the middle daughter, broke in. She did not share her younger sister's cool blond looks but had red hair, pulled severely away from her face, and a dusting of large brown freckles across her cheeks and forehead.

"I did become engaged in London but married in Liverpool very quietly," Victoria said. "My husband passed suddenly and then—"

"And then you had to go into mourning for what, twenty-four times longer than you'd been wed?" Matilda interrupted. "Outrageous, really, these customs of ours."

"Matilda has become quite strong-minded." Lady Redcake sighed. "She's working in the family business now. Do you do the same?"

Victoria gave in to temptation and reached for an apple dumpling. Penelope giggled. With a sigh, Victoria cut the fragrant pastry in half and slid a portion onto Penelope's plate, though she thought it would have been quite reasonable to keep all of the fruit for herself.

"Cousin Victoria has taken charge of me." Penelope poured cream from a jug over her dumpling, overflowing the plate. "And I'm quite a handful."

Victoria's fork stopped just over her sugar-iced pastry. "Penelope!"

Sir Bartley, Rose's father, chuckled. "The young lady has just proved her point. You will have a time managing this one. No children of your own?"

Victoria shook her head. "No, I wasn't blessed."

"Pretty girl like you, certain to find another husband," Sir Bartley said, his ruddy face creasing into a smile. "I'd offer you a son if I had any to spare."

"There's Lewis," Rose said. "Our cousin Lewis."

"Who makes the birds?" Penelope asked.

"Yes. I thought he was coming down for Christmas."

"I invited him," Matilda said, with a significant glance at her father.

"He's never been one to take meals," Lady Redcake said serenely. "Always fussing over some bit of machinery."

"Who is going to be at this house party you're attending?" Matilda asked. "Anyone from the neighborhood?"

"The earl's family, of course, the Gills. He has two sisters, his mother, and an aunt, I believe. A family called Dickondell," Victoria said.

Rose glanced up from her apple dumpling. "It's a large family."

"Ah. I only knew the name. Are you acquainted?"

"Yes. They are related to Hatbrook's family."

Victoria nodded. "My father will be coming. Honestly, I'm not sure who else. Are there Dickondell men who might marry some of the earl's sisters?"

Rose smiled. "There are definitely Dickondell men. Three sons, two of marriageable age. This is the Earl of Bullen? Why have I never met him?"

"I know the answer to that," Matilda said. "He's a scientific man, like Lewis. Awkward in company. He came to call with his mother and sisters once, shortly after we'd moved here. Barely spoke a word."

"I don't think he did speak," her mother said. "Lady Bullen is a forceful personality. How do you know the family, Lady Allen-Hill?"

"Connections of my late husband. Second cousins, perhaps? They all came to the wedding, and Lady Barbara, one of the earl's sisters, has become my frequent correspondent." Victoria passed the rest of her dumpling to Penelope after limiting herself to two bites.

"It sounds like a great deal of fun," Rose said. "The masquerade ball is tomorrow. We're all attending."

"Goodness, I'd forgotten about that," Victoria said. Her trunk had been sent on ahead.

"Would you like to stay until tomorrow and go in with all of us?" Lady Redcake asked.

"I think it would be best if I settle Penelope in now," Victoria said. "If a carriage can be spared." The Redcakes were all very pleasant, but this was a house full of women, not the kind of holiday she had in mind.

Lady Redcake nodded and called a footman to make arrangements. An hour later, Victoria and Penelope were on their way.

Snow dusted everything but the centers of the roads, giving the landscape a frosted appearance. Icicles pointed their teeth down from eaves and branches. The carriage would have been intolerable if not for a robust collection of hot bricks and lap robes.

"It does look like Christmas. I was afraid it wouldn't in the south," Penelope said.

"Christmas should be an internal feeling. That way it doesn't matter where you are. A feeling of innocent joy." A time, perhaps, of relief from the strict propriety of daily life.

"You sound like such a mother, Victoria."

She was startled by Penelope's comment. Did she really? Fascinating, when all her thoughts were of the possibility of illicit pleasure. Victoria stared out of the window, her hands anchoring her to the seat as the wheels occasionally slid on patches of ice. Her cousin huddled under the thickest robe.

Up ahead, she could see a shadowy patch on the snow: a large bush perhaps, or a fallen tree. But then, as the carriage rattled closer, she saw some kind of strange, wheeled machine.

Two figures bent over it. One stood, then, blowing on his ungloved hands. She could see wide palms, long fingers. The cap he wore gusted off his head as wind rushed through a stand of alders, revealing a thick shock of blond hair, the same shade as Rose Redcake's. He wore heavy clothes but gave the impression of solid strength and broad shoulders. The other figure was reed thin and tall, dressed similarly. A youth.

As the carriage drew alongside, the man turned and waved his arms over his head.

Did he need a rescue? Where had the horses gone? Only then did she notice the smoke curling up from the carriage: slow, sickly gray, and heavy. Maybe it was one of the new horseless carriages she'd read about in a magazine.

She tapped the roof of the carriage to make it stop, but it was slowing already. Penelope got to her knees on the cushion as Victoria opened a window and peered out.

The man didn't come to talk to her, though she could hear voices. He was speaking to the Redcakes' driver. She heard a chuckle, a responding male growl. Did they know one another?

A moment later, the carriage door opened and the man appeared, still hatless. "Hullo," he said with a friendly grin.

The way his lips curled at the edges, the dimples that were exposed by his smile, stunned Victoria into speechlessness. When she had hoped to make this house party a sensual idyll, she hadn't considered intimate relations with a servant, but perhaps she should have. Good heavens, did they make all the carriage drivers this pretty in Sussex? She'd been living in the wrong part of England.

Penelope poked her, and Victoria regained her self-possession. "May I help you?"

"We were out testing the Marquess of Hatbrook's new contraption and something's gone wrong," he said with a wave at Penelope. "Mind if we join you in the carriage? We can't force the engine to turn over, and it's getting colder by the minute."

"I certainly do," Victoria huffed. The cheek! And yet, his voice was surprisingly cultured. Could he be the marquess's butler or some other kind of upper servant? "We have not been properly introduced."

"You're Victoria Courtnay, are you not?" he asked. "I know your father. We're members of the same club, the Euphonious Commerce Society."

"I am Lady Allen-Hill now," she said. "But yes, Rupert Courtnay is my father."

"I remember meeting you once, at a holiday party, I believe. But you don't remember me." He injected a question into his words.

She wondered how she could possibly have forgotten someone so handsome. Perhaps she'd met him when she was newly engaged, two years earlier? No, she still would have noticed him.

But what did it say that he knew her father? If he was a member of the club, he'd likely be a businessman, not a servant. Someone like her father.

"I am sorry I do not recall being introduced."

"Perhaps we were not," he admitted with a sly grin. "But I saw you. I remember the curls in your hair and those lovely gray eyes."

He probably remembered what he wasn't saying. Her rotund figure. In fact, she was surprised he even recognized her, but maybe the coachman had told him who was inside. "Do you live in the area, Mr.—"

"Noble. Lewis Noble, Lady Allen-Hill. I live in Battersea, but I've been staying at Hatbrook Farm to work on this vehicle, and then I'm off to Pevensey-Sur-Mer Fort for the holidays."

"Oh," she breathed. "You are Lewis Noble. The bird maker."

His blond eyebrows lifted. "I am?"

"We spent much of yesterday with your cousin Rose. In fact, we stayed at Redcake Manor last night because of the snow."

"I make motor carriages," he said, with no hint of his previous levity. "And dabble in kitchen improvements."

"He's brilliant," said the youth, coming up to the carriage. He was in the super-stretched growing phase, though his voice had finished deepening, maybe fourteen. "He's the secret behind Redcake's, you see."

"You don't say," Victoria said, wondering who this brash lad was.

Lewis cleared his throat. "May I present Eddy Jackson, my apprentice?"

Penelope stuck her head out of the door. "Introduce me, Cousin Victoria."

Victoria did so, feeling acutely uncomfortable. One did not have social occasions on the side of the road in winter.

"Now, would you mind giving us a lift?" Lewis asked again. "Are you going somewhere with a telephone, or could you drop us at the next pub?"

"We are headed to the Fort," Victoria admitted. "For the house party."

"Jolly good. Can you give us a ride?" he repeated, rubbing his hands together.

Her eyes were drawn to those long fingers again, inventor's fingers. He did not have the hands of a gentleman. They were stained, callused, even marred with small cuts. "Is it safe to leave that contraption on the side of the road?"

"Nothing else to be done until I can get the part I need. I'll borrow a horse there. Waste of a day, but there you go."

"Can't you send someone to tow it back to the Farm and stay at the Fort? You don't want to miss the masquerade ball," Victoria said.

"I don't?" he replied. "I'm as social as the next man, but my work comes first."

"I'm not suggesting you leave the carriage to rust, just that you don't have to be the one to take care of it."

He regarded her with cool, solemn appraisal. Without turning his head, he said, "Eddy, when we arrive at the Fort, I'd like you to return with Robbie to the Farm to retrieve my bolt case. It's likely the case will have what we need to fix the carriage."

"Certainly, guv." Eddy grinned at Penelope and started telling a joke in an exaggerated Cockney accent. Victoria, resigned, made a welcoming gesture, and the pair entered the carriage and sat opposite them. Eddy leaned toward Penelope and kept talking, a practiced storyteller. The two passed the rest of the ride in youthful jollity, while the adults were silent.

Victoria's hat had netting that somewhat covered her eyes. She took advantage of it to peer at Lewis from time to time. When he caught her once, she turned away quickly, as if she hadn't been looking on purpose.

She wished he had more of Eddy's joie de vivre and would engage her in chatter, but the man was all business. He wasn't likely to be interested in a midnight dalliance. Although he had bent a little, deciding to send Eddy instead of going himself for tools.

And really, you never knew what a man might be willing to do in the middle of the night unless you approached him.

"Would you like a robe?" she asked.

Lewis shook his head without speaking.

Eventually, Victoria began to stare out of the window again. They drove through a small town, then climbed a hill. The landscape of dirt fields, dusted with pearly snow and bare trees waving in the wind, gave way to streams, then fens, and, finally, she could see the sea to the right. Through the trees, what looked like a fairy castle appeared, the high stone curtain wall broken only by arrow slits. They were all crenellated on top, with a tower at one end.

"Amazing," Penelope breathed in her ear. "Do you think Sleeping Beauty is asleep in that tower?"

"It looks as if the Fort is perched on the water," Victoria said.

"It is fronted by a moat and backed by a lake," Lewis said.

"Will we be staying in the real, medieval castle?" Victoria asked.

"There's a proper manor house inside the walls, rather than an old keep," he said. "The stone walls are a restored shell from the days when England was at war with France."

"Like your story," Penelope said to Victoria. "Will you tell me more?"

"Tonight, when I tuck you in," Victoria promised.

Lewis lifted a brow but didn't ask a question. They skirted the edge of the lake, watching the water undulate like liquid silver in a bed of mother of pearl. It seemed colder here, and Victoria could see her breath in the carriage. The four of them gusted little puffs of smoke into the air like dragons taken human form. She expected if her fairy-tale characters had seen a machine like Mr. Noble's horseless carriage, they'd have fought it with swords and maces as if it were the fabled creatures.

The bridge lay open over a moat between the curving road and the Fort. The tall, crenellated walls flashed golden yellow under the weak sunlight, and Victoria felt like they had entered an enchanted place.

But when she turned back and saw Mr. Noble, leaving black streaks on his cheek as he thoughtfully scratched with a finger, and smelled the machine oil emanating from him, it seemed all too real. Like home even, because her father often smelled of the same sort of substances—machine oil and dye and hard work—even though he only spent time in his offices.

Mr. Noble and Eddy Jackson separated from them, jumping out of the carriage as soon as they pulled up on the shell-lined drive in front of the main house behind the castle wall, a tidy red-brick rectangle that appeared to be about a hundred years old. Eddy waved at them with an open smile, but Lewis only nodded absently before they vanished around the side of the house. Footmen led the carriage around the drive, and maids took Victoria and Penelope into the house, where they were greeted in the morning parlor by the Countess of Bullen, the present earl's mother. The lady, thin and upright, her graying hair coifed over a narrow face, instructed a maid to pour tea.

She gestured for them to sit across from her on a firm-cushioned sofa. "I'm sorry you've missed my daughter, Lady Allen-Hill. She's shopping on the High Street, but I'm sure she'll be back in time for tea. Did you have trouble in the snow? We expected you yesterday."

Victoria and Penelope seated themselves on the yellow satin settee across from the countess's straight-backed chair with its embroidered cushion. She scarcely knew this connection of her late husband yet had the sense of being dropped into the middle of a long conversation.

"We only made it as far as Brighton on the train," Victoria confirmed. "We came into Polegate from there with Miss Rose Redcake and spent the night at her family home."

"Ah, yes. We'll see them tomorrow at the masquerade ball."

"Yes. We picked up Mr. Noble on the way here."

The countess smiled faintly, her upper lip losing little of its network of wrinkles in the process. "Mr. Noble and my son are cut from the same cloth. Men of machinery. They breathe nuts and bolts and tools."

"They were bent over a horseless carriage when we drove by," Victoria agreed.

"Mr. Noble and my son?"

"No, I'm sorry. Mr. Noble and Eddy Jackson."

"Who is . . . ?" the countess inquired.

"His apprentice. I believe the carriage belongs to the Marquess of Hatbrook."

"I did hope the Shield men would come and bring their ladies for a long stay, but of course Lord Judah's heir only came into the world last month, and the marchioness is expecting another small treasure sometime in the spring."

"They are all probably more comfortable at home," Victoria agreed.

"Yes, those times can be most vexing, and one does want to sleep in one's own bed. But of course you weren't blessed."

"No," Victoria said politely. "I wasn't."

"I did not hear who inherited your husband's title."

"A cousin. He resides in Bath. I've never met him."

"Such a pity," the countess murmured. "I have done my best to deliver a selection of gentlemen to the holiday proceedings, my dear. My son is too involved in his projects to travel to London, and my daughters have not had much opportunity to be in society."

Victoria brightened. If Lewis Noble was a sample of the men to be present, she ought to have a wonderful time. "Will your son be attending the house party?"

The countess sighed. "I expect he'll be holed up in the stables with Mr. Noble. Now, there is a waste of a handsome gentleman."

"A waste?" Victoria's wrist wobbled as she lifted her teacup to her mouth.

"They say he is ever pining for some lost love. He never even looks at a woman. One of my daughters would be perfect for him. He could spend even more time with my son if he lived here with us."

The countess put a hand to her mouth to cover her emotional outburst.

"He looked at my cousin," Penelope said, speaking for the first time.

Victoria slid her body into an angle on the seat to look at her cousin. The countess dropped her hand in shock.

"He did," Penelope insisted. "You'd think she was displaying her bosom, the way his gaze fixed on her."

"Penelope!" Victoria gasped.

"It's true." Penelope's eyes were wide with childish innocence. "He did look at you, the entire drive here, at least when you weren't looking at him."

The countess pressed her lips together. "If you can capture Mr. Noble's attentions, I assure you that you will be the envy of every young woman at the party. He's considered quite untouchable."

"I expect it was more a case of his scientist's mind assessing me," Victoria said, feeling sour as she recalled how much her body had changed.

"You'll see at dinner," Penelope said. "He'll be at dinner, won't he?"

"They often take meals in the stable. But I have insisted, you know, with guests present, that they stir themselves. Surely they can both take enough time away from their machines to settle their affections. It is not right for young men in small societies to stand apart from the ladies."

"Gentlemen do as they wish," Victoria said.

"Then there is your father," the countess said. "He has been widowed a great many years."

"I believe my mother's death was devastating to him," Victoria said. So this was to be a true matchmaking paradise, this party. Were any of the men aware of the countess's plans?

"That was more than a decade ago."

"Eleven years," she agreed.

"It must have been difficult to go through your wedding without her," said the countess.

"My father is very good to me, but it is true that I have a dearth of female relatives."

"Is the new baronet unattached?" the countess wondered.

"Yes, though I do not think he ever leaves Bath," Victoria admitted.

"Such a waste." The countess brightened. "But we do have a selection of fine gentlemen from locally and far away."

"Oh?" She noticed Penelope, looking bored, had worried at the edge of one satin cushion. Wincing, she saw a tiny tear in the fabric. She put her hand over the girl's to prevent her from causing further damage.

"We have been graced by the Baron of Alix, from Edinburgh. A lovely young man whose brother recently married into the Shield family. We met him at a party at Hatbrook Farm several months ago. Of course, he is distantly related to us as well."

"I've never met him," Victoria said.

The countess touched one index finger to the other, as if counting her guests. "Have you met the Dickondells? Clement and Ernest are the older young gentlemen. Very friendly with my daughters. Samuel will be here, too, but he's just twenty."

"No."

"Clement was at school with my son, which is how we came to know him; he is just a year younger. Very eligible."

"So that is five, no, six eligible men." But mostly from the same family. Still, two titles.

"Your father, of course, but not for you."

"I don't imagine he'll see himself as a prospect."

"A woman must have wiles, my dear. I thought of him for one of my daughters, though Lady Florence, my husband's sister, will probably make a play. She's incorrigible." The countess sighed into her teacup.

"I look forward to meeting her," Victoria said sweetly. The pickings here did not come to much. Two inventors, three locals, and a Scottish baron. She had promised herself a dalliance before remarrying according to her father's wishes, hopefully at some point in the distant future. He wanted someone to run the factories when he was gone, but he was not old yet. She wanted fun with a man she found attractive. The two goals were unlikely to mesh. She deserved some pleasure after being shut up in her father's Liverpool mansion for a year and a half after a month spent nursing Humphrey. He hadn't even found a home for them because they had planned a honeymoon excursion to Italy before building themselves a house. He had died in her father's house, and there she had remained until this very week.

So, she'd make a play for Lewis. With any luck, his sensual side would come out at night. Her next husband would not expect to find her a virgin, so why should she be one? She'd even packed precautions.

"We can hope for more guests," the countess said, looking at her with a puzzled expression. Had she been visibly woolgathering? "I admit there are a few too many females. My daughters and sister-in-law; Maud Wilson, the Dickondell cousin, who is nineteen and very pretty. Rose Redcake will likely be around quite a lot. She is particular friends with Adela Dickondell, who at seventeen should not really be invited, but that family does come as a package."

"Seven females of eligible age, then," Victoria counted. "You have set up an even complement."

"Adela and Lady Florence should not be counted."

"They should be if they are in on the game."

The countess tittered. "You are blunt."

"I'm a northerner. Sometimes I forget my pretty manners," Victoria admitted.

"We do need one more man for the table," the countess said, "as I do not like to eat alone in my rooms. I had not realized Miss Redcake meant to stay for the entire party until today. I have instructed my son to cable a selection of his friends. Someone is sure to come, or perhaps one of the masquerade guests will want to stay. Will your father arrive soon?"

"I certainly hope so."

"We can do nothing more for now. I shall have you taken to your rooms. Would you like Penelope to stay in the nursery?"

"Are there other children in residence?" The answer was, of course, yes, but she didn't want her cousin to be completely isolated.

"We could ask Matilda Redcake to stay," the countess said in a low voice. "She has that son. He is two years old."

"Not much of a companion for a nine-year-old."

"No, no, and we really shouldn't encourage Matilda, despite the Redcake money."

Victoria sighed. "She will have to stay with me, then, unless suitable children arrive."

"Very well. But we'll have a nursery maid take charge of her during the day, and I'll think of someone I can invite in from the village to play with her. I promised Sir Humphrey, you know, that I would see to your future as best I could. I was his favorite aunt, you see, and he wrote me on his deathbed."

"I wasn't aware," Victoria murmured.

"I could do nothing until you had mourned. But now . . ." The countess dropped her empty teacup into its saucer with a brisk clatter. "It's time to find another husband for you."

The countess rang a bell and instructed the maid who answered to take Victoria and Penelope upstairs.

The room they were led to had country charm, though the battlements blocked the sight of the bay beyond. But it was just a single room, without a sitting room. How was she going to have any fun when she had to share a bed with a nine-year-old? She would have to hope her male counterparts weren't as marriage minded as her father or the countess, and that they could find a creative way to help her lose her virginity.

CHAPTER 3

Lewis set his lamp on the table next to the comfortable brown velvet chair in his room. He could imagine himself falling into it, putting up his feet on the ottoman, and sleeping for the rest of the night. It would be good enough for him after such a long day. He would take that bargain instead of having to listen to the features of the room described and allow the footman to valet for him.

But he could never stand to be rude to servants. They worked harder than he did. The man stoked the fire for him and lit a lamp next to the bed before turning down the sheets.

"No gas or electricity in the entire building?" Lewis asked.

"We have gas lighting downstairs, sir. Would you like me to ring for food since you missed dinner? We have kitchen service until midnight during the holiday."

Not much of a holiday for the kitchen staff. He didn't want to disturb them, but his stomach growled, betraying his hunger. "Very well. Just some rolls and cheese. Nothing complicated."

"Very good, sir. Can I help you with your coat, find your dressing gown?"

Somehow, the footman managed to still be in the room when the food arrived, but Lewis found himself more comfortable, his muddy, damp shoes and socks removed, a thick robe over his shirt and trousers instead of a mud-spattered coat. The long day of going back and forth between the vehicle on the road and Pevensey-Sur-Mer Fort could finally be declared over.

The maid poured him a cup of tea and simpered at the footman. Now Lewis knew why the man had continued to find small tasks for himself for the last fifteen minutes. A romance was brewing. He'd take himself into the dressing room and give them some privacy if only Eddy wasn't already snoring away on a cot tucked against the wall.

He stirred himself and stood. "Thank you. That will be all."

The maid curtseyed and was followed out by the footman, who no longer pretended any eagerness to stay in the chilly room. The fire was inadequate, but judging by the number of blankets heaped on the bed, it wasn't expected to get any warmer in here. But then, he was an afterthought as a guest, here on the earl's order, rather than a true catch for the house party. Nicholas, the earl, had warned him that his mother had planned for the two-week party to be a grand event of matchmaking. They'd promised each other to steer clear of that nonsense as much as possible.

A small clock on the mantelpiece clicked to eleven as he sat down again. In an hour it would be Christmas Eve, and then Christmas Day. When he was a boy, he'd looked forward to the holidays. Though he'd lost his parents before his majority, the season stayed a happy one, because he was welcomed into his aunt's home. Her husband was an ambitious sort, and Lewis had put his nimble mind and mechanical hands to work for the family businesses. In his spare time, he made automatons, then became interested in horseless carriages. He'd opened a machine shop with a partner. But Alys Redcake had rejected his offer of marriage one holiday season three years earlier, and the next winter holiday had brought the sudden death of his business partner. Last Christmas had been thankfully pain-free. He and Eddy had spent it together quietly in religious observance. Trying to take the heathen out of Eddy was an uphill battle, but he'd made an effort at Christmas.

This year, he'd relented to a more secular holiday because he couldn't resist spending a couple of weeks assisting Nicholas with his submarine. Ever since he'd read Jules Verne as a child, he'd wanted to experiment with an underwater craft but hadn't lived anywhere suitable for such experimentation.

He drank down his tea and picked up a roll with ham tucked into it, wondering why he'd bothered to waste another full day on Hatbrook's vehicle. Especially when he was the husband of the former Alys Redcake. But his money was good and the prestige of placing a horseless carriage with him was high. One of these days, he ought to stop experimenting and just make the same vehicle more than once. He'd have fewer breakdowns that way, but the inventor in him couldn't stop tinkering.

A scratch came at the door. The footman again? Lewis swallowed his sandwich in one gulp and went to answer, but before he could turn the handle, he saw it start to move on its own. He stepped to the side as it opened into the shadows, and saw a ghostly figure in a billowing black wrapper and long dark curls step through.

The door shut gently, and the woman pressed herself against the back of it, as if frightened.

Lewis suddenly remembered he was at a house party, and hijinks were *de rigueur*. All he need do was lock his door to thwart the ladies, but then, he'd thought, who would come to him at this hour? Most of the women in the house were virgins.

Dear God. Surely no one was going to try to trap *him* into marriage with a nighttime tryst. He went to the mantelpiece and picked up a candlestick, then marched back to the door to see who she was, since she hadn't spoken.

The candle first revealed a substantial bosom, heaving behind a froth of delicate lace between the open lapels of her wrapper. The tantalizing view reminded him of the lusty grocer's widow he'd sported with after Alys had rejected him, when he'd first moved to Battersea. But then he lifted his candle higher and saw a heart-shaped face. The frank humor he'd seen in it in the carriage earlier that day had not vanished. She lifted her brow and tilted her lips humorously yet provocatively.

"Lady Allen-Hill," he said in a low voice, as if to speak in a normal tone might make her vanish back through the doorway, a ghost only imagined.

She put her hands to her belt tie, which only served to throw his attention to the substantial curve of her hips. My, but she had a true hourglass figure, even uncorseted. He shifted as his lower body came to attention. His throat went dry and his hand shook just once, involuntarily. A drop of wax spattered onto his wrist.

He swore.

She stepped forward, coming into the firelight. "Mr. Noble, did you burn yourself?"

He set the candle down next to his teapot and tugged off the small piece of wax. "It was nothing."

"Let me look." She took his hand, her fingers cool but silky with some feminine lotion. "I see a red spot."

Then she bent over his hand and blew, her cupid's lips pursing even more into a little bow.

He couldn't help himself; he was enchanted. And aroused. He hadn't thought to find a beautiful young widow here to hold his interest. Just a submarine. Surely she'd been widowed too recently to be on the prowl for another husband, and anyway, she'd be looking for a title, not for the likes of him.

"To what do I owe the pleasure of this visit?" he asked.

She looked up at him through thick lashes that matched her hair perfectly. They owed nothing to her maid's art. "I wanted to thank you for seeing to our comfort this afternoon on the drive here."

"On the contrary, you saw to ours, picking us up on the road as you did."

She smiled. "Then you agree I saw to your comfort earlier?"

"Why, yes," he said, not sure what she was getting at.

"Then I ask you to see to mine." She blinked slowly.

"Excuse me?" he said, unsure of her meaning.

She slid the fingers that were holding his hand up his arm, underneath the silk of his dressing gown until she reached his biceps. Squeezing, she sighed, a breathy little moan. "See to my comfort, Lewis. I can call you Lewis, can't I? In the privacy of night?"

"My lady, the door isn't even locked."

Her eyes glittering, she tugged him back, until her back was again against the door. With her free hand, she took his and guided his fingers to the key.

"One turn of the lock and I am all yours."

"You're awfully young for an assignation," he said. "I must be a decade older than you."

"I'm a widow. I'm allowed."

"You are?" He held back a chuckle, though his cock had hardened enough to make clear thought difficult.

"I've been locked up in my father's home for a year and a half."

He thought he saw a muscle twitch just under her right eye. "It is not right, what happens to young widows," he agreed.

"I'm lonely, Lewis. You're a nice man, and so attractive." Her fingers found their way up his other sleeve, so that she massaged the muscles of his biceps on both sides.

He hadn't realized how sore those muscles were, after a day of wielding a wrench. Imagine what such talented hands could do with his neck, shoulders, and back. Then his gaze drifted to her bosom, which was not quite pressed against him, and he imagined what he could do with the rest of her.

"You are so young, Lady Allen-Hill. You might conceive a child."

Her eyes gleamed. "I brought a rubber."

He blinked. "You brought a *what*?"

"A condom," she said patiently. "I understand that's what everyone calls them. I'm a modern girl, you see. I thought ahead. I want a bit of fun, like anyone would at a house party. Isn't that why you came?"

"I came to work on the submarine," he said, his thoughts about a million miles away from the earl's machine shop.

"You aren't going to work on it at this time of night," she said with a little pout.

"I might." Why had he said something so sulky?

"Stables don't have artificial light," she said, "so it's no use trying to work there in the dead of winter. All that cold, and only lamps. You'll need some other activity."

"I could sleep," he suggested as his cock twitched.

She pulled her hands from his sleeves and slowly lifted her arms until they were above her head in a provocative pose he'd seen on a theater poster. Her breasts lifted, and he could see the hard points of her nipples through her cotton gown.

His cock hardened into a thick, steel rod. He could think of nothing but undoing the laces that held the fragile lace yokes together and swirling those sweetly budded nipples with his tongue. His hands made the decision for him as he reached for the laces. Time seemed to slow. He thought she'd even stopped breathing.

His palm touched her breast and time sped up again. She inhaled sharply, and he saw the smallest hint of a pink tongue dart out to touch her plush bottom lip. Losing all sense of reason, he put one hand on the door, above her head, and tilted his face toward hers, angling for a kiss that would probably ruin what was left of his mind.

Behind him, a door slammed against the wall. "Eh, guv, there's no chamber pot in my room. Where am I supposed to piss?"

Lewis dropped his hands instantly. "Eddy," he said in a none-too-steady voice. "Go back to your room."

"Can't, mate, 'ave to piss. Why aren't you asleep already? Is there a pot behind the screen?" The boy stumped forward.

Lady Allen-Hill gasped and pulled her wrapper around her, hiding those amazing breasts and damned laces. Lewis turned protectively, trying to block her from the boy's view.

For a moment, they all stood in a tableau. Then Lewis remembered the locked door. He reached behind him and turned the key. The lady stepped forward and he opened the door, positioning her into the opening.

"Go," he said. "It wasn't meant to be."

"Can't he sleep somewhere else?" Her eyes were a little unfocused, as if she couldn't quite understand what was happening.

Lust had done that to her. She was normally rather sharp. "Go to sleep, Lady Allen-Hill. In your room."

He shut the door, then sagged against it.

Eddy's face broke into a wide grin. "I interrupted a tryst. Aren't you a lucky one."

"And aren't you a right bastard for interrupting me," Lewis snarled.

Eddy shrugged. "I'll get a chamber pot tomorrow. Then you won't 'ave to worry."

Victoria crept back into her room, her feet icy cold from the unheated corridor between her room and Lewis's. She had made her way in the dark, grateful that shadows hid the deep flush of thwarted passion and embarrassment. How could the simple, almost accidental touch of a man's palm against her breast make her feel so weak in the knees, so frustrated, so alive?

As quietly as possible, she shut the door behind her and willed her eyes to adjust to the dark so she could find her bed. If she quieted her own breathing, she imagined she could hear Penelope's soft breaths over the crackling of the dying fire.

She went to the fireplace, barking her shin on a low table as she moved forward. After she stirred the coals, she decided the ensuing warmth wasn't enough for a child, so she added more fuel. This brightened the room enough for the bed to come into hazy focus against the opposite wall. She thought she could see a figure sitting up in it.

"Mama?"

"It's Victoria, darling. Just fixing our fire."

Penelope's breath caught. "I didn't know where I was."

"I'm sorry. I hope you'll be able to go back home soon."

"Mama said she'd never see me again," Penelope said in a small voice.

Victoria frowned, her experience with Lewis dropping from the forefront of her mind. "You can't be serious. I wasn't told anything of the sort."

"She was in a rage. She yells, she cries, and she throws things." The girl hiccupped.

"What about your father? What did he say?"

"Just that I was to go with Uncle Rupert and he would take care of me."

"I must say I do not understand why he didn't simply hire a governess."

"It's the holidays. No time to hire anyone. Maybe later."

Victoria hoped so. After a year and a half in isolation, she didn't want to spend all her time caring for a child. She had a life to renew. "I'm afraid I don't know anything about that either. Do you want me to ring for some hot milk?"

"I'm not thirsty. Where were you?"

Victoria sighed. She didn't want to coddle the child, but she didn't want tales to get back to her father either. "I took a walk."

"Will you tell me more about Princess Everilda? It's been ever so long since you started the story."

"Where was I?" Victoria asked, leaving her wrapper at the foot of the bed and climbing in.

"Princess Everilda was angry that the dead queen was playing so lightly with Prince Hugh's life. Do you think Prince Hugh looks anything like Eddy Jackson?"

"You think he's handsome?" She reflected on the youth's reddish brown hair and sharp, freckled nose. "Aren't you a little young to find youths handsome?"

"I didn't say he was handsome," Penelope said in an injured tone. "But he's lively."

"Do you think the son of a queen like Avice would be lively?"

"More of a milksop, I suppose," Penelope said with a yawn.

"That's what I would think. Though he probably sits a horse well enough."

"I think I might like horseless carriages better than horses," Penelope said.

"But girls love horses," said Victoria, startled. She'd never been one for horses herself, but that was because she lived in the city, not a place where she would have learned to ride and care for the beasts.

"They smell," said Penelope, yawning again. "How many more difficulties will Princess Everilda face?"

"Twelve, of course. It is a Christmas story."

"Then what is number eight? You didn't finish the list."

"Let's see. Queen Avice sneered, of course, and said, 'Not that it will do you any good, Everilda, but I shall tell you the rest, so that you may have additional opportunity to despair.'

"The princess stared down from the dais, appearing unmoved, though of course she was shaking and sweating under her winter wool gown."

"Is she pretty?" Penelope asked, snuggling back against her feather pillow.

"As pretty as a very plump princess can be," Victoria said, leaning back against her own pillow with her hand tucked under her head. "'Cease your delay tactics, your highness,' said the princess, 'and explain.'

"'There must be eight tapestries unraveled,' said the queen with a roll of her undead eyes. 'Nine ribbons ripping.'

"'Go on,' said the princess, unmoved.

"'Ten castles uncastled,' said dead Queen Avice.

"The princess thought the fires in the enormous fireplace roared higher at this, as if they grew strength from the evil shade. 'You don't say,' she said pertly, for she could not show fear." Victoria yawned herself. When she closed her mouth again, she realized she was about out of ideas. She stopped speaking, hoping her cousin had fallen asleep, but the girl poked her.

"Just coming to the good stuff now," she promised. "'Eleven tigers will roast,' the shade snarled. 'And, finally, twelve masks must unmask.' "

"The tigers were a bit unexpected," Penelope said. "Tigers in old England?"

"They can't be simple tasks," Victoria reasoned.

"No. Now you'll have fun figuring out how to get the princess out of this mess."

"Do you think I'm making the story up as I go along?"

"Probably." Penelope rolled over. "Good night, Victoria. Dream up some more of the story, please."

"I will." Victoria pushed her pillow down and inched into a full recline. At least Penelope had given her the excuse to think of something more than her failed seduction for a few minutes. She still felt a little weak in the knees, though, a little tremulous in the heated flesh between her thighs. Resolving to banish Lewis Noble from her thoughts for now, she closed her eyes and tried to sleep.

"I wish I was old enough to attend," Penelope said wistfully the next evening, as Victoria straightened the green velvet draping over her Marie Antoinette–style panniers. In her dress, she was nearly four feet wide. She never would have dared such a style when plump, but now it felt like a delicious tease. Her low-cut bodice displayed an ample though very reduced bosom framed in delicate lace. Most of the fabric in this costume went into the skirt.

A tall blond wig covered her dark curls, giving her a feeling of invisibility even without the green mask attached to a stick that she could hold to her eyes. She had debated hiding her face more fully, but from whom? No one was trying to avoid her, and few in the crowd would even know her name.

She nodded to the maid when a knock came at the door. When a male voice rumbled, Victoria stood with a cry. "Papa!"

Tall, broad Rupert Courtnay strode toward her, resplendent in brocaded Louis XVI court dress. A curly white wig covered his graying, thinning hair.

"You look a decade younger in that costume!" she teased, tugging a curl before hugging him.

"You are almost as wide as you are tall, daughter," he said, shaking his head over the elaborate dress.

"I am sure others will be dressed as extravagantly," she said, hoping she was right. The masquerade ball was hosted by an earl, after all.

"I am sure most of the attendees will be digging into their attics," her father said. "You will be the belle of the ball."

"I wouldn't mind a little male attention. You'll dance with me, won't you, Father?"

He frowned. "I understand you are young and frustrated, Victoria, but I thought you would remain in half-mourning for another six months."

"It's a masquerade ball. No one will know me."

He pointed to the mask. "If you wish to be incognito, then that mask is insufficient. Let us trade."

She sighed and handed over her mask-on-a-stick. She didn't like the half-domino style with ribbons that he handed her. They tended to compress her nose and make her sneeze.

"Keep it on all night," he cautioned her. "I don't want you to be disgraced. This party is your chance to enter another level of fashionable society."

"I hardly think so, Father. Why, the earl never goes to London. The only other title I've heard mentioned is a Scottish baron."

"The Marquess of Hatbrook will be here."

She shrugged. "He is wed, and he has already attended your parties in London."

"I take it you've heard of no one who might interest you for a second husband?"

Her thoughts jumped to the curly white-blond head of Lewis Noble. But he was just another inventor, for all his good looks and working muscle. A step up would be a marriage into the peerage. At the very least, she should find herself another baronet so she didn't lose a title. When, of course, she was ready to wed again, which wouldn't be any time soon.

"Sussex isn't the place to find a man who will want to run factories in Liverpool someday," she pointed out.

"Then I'll have to live long enough for Penelope to find us a captain of industry." His smile loosened the beauty mark he'd applied at the corner of his mouth.

Penelope giggled. "Do you think I'll marry at eighteen?"

"I don't see why not. You're as cute as a merry lump of coal dancing in the grate." Rupert pinched his niece's cheek. "Now get yourself into bed. You won't grow if you don't sleep."

"Yes, Uncle."

Victoria reached up and pressed her father's beauty mark back into place. "Is it late enough for us to go downstairs?"

He held out his arm. "Put on your mask, my dear, and let us see."

She put the mask to her face and threaded the ribbons behind her ears. As her father tied them, she felt a sneeze coming on.

"Kerchoo!"

"You do not sneeze prettily," Penelope said. "Keep your mouth closed and wrinkle your nose if it itches. It is much more attractive."

"Who told you that?" her father asked with a frown.

"Mother."

Still frowning, her father pointed at the bed. "Go to sleep. Now, Victoria, I think you need a couple of beauty patches, too. It is amazing how they obscure the identity." He pulled a small case from his waistcoat.

He added one to her right cheek, then placed a second just above her top lip. "Yes, with that wig I would hardly know you. Lessen the speed of your speech. With your figure so reduced, you should be all but unrecognizable from eighteen months ago."

Victoria nodded. She put a finger under her nose to try to stop the next sneeze. Why had she wanted her father to join her at this party? He was dragging down the fun more every minute.

With a sigh, she took his arm and blew a kiss in the direction of the bed. The mattress squeaked.

"Will there be cake? Will you bring me some at midnight? Just as it is becoming Christmas Day?" Penelope asked.

"You would be better to pray upon the miracle of Christ's birth and think less about cake," her father advised. "We will see you in the morning."

They exited the room. As soon as the door was shut, Victoria whispered, "Why were you frowning when she mentioned her mother? What is going on with Aunt Clarissa?"

"Not now, Victoria," her father said in a voice that betrayed exhaustion. "It has been a long day coming here, and now we have this masquerade ball to get through. I cannot deal with family at this moment."

"We need to discuss the matter soon. You cannot expect to saddle me with a child when I should be courting," she protested.

"The right man will be too industrious to worry if you are caring for a child, Victoria. In fact, it will be a blessing because he will see how you are with children."

She rubbed the corner of her eye where the domino was scratching it. If a man saw her with Penelope, he would be more concerned than satisfied by her maternal instincts. "I allowed you to direct my courtship the first time, Father, but surely I have earned your trust this time around?"

"My dear, I found you a husband the first time," he said, the skin around his eyes creasing.

"I think I can find my own, now, what with the title and everything." Just hopefully not too soon.

"Your appearance is improved," he said. "We shall see if you can attract any attention on your own. Now you have not only your dowry but your late husband's funds as well. Of course, your age is against you."

"I'm twenty-one, not even on the shelf by nonwidow standards," she said.

"Marriage is business. You've lost a couple of years of childbearing, I don't deny it. But we shall see what we can manage." Her father looked away as they reached the staircase.

Victoria stepped down carefully, in front of her father, as they both could not fit. It was for the best, really, because she might have slapped him if he'd been alongside her. How dare the man who loved her best insinuate she was second-class material on the marriage market? She blinked rapidly, trying to hold back tears that might stain the velvet. Tears wouldn't do. He couldn't possibly be correct.

CHAPTER 4

Tears were never acceptable in public, and this descent was most assuredly not private. The stairs had a slight curve to them, and as she stepped down, she first saw the tops of heads, decorated boldly in holly sprigs and wigs, feathers and hoods. Not to be missed were the hats, both fashionable and military. Next into view were the faces uptilted in laughter. Then, as she reached the bottom, the costumes became more obvious. The obligatory Tudors, the fantastic military display of lobsterback coats. The eighteenth-century gentlemen, with their falls of lace, and rotund women in the evening dress of early in this century that so admirably cloaked size. She knew, for she had worn those costumes herself during her engagement, while Sir Humphrey had gone about dressed in his admiral grandfather's black tricorn atop a regular modern evening suit, since he refused to wear a costume. He had been a stolid, unimaginative man, very proper and most kind. She could not imagine how her father's businesses would have thrived under him, except that he might have been able to bind excellent employees to him by his sheer goodness, if he had the presence of mind to hire correctly.

While she had been visiting graying memories, her slipper-clad feet had reached the marble floor. All came into sharp relief again:

the laughter, the music, the bright colors. Should she be ashamed to be here in her pretty white and green costume? Sir Humphrey had been proper, true, but he had known he was robbing her as he died. He would not grudge her a little masked fun so long after his death. Blast Queen Victoria anyway, for making mourning such a state of desirability.

Her father stepped down behind her. She turned to ask him whether he wanted to go into the ballroom, the dining room, or the game room, when a girl with long, flowing blond hair, clad in a mid-sixteenth-century gown embroidered with seed pearls at the bodice stopped in front of her. With a red wig, she might have been a young Queen Elizabeth. Instead, Victoria recognized Rose Redcake, waving a dance card, her mask tied around her neck instead of covering her eyes.

"I saved one for you," she said, a little out of breath. "Where have you been? I thought you would be one of the first to arrive, since you are staying here."

Victoria took the card with a smile and tied it around her wrist. "Father, this is Rose Redcake."

Her father bowed slightly, causing his wig to slip down over his eyebrows.

Victoria laughed and helped him right it. Rose laughed, too, then put her hand to her mouth and coughed.

"Suffering from the aftereffects of a cold, Miss Redcake?" her father inquired.

"No, sir, I am well."

Her father nodded, but Rose colored and looked at her slippered feet. A path through the crowd opened, and Victoria saw a trio of broad-shouldered, dark-haired young giants, full of masculine energy. Rose followed her gaze and turned, her own expression darkening.

"Who are they?" Victoria asked.

"The Dickondell brothers. That is Clement, Ernest, and Sam; he's the youngest, younger than we are."

"Clement is unwed?" Victoria asked, eyeing the man who was clearly the eldest brother, in his late twenties, with just the faint touch of creases around his eyes.

"He is not adverse to flirtation, but I am not convinced that he does not have his heart set on his cousin Maud. She is nineteen now, so I do not understand why he hasn't spoken for her."

"Does she have any money?"

"Not that I'm aware of, but that can't be it. I have an excellent dowry and he hasn't shown me any special attention," Rose said.

"His parents may disagree with his desired match, and his heart has not reconciled him to that," said Victoria's father.

"You speak with authority on the matter," Rose said.

"I saw it work so with my brother," he said.

"Did he ever marry?" Rose asked.

"Yes, to the woman our parents wanted for him."

"It ended well?"

"He is speaking of Penelope's parents," Victoria said.

"Oh, has she been orphaned?" Rose asked, missing the nuances of the situation.

Mr. Courtnay shook his head. "No, but she is with us for a time."

Victoria hadn't known the match had been forced upon her uncle. "Were you forced to marry Mother?" she asked.

Her father smiled. "No, dear, I was lucky to love someone who was acceptable to your grandparents. I only regret we lost her so young."

"You should remarry," Victoria said. "You have been alone for eleven years, Father. What better place to fall in love than a holiday party? Your parents are no longer alive to have an opinion on the matter."

He chuckled. "I was always stronger-willed than my brother. My parents would not have been an obstacle."

"Even so. Rose, will you not help me choose a suitable bride for my father?" If he were occupied, he would not watch her actions so carefully.

She thought Rose would immediately suggest Lady Florence, who at forty was just a few years younger than her father, but Rose did not respond. "The countess thought Lady Florence."

Rose tilted her face up to Victoria's father. "No, she will not do."

He smiled. "Will you give me a dance, Miss Redcake? We can discuss my options further."

Rose pulled her mask from her neck and held out her card. While her father signed it, Rose tied the mask over her eyes. Though she had freckles and a pale countenance, she was rather lovely. Victoria felt a shiver of precognition excite her marrow. But her father had never fallen for a pretty face as long as she could remember. Why would Rose find a middle-aged man interesting when she didn't need his money to be comfortable?

Without her quite realizing it, her father and Rose had relocated a good ten feet away, clearing a path through the crowd hovering in the hall. Victoria looked up, wondering if she should follow, or even try to cadge an introduction to Ernest Dickondell from someone they both knew. Before she could move, she saw a mop of white-gold curls lit by the gasolier.

The man had been standing along the wall, speaking to someone dressed like one of the King Charleses. He wore a pleasingly snug, high-necked blue coat faced with white satin over an open shirt edged with lace. Tight, very tight white breeches showed every morsel of the delectable male body to perfection, and she could see his stockings needed no padding to fill out the calf. Dress slippers looked almost absurd on such large, manly feet, but really, Lewis Noble was perfection in his nearly century-and-a-half-old naval uniform and totally identifiable despite the black domino.

"Oh, my," she whispered.

He approached her as if no one else was in the room. She saw a woman lift her fan in his direction. No response. A man held out his hand, but Lewis Noble didn't seem to see him.

Then he was in front of her, bowing in the flowing style of vanished days.

"Mr. Noble," she murmured.

He lifted his gaze. "Lady Allen-Hill. Such a pleasure to see you out of mourning."

She gave him a tight nod, not sure if he was truly praising or subtly indicating his disapproval. But he was not supposed to be a man of subtlety. He said what he thought, so she said, "Thank you. I could not have a drab Christmas. Though the mask is intended to protect my identity, of course."

"I do not blame you for wanting to wear a pretty gown. You are too young to dress like a crow. I'm sure your mask will have the intended effect, for most people."

But not for him, who had known her somewhat intimately. She felt her bodice constrict as she tried to draw a deep breath.

"Your costume is exquisite," he observed, his gaze lingering on her exposed bosom.

"I didn't see you all day." His gaze heated her, reminding her of what they might have shared the night before, if only they hadn't been interrupted.

"I was busy with the earl." His gaze drifted down her skirts and back up again.

"I was sorry we were disturbed last night."

His gaze fastened on her face, his eyes widening.

She should not have been so bold, but then again, her words were far less bold than her actions had been. He smiled, giving him a hint of boyish naughtiness.

"I am sorry, too," he said. "But Eddy sleeps in my dressing room."

"I don't suppose there is a lock on that door."

He chuckled. "I can't lock the boy in. What if there was a fire?"

"I share my bed with Penelope. I didn't expect house parties to be so complicated." She made a face. How did people manage? And had she really just spoken so frankly? She had exposed her naïveté, true, but also her lust.

"I was honored by the attempt." He glanced down at her wrist. "May I?"

She held it up, the card dangling. He laid it on his own palm and wrote his name down for two dances.

"No one else has spoken for you yet?"

"I have just arrived. I don't know anyone except the ladies of the house, your cousins, and you."

"I see." He offered her his arm and was soon placing her in front of the Marquess of Hatbrook and insisting he take a dance. Then they moved to Sir Bartley Redcake, who was also persuaded into a dance. Lastly, he brought her to the Earl of Bullen, who looked shocked at the notion of dancing at his own ball but agreed to a reel. Victoria followed in a daze as Lewis made the introductions.

"There," Lewis said with obvious satisfaction. "No need for you to interact with any other gentlemen."

"It might be said that you introduced me to the most eligible bachelor in the room," she said, flattered by the way he had taken charge of her evening. When he gave himself a goal, it prompted a whirlwind of activity. She followed him to the foot of the staircase.

"Oh, Nicholas?" Lewis said with careless satisfaction. "He has yet to discover the pleasures of the fairer sex. His brain is too full of maritime vessels."

"Then you were not displeased by my boldness?" Her voice caught on the last word. She still felt a little shy around this intensely masculine creature, though she was increasingly sure that she would, in the end, become his bedmate. Her body positively quivered with sensual awareness.

They were interrupted by a hand on Lewis's shoulder. "Noble. I hope you aren't trying to hide a pretty lady from the rest of us."

"Trying," Lewis said to Ernest Dickondell, who had a cheery grin on an unshaven face.

"I have thwarted you. Introduce us. We're at a private ball. The rules can be relaxed."

"They have to be relaxed very far to introduce such a reprobate." Lewis sighed dramatically. "But if I must. Lady Allen-Hill, may I present Ernest Dickondell, feared pirate of the seven seas?"

Victoria stared doubtfully at the child's cutlass tucked into a sash around the man's broad waist. He wore clothing not so different from Lewis's, but in purest black. A tricorn hat of ancient lineage was pushed back on his head. "No eye patch?"

"Couldn't find one," Ernest admitted. "Rather spoils the effect, I admit."

"You could wink a lot," Victoria suggested.

Ernest smiled, displaying large white teeth that looked entirely too well cared for to belong to a pirate. "May I have a dance?"

"Card's full." Lewis's grin bared his teeth. "Sorry, Captain."

"What are you then, Lewis? Seaman Noble?"

"Major General Lewis Noble of Her Majesty's Marine Forces," Lewis said, deadpan. "I shall pursue you to the ends of the earth, you scurvy dog. And win the girl besides."

"She has to want to be won. One look at you after a hard day in your machine shop and she'll run straight into my arms." Ernest winked at her.

"Lady Allen-Hill?" Lewis countered. "I don't think so. She grew up among her father's machines, right, my lady?"

"Something like that, Major General," she said, then blushed at the lie. "Actually, I never went near the factories."

"You probably have her confused with your cousins, Lewis," Ernest said. "It was the Marchioness of Hatbrook who grew up in the factories. It only takes one look at this lady to see she is more gently bred."

Lewis's brows narrowed as his expression grew hard. "I will not have you insulting Lady Hatbrook."

Ernest held up his hand and favored Victoria with another slow wink. "I just thought the lady should know where your loyalties lie. Madam, my heart is pure and untasted, whereas you see before you a most compromised seadog."

Victoria glanced at her dance card, suddenly wishing she had a dance to spare for this naughty Dickondell. She'd like to hear more about Lewis's compromised heart, even if all she'd really been looking for were his embraces. Why was it so hard for a respectable widow to get some amorous congress with a decent man?

"The Fates are conspiring," she muttered, then looked up at the men's startled expressions as she realized she'd said it aloud.

"Not against you, I hope, my lady," Ernest said with an exaggerated frown. "Never against you. If I cannot have a dance, may I partner you to dinner?"

Lewis opened his mouth to protest, but Victoria spoke first. "By all means, my gallant pirate. I cannot wait."

Ernest winked yet again, bowed, then disappeared into the throng.

"Why would you want to dine with him?" Lewis growled. "He's a known rake, on the prowl for a rich heiress."

"I am a rich heiress," Victoria said softly.

"I thought you were interested in me. Was that all a mistake?" His expression stayed closed, remote.

"Will you be dreaming of some other woman when I'm in your

bed?" Her retort shocked her. She was acting like a jealous lover, not a flirt.

He stared at her for a long moment. "If I allow a woman into my bed, she is going to be the only thing I think about. The only thought I will have will be her pleasure; my only concern will be her satisfaction."

She felt her intimate flesh contract in a hard burst of pleasurable shock. "Are you ready to allow it, sir?"

"Are you?" His gaze narrowed. "You seem to be having second thoughts."

"I never have second thoughts at midnight. Only at other times of the day," she said lightly, wishing she could run her hands over his elaborate jacket and feel the outline of the hard muscles underneath.

"Then we will make an assignation for some midnight," he said. "But not tonight. I need time to make arrangements for Eddy."

Sir Bartley Redcake lumbered up to them, ready for his turn on the dance floor. Lewis nodded to her and turned away, vanishing into the crowd.

The next day, after hours of church services, Victoria found herself faced with a roomful of women. The men had all moved onto masculine pursuits, leaving their feminine counterparts to huddle by the fireplaces in the warmest parlor. The four ladies who comprised the female household of the earl all held embroidery hoops. Victoria and Penelope both had knitting needles and Rose Redcake, who'd stayed behind after the ball because she'd nearly fainted after three dances in a row and had been sent to rest in the countess's bedchamber, was exclaiming over the talented stitchery of Lady Florence.

"Will you tell me more of the story before I expire of boredom?" Penelope whispered.

"It may just keep me awake," Victoria said. "Let us see. The princess and our evil queen were facing off. The princess pulled off her veil and stared directly into the evil shade's wavering, ghostlike face. 'You make it too easy for me,' she sneered."

"Are you telling more of the story?" Rose asked, coming to perch on a sofa arm. "Have I missed anything?"

"Yes, I revealed the rest of the clues," Victoria told her. "The last was twelve masks unmasking. But now Princess Everilda must decide how to save her betrothed."

"She needs a friend," Rose said. "Someone to talk to, someone to advise her."

"Good idea," Victoria said. "Princess Everilda sneers some more. 'Begone, dead hag!' she cried. 'For you waste my precious time.'

"Strangely enough, Queen Avice's shade bestowed a look of pity upon the princess. 'Save my stepson if you can,' she intoned. 'Find the character I know you have lacked.' Then, with a puff of sickly, yellow-tinged smoke, the queen vanished. Everyone in the room gasped, then started coughing from the pestilent odor of the grave left behind."

Penelope wrinkled her nose. "Did it smell as bad as London did when we left?"

"Exactly the same," Victoria said. "Like the train station."

Rose chuckled, then covered her mouth with a lace-edged handkerchief and coughed delicately. "And everyone ran outside to breathe the fresh-smelling air until the stench dissipated."

Victoria nodded. "That would be most sensible. Everyone stood in front of the castle, staring out across the water to the tree line, wondering if they'd all had a stench-induced hallucination, and if they would soon see Prince Hugh on his destrier, galloping toward them. But of course, it was not to be, for in that distant time shades were very real, and Princess Everilda had brought disaster upon herself by refusing the mince pie.

"Eventually, the princess sighed and gestured to her liege men to go back inside, but she climbed the battlements, taking only a fur her handmaiden had provided. She stood vigil for many an hour, puzzling over the Herculean tasks the queen had imposed upon her. Did she start at the first or the last? The masks or the merman?"

"Are mermen real in this story?" Penelope asked.

"I should think so," Victoria said. "There is magic enough."

Penelope smiled and bent her head to her knitting. She was making a baby cap destined for a workhouse child.

"Eventually," Victoria continued, "she decided to start at the top, as it were. Twelve masks must be unmasked. She resolved to search her father's very large castle until she could find them."

A maid opened the double doors that led into the parlor. "My lady? Visitors have arrived."

Everyone's attention turned to the door.

Lewis stepped into the foyer of the Fort, his stomach rumbling. He'd gotten up early, ready to help Nicholas with an experiment, and had been too full of the previous night's cake and champagne for breakfast. Now, however, after several hours in the chill air, wading through the lake, he could eat a bear. Nicholas had pulled out a stale loaf and cheese in his workroom, but Lewis wanted meat and resolved to appear at the formal luncheon he knew would be served in the dining room.

As his eyes adjusted to the lower light indoors, his gaze was struck by the ingress of new people. He hadn't expected the Fort to have visitors on Christmas Day. There were only two of them, a man and a woman, both richly dressed. He recognized them then, for he knew one of them as well as he knew himself: his cousin Alys, Marchioness of Hatbrook, and her husband.

He'd managed to avoid Alys all last night and hadn't expected to see her at the Fort again. Why had she returned?

As if sensing his approach, Alys turned. She blinked when she saw him, as if she couldn't quite believe it.

He looked down at himself and wanted to groan. He'd have felt more comfortable meeting her in a naval uniform than stained, baggy wool pants and a thick, shapeless coat, items that were suitable only for machine work.

"Your hair is longer than when I last saw it," his cousin said. "I had forgotten how curly it could be."

He touched his matted hair. Must have lost his hat underneath something. "Are we speaking? I did not realize."

"You have avoided me," she said. "I never avoided you."

As Hatbrook turned around, Lewis said, "I never thought you to be a liar. You never called upon me all that time you were running Redcake's. You left it to Lord Judah to contact me to repair all the bakery equipment. But then, I should have known you were one for avoidance. Look how my proposal to you went."

"Still holding a grudge from three years ago?" Hatbrook asked. "Beneath you, isn't it, Lewis?"

"I have no grudge against you," Lewis told the marquess. "Just my cousin, for making my exit from her father's house such an awkward one."

"I didn't ask you to propose to me," Alys said, her chin lifting. "We were good friends once. Can't we be again?"

He looked at the woman he'd once worshipped. At twenty-nine and used to her title now, she did not much resemble the young factory girl she had been when he'd first come to live with her family. She had been a changeable girl at first, but eventually she'd settled down, with a focus on her work that rivaled his own. He had never thought she'd use her new position as a knight's daughter and her dowry to land a premier nobleman. But then, why would such a man find her unworthy?

Staring at her, feeling the love in his heart that wrapped her fiery red hair in some kind of heavenly nimbus, he scarcely knew what he said, just that he mumbled it and took a corridor blindly. He walked briskly until he was out of sight, then pushed his way through the first door he found with his December-iced hands. Why had he chosen now to confront her when any time in the past three years might have done just as well? And her expecting a child. He'd been unconscionably rude.

Unfortunately, he'd chosen a door unwisely. At least five pairs of female eyes went to him and his filthy clothing as he shut the door behind him.

"I see you have been busy with my son," said the countess.

Thankfully, her voice held a note of refined humor. She was never rude to a potential husband for one of her daughters, who were also in the room. Both girls were still just young enough to be eligible but were fading fast as marriage mart material. Alys had been older still when she caught the marquess, but then, she was exceptional.

The room also held Lady Florence; his cousin Rose, who was Alys's youngest sister; and, unfortunately, Lady Allen-Hill and her cousin. Unfortunate, because he had enough pride to want to look his best in front of a woman who frankly desired him. Her large gray eyes regarded him with more concern than amusement. He understood she could see he labored under some distress and wondered how a near stranger could read him so well.

Nodding to her, he went to the tea tray in the corner and poured himself a steaming cup. Wishing for something sturdier than the nearly paper-thin china, he lifted delicately but drank with vigor, then poured again. When he turned back, all the female gazes were still upon him. He was an elephant in the gazelle house.

His cousin stood, looking far too frail in a borrowed gown that revealed a couple of inches of her thin wrists.

He cleared his throat. "What are you doing here, Rose? I didn't know you had stayed."

"I am to return this morning with Alys."

Behind him, he felt air moving and gentlemen entering the room. He recognized the dye magnate, Rupert Courtnay. The man shared his daughter's crystal-clear gray eyes, but other than that, the lady must resemble her late mother, for he had nothing of her apple-cheeked beauty.

"Miss Redcake," Courtnay said, inclining his head to Rose.

Behind Courtnay, the youngest Dickondell brother grinned at the throng of women. Most men would be intimidated, but this boy was too young to be caught in any of their clutches.

"You should stay," Victoria said from her position on a sofa. "You will miss my fairy tale if you go now."

Rose smiled wistfully at her. "I hope the countess will extend another invitation to me, one for which my wardrobe would be better prepared."

A maid peered around Samuel Dickondell. "Miss? We're bringing your things to the carriage now."

Rose approached Victoria, who stood to clasp her hand. She made her good-byes to the Gill ladies.

"Why do you not come on January third?" the countess said. "We are having a large dinner that evening and you can spend a few days with your friend before she returns to London."

"I should like that very much," Rose said. "Thank you, my lady." Rose squeezed Lewis's arm as she left the room.

He followed her out. "You're quite friendly with Lady Allen-Hill."

Rose turned to him, her eyebrows lifting. "Does that matter to you?"

Lewis looked at a masterful, though bloody, painting of a broken stag over his cousin's head. "Do you have any warnings for me about her?"

Rose tilted her head. "You can't propose to her. Not unless you want to live in Liverpool and manage her father's factories."

"I used to hear that about her, but that was a couple of years ago. Haven't they found anyone else by now?"

"Her husband," Rose said pertly. "He died, remember?"

"Then I can't develop an interest in her," he said grimly. "Everything I have is in Battersea."

"And Leeds," she pointed out. "That's farther north."

"I have suppliers in Leeds, not business interests."

"At least," his cousin said, "you are showing some interest in a decent female for the first time since Alys rejected you. I am glad, because I think you will make a good husband to someone."

He felt the need to protest. "I was pushed to propose to her, you know, by what your father was doing."

She rolled her eyes. "You would have preferred to worship Alys from afar, a gentle, perfect knight. I know that's what you thought, Lewis, but you're a flesh-and-blood man. It's silly to be so idealistic. Find a wife. Women are real people, you know, not statues. We have faults and strengths, just as men do."

"You've turned into quite a philosopher." The words came out sourly.

"I'm not proud of things I've done and said," Rose said quietly as her sister and brother-in-law appeared at the end of the long corridor. "I've had a lot of time to think, stuck as I am in the country, trying to breathe."

"Has Hatbrook forgiven you for your interference?"

"It's not him I care about, it's Matilda, for my part in making her think she could seduce her son's father into marriage. She's the person I most injured by my dangerous gossip."

"Then it's true; you really did see Alys and Hatbrook together before they were wed?" Lewis had never quite believed it.

"Alys is a real person, not a statue," Rose repeated. "Just like other women. They desire, they crave." She bit her lip tightly.

Lewis realized this cousin of his was lonelier than he had ever been. Could he help her find a family of her own? "Do come back on the third," he urged. "There will be gentlemen here. I'll suss them out for you over the next week."

She laughed gently. "See to your own needs. You have a decade on me. *Vita brevis.*"

Lewis watched her as she went down the corridor, her slightly too short skirt showing off her stick-thin ankles. He wondered what Victoria's lower limbs looked like and resolved to make an assignation soon.

CHAPTER 5

Vita brevis. Life is short. Lewis pondered this thought as he paced in front of the fireplace in his room just before midnight on Christmas Day. Eddy had gone to bed so stuffed full of sweets that he doubted the lad would stir before noon unless he was kicked awake. This would be a perfect night for Lady Allen-Hill to scratch upon his door, but he had waited for an hour and she hadn't come.

As with Alys, he must have made a hash of things with this woman. Dare he go to her door and make his plea in person? Or would young Penelope answer? Victoria had seemed interested when they spoke at the ball last night, but he hadn't said a word to her today. Had she found greener pastures? Ernest Dickondell, for instance? Was she looking for a husband or a lover?

He gritted his teeth at the idea and turned around. A short stroll around the corridors might be in order, just to stretch his legs and clear his mind. The countess had provided a seven-course meal and surely light exercise would be in order after such a banquet.

With resolve, he went to his door and opened it, only to find the lady herself with her hand lifted toward the wood, a surprised expression on her cherubic face. His heart thumped an extra beat out of sheer surprise.

"I did not tread lightly?" she asked with a wide-eyed gaze.

He knew he was smiling like an idiot. Just the sight of her put his cock to half-mast. "I did not know you were there. I was about to leave my chamber."

"I see." She stepped aside, still appearing confused. "I do not wish to interfere with your plans."

"My dear lady," he said, taking her arm and drawing her inside, "you *are* my plans."

She shut the door softly behind them. "What of Eddy?"

"He is stuffed too full to wake."

She smiled ruefully. "Penelope is the same. Why, she is snoring. I do not think I shall be able to sleep with her tonight."

"I am pleased to be your alternate companion." He inclined his head.

Her lips bowed upward. "What a waste that would be, if people came to house parties merely to find a different sleeping companion. So much duller than what you understand the reality to be."

"I thought you a seasoned adventuress," he ventured. "But this is a new game for you?"

"Not at all, Mr. Noble. I am merely curious. I've never even been to a house party before, especially one where matchmaking is intended."

"I am your safe harbor?"

Her lids dipped half-closed over her stunningly clear eyes. "Rather, my uncharted territory."

"They say all women, and men too, are the same in the dark." As soon as he made the joke, he knew it had been a mistake.

She winced and turned away, staring into the fire. After a moment of silence, he touched her shoulder. "I did not mean to offend. Or course your husband—" Had she been in love with the man rather than the title?

"We will not speak of Sir Humphrey," she whispered.

"No, of course not. I suppose I've ruined things." He cleared his throat and tried to press through her change of mood. "Would you like a glass of wine? I sneaked a bottle up here. The underbutler is an old friend; he was a footman for the Redcakes once."

"That would be lovely," she said, still in her pensive mood.

He pulled the loosened cork from the bottle and poured half a glass for each of them, then invited her to sit by the fire. Instead of sitting next to her, he perched on the table between the sofa and the fire. Firelight danced on her features, drawing red streaks through her dark hair. For the first time, he noticed her clothing, her figure, and damned himself for being the kind of man who could spend five minutes alone with a woman and not notice these things. He would never be a true rake.

"Your dressing gown is a work of art," he observed. The stiff white fabric was heavily embroidered with vines and purple and blue flowers.

"Forget-me-nots," she said ruefully. "A wedding present from Sir Humphrey. Silly of me, not to mention inappropriate to wear it, but it is so pretty."

"I do not like mourning customs," he told her. "Why turn young women into crows? Their husbands no longer care."

"I expect a scientist like yourself has many unconventional notions."

"It comes of thinking too much." He felt cheerful all of a sudden. The wine was good and the fire had made the room pleasant. And now he'd taken the time to notice that her gown, which peeked from under the fanciful robe, was cut low enough to show the tops of her high, rounded breasts. Breasts he'd touched once and, God willing, would touch again.

She put the glass to her lips and took a long sip of her wine. When she pulled the glass away, there was a bubble of deep red on her upper lip. He sat, mesmerized, as she licked the bubble away, then smiled at him. "It got away from me."

He leaned forward and took her glass from her, setting it on the table.

"Are my table manners too upsetting for you?" she asked.

"On the contrary, my lady, you are driving me mad." Indeed, his cock was fully hard now, straining against his clothing.

Her pleasured chuckle gave him the encouragement he needed. He bent forward and found her lips with his own. *So sweet.* She parted beneath him with a gasp and he found no barrier to deepening, intensifying, the kiss. And why not? This was no exploration of a prospective mate but a furtive encounter at a house party. He slid his lips against hers, then tasted her tongue with his own, learning her flavor of caraway beneath the grape. Her mouth opened wider, so he angled in, feeling his body twitch in response. Crouching before her, he found her upper arms, the silk threads of the embroidery rasping under his fingers, then the tops of her breasts. He slid forward on the table, eager to get closer, to touch more. Her hands gripped his biceps, and the next thing he knew, one of them had overcalculated their movement and they were falling.

Their lips lost contact as he hit the floor back first. He let out an inelegant "ooof" as her body dropped heavily on his, their legs tangling together. Her chin hit his chest and she gasped at the impact.

"Sorry."

"It does not take much wine for us to lose our balance," she said, grinning at him as her long braid of rich dark hair tickled his neck.

"Or rather, not much kissing," he replied, wrapping his arms around her and finding her mouth again.

They kissed tenderly until the shock of the fall left their bodies and only passion remained. Some minutes later, Lewis flipped their positions, moving the table so that she could roll to the floor. He lifted himself on his elbows and gazed down at her chest.

"Out of breath?" he asked.

"My belt tie is digging into me," she told him.

"We must remedy that." He found the offending knot and undid it. The thick fabric of her dressing gown fell away, leaving her low-cut cotton nightdress open to view. Her erect nipples thrust the textured needlework at the top of her gown into high relief. When he glanced back at her face, he saw she'd flushed pink. "What?"

"You must think me wanton."

"I hope for it, my lady. I dream of it." He nuzzled her neck.

"How gallant." She relaxed back to the floor.

Cursing himself for his inattention to her comfort, he pulled a cushion from the sofa and tucked it under her head. As he moved, making the adjustment, she let out a small gasp.

He glanced down, concerned. She was biting her lip with strong, white teeth.

"What is it?"

"You brushed me," she said, blushing more brightly than ever.

He slid back on his heels and glanced at her. After a moment's perusal, he decided her nipples looked even more tightly budded than before. "Madam, I am of a scientific bent. I must learn more."

"Yes," she whispered. "You must. I can see that."

He undid the tiny buttons holding her bodice together. Slowly, her flushed skin revealed itself to his eyes. After a moment's effort, he had her beautiful, bountiful breasts bare. The globes were perfection, all cream tipped with pink. His mouth watered and he ached to taste her. Now the game would truly begin. His cock twitched again, urging him on.

"We need to know what made you gasp, Lady Allen-Hill. The only way to do that is to perform an experiment."

"Victoria," she whispered. "Call me Victoria."

He nodded absently, his attention focused on using his hands to plump up her soft breasts. "I shall test your sensation with various techniques."

"Such as?"

Her throaty voice, with that little catch, made him crazy, but he kept his voice level. "Blowing. Licking. Rubbing. Flicking. Biting."

Her breath hitched. "Biting?"

"Of course. We must test strong sensation." He realized he'd never been so hard in his life. He could use his cock to break a knight's shield. That thought reminded him of his old chivalric bent, how he used to consider his love for Alys as something out of an old story about the Round Table. A pure, bright love that didn't need kisses to maintain it.

Surely an earthier love had its merits. As he stared down at Lady Allen-Hill, a flushed, pretty widow, he willed himself to stay in the moment, to provide her the congress she so ardently desired.

"Lewis?" she whispered, a hint of doubt creeping into those lovely eyes.

"I'm sorry," he said. He couldn't behave like this. Dust sheered the floor under the sofa, the floorboards were hard, and she was a lady. "You must think I'm a madman to assault you on the floor. I do apologize."

"Lewis," she said again. "I was enjoying myself. Weren't you?"

He shook his head slightly, not knowing what to say. Her fingers shook as she rebuttoned those tiny buttons that had been such an object of desire to him only moments before. She sat up, then stood.

"When did you decide I repulsed you?" she asked, exhaling sharply.

"You don't repulse me." Surprised by her question, he took her hand and held it between his own much cooler digits. "Not at all."

"Then what?" She pulled her hand away and tucked it behind the other.

"I realized I had never conducted myself in this manner. I realized it wasn't like me." He came to his feet.

"I don't think I understand. I mean, you have been with women, yes?"

For a moment, he didn't know how to respond. Men didn't blush or simper. "I have never engaged with a titled lady at a house party," he said.

"I was plain Victoria Courtnay before I married," she said. "No better than Lewis Noble."

"I misspoke. I have never trysted at a house party, any more than you. We are both novices."

"I see. Such antics are beneath you. I suppose that is better than you finding me repulsive." She crossed her arms over those delectable breasts and shifted from side to side.

"I am sorry. Your beauty went to my head."

"I apologize for disturbing you."

He heard the break in her voice and felt absolutely terrible. "I will escort you to your room."

"No need. We are on the same corridor, Mr. Noble." With a stiffness in her gait very different from her usual flowing, hip-centered walk, she pulled the edges of her wrapper under her chin and stepped to the door. Without looking back, she opened it and departed.

Lewis closed his eyes as the door clicked decidedly behind her, as if it chastised him. What would have been more gentlemanly under the circumstances? Refusing her or agreeing to romp?

Victoria felt more restless than she ever had in her life as she sat with Penelope and the Gill women in the morning parlor the next day. Should she depart? Her father had moped at breakfast as well, making her wonder if he'd had a tryst go wrong, too. Some things could not be discussed between father and child, but somehow she knew they were feeling a similar level of disappointment.

"Victoria, stop woolgathering," Penelope ordered. "What is Princess Everilda going to do?"

Victoria cast her thoughts in the appropriate direction. "She was meant to search her father's castle for the masks."

"What did she find?" the girl whined.

Victoria dug deep into herself for the next kernel of story, hiding behind her fretful thoughts of Lewis. "She was at the highest level, so she searched the attics first but found nothing. Then she went to the floor on which the family lived. She searched the bedchambers and the solarium, then the chapel, all to no avail. On the ground floor, she investigated the main hall, even peering up the massive fireplace until her face was covered with soot. This was particularly troubling because, of course, the prince was expected to arrive that day and she hadn't quite given up hope that he would appear. But the day progressed and even when her face was clean Prince Hugh had not arrived."

"She knew the curse was real," Penelope said. "By then."

"I am afraid so," Victoria said dully. Everilda had lost her prince, and Victoria couldn't lose her virginity to save her life. Idly, she wondered if Ernest would be up to the adventure. But Lewis had kind eyes, and she was worried about the pain and perhaps even some blood. And he made her insides feel like they were melting. She expected if she told Ernest she was still a virgin he would refuse her for fear of entrapment. Or maybe he would want to be trapped by a rich heiress. Then she'd be forced to remarry much sooner than she wished.

"Where did Princess Everilda go after she cleaned her face?" Lady Florence asked.

"To the kitchens," Victoria said. "She looked in the fireplace there, though far more carefully, because a boar was being roasted on a spit just in front. She opened and sifted through every basket and cask. Finally, there was only one more place to look."

"The dungeon?" Penelope asked.

"No, no dungeon, but there were twelve storerooms down a dank staircase. This castle was close enough to the sea that there were floods at times, so all the rooms had benches erected higher than the waterline, and that's where the foodstuffs were stored. She despaired, as you can imagine, when she saw the barrels in the deep recesses of her father's castle. Unfortunately, though there were many barrels to go through, there was little fresh produce, hanging meat, and the like. She wondered how they would ever get through the winter without men to hunt for game and fish."

"You would think the first task wouldn't be so difficult," Penelope complained.

"That's just it," Victoria said, thinking quickly. "As Princess Everilda held her torch high, she saw a door in the far wall of the long corridor leading between the storerooms. She'd never noticed it before."

Lady Florence bent forward over her embroidery. "How exciting."

"The door was locked," Victoria continued. "Of course the princess was the castle's chatelaine, so she went through every key in her possession until she found one that fit."

"Was it a strange key?" Lady Florence asked.

She was surprised by the older woman's enthusiasm. "Definitely. The metal was a kind the princess had never seen before: vaguely marbled, with a sickly green cast to it, like moldy fingernails."

"How vile," the countess murmured, proving she had been listening all along.

Victoria hid her smile. "She inserted the key and voilà! The door creaked open. She held her torch in front of her and tiptoed inside. The torch cast eerie shadows on the walls and the air smelled strangely clean and salty, as if the room were exposed to the sea. Eventually, she noticed slits in the walls, narrow slits like archers had used in times of war. She put her torch into an iron circle in the wall and looked around curiously.

"She saw the room held twelve statues of knights in two long rows along the center of the room, cut from the same greenish marble of which the key was made."

"Were they wearing masks?" Penelope asked.

"No, the masks were carved out of the same marble." Victoria smirked. "And they weren't over the knight's eyes either, but took the place of fig leaves."

Lady Florence giggled naughtily. The countess frowned.

"I suppose that made it unlikely that a lady of gentle birth would try to remove them," Lady Barbara said.

Victoria shot a glance at her friend, but Barbara's expression was placid. "Our princess was made of sterner stuff than that. She took her torch from the wall and thrust it toward the first mask. To her surprise, the knight moved back with a clang. The mask burst into flames.

"She moved down the line of knights, thrusting her torch at each one in turn. In the end, the masks were gone, but the knights held their line. As she stood, staring at the strange figures, each one lifted his sword. She felt a moment of fear, afraid they meant to skewer her, but they touched their swords to their helmets in a salute.

"Were they naked?" Lady Florence asked.

"No, they had armor on."

"Tragic," Lady Barbara muttered as her mother sighed.

"Then they all turned toward the door and marched out. Victoria tried to follow, but wind rushed through the arrow slits, preventing her for a time. When she was able to get through the door, it slammed behind her. She turned around, and the stone wall held no hint of the door she had just exited through. But all of the twelve storeroom doors were open. Not only that, the damp smell was gone, as were the watermarks. And every room was bursting with food. Baskets of fresh berries, hanging herbs, barrels of root vegetables, plucked fowl, salted fish. Every foodstuff she could imagine, fresh and perfect."

"What about mince pie?" Lady Florence asked.

"One room was stacked with them," Victoria said. How had Florence Gill heard about the start of her story? "Of course."

Penelope giggled.

"All this sudden largesse made the princess wonder how long her father's castle had been cursed. They had not been prosperous in a long time and she had blamed the war. But now, she had enough food for a fine wedding feast, if only she had a bridegroom. She went up to her solarium, tucked her feet under her gown, and began to think."

"Better she had gone to her chapel and prayed," said the devout Lady Rowena, the youngest of the countess's children.

"She isn't scared enough yet," Victoria said impishly.

"Were there any knights at the masquerade ball last night?" Penelope asked.

"No, dear," Lady Florence said. "Armor is too cumbersome for dancing."

"Lord Cuthbert came in armor one year," the countess said. "The odor was unspeakable after a couple of hours."

"I remember that," Lady Florence said. "My, that was twenty years ago or more."

"Everyone wore masks last night?" Penelope asked.

"Of course," Victoria agreed, "but there were more than twelve of us."

"What comes next?" asked the girl.

"Tigers," Victoria said as the door opened and her father came in, trailed by a collection of Dickondells. She balled up her knitting and dropped it into her basket, giving up the pretense. Her belly tightened as she looked Ernest over, trying to decide if she dared to approach him. Would Lewis relent if she gave him time?

"Why don't you join me for a game of chess, Victoria?" her father said, interrupting her perusal of Ernest.

"Penelope is learning," she told him, hoping he would take the hint and entertain his niece.

Instead, he crooked his elbow and pointed it in her direction. With as much grace as she could muster, she stood and took his arm. When they moved past the Dickondells, she made sure to let the satin ruffle at the base of her gown trail over Ernest's shoes, but she didn't dare look back to see if he noticed or reacted.

Penelope trotted in their wake without being invited to join them, standing to the side as they seated themselves in heavy dark chairs around a small table inlaid with black and white squares. A carved chess set of blocky figures was already in place.

"Back to your sewing, please, miss," Victoria's father said.

"I want to watch." The whine was back in the girl's voice

"Never disobey your elders. You need discipline, girl. Please ask the countess to ring for the nursemaid so that you may be returned to the nursery."

"Father, she's sharing my room," Victoria said.

He lifted his head, his gaze piercing hers. "Remedy that at once.

You will not have time to play mother to the child for the rest of the gathering."

Penelope stomped her foot. "She's not my mother!"

"I wasn't playing mother. There simply aren't any other children around." Victoria spoke quietly, hoping to avoid a scene.

"I'm sure the countess can bring in some tenant children or the like. Now run along, Penelope."

Victoria saw the bright sheen of tears in her cousin's eyes as she turned away, and the drag of her steps. "You have been indulgent to her before now, Father. What is wrong?"

"She needs discipline." He pointed his index finger at the table. "Now, play. Show me that intellect you frequently claim to have."

Victoria shot her father a murderous glare but held her tongue. The temper he unleashed so famously at his factories was never in true evidence at home, and that was for the best. "Never poke a sleeping bear" was a phrase she'd read in a dime novel once, and it applied to her relations with her father. She watched as the countess gestured to a hovering maid to escort Penelope from the room. Once the girl was gone, she considered her options.

Since she had white, she moved a pawn forward in a classic Queen's Gambit. "I find it hard to believe you really want to test my chess ability."

"On the contrary, daughter. I find chess is an excellent measure of a man."

"I'm a woman."

"Exactly," he said absently, moving his pawn in the Queen's Gambit Accepted response.

"Then what is your point? Surely you aren't going to consider allowing me to learn your business."

"You aren't educated for that. What is your next move?"

She ignored his dismissive comment for the sake of peace. After all, she'd had nothing to do but educate herself for the past eighteen months. They continued their game, moving knights into play. Victoria recalled her fairy tale, and the naughty knights with masks covering their privates. She held back a smile.

Her father caught her expression with a frown. "You are not going to win."

She shook her head slightly. "I am sorry, I was thinking of something else."

Her father's chin lifted and she thought he would reprimand her, but then his head swiveled toward the door. She kept her expression impassive as she realized she'd been outmaneuvered by her father yet again. He'd brought her here to the chess table to make sure she was in a pretty pose, suitably demure, so that he could display her.

To Edmund Parker-Bale and Percy Dandy-Willow, no less, who had just come through the parlor doors, accompanied by the butler. She hadn't realized the pair ever left Liverpool. Distant cousins, they were both descended from an earl whose direct male line had ended fifty years before. Mr. Parker-Bale's distinguishing characteristics were a receding, mouse-brown hairline, a twiglike body, and piercing blue eyes. Mr. Dandy-Willow looked like he belonged on a long-ago battlefield. Though he had a somewhat protruding belly, his arms were thick, which made his tailoring suspect. His hair was bushy black with eyebrows to match, and Victoria suspected he had to shave at least twice a day. At times, he sported a luxuriant mustache, but it was gone for now.

What on earth were they doing at the Fort? She could see the light firing in Lady Rowena and Lady Barbara's twin hazel gazes as they saw the two young men. Though not in their first youth, they were a couple of years north of Lady Barbara's twenty-five years.

Her father stood to shake their hands and draw them into the room. Victoria sat at the chess table as he introduced the men to the countess. She could tell the countess was not surprised by their arrival. Had it been planned all along, or had her father finagled the invitations for the rest of the Twelve Days? And how would she be able to be naughty with men around who could carry tales back to Liverpool? Assuming she decided to approach Ernest, she would have to be very discreet. The thought gave her a hollow feeling in the pit of her stomach. A novice at the game of love needed fewer roadblocks.

She remembered the sight of Lewis in his naval finery at the masquerade ball. Something about that white-blond mop of tightly controlled curls made her want to tug his head against hers. Ernest and the two latest arrivals were dark. Perhaps she did not find dark men attractive. Sir Humphrey had been ash blond. She clasped her hands in her lap and sighed. If the two new arrivals were kept busy by the daughters of the house, perhaps she could stroll to the stables and see what Lewis and the earl were doing. Her father might protest, but she could claim she'd set her cap for the earl. He might want her to find another husband to run the factories for him, but if he thought she could land an earl, she couldn't imagine he would protest. Even he didn't associate with noblemen of that caliber very often.

She stood, thinking to sidle out of the room while the men were occupied, but Mr. Parker-Bale saw her. He went on point like a hunting dog, his nostrils flaring. Cornered by those piercing eyes, she didn't move as he stalked her, and, upon reaching her side of the room, bowed deeply.

She had almost forgotten his flair for the Continental; he took her hand in his cold, greasy paw and bent over it, then kissed the backs of her fingers. At least she was spared his cousin's perpetual stubble marring her skin with hot pinpricks.

"Many felicitations of the season, Lady Allen-Hill," he exclaimed. "*Joyeux Noël.*"

Oh, yes. The French. "*Merci,*" she said, mocking him, though he didn't realize it.

He released her hand as a meaty paw descended on his shoulder. Mr. Dandy-Willow bowed, then laughed heartily.

"I hope you had a most happy Christmas, Lady Allen-Hill," he boomed.

"It could have been," Victoria muttered, thinking of her aborted tryst. "What brings you gentlemen to Sussex?"

"Change of scenery. Too much snow up north."

"We had snow here, too," she said sweetly.

"There isn't any on the ground *à cette heure*, madam," Mr. Parker-Bale demurred.

"I haven't looked outside all day," Victoria told them. "In fact, I was just thinking of taking a walk."

"You mustn't, you might take a chill," protested Mr. Dandy-Willow.

"You must allow *moi* to accompany you," said Mr. Parker-Bale.

"I saw you met Lady Barbara and Lady Rowena," she said. "A charming pair, yes? Lady Barbara is a particular friend of mine."

"Neither of them holds a candle to *vous*," said Mr. Parker-Bale.

"I was not fishing for compliments, sir, merely stating what I consider a fact."

"We could all five of us stroll," Mr. Dandy-Hill said, a bit too loudly. "Parker-Bale and I could do with a walk after so much time on the train."

She could do with some fresh, even accompanied, air. Both ladies were peering in their direction and she mimed wrapping her neck in a scarf and putting on a hat. They both nodded happily.

"You are in luck, gentlemen. I leave it to the two of you to figure out how to entertain three ladies."

Both men laughed heartily.

"Always ready to rise to the occasion, my lady," Mr. Dandy-Hill boomed.

With her current bent toward amorous congress, Victoria could not help but lift a brow at the man's phrasing. A large man in frame, she wondered what else might be large. Alas, she could not assuage her sexual curiosity with a man from Liverpool. She'd just wind up married to him, even if she decided he would never do.

CHAPTER 6

Though it was Boxing Day and the servants should have had the day to relax, the countess had persuaded her staff to take their half day in the morning and spend their afternoon preparing a feast and their evening serving it to the house party guests and a number of other visitors. She had confided to Victoria at tea that she'd done this for years and could count on a selection of interesting people at the party because she would be the only person in the area having one. Victoria, however, would not mar Boxing Day for her servants if she had her own home. She'd even kept her maid in Liverpool because the girl was recovering from measles, effectively giving her a two-week holiday.

This left Victoria with the haphazard assistance of Lady Florence's rather decrepit maid and her cousin Penelope as she struggled into her dinner dress, constructed mainly of black velvet with white cashmere accents. While the dress was appropriate for half-mourning, it exposed far too much skin to the castle drafts.

"I shall need a heavy shawl," she told Penelope as the exhausted maid pinned holly to either side of her head.

One of Victoria's black silk gowns had torn at the hem in London just before she'd arrived. She had the gown with her and had decided to give it to the maid in thanks at the end of her stay. The woman could do it over to suit herself, or sell it for quite a bit of money. Mourning clothes were of necessity a popular item in secondhand stalls.

"The holly looks well wi' your hair, my lady," the maid said.

"Thank you." Victoria would rather it have been mistletoe, though such things often attracted the wrong man's lips.

Lewis had barely noticed her when she'd visited the stables with her two suitors. In fact, she'd wondered if he deliberately hid away. The earl had shaken hands with the two men and welcomed them, but it was obvious they, and their assistants, were completely focused on their submarine project. The earl had said something about "trials" coming soon.

Victoria had looked at the long, iron cylinder with its mushroom-style windowed front and thought of something far different from marine exploration. At least the men weren't building the aquatic vessel to fire torpedoes, which is what most governments wanted them for. At one time, she recalled, the Fenians had been working on them to harass the British Navy. The Irish rebels had been of special concern in Liverpool ever since they had tried to blow up Town Hall earlier in the decade.

She had brought up the subject on the way back to the Fort and her suitors had been kept busy arguing the merits of the Irish question until teatime. After congratulating herself on a successful diversion, she had enjoyed some time with Lady Barbara, dissecting the merits of the Dickondell brothers. Her friend preferred Samuel for personality but thought Clement the best-looking.

"Here is your shawl," Penelope said, fingering the creamy white wool.

"Don't look so downcast. At least there will be other children at the nursery dinner tonight."

"Babies," Penelope said with a frown.

"Some of them are old enough to talk. They will be fun to play with," Victoria assured her. "They will idolize you. Also, your dress is very pretty."

The girl's costume was black velvet with a green collar and trim. "Mummy made it for me." Her lower lip trembled.

Victoria needed to get to the bottom of the situation with her aunt and uncle. Penelope missed her mother, so there was no lack of affection there. Why had they been separated? She glanced at herself in the mirror, knowing it was a problem for another day. Holding out her arms until Penelope came to her, she folded the girl into a hug, then offered her a dab of rose-scented Creed eau de cologne on each wrist as a special treat.

A knock came at the door and the maid, sweaty and with her cap askew, opened it. When Rupert Courtnay was revealed, the maid bobbed a swift curtsy and disappeared, no doubt to visit yet another guest who was in need of her services.

"Another night, another party," her father said, rubbing his hands together. "Who is on the guest list this time?"

"Many of the same faces as the masquerade ball two nights ago," Victoria said. "But Lady Barbara said Lord and Lady Judah Shield are coming down from London. Their new heir is staying at the nursery at Hatbrook Farm, though."

"Member of my club," Courtnay said. "I always like the soldiers. Practical lot."

"Yes, sir," Victoria agreed. "Lady Barbara also said the Baron of Alix has recovered from the chest cold that has left him out of the festivities until now, so we shall finally meet him."

"A Scotsman." Her father nodded thoughtfully and rubbed his chin. "What about all those Redcakes? Coming along with Hatbrook and his lot?"

"Mr. Noble is staying here for the duration," Victoria said. "As there are no other eligible gentlemen in that family, the subject of the Redcakes did not come up."

"Still, rather likely we'll see them," her father said with a thoughtful look.

Victoria stood and took Penelope's hand. "Run along to the nursery, darling."

Penelope's expression was mulish until she caught sight of her uncle's stern expression. "Yes, Victoria."

They followed her out of the room. Victoria wondered if her cousin would fall asleep up there before the long dinner was over. Might she have a room to herself that night? As far as she knew, her father hadn't given any orders about the girl.

"We are early," Victoria realized as they reached the main stair-case. "Why don't we go into the picture gallery for a few minutes? I believe they have a Rubens *Venus*, as well as a number of paintings done in his workshop."

"I don't wish to look at paintings of chubby nudes with my daughter," her father said in a dry tone as she led him through the door into the long gallery.

"Would you rather visit the mirrored gallery? I understand they have quite a fine one, a small version of the Hall of Mirrors in Versailles re-created by a countess who fled the Revolution and married an Earl of Bullen."

"No, this will be fine."

The space had been improved with gas lighting, but it was not bright enough to do the paintings justice. The moon was a mere sliver in the sky seen through a trio of small windows set into the wall and didn't lend any brilliance to the room.

"We need a lamp," Victoria muttered.

"Come back tomorrow," her father advised.

Instead, she sat down on a bench in front of what she dimly thought was a Cromwell-era family portrait. She patted the bench next to her.

Her father sighed audibly and seated himself. "What is it, Victoria? Are you planning to berate me for inviting Dandy-Willow and Parker-Bale? Because I will not apologize."

"You want either of them managing your business interests?" Victoria asked.

Her father ran his tongue over his upper lip. "I can train anyone with a good brain. They are both well-educated."

"Nincompoops," Victoria said.

"Give them a chance. I'll take a look at this Scotsman."

She nearly blurted out Lewis's name, but there was no point. Her father knew him already. "Very well. I shall do as you ask."

"Anything else, my dear?"

She couldn't stop herself. "Find out if Lewis Noble would relocate from Battersea. He has just the kind of scientific mind you could use at your factories."

"I will investigate. Anything else?"

"Yes, Father." She drew herself up. "Tell me what is going on with Penelope."

"She's visiting you for the holidays. Her father didn't want to leave her home with the staff when she had a perfectly nice party and cousin to come to."

"Why isn't she with her parents? She is an only child. Surely they want to see her."

Her father pulled his watch from his pocket and glanced at it. "We do not want to be late, my dear."

"Why won't you answer a simple question? You do realize having her underfoot disrupts your desire for me to husband hunt."

"On the contrary, it makes you seem more feminine," her father said. "It softens you."

"You think I appear hard?" The thought was beyond comprehension.

"I think you appear disinterested, and it won't do. You need to remarry. I won't have you wasting your best years. I expect to see you wed next year."

She wasn't disinterested in men, just marriage. "Or what, Father?"

"Or what indeed," he rejoined. "You shall be very bored, living all year around in Liverpool with nothing to entertain you. I don't need you to manage my household and I won't have you near the factories. So unless you plan to engage in voluminous good works, you're going to have nothing to do but pay calls and embroider."

She swore under her breath, not caring that her father could hear. It was his fault for saying such things in her earshot all these years.

"You weren't married long enough to have earned your freedom, Victoria. And you were robbed of children by the situation. Let's remedy that in 1890, shall we?" He patted her knee and stood, then walked out without looking back.

He wanted grandchildren. This torturing of her could have no more reason than that. But all she wanted was a little adventure before settling back into Liverpool. Really, the only thing being married would get her was a household to manage on her own. Other than that, it would be calls, good works, and embroidery regardless.

"Blast it," she said aloud. In the end, she probably would want children, if only to distract herself. But 1890 was only a few days away.

Realistically, a Scottish baron would not be a suitable son-in-law for an English manufacturer, as he presumably had lands in the north, but to her, anyone would be better than the Liverpool suitors. And Lewis Noble . . . she had not gotten anywhere with him, not even as a successful partner in trysting. Those Dickondells were a problem, but she wasn't prepared to avoid their company for fear of proposals quite yet. One of them might possibly become her lover. However, she was probably safe from an offer of marriage there, exactly as she wanted to be.

She stood and searched for the Rubens, finally finding a *Venus* in the center of the far wall, opposite the fireplace. Caught by the image's flowing hair, she realized the goddess had the same hair color and curls as Lewis Noble. Compared to the other men here, he was a god, though a much more physically spare one than this fleshy and bejeweled creature made from imagination and oil. Even Venus would probably want to toy with Lewis Noble.

One more chance: that was all she would permit herself. One more chance to see if she could make her way past Lewis's resolve. Then she would find an alternative.

The countess had seen fit to seat her unmarried guests by alternating the sexes. Her Boxing Day feast must be a matchmaking party. Victoria found herself between Mr. Dandy-Willow and Mr. Parker-Bale, not the men she would have chosen. Lady Barbara was on Mr. Parker-Bale's other side, her other dining partner the senior Dickondell son. Lady Rowena had Dickondell's left, demonstrating the countess's interest in the young man for one of her daughters. Seventeen-year-old Adela Dickondell had the earl as her first dining partner, and Lewis was far down the opposite end of the table, dining with Lady Florence and Maud Wilson. The countess must be trying to distract Clement away from Maud. She could hardly see Lewis over a clove-studded orange topiary.

As a plate of raw oysters on crushed ice was placed in front of her, Victoria felt her left foot nudged and—for lack of a better word—tickled by, presumably, Mr. Parker-Bale. She kept her expression neutral as she slurped her first briny oyster. Her lack of notice emboldened the man, whose shoe dipped under her skirts and began to travel up her calf. He had never been so bold back home, but she didn't want him as a lover.

She bent forward slightly, trying to catch Lady Barbara's eye in the hopes that she would distract the man. But her friend was deep in a conversation about cocker spaniels with Clement.

Mr. Parker-Bale's questing foot reached her knee. She jerked away. Her right elbow moved, cashmere landing in one of Mr. Dandy-Willow's oysters.

"I say," he said.

She whipped her head toward him, gasping a horrified apology.

"Lady Allen-Hill, if you wanted to converse with me, all you had to do was ask," Mr. Dandy-Willow said, his eyes dancing merrily under those absurdly bushy brows.

"Perhaps you are quite a nice man," she said aloud without meaning to.

A grin appeared and widened. Oh, dear; she had encouraged the man. If only he didn't have quite so much hair. She imagined birthing a baby that looked more like a bear cub than a human.

On her other side, Mr. Parker-Bale's foot had returned to its original position under the table. She glanced around, hoping her disturbance had been unnoticed, but found her father's gaze on her. He had Lady Florence on one side and Rose Redcake on the other. Rose gave her a little smile and turned back to Victoria's father. Victoria wondered how Rose had managed yet another invitation to dinner, given that she could distract the available men from the Gill daughters.

Thankfully, a footman removed her oysters and placed a clear soup before her.

She had learned to fill up on soup so that she was not too hungry when later, more voluptuous courses came along. Applauding herself when she was able to keep herself to one small bite of fried fish in a rich white sauce during the next course, she initially did not think anything of a sturdy foot nudging her own on the right. Instead, she tucked one slipper over the other and continued eating.

Next came potatoes, sweetbreads, vegetables, and, finally, one of the main courses, a stuffed game hen. She took one bite of the well-seasoned meat and closed her eyes. *Heavenly.* As she chewed her second bite, though, she found the tip of that interloping shoe on her ankle. She had no way to move unless she tilted her entire body toward Mr. Parker-Bale. Unfortunately, she had to speak to the man unless she wanted to visibly snub him, so she did just that, pasting a smile on her face as she slid as far to the left on her chair as she could.

His piercing blue gaze held no hint of either mischief or reproach, and they spoke cheerfully of the sights in Sussex until a vegetable salad was served. When he turned to his other partner, she scooted back to the middle of her chair, forgetting Mr. Dandy-Willow's foot. But there it was, back again. When she attempted to give him a setting-down glare, he smiled with the innocence of a child, just as his cold shoe tip found a sensitive spot at the center of her calf.

"That's quite enough!" She stood, dropping her napkin over her salad. Lady Barbara looked up at her, her blonde brows raised.

"I am indisposed," Victoria hissed and stalked off, her shawl dropping to the floor behind her. She was too embarrassed to pick it up. Her shoulders slumped as a footman opened the double doors of the dining room for her. Surely she was too mature to react so to a mere tickle? But the dinner had been so uncomfortable, she couldn't stand it.

If her father thought she would marry one of those two nodcocks he was a few pennies short of a pound himself. She knew a man who would woo by playing footsie under the table would be doing the same to some girl at a house party a few years hence, married or no. They weren't worth having, their educations notwithstanding.

She wandered for a while, until she found herself in a corridor she didn't recognize. Double doors were set into a recess in the middle and she opened them, hoping to find a library or some other place where she could compose herself. She turned a knob, hearing her fast breaths puffing against the door. How had those two suitors brought her to near hysteria? She pushed the door open, knowing it wasn't the men but everything. Being back to where she'd started, forced onto the marriage mart again, when she had thought she was finally secure with a husband to please her father. Instead, she'd lost two years of her life with nothing to show for it. And now she had nothing to show for her bold attempts to lose her virginity with Lewis, either.

All of a sudden, her stays felt much too tight, a sensation that had become unfamiliar since her figure had reduced. She bent as much as the steel would allow.

"Who is there?" a man asked. "Madam, are you well?"

She felt a firm hand at her back and was led deeper into the room, which seemed to be lit by a soft glow. A fireplace was lit at one end. The man pushed her down onto a cushioned bench. She attempted to compose herself and looked up into a sea of eyes.

She cried out, hunching against the wall, and felt a cold, smooth surface against her bare shoulders. Opening her eyes wider, she realized she was staring into a wall of mirrors. The man next to her had strangely striated reddish brown and amber eyes reminiscent of tiger's-eye gemstones.

"Dear God," she said, putting a hand to her heart.

The man moved slightly, and he came into fuller relief. Either that or her vision was clearer. She had nearly swooned.

"Lord Judah Shield," she blurted, recognizing him.

He bowed slightly. "At your service, madam."

"All those eyes," she murmured. "I was quite taken aback for a moment."

"I understand. In the firelight, the effect is unnerving."

She made an effort to compose her breathing. "I am Lady Allen-Hill."

He inclined his head. "You may not remember meeting me, but you showed me a cake once at a party."

"Oh, yes," she recalled. "I wore a dress not dissimilar to the cake."

He smiled. "Fashion."

"You ended up marrying the girl who came in after us, no?"

"That is correct. My wife Magdalene. You married as well?"

"And was widowed." She sighed.

"I am sorry."

"It is no matter. It feels more like a dream than an actual part of my past. Sir Humphrey became seriously ill so suddenly."

"I had not put Victoria Courtnay and Lady Allen-Hill together until just now. You met Lewis Noble on the road, I believe. He mentioned you when I saw him earlier."

"Yes. His motorized conveyance had broken down." Why had Lewis spoken of her? Was he investigating her intentions?

"Not surprising," Lord Judah said with a chuckle. "He never stops playing. Instead of perfecting one machine, he moves on to the next. Therefore, they are all perpetually in need of repair."

"He's a restless soul?"

"I don't think he knows how to set down any roots. I sympathize with that, but I wish, well . . ." Lord Judah shifted from side to side. "Any man who is happy wants the same for his friends."

"And Lewis Noble is unhappy," she said. "I agree with you."

"You like him?" Lord Judah asked.

Victoria chuckled. "Such an improper question, sir."

"You seem unusually interested in the topic of Lewis. I'd like it if a good woman took an interest in him. He needs to settle down."

"I don't plan to be a good woman," she murmured.

Lord Judah laughed. "I'm sure you won't be able to help yourself. I have never heard any outrageous gossip about you. Your father is a bit mysterious, though."

"He keeps everything close to his chest." She thought of Penelope again. "But I think he's a good man, and probably as lonely as Mr. Noble."

"It's good that you are both at this house party. You can drag him away from that blasted submarine."

She glanced at him, amused. "You think this is a good occupation for a lady?"

"I think your patience would be rewarded. You're just the kind of lady Lewis needs." He bowed again and walked away, his shoes clicking on the parquet floor.

Victoria sat back and closed her eyes. Lewis's friend had all but given her carte blanche to pursue him. But his friend didn't speak for him. He was simply a happily married man who wished for his pleasure in marriage to spread in his social circle.

Still, he gave her the confidence to give Lewis one more go before trying to find an alternate lover. He had spoken about her, after all.

Smoke drifted around the men as they departed the dining room on their way to the ladies in the drawing room, reminding Lewis of his machine shop. He hung back as card games were arranged and the Gill sisters bickered over who would play the piano first and who would sing. Maids brought in trays, staring resentfully at the relaxed guests when it was they who should be enjoying Boxing Day. Eventually, everyone was settled, but he hadn't seen the one person he'd been curious about.

Lady Allen-Hill had jumped up from the dinner table in some alarm. From the daggered glances her two dining companions had given each other, he thought they'd had something to do with it. Had they reached for her limbs or something similarly inappropriate?

Lewis couldn't help wondering about those thighs. Slender and hard? Soft and dimpled? She and her little cousin took long walks in the gardens every day, he was told, so she probably did have some strength in her limbs. He wondered if she rode, and the thought of her astride a horse in the way he'd once seen on an erotic postcard had him facing directly into the fire until he composed himself.

Where was she? He glanced around again and caught Lord Judah's eye. The man detached himself from Ernest Dickondell and came forward.

"You look irritated. Submarine project going badly?" his friend asked.

"No, no, going fine," Lewis said.

"Dickondell was just inquiring after Lady Allen-Hill. I take it she is the catch of the house party."

"Whatever do you mean?" Lewis growled.

"I heard about the dustup at dinner."

"I heard no such thing, though she did leave abruptly."

"I found her in the Hall of Mirrors," Lord Judah said.

"You did? Is she there now?" He glanced at the door, ready to leave.

"I expect she retired." Lord Judah's unusual eyes caught the firelight, making them appear more golden than usual.

"Awfully early to retire," Lewis mused.

Lord Judah smiled. "Someone should entice her back to the party."

"Or not."

Lord Judah clapped him on the shoulder. "She likes you, you know. I think you should go to her before Dickondell does."

"What if she has a headache?" He spoke without thinking.

"You can provide a cure for that." His friend lifted an eyebrow.

"I'm not at ease around the woman," Lewis confessed. "Just when I think I can relax into the ways of a house party, something stops me."

"Maybe because you find yourself unable to think of the lady in a casual fashion?"

"Hardly," Lewis scoffed. "She's the Liverpool heiress, you know. I'm not going to leave London."

"I think she'd be happy if you simply paid attention to her," Lord Judah stated. "But if you really don't want to, a signal to Dickondell will allow him to formulate his own plans."

Lewis narrowed his eyes. "Think she's back in her room? With that cousin of hers?"

"The cousin is up in the nursery with the other children. They have quite a party going. You can hear the laughter from the stairs. And Eddy's in the stable with the hands, playing dice."

"Great," Lewis muttered. "He'll probably skin the lot of them."

"Nonetheless, it is a rare chance to speak to her without fear of interruption."

Except from my own tortured thoughts. He forced a smile for his friend. "You are right, of course."

Lord Judah gave him a knowing glance, then clapped his hand on Lewis's shoulder again. "You had best go now, before Lady Florence comes up for a chat. I can sense her lurking now."

Lewis nodded and departed without further comment.

The front hall, stairs, and corridors of the guest wing were surprisingly free of servants. They must be taking any chance they could to celebrate the end of their holiday. Candles burned so low on the walls that his path seemed like one from a waking dream. When he found Lady Allen-Hill's door, he knocked, wondering what he would find: welcome or dismissal?

CHAPTER 7

The door cracked open. Lewis saw Lady Allen-Hill still wore her evening dress, though her thick hair had been released from some of its more tortuous braids, which had earlier been tucked and pinned so that they hung down the back of her neck. Her mahogany curls now fell down her left arm, cradling the outside of one magnificent breast.

He inhaled sharply, searching for a peek of nipple as his gaze outlined her feminine curves. "You left dinner rather suddenly."

She nodded. "My dinner companions were not congenial."

Lust had him blinking, trying to remember who she'd been seated with. "They came down from Liverpool especially to see you."

"I can only manage one at a time." She smiled, but the expression did not reach her eyes.

His trousers felt uncomfortably tight and he wondered if his voice was higher than usual when he spoke again. "Is your father hoping you will choose one of them?"

"I cannot imagine they would be here otherwise, but the countess may have plans for them. She is far more marriage-minded at this time than I am."

He leaned against the doorjamb as his center of gravity continued to shift. "Do you have a preference between the two?"

She inhaled, her lips parted slightly. Could she smell his arousal?

On her, from this slight distance, he could smell some kind of hair pomade made of coconut oil. It made her hair shine as if it drew light from any available source.

"I have a preference for you, Mr. Noble, but you seem to no more than pull me in before you push me away." Her voice caught.

"I am sorry for that." He stared into her eyes, admiring her boldness. "I would much rather pull you in than push you away."

"Then please stop doing so."

He nodded.

She crossed her arms, one over the other, and tucked them underneath her bosom. "Well?"

He tilted his head, wondering what she was waiting for, given her straightforward nature. "Are you going to invite me in?"

"Penelope," she said with an air of exasperation. "She's staying in the room with me."

He smiled. "I'm told the children are happy in the nursery, and therefore she is unlikely to surprise us, but perhaps you would rather join me in my room?"

"From a practical standpoint, that is not a good idea. This dress will be impossible to manage without a maid." She unbent enough to lift a finger. "And don't tell me you can act as my maid. You would be certain to rip something. I shall ring for one, and then meet you in a bit."

He nodded, wondering if he would hear from her again that night. Might she have second thoughts? She closed the door with one last, lingering glance that told him she might come after all. Strolling down the hall, with the lights flickering, he kept moving past his room until he reached the end of the corridor. A blacker rectangle of light was a window that had probably once been an arrow slit. He peered out, hoping to see something of the wintry landscape outside. Perhaps the sight would cool him down. The frigid cold of the corridor was not reducing the heat in his loins. He could see nothing but blackness, a pit similar to the state of his mind, wiped clean for once. Just accepting, willing, instead of analyzing.

Eventually, he heard a door open a ways behind him and turned back toward his room. At his door, he met Lady Allen-Hill, who was now wearing the casual sort of dress a woman might don to do inventory on her jams and jellies.

"I've become used to seeing you in a dressing gown," he commented as he opened the door.

She passed through. "It's much too early to risk that. But this dress is easy to manage."

"If we are caught, I shall tell the interloper you are dressed to help me make a repair on the submarine," he joked, following her in.

She fixed him with a gimlet stare. "You do not like my attire, sir?"

"It is too plain for you," he said. "I like all the feminine, embroidered details on your clothing. This dress reminds me of what my cousins used to wear in Bristol, when we lived there." And there it was, another reference to Alys. Why did he torture himself so? She would not enter his thoughts again during this tryst. He forbade it.

To set his thoughts in motion, he shut the door and put his hands on Lady Allen-Hill's waist, drawing her forward. As her hips brushed his, her hands went up to balance on his rib cage. He glanced down. From this angle, her manicured fingers were the epitome of feminine grace. He bit back a groan at the thought of what they could do to his shaft. And she was a widow, too, not a blushing young miss. She might actually be willing to do some of the things he imagined late at night, when he was too tired to think about machinery.

He forgot about her fingers when her hips touched his again. She was not as tall as he, so she must have extraordinarily long legs. His erection tightened to an almost painful intensity at the realization. Long legs, wrapped around him. Legs in the air, spread for his maximum penetration. Slender legs bent at the knee, feet pressed into the mattress, so her hips could gyrate against his as she cried out in inelegant, undeniable ecstasy.

His fingers tightened around her upper arms.

"Too many clothes," he croaked.

"I agree," she said in a choked whisper. "But here, I need to give you this." She handed him a tin box.

"What's this?"

"My rubbers." She looked up at him hopefully.

He smiled and took the box. "Thank you."

She reached for his tie at the same time as he reached for the buttons down the front of the dark blue gown. Their fingers and arms tangled. She squeaked, he chuckled. They apologized, arms flailing as they tried to work out who could go first.

"Let's take off our own clothes," he suggested.

"Good idea," she agreed.

He found difficulties presented themselves with this as well, since he couldn't take his eyes off her as each bit of underclothing, then pearlescent skin, revealed itself. This must be how it was to undress himself as a wee lad in skirts, all fumbling and missed opportunities to unbutton. The lady chuckled as a button on his waistcoat refused to go through the hole for a third time. By then, she was down to her combinations.

"Let me," she said, shaking her head.

He could smell her skin, and a hint of soap, when she stepped close enough to take over the unbuttoning from him. Fine dark hairs stood up from her bare arms.

"You're cold," he whispered.

"You will warm me," she said in a practical manner, tugging his waistcoat off his arms. Then she pulled his shirt from his trousers and, after loosening his tie, set to work on the buttons.

He stood mute as she took out his cufflinks and dropped them on the mantelpiece, then removed his shirt, wondering if he'd ever been so undressed in front of a woman in firelight.

She ran her fingers up a vein on his bare arm, as if playing piano. "You have beautiful muscles."

He flexed instinctively, making her laugh. "I could already tell they were large, Lewis. Such intellect and brute strength do not often go together."

"I lift a great deal of heavy metal items," he told her.

She nodded thoughtfully, then whipped his undershirt over his head. When she drew in a sharp breath, he looked down and saw his nipples had hardened to tight little points.

His gaze shifted and he saw her tongue dart over her lower lip, as if she wanted to taste him. His cock twitched and his throat went so dry, he'd probably lost the power of speech. Mutely, he reached for her combinations, tearing down the front placket, scattering buttons across the floor. He pushed her down until she sprawled along the sofa in front of the fireplace and settled himself on top of her, think-ing nothing but "Mine. Now."

One hand went into her hair, the other to a soft globe of breast. He tweaked her nipple, willing it into the same peak as his as his mouth crushed hers. She squirmed, which allowed his pelvis to settle against her soft warmth. One of her legs drew up along the cushions. He let go of her hair and took her leg instead, grinding against her. The real-ization that layers of cloth kept his cock from her hot depths was enough to make him want to curse the skies. He drew up his knees and lifted himself off her, though he did not release her from their kiss, and fought his trouser front.

Her hands moved from his back to his waist. She helped him undo buttons and push down fabric, until the only thing between his cock and her was her combinations.

"Lift," he urged, hoping to pull them off her.

"Use the slit," she said, pulling him back down. "I don't want to wait."

"Amazing woman," he said, reaching down to separate the fabric. He took both edges and ripped up until the tear reached the open front. Then she was bare to him, bare to his gaze and his body both.

He saw a triangle of curls matching her dark head, smelled a faint scent of coconut there, too, as well as musk. Dipping his fingers to that forbidden place, he found her hot and damp. His fingers made her gasp and move even closer to him. He opened the tin box and took out a long sheath, then carefully pushed his cock into it, wetting the tip. She put her fingers to his cheeks and pulled his mouth back to her, kissing him openmouthed. He raked her tongue with his, learn-ing the contours of her mouth as he settled against her, his cock rub-bing along her secret place. When she jerked against him, he knew he'd found her pearl. He moved along her again, generating more re-sponse from her. The third time she groaned, her long legs lifting and folding until they wrapped around him, just as he'd imagined.

He reached down and spread her wide for him, then moved his cock to her opening and thrust home in one smooth movement.

She cried out, bowing back, and he wondered if he'd given her the ultimate pleasure so soon. What a sweetly responsive woman. But then he opened his eyes and saw a look of tension on her face, quite the opposite from what he expected.

A little of the fog left his brain, for all that he was buried inside her. "Did I hurt you?" Involuntarily, he pulled back a little.

But she found his buttocks and gripped them hard, digging her fingers in, her jaw taut with determination. "Keep going."

He bent his head to her hair and did as she ordered. After a few slow strokes, she seemed to relax, and he realized it had been a while for her. She hadn't been married for long. Perhaps he was the first man she'd sported with since her husband's death. The thought made him feel tender. She moved her hands up his back, stroking his skin. He kissed her temple, tasting salt. His knees rasped along the cushions. She shifted, allowing him to further penetrate her secret depths. The way she felt was everything. He thrust inside her in a kind of tropical haze. The fire kept them warm, and her smell was a nautical one. It was as if he rocked on the sea, as well as inside her. His completion caught him by surprise. He arched his back, thrusting spasmodically as the orgasm took him, and then fell back to earth with her still gripping him.

He opened his eyes and found her regarding him with a frown between her eyes. "I'm still hard. I'll keep going for you."

She shook her head. "Do not trouble yourself."

He grinned and found her mouth with his, determined to overwhelm her, to drive her to the ultimate completion. Not trouble himself, indeed. Changing position so that he could rub her pearl directly, he began to stroke her, holding her legs as far apart as he could in the narrow space. Soon, she couldn't kiss him anymore, and her gaze went soft and unfocused. He nuzzled her neck as she came apart beneath him, cooing with surprise. He felt the pulsation of her heartbeats against his chest.

As soon as her breaths slowed, she pushed against him, and he realized he had his full weight on her. He shifted to the cushions, attempting to stay inside her as they moved into a side-to-side position. She, however, pulled back, disengaging.

"Don't you want to be held?" he asked.

"I must go. What if Penelope comes back?"

He could tell she was still out of breath. "The maid will stay with her until you arrive. We can do this more than once, you know. Just relax with me for a while and then I will be ready."

She moved back so quickly that she lost her position on the sofa. He grabbed for her as her bottom hit the carpet.

"Ooof!" Her hands went to her knees and she pushed them together. The slim, firm thighs had him already longing for another go.

"I'm so sorry," he apologized. "We should have gone to the bed." Wary of his own balance since his clothing was still around his knees, he crouched next to her and put his arms around her. "Come, let's test the mattress."

She shook her head. "I need to go, Lewis, truly."

"I'll get you a towel," he said, feeling a hundred kinds of fool. Somehow he had failed her. Not enough experience, and none with a lady. Had it been wrong to impose *la petite mort* on her? Perhaps she had really wanted him to stop.

Turning away, he removed the rubber, pulled up his small clothes and trousers, then went to get a basin and towel. She had her dress over her head before he arrived, but she took what he offered and went behind a screen in the corner. He gathered the rest of his clothes and seated himself on a chair, his senses still swimming from his release and the heavy, sealike scent of sex in the small room. Closing his eyes, he allowed himself to drift until he heard the sound of the screen moving back.

Victoria put her hand to her chest to still her racing heart. Her first orgasm, followed by an embarrassing fall to the floor, her first lover's obvious fear that he hadn't satisfied her, all had her senses on overload. But over and above all that, she was frantic to leave before he saw her again and realized she had blood on the fabric of her combinations, which was, in truth, still bleeding.

Now that she was a widow, no value would have been placed on her virginity. No one had cared about virgin widows since King Henry VIII's wife, Katherine of Aragon, had so ardently pleaded that she hadn't slept with her first husband to stave off losing her position as Queen of England. But nonetheless, Victoria didn't want Lewis to *know*. To realize she hadn't known how to find completion, to keep him from making all that extra effort when she was certain, as she'd been told by friends, that all a man wanted after exerting himself was to sleep.

She had done it all wrong. Pushing back the screen, she peered out, hoping that Lewis had indeed gone to sleep. She could see his eyes were closed, proving the truth of what her friends had said about men after lovemaking. She tiptoed out, but her hip caught the edge of the screen. It squeaked, and he opened his eyes.

"Drat," she muttered. Even with reducing, her hips were generously built.

Lewis leapt to his feet, his muscled chest still gleaming with sweat. "What?"

"I am so sorry to wake you. I bumped the screen."

"I wasn't sleeping. I was waiting to escort you . . . if you really feel you must go, of course."

Victoria sidled to the door, careful to keep the front of her body facing him for fear that the blood would soak to her dress. Her fault for not wearing a petticoat. "No need," she assured him. "I am just down the hall."

"I want to be a gentleman," he said.

"I know you are a gentleman," she said, walking sideways, as if she were a crab. "But I shall be fine. Err, thank you for an illuminating experience."

His expression lost much of its buoyancy. "I didn't please you, did I? I am so sorry. I'm not used to your sort."

Victoria felt her expression freeze into place. "I can explain," she began. Dear God in Heaven, should she have told him she was a virgin? She'd been afraid he would not take her if she had.

"Explain? No, dear lady, the fault is all mine. I do not associate with Society. Indeed, I'm just here as a mechanic for the earl, truly. I never should have reached so high. You are too special."

"A mere mechanic? You aren't anything of the kind," Victoria protested, almost not hearing his compliment. "Of course you are a guest, not just a mechanic. The countess spoke of you from the start. You have been at all of the holiday celebrations. You are simply a gentleman who is good with his hands."

She realized her cheeks were flushed as his chin tilted up to enable him to make a closer examination of her. "I didn't mean . . . well, I did mean, of course. I shall simply say good night."

Keeping her skirts tucked behind her, she reached for the door and undid the lock before slipping out, back first. The last thing she saw was his bemused expression. But she heard his words again, like a caress. *You are special.*

When she reached the inside of her room, she sagged against the door. She wanted to ring for a maid and order a bath, but no one must know what she'd done. Smiling, she closed her eyes and tucked her arms around herself. She, Victoria, was no longer a virgin. She had finally become a woman, and as awkward as the aftermath had been, the sensations he'd evoked in her had been heaven. The question was, would Lewis Noble ever be willing to touch her again?

In almost a parody of her life, Victoria sat with her cousin the next day in the morning parlor. The ladies of the house party were all seated around the room, and Victoria wondered if any of them thought she appeared different. She felt altered, as if her walk was that of a sexually experienced woman. The slight soreness between her legs contributed to this, of course, but it didn't stop her from thinking about what had happened every couple of minutes, and wondering when she would next experience lovemaking again.

Lewis had been so humble; endearing, really. She wished she had known how to please him, but that had been the point, after all: to gain experience. Her father would continue to insist she marry again soon, and her husband would expect at least a nominally experienced woman. Last night had taught her that some men, at least, wanted a woman to find pleasure in the act. She found she quite agreed with that notion. Her only quibble was that she needed to learn how to do it without subjecting a tired male to additional exuberance that he was ill prepared to offer.

"What are you thinking about, Lady Allen-Hill? You look so pensive," the countess said.

Victoria smiled blankly. "I was recalling, err—"

"Our fairy tale?" Rose asked eagerly from her position on one end of the sofa. She had a half-finished sock in her lap but had not been working on it.

"*My* fairy tale," Penelope corrected with a lift of her sharp chin. She had fought with Victoria that morning over what dress she would wear and had a pinched look to her features.

"Penelope," Victoria admonished. "No one owns a story. And besides, Rose is right. I did have something to report. It seems our fairy tale is coming true yet again."

"Is it really?" Penelope asked with wide eyes.

"Yes. First we had the masquerade, just like the twelfth challenge in the story, and then, last night, I had the eleventh one, in real life."

Rose's knitting needles clattered to the floor. She grabbed for the sock, trying to keep the stitches intact. "Do tell, Victoria."

"It was Lord Judah. I went into the Hall of Mirrors and there he was. The mirrors reflected the fireplace and his tiger eyes. Stunning really, to see Queen Avice's prediction come true right here in modern times. At least in the sense of tigers, if not precisely eleven of them roasting." Victoria smiled in satisfaction.

"But only you saw it," Penelope whined.

"Perhaps Lord Judah will repeat the illusion for you, if you ask him nicely," Rose said.

"He has already departed for home," the countess said. "I am sorry to disappoint you."

Penelope rubbed her nose. Victoria handed her a handkerchief.

"Countess, you said I could do puzzles?" the child asked. "May I take Cousin Victoria with me, or does she need to stay with you?"

"Go ahead, dear," said their hostess.

Rose leapt to her feet. "I shall join you. I adore puzzles."

Victoria nodded to the countess and stood, happy to have something to busy her hands and mind. As it was, the ladies would continue to ask questions about her thoughts, and they were far too indecent to share. The three of them walked to the sitting room, where several puzzles were set out. In fact, she noted ten different puzzles on the tables. Each puzzle was of a different English or Scottish castle.

"Here we are in our fairy tale again," Victoria said.

"What do you mean?" asked Rose.

"Remember? Ten castles uncastled." Victoria made a grand gesture across the tables.

Rose looked around, her lips parting in a grin. "My goodness, you're right!"

Penelope danced around the tables, twirling her velvet skirt. "I wonder what will happen at our end of the fairy tale."

"In your cousin's story, one hopes the princess will save her prince and marry him."

Penelope screwed up her nose. "That's no fun. I do not want a husband."

Rose tilted her head, her expression becoming wistful. "You are too young. You will change your mind in a decade or so."

"I will not," Penelope said, stomping her foot. "What is next, Victoria? If it is only boring old husbands we are seeking, then I would like to get through the story as quickly as possible."

Victoria thought. "Ribbons ripping comes next, I believe. We shall have to wait and see how that comes about."

They seated themselves at the table with what appeared to be a puzzle depicting Pevensey-Sur-Mer Fort and began to sort pieces.

"Is this the moat or the sky?" Rose asked, holding up a piece about half an hour later.

The door opened before Victoria could speak, and Lady Barbara stepped in, looking pensive. She held letter paper in one hand and a handkerchief in the other. Her ash brown topknot had been knocked askew, as if she'd been worrying at her pins as she read.

Victoria intuited that her friend wanted to converse. Since Penelope seemed to be calming under Rose's influence, she stood and gestured to the fireplace. Lady Barbara shook her head slightly and turned back to the door. Victoria followed her into the hall, closing the door behind them.

"What is wrong?" she asked, observing that the letter paper wasn't lined with black, a sign the letter might be a death announcement.

Lady Barbara took her hand and pulled her into the library on the other side of the corridor. A more masculine room, its wood paneling darkened the space. Without a fire, the room held little warmth either in temperature or atmosphere.

Victoria glanced at the letter again. "Bad news?"

"News I could not share with the little one present or, indeed, a near stranger."

"I am not entirely clear why Rose is here still," Victoria ventured.

"My mother invited her for purposes of her own," Lady Barbara said.

"Such as?"

Her friend pressed her already rather thin lips together. "I believe she intends to thwart some plan of Aunt Florence's by the offices of Miss Redcake."

"How intriguing." Victoria chuckled.

"You sound so naughty when you laugh," Lady Barbara said. "It always seems as if you have the most delicious intrigue in mind. One of the reasons I like you so."

Victoria's thoughts rambled toward her stolen moments with Lewis Noble.

"Ah, now my friend has become pensive," Lady Barbara observed. "If you will not share your secrets, I can at least share mine." She thrust her letter at Victoria, who took it and moved to a chair directly under a gas sconce so that she could read it in the dim room.

Lady Barbara went to the window and pulled back the heavy green curtains. Outside, tiny snowflakes mixed with rain dampened the windowpane. She breathed against the glass and began to draw in the white mist with her finger.

Victoria forced her attention to the letter. "Where did this come from?"

"A cousin of mine who lives up north. One of those women who never leaves her home yet all the news comes to her as if by some strange alchemy."

She perused the light, crabbed handwriting, wishing her family's secrets had not reached the hand of a gossip. How was it that a complete stranger, a relative of her late husband, knew more about her family than she did?

"Is this correct, do you think?"

"It does explain why Penelope isn't allowed to reside with her mother."

"I don't believe it. Aunt Clarissa tends to hysteria, but she's not a lunatic. She was always such fun when I was a child. And Penelope adores her. She's said nothing about any trouble."

"Was she terribly religious?"

"No more so than anyone else, at least not until recently. It is not as if she read sermons. I believe she was involved in Methodist Temperance, but that is not a bad cause."

"No," Lady Barbara agreed. "But it does seem as if your uncle has cast her off."

"And that she is somewhere near the Fort," Victoria said. "I wonder if Father has been to see her. I cannot understand why he feels he must keep me so in the dark. It is one thing to keep his business matters away from me, but this is family, and female family at that."

"Your color is quite high today," Lady Barbara observed. "Is this all that is troubling you? The issue of Penelope?"

"No. Please, tell me everything you know about Lewis Noble," Victoria said, feeling her cheeks warm.

CHAPTER 8

Lady Barbara told Victoria everything she knew about Lewis Noble, but nothing new came to light. The man himself had disappeared into the earl's workrooms in the stable block, and neither of them appeared at dinner. Victoria considered going to his room late that evening, but Penelope had been very clingy, and her compassion for the girl's difficult situation, coupled with a vague fear that she might be coming down with a cold, made her stay in. No one knocked either.

The next day, she was back in the parlor with the women, sorting embroidery silks. This reminded her of ribbons ripping, the ninth task of Princess Everilda, and she was happy to continue spinning her tale when Penelope, her hands full of red, orange, and yellow silks, begged her for more.

"As you may recall," Victoria began, "Everilda was in her solarium, having experienced her first Christmas miracle at the hands of Queen Avice. Well, time is short for both the princess and us, so it should be no surprise to you that Everilda fell into a kind of daze."

She paused dramatically. "And then a parade of tigers entered."

Lady Barbara's hands went still on their bed of blue and purple silks. "Real tigers?"

"No, she was dreaming," Victoria assured them. "They streamed toward her. First, nothing but bright light, then breaking into shades of tawny reds and blacks, then finally the vague shape of feline faces, and then the eyes. Those eyes blazed into Everilda's own gaze, all eleven pairs. Yes, eleven tigers, all came to stand around her in a circle, faintly glowing.

"The princess woke with a start and looked at the cushion where she had been perched. It had been a simple blue wool before, but now the fabric was dotted with eyes. She traced them with her fingers, counting twenty-two. 'Be gone,' she commanded, and the cushion burst into flames. She jumped back with a shriek and reached for a ewer of water, which she threw into the flames.

"An old retainer woke from her slumber and tottered forward, peering through the smoke. A shape seemed to coalesce behind the wall of gray froth. Everilda reached in and drew out a shiny, supple black shift. But as it came through the smoke, the fabric disintegrated, the strands unraveling until her hands held nothing but black threads that became soot, then nothing at all. The old woman fell to her knees and began to implore the Mother of God for intercession on the princess's behalf. But other than irritation at the loss of her favorite cushion, Everilda was unmoved."

"It's like a warning," Lady Rowena said with a nod of satisfaction at Victoria's including of a religious element. "If the princess does not have that shift by the end of the quests, she will never see her prince again in this life."

Victoria held her hands tightly in her lap, refusing to give in to scratching the itch in her left eyebrow. She had no idea how to resolve this fairy tale, any more than she had of how to deal with the absent Lewis. Surely an ardent lover would make an appearance, send a note, something. What magic must she work to win him into her bed for the remainder of this house party?

"The sleet appears to have stopped," she said. "I believe I shall take some air while I can."

"Do you want company?" Lady Barbara asked absently, separating a lavender strand from a royal purple one.

"No," she said quickly, for she planned to visit the submarine crew.

She went up to her room and found a sturdy fur-trimmed coat and warm bonnet, then changed into boots. A few minutes later, she was ready to visit the stables.

Lewis turned away from the blacksmith, who was at his forge in the stable yard, making a replacement for a panel that had been damaged, and went back into the warmth of the stables. Though horses had not been in this space for close to a year, it still smelled strongly of livestock, overlaid by the acrid scent of electrical batteries. The earl had asked him to gather the order of dry cell batteries and get them installed so that trials could begin soon.

Lewis went to the shelf and reached for a handful of the zinc cans. As he turned, two workmen went by carrying a wooden bench upholstered in leather, meant as a seat for the submarine interior. The inside would be as luxurious as the outside was practical. Looking at the bench inevitably reminded him of his interlude on the sofa in his room, and he wished he'd found the time to see Lady Allen-Hill again. In a less-isolated locale, he might have walked to the village and purchased her some small token of his appreciation. But since she had not searched him out either, he had to consider that he'd not pleased her well, as he initially hoped. Or she had not intended that they share more than one night.

When the bench had passed, he could see a woman walking toward him. The lady of his thoughts, her dark hair tucked under a jaunty hat, moving with purpose in his direction. Her hips swayed visibly, even under her coat, waking his cock. As if in a dream, he put down the cans and walked forward, sawdust tickling his nose.

"Mr. Noble," she said in her husky voice as she stopped in front of him.

Not sure where to begin, he stood, tongue-tied. She winced, which called him to action. Reaching out, he clasped her arm. She looked down, then jerked back. With dismay, he saw he'd left dark fingerprints on the gray fabric of her coat.

"Terribly sorry," he exclaimed. He reached for a handkerchief but didn't find one in his pocket. She pointed to his neck, and he realized he'd tied a large red pocket square around it at some point.

"What a dirty boy you are," she said.

In that dulcet tone, he wasn't sure if she were referring to his physical disarray or their activities of Thursday evening. "My apologies. I did not mean to muss you."

She lifted her eyebrows. "I haven't seen you at meals or, indeed, anywhere else. I was afraid you and the earl had drowned in that contraption of yours."

"Not yet," he said cheerfully. "You shall have your chance to worry soon enough. But, on a more serious note, we have been at the infernal beast all night. I haven't left the stable in at least thirty-six hours."

"You should get some rest before you become silly," she said, lifting her chin to his neck again.

Shaking his head, he untied it and handed it to her so that she could dab at her coat.

"Water might help, but I think the trough is iced over," he said ruefully.

"I'm sure one of the maids can fix it." She wiped harder.

"I wouldn't wait long. I might have had acid on my hands."

She tsked. "Wouldn't that damage your skin?"

He shook his head. "Immune, after the years of foul substances that have coated me."

"I did notice the black lines on your palms. Permanently baked in, I suppose."

"And under my nails," he agreed. "Mechanical work is a foul business."

She nodded. The brim of her hat shaded just enough of her right eye that he couldn't quite gauge her emotions. He waited for her to speak, to give him some clue of how she wanted him to proceed.

"I did miss you last night," she said softly. "This is my first experience, of, err, house-party antics. I was afraid I didn't please you."

"Not at all, my dear." He leaned his head toward hers to give them some privacy, but it only served to garner attention from the workmen, who were returning to pick up the next bench.

"The earl wants us to be ready to start testing tomorrow. It is so busy here that I am afraid you will be hurt." He didn't mean for his concern to sound like a dismissal, but she took his sleeve in her hands, pulling his palm toward her, and placed the red handkerchief in it. Then she turned away.

"Lady Allen-Hill," he said, "please don't go. Wouldn't you like to see what we are doing?"

He knew she wouldn't, of course. Machinery did not fascinate women.

"You are busy." She shook her head. "I should not have interrupted your work."

As if to prove her point, he heard the earl's voice coming from the other side of the stables, calling for him.

"I would like to talk to you some more," he said. "Just not now. I would like to come to your room later."

She stepped up to him and touched her lips to his. The warmth of her surprised him, and he parted his lips, meaning to speak. Her response was tender and innocent. A different woman might have tangled tongues with him, but she kept her lips closed in a sweet bow. He wondered how much this naughty widow really knew about lovemaking. Had she chosen him to teach her?

But he could do nothing now. The earl called again, and if they were spotted in this compromising position, especially with her father in residence, he might find himself engaged to the Liverpool heiress with alarming speed.

He put his hands on her cheeks and gently moved her. Her hands went to the places where his fingers had touched. Of course he'd left marks again, and this time on her skin. She stared at him, wide-eyed, a picture of maidenly confusion.

Lewis felt hot breath at his ear and turned to find the earl uncomfortably close.

"Lost my spectacles," Nicholas said. "Can't quite see who this lady is."

"It's Lady Allen-Hill, my lord," she said, flashing Lewis an impishly relieved smile. "I was taking a walk."

Without his spectacles, the earl would probably not be able to discern the marks on her face. He was notoriously farsighted.

"I would confine your movements elsewhere," the earl said. "Dangerous around here. Now Noble, can you get those batteries connected, if you please?"

"Of course," Lewis said. "Straightaway." He nodded at the woman with the black dots on her face and followed the earl back into the barn, wondering what she wanted with an absentminded inventor like him.

Victoria continued to walk, bemused by the carnality of Lewis's kiss. Underneath her combinations, her thighs were damp with desire. She wanted more. Behind the stables, she glimpsed the lake and walked to it, catching the gleam of the submarine's metal outer shell where it rested on blocks. She continued east, following the edge of the lake so she would be able to find her way back to the Fort even if it went out of view.

While she walked, she pondered the mystery of Lewis Noble. She'd still had no glimpse into the workings of his brain. She could not even theorize if he liked her. That kiss had been the first time she'd ever been truly certain he found her desirable. He'd forgotten himself enough to touch her face.

She walked down to the edge of the lake. Sparkling ice dotted the lower levels of vegetation, but beyond that the water was clear. Leaning over, she attempted to capture her reflection. When she touched her cheek with her gray wool glove, it came away with a bit of dark grease. She had suspected as much. Lewis had left his mark on her skin, too. She pulled off a glove and dipped a hand into the water.

"Ah!" she gasped as the cold touched her skin. Quickly, she scrubbed at her face, then wiped the grease off with a handkerchief. Eventually, she felt presentable again. She tucked away the handkerchief and pulled on her glove.

When she turned away from the lake, she saw a man watching her. At first, she assumed it was one of the earl's workmen, but then her eyes focused and she recognized Ernest Dickondell.

He grinned at her as she recognized him and jumped off a small rise. She stepped forward to meet him.

"Good afternoon, my lady," he said with a slight bow, diminished in formality by a knowing grin.

"You are underdressed for taking the air, sir. Where is your coat?"

Indeed, his clothing was of suitable tightness to promise the viewer that there was no long wool underwear lurking underneath it.

He wore town clothes, with no condescension toward winter. She suspected he knew he looked his best in spring fashions and dressed accordingly for all seasons. With her newfound knowledge of the male physique, she could see he had much to display.

"I believed the sun and followed her," Ernest said.

"You will catch an ague." Victoria smiled vaguely as she decided where to go next. Should she continue along the lake? She wasn't sure how far it went, and she'd need to be back with time to bathe before her next change of clothing.

"I have never felt cold in my life."

When she regarded him curiously, he shrugged. "Strange, I know, but unless there is precipitation, I never concern myself with outerwear."

Or underwear. She wondered how she could have such a naughty thought when she had hitched her star to Lewis's cart. Surely she wasn't capable of changing beds in only the course of a few days. Ernest was handsome, to be sure, and far more rakish than Lewis, but she liked the inventor's quiet self-assurance. She also knew he was a man of strong interests. Ernest was an enigma, but the kind that wasn't terribly interesting to her. You could assume you knew what he did with his days. Some form of exercise. Drinking, gambling, adventures with unmarriageable women.

Unlike Lewis, he might be willing to move to Liverpool, however. Did he have the intelligence to succeed her father in the family business? She knew, Lewis or not, she needed to give Ernest the opportunity to impress her, because her father would certainly be checking him out as a prospect. If she decided to dislike him, she needed to know now.

So, with Lewis's kiss still fresh on her lips, she smiled at the second Dickondell son. "I do hope your good luck continues, sir, as I should not like you to become susceptible."

He nodded. "May I offer you my arm, Lady Allen-Hill? There are plenty of depressions in the ground. Trouble with moles, I believe. Common around here."

She took the proffered arm, feeling strangely adulterous. "I have always been a city dweller. No experience with rural complaints."

"Do you plan to return to your city ways after the holidays?" He drew her in the direction of the house.

She bit her lip, not wanting to head in Lewis's direction, but not knowing how to demur without Ernest thinking she wanted to be alone with him. "Oh, yes. I make my home in Liverpool, with my father."

"You have a young charge, too?"

"My cousin, but she does have her own family. Mr. Dickondell, I did want to see the rest of the lake. Is it a long walk around?"

He stopped. "It might take an hour to walk it."

"Would it be improper to ask you to accompany me?"

"Not at this time of day," he said with a knowing smirk. "Any number of people are likely to be around, especially with Bullen playing his water games."

"I suppose it is handy to have a body of water when you are testing aquatic equipment."

"Oh, I don't see what good a pond will do him," he said dismissively. "He needs to take that submarine of his into deeper waters."

"I shall be romantic and hope there is treasure buried in the center of the lake."

"Then we shall indeed perambulate its length, so you can have the pleasure of describing it to all of your friends when the pond becomes famous."

"You are too thoughtful," she murmured.

He was quiet for a few moments as they reached the edge of the lake and began to walk above the vegetation at the edge. The sky was a solid gray, with a wall of darker color to the south. "I say, your father is a dye manufacturer, I believe?"

"Yes. Papa has been very successful."

"But he has no sons." Ernest's dark eyes became shrewd.

"That is true," she agreed, knowing he ought to be asking these questions elsewhere. Had she caught his eye in such a way that he'd addressed her due to a personal interest and not a financial one? Such fantasies on a girl's part let fortune hunters flourish.

"I've never been to Liverpool," he mused.

"It's not all shipbuilding and banking," she said. "We have one of the finest concert halls in the world in St. George's Hall. Papa and I often attend operas there."

"So you attend to culture and he attends to business?" Ernest said.

"Which do you prefer?" she countered, wanting to learn more about the man, more than his dandified appearance could tell her.

"One way or another, I shall have to make my own way in the world," he said. "I don't suppose it should matter to someone like you."

"Why do you say that?" Did the man dislike wealthy women? That would be unusual.

"Because I'm sure you are looking for another title to marry. Why marry down?" he asked carelessly.

She stumbled on a clump of pebbles. He attempted to right her but had difficulties, and by the time she was steady again, she found herself in the man's arms.

His full lips curved and she found herself staring at a hint of incisor. She thought of wolves and stepped back quickly.

"Were you afraid I'd kiss you?" he asked, the predator's grin in place.

She gave him a reproachful glare and he put out his hands. "Do not worry. I shall be a gentleman, though your beauty quite overwhelms a man. I must admit I've imagined what you must look like with all of that luxurious hair down and wrapped around your shoulders, and, err, bosom."

"As you said, Mr. Dickondell, any number of people could be around us at any time. I would prefer you comport yourself as if we were in public."

"Does that mean we might comport ourselves differently in private?" He leered, but she could see the humor in his eyes as he squinted down his nose at her. "A widow has more options than a maiden."

Which she had exercised, though he didn't know it. Still, she had some power in the courting game, courtesy of her money and title. "Mr. Dickondell, really. Without a declaration—" she trailed off delicately.

"I declare myself to be fascinated," he exclaimed, holding his arm out to her. "I thought you were only willing to converse with Lewis Noble."

"How ridiculous," she said, feeling guilty, wondering how many people had noticed her shameless pursuit. "I have formed a dear friendship with his cousin, Rose Redcake, you know. One does wind up in his company at times."

Ernest snorted. As she took his arm again, they began to walk, buffeted by winds that made the tall grasses dance around the lake. She enjoyed the movement of green and yellow in front of the gray-blue waters. "Do people swim here in summer?"

"If they did, I imagine someone would have found your buried treasure by now. The area is considered to be cursed."

"My goodness, by what?"

"A French mermaid, I believe. Some silly legend. Can't remember, exactly."

"Just the bit about the mermaid intrigued you, then?"

"If you must know, yes." His eyes twinkled. "They don't wear clothing, you see, and I first heard the tale as a lad of twelve or so."

She blushed, knowing what part of female anatomy Ernest found attractive. Between the mermaids and his fantasy of seeing her only clothed in her hair, he had a fascination for breasts. Luckily, despite her reducing, she still had a fine pair. If she wanted to snare him for her bed, she knew how to dress from now on.

"I have never met a lad of twelve who wasn't beastly," she mused.

"Very true. I am ashamed that I ever was such a craven creature."

"What do you do with your time, Mr. Dickondell?" she asked, squeezing his arm as she stepped around a visibly muddy spot. His forearm muscles felt firm and rounded. She suspected he enjoyed physical activity.

"Help out with our farm. We're cousins to Hatbrook, you know, and my family is attempting to learn from him. Diversification and all that. But I couldn't support a wife right now, to be frank."

Meaning he probably intended to marry for money. "What interests you other than farming and mermaids, Mr. Dickondell?"

"Travel, definitely. I'd like to expand my horizons, but I've never even been to France."

Yes, money was his game. "I have never traveled, either."

He helped her around a slimy pool in the middle of the path. "Perhaps someday we will toast each other in Rome or Paris."

"Someday," she agreed with a smile. But not anytime soon, if she had a choice in the matter.

They didn't speak much more as they walked around the far southern end of the lake, but exchanged frequent smiles. Victoria kept hers short of romantic amusement, not feeling comfortable with kissing a second man in one day, but she could see Ernest had possibilities. When they rounded the final stretch, they saw a flurry of activity and assumed something exciting was happening at the submarine.

"Not the submarine," Ernest said when she offered her opinion. "I believe it is the Professor with his theater."

She could just make out a gaily-colored stage being set up in the distance. "Oh, are we going to have a Punch and Judy show? How entertaining!"

"I expect it will be mostly for the children. Don't suppose we'll see the hanging today."

"The countess does seem rather strict," she agreed. "But I do hope they bring in the crocodile."

"I shall request it of the Bottler, if there is one," Ernest said. "Will you sit with me at the show?"

"I don't see why not," she said, smiling at him.

He stopped on the path and put his hand over hers, then drew it off his arm. She watched, wide-eyed, as he bowed and turned over her hand so that it lay palm up in his much larger one. Birds rustled the leaves in the trees around them as they left their perches and climbed into the air, creating a tangible sense of chilly movement that left her shivering even before his lips touched her palm.

Instinctively, she snatched her hand away from his. Her breath rattled in her chest.

"I go too far, my lady," Ernest said, straightening. "You are irresistible."

She put her hand to her chest, hoping to slow her respiration. Why had this affected her so much? He didn't mean anything to her. But she was a girl who had been all but a wallflower until now, not used to a practiced flirt.

As she attempted to catch her breath, his glance became speculative. "I shall have to take a train up to Liverpool. Perhaps your father will invite me to dinner some evening next month?"

She'd never heard a more blatant indication that a man wanted to court her, and his willingness to go north said it all. Here was a true candidate, title or no. The question was, did she like him enough to say good-bye to the title she possessed when she was ready to wed again? Her father would have to decide if this man had a good head for business.

"I think the booth is ready now," she ventured. "Let us join the others."

He nodded and offered his arm again, but she shook her head and merely walked alongside him. It was too soon to make what amounted to a proclamation that they were courting. She couldn't imagine Lewis doing anything so public.

She saw her father standing with Penelope and Rose Redcake to the left of the stage. Behind them, footmen were arranging chairs, and to the right, maids were adjusting rugs so the children could sit close to the stage. A long table had been set with steaming teapots, ready to warm the audience. Victoria longed for a hot cup of chocolate instead, but she would not turn to gluttony now, after so many months of abstemious behavior.

"Shall I bring you a cup?" Ernest asked.

"Let me introduce you to my father first." She took him over to the trio and made introductions.

Her father nodded at her companion and made general inquiries appropriate to the occasion, while Penelope took her hand and pulled her a few steps away from the men. She was pink with excitement, while Rose had a white scarf tucked up over her mouth.

"The nursemaid made me wear a coat and hat, but your friend isn't wearing any. I'm not cold. Can I take my coat off?"

"You'll get cold once you're sitting down," Victoria said absently, her eyes scanning the crowd for Lewis. She saw the earl standing with some of his workmen. Women who were likely their wives were streaming around the far side of the castle, a dozen or more children in tow.

Penelope clapped her hands, eager for more playmates. Victoria didn't see the harm in one afternoon with the village children. As her cousin ran off, Lady Barbara joined her. They were out of earshot of both Mr. Dickondell and Victoria's father.

"What are you playing at?" Lady Barbara said in a low voice.

"Mr. Dickondell spoke to me when I was out for a walk and continued on with me."

"He's a very naughty gentleman," her friend warned her.

"Even naughty men can settle down." At least she hoped so.

"He's twenty-four, Victoria. Hardly mature."

"He's young enough to want to train with Father," she said, piqued. "He's already spoken of coming up to Liverpool."

"Culled you from the herd, has he?" Lady Barbara said.

One side of the stage began to rock, and some of the earl's men ran up to stabilize it. A child capered between the men's legs, unaware of the danger if the stage collapsed.

"Why so sour? He is younger than you; surely you did not want him?" Not that she did, but she couldn't understand her friend's mood.

Lady Barbara pressed her lips together and looked away for a moment. "Of course not. I'm an earl's oldest daughter."

"For Lady Rowena, then?" Victoria asked.

Her friend was too much of a lady to shrug. "You may have a battle on your hands."

"Will she be the Queen Avice to my Princess Everilda?" Victoria joked.

"I just wanted to make you aware that my sister may have plans for Mr. Dickondell."

"Why? He has no money and, I have the impression, not a great deal of education."

Men came from the stables with boards and took them behind the stage to stabilize it.

"We need someone interested in farming in the family. My brother is not the person to make the best use of our land. Mr. Dickondell would suit us fine here."

"I feel for your sister, since Mr. Dickondell approached me," Victoria said.

"My sister may not be beautiful, but she is stubborn," Lady Barbara said with a smile. "She generally gets what she wants."

Victoria sighed. What she didn't say was that this party wouldn't last much longer, and they'd be free of Pevensey-Sur-Mer Fort. Mr. Dickondell could go where he wanted, then, even as far north as Liverpool. Lady Rowena could have no effect on their courtship from here, assuming she wanted to pursue it. In fact, the lady had very little claw with which to swipe at her.

CHAPTER 9

Though Ernest Dickondell soon returned to her side, Victoria couldn't stop looking for Lewis. He still hadn't appeared from the direction of the stables. However, her two Liverpool suitors, Mr. Dandy-Hill and Mr. Parker-Bale, appeared from the Fort, walking together. She did find it odd that rivals for her hand would be such close companions. But then, she had avoided their company in the day and a half since the disastrous dinner. Lady Barbara drew away, giving her one last significant glance of warning, as two of the village mothers approached her.

The thought came that they had planned that simultaneous attack on her lower limbs the other night. But if so, what had they hoped to accomplish? Did they expect her to distinguish one of them from the other when their behavior was the same?

"You look pensive, Lady Allen-Hill," Ernest said, taking her elbow and directing her to two newly placed chairs.

"My father wishes me to wed again soon," she said bluntly. "Do you know those two gentlemen?"

He nodded. "Imported from Liverpool, yes? I didn't see why they had to come here and ruin the fun for the rest of us. You could speak to them when you are in residence again."

"Perhaps that is exactly why my father sent for them, so that I did not marry someone who lives in the south." She shifted on the flimsy chair. "The house party invitation came courtesy of my late husband's relation to the Gills. My father did not orchestrate it."

"You need a rug," he said. "It's dreadfully cold. Shall I fetch one?"

"Just ask a servant when one wanders by," she said. "I am still rather warm from our walk."

"A cup of tea, then?" At her nod, he lifted his chin to a passing footman with a tray and received two steaming teacups.

"Thank you." As she took her cup, the curtains on the stage began to wiggle, as if there was action going on behind it. Was the Professor ready to begin?

"Just because a man lives in Sussex doesn't mean he wants to stay there forever," Ernest said. His cut-glass jaw looked uncharacteristically tense.

The Bottler came out from behind the stage and rang his bell, announcing the performance. As the children quieted, he began to instruct them on how to behave during the show. Victoria remembered how much fun it was to call out reactions and instructions to Punch and the other characters as a child. In most circumstances children were meant to be quiet in public, but not during a Punch and Judy show.

Ernest's face relaxed as he smiled at her. "A bit of childish nonsense, eh?"

"No harm in it that I can see," she told him.

Her suitors came up to her and bowed in tandem.

"May we sit *avec vous*, Lady Allen-Hill?" Mr. Parker-Bale asked. With a hat covering his thinning hair, she could see he had a handsome face, if not a handsome personality.

She nodded reluctantly, and he sat in the open chair to her right, the other man sitting on Parker-Bale's far side.

"Of course not," Ernest said. "But we do not have to sit through it. Wouldn't you rather go warm yourself in one of the parlors? I understand there is a puzzle room, or you could play the piano for me. I would love to sing with you."

She found herself irritated at his suggestion. Toby the Dog had come out and was lolling his tongue at the children. "I'm happy to remain here, Mr. Dickondell, but thank you for your concerns for my comfort."

Her companion sat back in his chair and sipped his tea in silence, occasionally bumping her elbow in a way that she thought was deliberate. However, she couldn't find fault with that . . . not exactly.

The Liverpudlians, on the other hand, were guffawing at Toby the Dog with the glee of children. While they were both older than Mr. Dickondell, they did not have his air of assured masculinity.

Her thoughts wandered to Lewis in comparison. Thirty-two years of age, she'd been told by Rose Redcake. He knew who he was, for certain. A man who had work he felt passionately about did excite a certain admiration. His looks were flawless, his body muscular perfection. And his touch . . . well, she'd found heaven indeed.

She lost track of the show, remembering their passionate encounter. Really, she couldn't possibly imagine doing *that* with another man. Had her father done any investigating as promised? Could there be a chance that he might be willing to live in Liverpool? She didn't really think he would be insolvent, though. He struck her as too careful a man. Still, any inventor might overextend on the cost of making prototypes. A couple of her father's associates had lost their fortunes on failed dreams.

Judy brought the Baby onto the stage. The children laughed as they saw how ugly it was. Punch complained in his Swazzle voice. *Babies.* The reason Victoria was in this mess in the first place, instead of reveling in a widow's independence. Her father wanted grandchildren.

Punch threw the Baby, and Judy appeared with her stick. They began to battle, and Victoria was horrified to see the two Liverpudlians begin to mimic the actions of the warring couple, slapping each other on the back of the head.

"Gentlemen!" she cautioned in her most reproving voice, one she'd only developed recently in response to Penelope's antics.

Mr. Parker-Bale giggled, but they both subsided. On the rugs below, the children, Victoria saw, were keeping their hands to themselves for the most part. Honestly, her father had found men for her who were less mature than a set of village children. She found herself subtly shifting her bottom in her chair to move toward Mr. Dickondell.

The Beadle made his appearance to arrest Punch, and she glanced away from the stage. Lewis had appeared, standing just past the children. He was staring right at her, a line between his eyebrows as he frowned. No, that wasn't his expression exactly; it was more like hurt.

She wanted to melt into her chair and disappear. Not an hour before, she'd kissed this man, and now she was sandwiched between multiple suitors like some kind of . . . what, belle of the ball? She felt her spine straighten even before her mind recognized her right to pride. Why not make the man she desired realize that she was desirable to other men?

He didn't approach her; indeed, he disappeared before the end of the performance. However, he did reappear while she sat in the drawing room before dinner with the rest of the house party guests. He didn't work his way through the crowd either but came to her directly upon entering the room with the earl. Not only that, but the earl looked surprised by his henchman's defection.

She didn't smile as he approached yet could not help drinking in his broad, lanky form. His hair appeared to be growing longer by the day, curling over his brow. He'd look like a faun if he wasn't careful, with tufts over his ears. The thought made her smile.

"May I sit with you?" Lewis asked, smiling in response to her expression.

She held back a giggle. *Control yourself, my dear.* "Of course, Mr. Noble."

"Why are you sitting alone? You have so many friends and admirers here."

Was this a rebuke? She could not say because his tone was so mild. "Your cousin and my father were seated with me, but Rose began to cough and my father took her away from the fire."

"They are getting along very well," Lewis commented.

"My father is a gentleman," Victoria countered. "What else could he do with her in distress?"

"Indeed," Lewis said, glancing at the fire. Thankfully, a servant had tended to it, and now most of the smoke was headed properly up the flue. "I cannot help but notice your general popularity. There is a rumor that you are spinning a fairy tale. I should like to hear it sometime."

Ernest Dickondell entered the room, followed by the Gill sisters, who took up posts on either side of him and began to converse with much gesturing of fingers and fans. "Do you like fiction, Mr. Noble? Many men do not."

"I admit I am more a reader of scientific journals and the like, but I would like to hear what you have created."

She paused at that. "So you think to judge me on the basis of one silly tale?"

He adjusted his position on the sofa so that he was subtly focused on her. "No, I judge on the entire person. But you are more than a lovely form, Victoria. I want to know more. I crave it."

Her heart seemed to catch in her chest at his use of her first name. How bold he was being. How complimentary. Perhaps her inadvertent show of beaux had done some good after all. She must discover whether there was any chance of him leaving Battersea for Liverpool before her heart became entirely broken. An engagement to someone else while her mind and soul were full of regrets for Lewis was not what she wished for herself.

"I will be happy to tell you my tale-in-progress, but not here. It always draws a crowd, as you have heard. Besides, I have no idea where it is headed."

"You make it up as you go along?"

"Exactly," she confessed.

"I often design the same way. Not with actual components, of course; they are too expensive. But on paper, it is all about flights of fancy."

"A fairy tale is nothing but exactly that," she said ruefully.

"The rumor is that your fairy tale is coming true," he said.

"If that were so, and I was my princess, I could look forward to a very happy ending when this house party is done." Unable to meet his gaze, she stared down at her clasped hands. The pearl on her ring had slid to the side and she righted it.

"It's early days yet. You shall have to see what Twelfth Night brings." The corners of his eyes crinkled at that, and she thought he might appear at her door during the wee hours that night. The thought caused a cascade of reactions throughout her body, culminating in an electric sensation between her legs that she was only beginning to understand was mature, knowing desire.

The first footman came in to ring the ancient dinner gong. She wanted to whisper something provocative, something erotic, but the crowd was assembling in order of precedence and she was too far above him to take his arm.

Instead, she found herself escorted by John Alexander, the Baron of Alix. At twenty-seven, the handsome Scottish nobleman had the slightly anxious air of a fox at the start of a hunt; he knows something bad is coming but isn't certain what. When she saw him flinch at the sight of Lady Florence, she suspected the countess's sister had already made her move.

She squeezed his arm. "You're safe with me," she whispered.

"Why is that?" he asked in a low brogue.

His breath danced over her ear, but she was pleased to see it didn't create any sensuous raptures in her. "I'm destined to spend my days in Liverpool."

"Ah," he said. "I understand your point. I am bound tae the Lowlands. We can be friends, then."

She smiled at him. "Exactly. We can likely both use a friend."

"Are ye close tae any of the ladies of the house?" he asked.

"Lady Barbara is my friend," she said, noting his nostrils were still reddened from his recent cold. "And I know Lady Rowena has her eye on a certain gentleman."

"Not me?" he asked.

She laughed. "No. I wouldn't tell you if that were the case."

"I haven't been social enough for any lady tae form a connection," he said ruefully. "Dratted illness."

"Are you looking for one?" They were seated next to each other, which pleased her because this had to be one of the more intriguing conversations she'd ever had with a man.

"My brother is so happy with his new wife that I've been made quite jealous. And we have bad weather in Scotland, ye know. It's wonderful tae have a warm cuddle under the furs at night."

"Still sleeping in caves under furs, then?" she teased.

"I guess ye will never be permitted tae find out," he said with a mournful cast to his mouth. "What with your ties tae Liverpool."

"Ah, I think I will be a better friend than a lover to you," she told him, keeping her voice low.

He winked. "Don't underestimate yourself."

"Ah, but I am a widow, sir. I should know these things about myself."

"I believe that the advent of a new person in your life can change outlook, behavior, even personality tae some degree. Man is a social animal." The baron looked with disfavor at the soup placed in front of him.

"What is the matter?" she asked, then drew back herself when she saw the greasy lump of skin-on chicken in the bowl. "The hazards of hiring a French chef, I suspect."

"The man must be in a terrible snit," the baron agreed. "I'd rather eat haggis."

He grinned at her, and they spent a delightful meal together, trading anecdotes. She all but ignored her father, on her other side, but he seemed wrapped in conversation with Rose Redcake about one of Sir Walter Scott's novels. Her father had read novels? She'd never seen any. If there were a secret chest full of novels in the house, she'd have to investigate and find it. She never had enough books to read.

"I think I shall ride tomorrow if the weather is fine," she announced.

"I will be happy to escort ye," the baron said. "Would your friend Lady Barbara care tae go with us?"

She grinned. So that was where his thoughts lay. "I shall endeavor to add her to our party."

"And who would ye like me to invite?" he inquired playfully.

She sighed. "He would never go, so Ernest Dickondell, I suppose. He is amusing. It would be best to spend some time with him in a crowd."

The baron nodded thoughtfully. "A picnic, do ye think?"

"At the end of the year?"

"My lady, I am Scottish," he said. "The weather here is balmy tae me."

"I thought you were from the Lowlands."

"There is still rain and damp."

She detected an air of defensiveness and proceeded to tease him through the pudding course. After, the baron stayed close to her once the men returned from their cigars but made eyes rather blatantly at her friend, who was all but oblivious to him as she chatted with her siblings in a tight family circle. Victoria wondered if she stared at Lewis so desperately and obviously. The thought gave her a headache and she went up to bed, reminding herself that Lewis had looked rather hapless himself today when he saw her at the puppet show.

She went to bed with the copy of *Ivanhoe* that was on the shelf in her room. It didn't hold her attention long, and the candle was still burning on the wall above her when she was awakened by a knock at her door. She bolted upright, breathing hard. Her hand was over her heart when she heard the scratch, not nearly the verbal assault her dreams had made it seem. Had she locked Penelope out?

Still half-asleep and rubbing sand from her eyes, she rose to unlock the door. Instead of her diminutive cousin—or, even better, Lewis—she found Ernest Dickondell smirking at her.

She glanced down and nearly shrieked when she discovered she had forgotten her dressing gown. Her nightgown, made from thin cotton since she slept warm, did not leave much to the imagination.

He held up a bottle of corked champagne and two glasses. "I overheard that your cousin was feeling a bit poorly and was put to bed in the nursery. Care to celebrate?" His voice slurred a bit on the last word.

She slid behind the door, only allowing her face to peer out. Her hair had half fallen down, drifting to one shoulder. The weight of it pulled her head to the side. "No," she said. "Don't be indecent. I will see you at our picnic tomorrow."

"Come now," he coaxed. "It is the holidays. Relax a little. I know you like me."

"Not that much," she whispered. "Go away, Mr. Dickondell, or I shall be forced not to take you seriously."

His lips curved. "You should take me very seriously."

As she watched, he flexed his hips, as if to bring his male appendage in closer proximity to her. "I was not looking for an assignation," she hissed, aware of the irony, given that if he'd been Lewis, she'd have been all but overeager. What would her lover think if he saw another man enter her room? She'd lose all hope of another sensual experience with him.

"One can be seriously inclined and have a bent for fun," he told her. "One is not exclusive of the other."

Yes, and she could just imagine five years hence, when she had lost his marital interest after a child or three and a couple of stones returned to her hips. At some future house party, he'd be drunkenly holding up his bottle of champagne for some other woman. He wouldn't be the worst choice in a husband, but hardly the best either.

With a painful rush of longing, she wanted her awkward, distracted, beautifully muscled Lewis. One thing she was certain of was that he would never be so louche. Champagne and hip thrusting indeed. "Good night, Mr. Dickondell. Might I opine that you have already imbibed enough for this evening?" She shut the door in his face and went back to her bed.

Once there, she found her dressing gown and secured it over her person instead of getting back into bed. Mr. Dickondell had woken her fully and now she knew Penelope would not be returning. Did she dare go on the hunt for her man?

She dithered over her prospects for a good ten minutes, until the clock marked the eleventh hour. Most of the house should be abed by now, and Mr. Dickondell was certain to be long gone. She crept out of her room and down the hallway, then scratched at Lewis's door. After about thirty seconds, it was opened by the freckled Eddy Jackson, Lewis's assistant.

"Hello, my lady," he said with unusual cheer for the hour. "Wot can I help you with?"

She cleared her throat. "I was, err, looking for your master."

"Down at the stables," the lad said cheerfully. "The earl was forced to attend dinner by his mum's orders, but they are back at work now. Trials tomorrow, you know."

"They work very long hours," she said for want of anything else to say.

"I was sent back because I have a sniffle," the lad said, scrunching up his nose for effect. "Bloody boring in here, pardon my manners."

"Best to rest if you aren't feeling well," Victoria offered.

Eddy sighed, then brightened. "Fancy a game of chess? Lewis has been teaching me."

Victoria glanced down at her dressing gown. So inappropriate, yet Eddy was little more than a child, and she still felt electric prickles of excitement racing through her body. They would take time to dissipate, but how thrilling it had been for those few moments when she had walked to the door, hoping for Lewis. A game would calm her. "I'm not very good."

"Neither am I. Best we both practice, then." He opened the door wider and she stepped inside.

They played for an hour and a half. He'd won two matches to her one by the time she yawned and noticed his eyes were at half-mast. "Let us say good night," she said. "Time for you to get some rest."

He nodded and stretched. "I'm sorry Lewis didn't come back. I thought he might, if he remembered he was meeting you."

She shook her head. "We didn't have plans to meet."

"Then why did you come?"

His gaze was so clear-eyed and probing that she didn't quite know how to treat him like a child. "I missed him, I suppose. I find myself drawn to him, even though he scarcely notices me some days."

"Always proving himself," Eddy said.

"To whom?"

Eddy shrugged. "Doesn't matter, does it?"

She schooled her expression to be as probing as his. "I think it does. Is he in love with someone?"

"It would only hurt you to know, since you're in love with him."

"I haven't said so," she protested. She couldn't love him; he was almost a stranger.

"I wasn't born yesterday." He lifted his eyebrows with disarming humor. "I'm not even all that young."

"You're too young for this conversation," Victoria said in her tartest voice. "You needn't tell him I stopped in."

"I think I shall tell him you spent the night pining away, sobbing on my shoulder." His grin offered the shadow of a future rake.

"You'll do no such thing." She stood, as did he, and she saw he was taller than her by at least three inches. Not such a boy after all. "Now, get some rest. Do you want me to ring for tea or a mustard plaster or anything?"

"No, I'll be fine." He paused. "My lady."

She patted his shoulder. "Good night, Eddy."

"G'night." He reached for the door, with arms that were longer than hers, and opened it.

She nodded to him and went into the deserted hallway, making it back to her room before anyone saw her, though she heard footsteps on the stairs at the far end. They sounded too light to be Lewis's, though. He would probably be in heavy workman's boots rather than some light evening shoe.

Lewis caught an earful from Eddy the next morning, about a certain lady's visit to their rooms the night before, and why was he working on the submarine in the middle of the night when he could be trysting as a man should during an upper-crust house party.

Only the boy's raspy cough ended his tirade, and Lewis gratefully escaped to the breakfast table, where he expected to discuss final details with the earl over oatmeal and toast. If he had known Lady Allen-Hill was planning to visit him the night before, it would have only made matters worse, given that he couldn't disappoint the earl, who was, after all, paying him for his labors. And on a submarine, no less. Lewis might have paid for the privilege of working on one himself.

Still, he found himself ruminating on the might-have-beens with the lady. He was gratified to know that while she might have been flirting with her various suitors, at night she wanted him. His body did not agree with the conclusion his mind had made to choose submarine construction over sex, and he found his nether regions at an uncomfortable half-mast at the mere thought of what the lady had intended as he entered the dining room.

Thankfully, a footman waited at the sideboard and he was able to slide into a chair and place a napkin over his lap without the embarrassment of making up a plate for himself in his condition.

John Alexander, a Scottish baron whose title Lewis couldn't remember, was already at the table, studying the local newspaper. He glanced up and offered a sheet to Lewis, but he shook his head. His brain was full of diagrams for the submarine, and he decided they might as well stay at the forefront of his mind.

Lady Florence came in, her hair pulled so tightly back at her temples that it revealed her true age rather than ridding her skin of wrinkles, chattering excitedly with Lewis's cousin Rose.

"Can you believe it? Found in her bed? I'm appalled at the chit, but I suppose she got what she wanted."

The baron's head rose over his papers.

"Shhh," Rose hissed. "You mustn't gossip. It's unseemly."

"Come now, Miss Redcake," Lady Florence said, putting her hand on Rose's arm. "It's too delicious."

Rose shook her head.

Lewis noticed she was quite pale, but out of distress or because of her asthma he didn't know. He stood and guided her to the seat next to his own.

"I do not gossip," Rose said. "I have learned it is never the pastime of a lady."

"Why, Miss Redcake, I think I should be offended," Lady Florence drawled, sitting down. "Toast and coffee, please, Jeremy."

The footman nodded. "And for the young lady?"

"The same, thank you," Rose said. "I am sorry to offend, Lady Florence, but telling tales never did anyone any good."

"I disagree. It is so amusing."

Rose pursed her lips, then turned to Lewis. "How is the submarine? I saw the earl walking out the front door muttering to himself as we came down the stairs."

Lewis groaned. "I'd better eat quickly and be on my way. Trials today, but if he's thought of something else, we'll have work to do first."

"Oh, is everyone invited to watch?" Lady Florence cooed.

He took an enormous bite of oatmeal and swallowed without chewing. "We'll send someone to the house if it actually happens today. Then you can bundle up and come down."

"How charming," the woman said in the same syrupy voice.

He decided he was lucky Victoria came to his door at night, rather than this lady.

Just then, that lady herself entered the dining room. His intention to shovel down his oatmeal and bolt for the stables fell away when he saw how charming she looked in a dress of dark blue velvet. He could well imagine peeling away the formfitting garment from her marvelous breasts, exposing the tips, which would already be puckered and waiting for him.

"Are you well?" Lady Florence inquired.

"Whatever do you mean?"

"I thought I heard you groan, sir," she said sweetly.

He glanced up and saw Victoria regarding him curiously. While he wanted to go to her, he could not; his erection had taken another leap in turgidity when his imagination flowered. Good God, he was stuck here, between his desires and this shrew of a woman.

"Lady Allen-Hill, did you hear the news?" the older woman brayed. "A tryst, at our very own house party!"

The lady's glance went immediately to Lewis. He shook his head slightly, hoping to indicate it was not their lovemaking that had been discovered.

"I see," she said slowly. "I hope it is not too scandalous, for the countess's sake. She seems to me a very moral lady."

Lady Florence snorted. "Her legs were all but glued together years ago."

If anything, Rose went even paler at that coarse remark. Lewis rose, forgetting the condition of his lower body, and turned to his cousin. "Let me take you to your room," he said into her ear.

She looked at him gratefully, and it wasn't until he caught Victoria staring at him in bemusement that he realized she had probably caught sight of the state of his trousers. He shook his head ruefully as he went out, hoping she was intrigued rather than horrified by his condition.

CHAPTER 10

Victoria had gone to church with the rest, it being Sunday, but the mood of the house party had been far from pious that morning. The guests of the Gill family—and, indeed, the family members them-selves—glanced around, looking to see who was missing. Victoria noticed Ernest and Clement Dickondell were both absent, as was the Scottish baron. Lady Florence was in attendance, along with Lady Barbara, but the earl, his mother, and Lady Rowena were absent as well. Rose Redcake had not walked through the frigid air to the church, but Lewis had. He had not spoken to Victoria when their party assembled in the front hall, though his cheeks had colored slightly when he saw her. She wasn't sure why.

Now, he sat in front of her. In fact, she spent the service staring at the back of his neck. The church was frosty cold and he kept his coat on but didn't have a muffler, so she could see how his blond hair curled against his neck. She imagined he had been a very beautiful child, with ringleted hair and round, rosy cheeks. If they had a child together, would it have his blond hair or her brown? Perhaps some kind of sandy compromise? Foolish to imagine, but every woman was guilty of such fancies when considering a handsome male specimen.

Soon, her thoughts turned from babies to more sensual longings. She thought of what caresses she might offer to that vulnerable nape.

Her fingers itched to carve their way along his scalp again, as they had in a passionate moment. She wanted to hold that head in her hands as she reached the fulfillment only he had ever offered her.

Her thighs twitched as her center heated, dampened. So close to him, yet so far. The vicar droned on and on, his muffler half-covering his lips so that all his words during the service were indistinct. She could smell paint, as if the damp in the air had kept the church's walls from ever drying, and wet wool from the coats around her. More snow could come today; it was nearly cold enough. She wondered if the submarine test would be delayed. Would Lewis have more time for her, then? Did it matter? She had arrived on a Monday and there was a week gone already. The house party was nearly half over.

No, she needed to forget her longings for Lewis and focus on getting to know the other suitors, in case her father presented a serious candidate. With a sigh, she wondered if her father's businesses could somehow be moved to Scotland. Glasgow might be suitable. She didn't like anyone here but the baron and Lewis. Time for a firm conversation with her father. She needed to make it clear that neither of his Liverpool-based choices were acceptable. In fact, she'd prefer to have them both chased out of the Fort. And Mr. Dickondell, so briefly a perfect candidate, had proven himself craven.

She stared at Lewis's curls again, biting her lip. Her hands pressed tightly against her abdomen so she could resist the urge to touch him. If she bent forward, would she smell that faint odor of sandalwood and machine oil? Or would he just be wet wool–scented like all the rest?

Penelope, recovered from her indisposition, joined her on the walk back to the Fort, and they continued the fairy tale. She spun her way through ribbons and tapestries—nothing too exciting there—then talked at length about the six tarts untasted. Princess Everilda had decided to be as conscious of her figure as Victoria. She could not make herself fat while Prince Hugh suffered who knew how much.

The five melting coins cold stymied her, so she was glad to make it into the Fort at just that moment. Her nose burned from the chilly air, a reliable signal that snow would fall within the hour. Hopeful, she looked around for Lewis, but he'd gone straight to the stables.

Rose came down the hall, exclaiming her jealousy when Penelope told her that more of the story had been revealed. She made Victoria tell about ribbons, tapestries, and tarts all over again; then they worked on an enormous puzzle until it was time for tea.

Victoria found the full complement of the household in the dining room, where they had been invited to assemble instead of in the parlor. All the men had arrived, not just the ladies. The earl looked solemn at the head of the table, his youngest sister at his side. Instead of making some grim announcement, he gestured to the butler, who crooked his finger at the doorway. Footmen came in with bubbling glasses of champagne.

The ladies began to smile and whisper. Clearly, whatever had happened overnight had borne fruit. When Lady Rowena's lips curved in a cat's satisfied smirk, Victoria knew what must have happened: Ernest Dickondell had been rejected by her for a tryst, then caught in another's snare.

She listened, her expression calm, though her heart was thudding, as the earl announced the engagement of his sister Rowena to Mr. Dickondell. The ladies would mutter on behalf of Lady Barbara later, for she was the elder sister and should have married first. Her family had not put her on the shelf quite yet. Victoria wished she could press her friend's hand in sympathy, particularly because Mr. Dickondell had not been won in honest wooing but nighttime eroticism. Lady Barbara was standing next to her mother, though, too far away.

It was possible no one but Victoria realized the true sequence of events. Everyone toasted the future bride and groom with their glasses. She noticed the earl and countess both drained their glasses instantly, while Lady Barbara barely tasted the liquid. Lewis, standing slightly down and across, lifted his glass to her, and she nodded back, gratified by the special toast, though she had no idea what he meant. Would he be in his room tonight? Probably he had no control over his plans. And not only that; Eddy, ill, would be there.

Victoria ate more of the tea treats than she had intended, polishing off both a lemon and a jam tart, as well as several sandwiches. Thankfully, the earl announced, his chest puffed out with pride in a way it hadn't been when he told of his sister's engagement, that they were ready for their first submarine trial, and invited everyone to watch.

Victoria looked out the window as she left the dining room and saw the snow had held off for now. It wouldn't much longer. She went up to the nursery to collect Penelope, then bundled them both soundly in coats, gloves, mufflers, and hats. Then they walked hand in hand to the lake. Penelope was fascinated by a family of swans, the purity of their feathers set off by black masks over their eyes, but Victoria found herself distracted by the sight at the back of the barn.

First, the rear doors opened, and the snub-nosed metal submarine peeked out of the building that had housed it. The metal gleamed bronze in the sharp winter sunlight, making it hard to look directly at it, as if it were some celestial being. The first man appeared, holding onto a handle on the side of the watercraft. Iron chains secured it to a wagon base with sturdy wheels. She wondered why they weren't using horses to pull it, but perhaps the earl didn't want to take the risk. Instead, it seemed that every man on the estate had been called to push or pull. From the side opposite her, better-dressed men spilled out from the barn doors. The earl, Lewis, and a couple of their regular men appeared. Even Eddy and the Baron of Alix were there to shout orders as the wagon began to pull to the left instead of moving straight ahead.

She saw a dock had been built at the reedy edge of the lake, where it lowered into the water so that she couldn't see the final edge of the planking. Someone had thought about this launch process in detail. They had chosen a spot behind the barn, where the ground sloped gently toward the lake. Of course, she had to wonder how much more difficult it would be to get it back out of the lake again after. Did the earl plan to have it remain in the water forever?

A hatch at the top provided an entrance to the inside of the submarine. She wondered if anyone was inside, or would the explorers swim into the lake and climb in after? None of them were dressed to go in the chilly water. In fact, some of them, Lewis included, had stripped off their coats during their exertions, as if there were no ladies present. Lewis had even loosened his tie and undone his collar. As he came closer to the edge of the lake, Victoria could see the muscles of his strong throat move as he shouted words of encouragement to the other men. He danced nimbly out of the way as the earl stopped moving unexpectedly. His grace made her knees weak and her stomach tighten. Some place between her legs that had been awakened by his touch twitched, as if coming alive at the sight of his smooth-working muscles, his virile movements, his passion.

"You're gaping like a goose," Lady Barbara said.

Victoria's chin tilted back, her mouth snapping closed as she noticed her friend right next to her. She hadn't even seen her coming down from the house.

"Is the submarine that fascinating? I hadn't thought so." Lady Barbara wrinkled her nose.

Victoria watched the alarm of the men as they realized the wagon's speed was increasing as the ground sloped. "I just hope no one gets run over."

Lady Barbara's expression calmed. "I can think of a couple of people I would cheerfully allow to be so trampled."

Victoria touched her friend's arm. "I should have let him come into my room. I sent him off and this is the result. I'm sorry."

Surprisingly, Lady Barbara smirked. "Are you serious? My sister was his second choice last night?"

Victoria saw her cousin coming back from the edge of the lake, into earshot, so she merely nodded.

"How delicious," her friend said. "I may appear the loser, but at least I now know the truth of my sister's grand passion."

"Not so grand," Victoria agreed.

"What isn't grand?" Penelope asked, rubbing her nose on her sleeve.

"Handkerchief," Victoria scolded.

"I can't find it." Penelope sniffed. "What are you talking about?"

Victoria fished a cotton square from her coat pocket and handed it over. "The submarine. Isn't it grand?"

Penelope shrugged. "I like the swans better."

Lady Barbara smiled and patted the girl's shoulder. "If you can keep a secret, I will confide that I do as well. I hope we do not lose the fowl to my brother's project."

"But he is going to find treasure, isn't he?" The girl blew her nose.

Lady Barbara's smile widened. "We can only hope, so he can defray the cost of this mad project. Lewis Noble will be able to build a castle of his own on the proceeds."

"Why do you say that?" Victoria asked.

"He supplied all of the materials, and half of the men working on the submarine are his. Not to mention he invented various parts of the machinery."

"Indeed." She'd known of his talents, but here was confirmation. Surely her father would approve of such a suitor.

"Oh, yes. I believe they hope to sell the project to the military in the end, and make a fortune that way. Better than betting on horses, I suppose."

"Gracious," Victoria murmured. "I knew he was brilliant, of course, but I didn't realize quite how involved he was."

"Mr. Noble is a very humble man, but to my tastes that makes him all the more appealing. Because he has no need for humility."

"I quite agree." Did Lady Barbara have a romantic interest in Lewis? She glanced over to the men and saw Lewis's arm muscles flexing as he helped to slow the wagon. Heavens knew that she did. Why was it that she thought of him in terms of being a suitor instead of just a lover? It was her father's fault, with all his talk of a speedy remarriage.

"But for all his unassuming ways, I have observed how easily he leads his men. Why, even my brother sharpens to Mr. Noble's directives. He is the one in charge, not Bullen, no matter how it seems."

Victoria looked with new interest at the path to the dock. She now saw that horses were involved in the process. In fact, they had been harnessed to the back of the wagon, facing toward the barn. Someone—most likely Lewis—had foreseen a need for brakes after all.

He let go of the rope and thrust his arm in the air, a finger pointed toward the barn, shouting orders. So, she imagined, a commander would bark orders in the midst of battle. Oh, she saw beneath the unassuming exterior to the real man now. She would not underestimate him again, and she would not turn her focus to another man either. She wanted this one, and him she must decipher, entice, seduce.

There might be more than one angle to pursue. How could she

turn her father away from his insistence that she reside in Liverpool? That must be resolved.

"I have lost your cousin's interest again," Lady Barbara told Penelope. "I had no idea she found submarines so interesting."

"She is probably dreaming up the next part of her fairy tale," Penelope said with a sniff. "I long to hear more about Everilda's adventures. Five melting coins cold; that is where she left the story."

"Have you figured that out?" Lady Barbara asked.

Victoria smiled. "Maybe I have."

Lewis ate bread and cheese in the barn that evening, ignoring the sound of the dinner gong ringing over the property. The submarine had exhibited a pinhole leak and he had to find the source of the problem, and then have the part remanufactured.

"No water," the earl said, poking his head out of the hatch.

"It's not that side, then. I wonder if we've got a problem with the bottom. We've tested everything else." Lewis regarded the metal cylinder with disfavor. He preferred designing to testing.

"Do you want to turn it upside down?" the earl asked.

"We could pour water over the floor and see where it drips out."

"I don't like that idea. Might damage the interior."

"It's already wet," Lewis growled.

"No need to snarl." The earl grinned at him. He never minded spending time in the submarine, regardless of the reason for it.

Lewis wanted flesh. First of all, he wanted a good leg of lamb, properly prepared. Then he wanted a woman. To think a willing one waited for him in the Fort, but only if he could get to her. That had been the impossible part. Could he chuck the project and focus on Victoria instead? But if he did, the earl would probably send him back to Battersea, not let him remain as a houseguest. His connection to the aristocracy was much too tenuous to make him a suitable visitor.

"You know, Noble, I feel as though I am losing your attention." The earl pushed the hatch completely open and used his arms to lever himself out of the submarine. He sat on the edge and clasped one knee to his chest. "What's troubling you, old man?"

"We're done for tonight," Lewis said. "If we have to flip this bastard over, we'll need all the men."

"Will it damage the instruments?"

Lewis shrugged. "We can do it in the water. That will be easier on the men."

"I was asking about the instruments."

"I don't bloody know. I wasn't planning to flip the thing when I designed it. What does it matter, anyway? If we break something, we'll fix it."

The earl nodded. "Fair enough. Best to let her dry out a bit. We'll resume tomorrow."

Lewis found his shapeless old coat and stomped back up to the house, the earl at his side. "So tell me, Nicholas, was this party designed just to find your sisters husbands, or were some of the ladies supposed to be dangling after you?"

The earl let out a dramatic sigh. "I can avoid the lot of them when I work in the stables."

"You have to fill your nursery one of these days."

"I hope to unload my sisters first. I would love to send my aunt away, too, but I don't know how I can manage that. Too many women in the Fort, if you ask me. I'm not going to add another."

"You don't have to reside here. You and your wife could live in London."

The earl was shaking his head as they reached the back terrace. "I like it here. They can go, instead of rusticating here. But what about you? Who is mending your shirts these days?"

"I don't have a title to secure." Lewis pulled open the door and they stepped into a corridor outside the ballroom.

"No, but you seem far more interested in the women than I am. I've seen you looking at Lady Allen-Hill with a certain gleam in your eye. No surprise, in truth. She has blossomed since marrying my unfortunate cousin."

Lights flared on in the corridor. Someone had lit the lamps. A footman, probably, to make sure all was in readiness as the guests moved into the ballroom for a few sets of country dancing.

"I cannot deny that she is appealing." Lewis's eyes adjusted slowly to the light, after the darkness outside. "But she's not for me. Liverpool, you know."

He heard a low-pitched laugh and recognized the voice instantly.

Lady Allen-Hill; Victoria. Had she heard him? But what did it matter? She knew he was settled down in Battersea, like an old ship, no longer seaworthy, docked for a final time.

The group of women reached them. Victoria, Lady Barbara, Rose Redcake, even Maud Wilson, the Dickondell cousin. He supposed they were all dressed to dance, but only Victoria's ebony, low-cut gown caught his eye.

"How delightful," Lady Barbara said. "Are you going to dance with us, Bullen?"

The earl stopped, his gaze fixed on his sister in a kind of mute horror.

Lewis traded glances with Victoria, but then his stomach rumbled loudly. "Off to dinner," he said.

"Oh, but you must dance," his cousin Rose insisted.

"I think Mr. Noble would faint dead away from hunger if forced to," Victoria opined. "No, we will have to do without them tonight."

"I think I will go up to my room," Lewis said, hoping she understood his point. "Have a tray sent up."

The women turned into the ballroom, their heads held stiffly in that position of wounded feminine pride so familiar to men who had thwarted desires.

"Why don't we retire to the billiards room?" the earl suggested. "We can order sandwiches and have a cigar."

"And talk submarines to the wee hours. No, I think I prefer to ruminate quietly," Lewis said. "Go dance with Lady Barbara. She could use some attention after finding out your younger sister is to be married first."

"Why, Noble, you sound positively feminine."

"I lived with my cousins for years. I remember how important things like who became engaged first were."

"I suppose you are right. If I don't stroke her ego, I'm sure to pay in a dozen little ways." The earl directed his attention to a group of men walking toward them. "Off to dance? No time for brandy first?"

The Baron of Alix offered a rueful smile. "Engagement party, you know."

Lewis saw Ernest Dickondell in the middle of the crowd. From the blurry gaze and off-kilter tilt of his tie, he suspected the man was blind drunk already. It was time to go before he was forced to join the party. The corridor seethed with people, some he recognized and others he did not. He suspected there would be a late start on work the next morning as everyone in the castle would be celebrating.

When he reached his room, he rang the bell to order food, then cast himself onto the sofa. Expecting silence, he started at the sound of Eddy's congested "hello."

"Good gad, I'd forgotten all about you," Lewis exclaimed.

"S'all right." Eddy sniffed. "I can ring for anything I need."

"Not any better?"

"Worse," he said with a cough. "I hope no one else gets this, though the maid who brought me tea earlier was sniffling."

"I should send you home now," Lewis decided. "You'll be down for the rest of the house party."

Eddy's face contorted in mock outrage. "Don't put me on a train now, guv. Not when I can be sick in comfort."

Lewis checked his conscience and decided it would be cruel to send the boy away, no matter how convenient it might be for him. He had made himself responsible for Eddy, and who knew how much trouble he could get up to between here and London? "Very well. Go and rest. I'm going to order food. What do you want?"

Not surprisingly, the boy had no appetite.

An hour later, Lewis had eaten and bathed the lake muck off his chilled body. An hour after that, he was pacing the hearth rug, thinking over each and every rivet in the submarine's skin, trying to decide if there was a way of finding the leak without flipping the fragile craft. Seams ran between the wide wood planking of the interior floor. Could he test their seaworthiness without damaging anything?

Probably not. But if he pulled out the benches, and then the planks, he could reach the exterior from the inside and do a water test. As long as they didn't strip any bolts, it would all go back in smoothly enough.

After twenty minutes, the hearth rug became too small for his pacing. He could hear Eddy's raspy, congested breathing from his bed. At least the lad slept soundly. Lewis went into the corridor and walked down to the staircases leading to the next levels and then back again. When he reached his door, he saw a light flickering at the other end of the hall, near the window that looked out to the lake. The servants had never left a light there before. He walked toward it, eventually distinguishing a dark form huddled over something.

"Lady Allen-Hill," he said when he came close enough to see it was her, still in her evening dress, but with her dressing gown thrown over the deliciously revealing, low-cut confection. "Writing letters at this late hour?"

She glanced up, seemingly shocked out of deep thought. "No. I was thinking about five melting coins cold."

"What does that mean?" Bemused, he sat across from her in the other armchair in the alcove.

"My fairy tale has a princess who has to solve riddles to win her betrothed back from the clutches of her stepmother's shade, but I imagined myself into a corner. I don't know how to solve the riddle of five melting coins cold." She smiled ruefully, folding her hands over her dressing gown.

"Metal is forged and tempered. In other words, heated and then cooled. Metal for coins has to be melted, then formed into rods for slicing. I don't know the actual process, but perhaps the rods are tempered."

"I guess they will have to be in my story," Victoria muttered. "Evil coins? Cursed coins? Blessed coins?"

"Coins forged in hell?" he suggested.

She narrowed her eyes. "Now you are teasing me, but I don't want to be a storyteller with a bad story."

"How about a creature with hands of fire who melts metal, then passes them to a creature with hands of ice?"

"What would Princess Everilda have to do to achieve her quest?"

"They could appear and start juggling the burning and icy coins around her. She'd have to escape them."

"Not bad," she said. "I could work with that. Thank you, Lewis." She leaned forward and kissed him on the cheek.

"Mind the candle," he said, pushing it out of the way.

"I was." She reseated herself, holding her dressing gown at the throat. "How is Eddy?"

Somehow, this was not the way he had imagined their first private encounter in days. She seemed distant. Had he lost her interest already? "Sick. I wanted to send him home but had second thoughts."

"Penelope was unwell, too."

He drummed his fingers on the armrest. "They don't give us much chance to speak. Well, that and Bullen's project."

"I thought perhaps you considered that to be for the best." Her voice was quiet.

Her words made him louder. "Really?"

"I should not have said that." She glanced down.

He took a deep breath, remembering what Bullen had said about stroking the egos of ladies to keep them from causing unpleasantness. "I like you, Lady Allen-Hill."

"It is a very partial affection," she said softly.

He saw the hurt in her expression and so found himself rising, blowing out the candle, and letting the smoke drift around him as he lowered himself to the table at her knees. Wasn't lust enough? "I ache for you."

She leaned forward. One hand moved. She placed it against him, at the top of his trousers. Then she slid it down. He felt himself strain against the weight of her palm, wondered if she would trace him through the wool. What would she do next? He longed for curtains to hide them away from prying eyes.

"This is where it aches," she whispered. Then her fingers left his manhood desolate as they rose. She rapped her nails against his forehead. "Not here." She moved her hand again, over his heart. "Or here. I must at least have your thoughts or you will never think of how we are to be together."

"And if you had my heart?"

"Then I would fight to have you."

He exhaled, the ache in his groin becoming a flame he wanted to douse inside her. "I believe you would, Lady Allen-Hill."

"Call me Victoria," she breathed. "I hate that name. I never really earned it. If he hadn't died, the marriage could have been annulled for all that he never touched me."

"But—"

"You are the only one."

Her fierceness burned into him despite the dark. The force of her words bit like shrapnel. "I took your virginity?"

"I gave it to you. I gave it to myself." She lost a little of her heat as her tone turned wry. "A virgin widow is absurd."

He felt confused yet strangely seduced. "I do not know what to say. What do you want me to say?"

He felt her breath puff on his cheek. "Only that you want me, Lewis."

"You know I do, but where could we go tonight?"

Only silence for a moment; then he heard the whisper of her skirts. "I didn't say I wanted you to desire amour with me, just me."

"Isn't that the same thing?"

"I don't know. I don't have enough experience."

Frustration rising, he stood and pulled her to her feet. Without knowing quite what he was doing, he led her to the window and pressed her against the icy pane. When she gasped, he took her open mouth with his, pressing his entire body to hers. Her mouth moved eagerly with his, her tongue darting out to touch his lips. He responded by exploring the insides of her mouth, stealing her every breath. As if in surrender, her head fell back and her hands came up, sliding along his hips, reminding him there was more to discover than just her mouth.

"Victoria." His fingers crumpled into her skirts, lifting them. The lavender scent of clean linen and warm woman diffused around him as she changed her stance, widening her legs. He pushed through the slit in her drawers and found her heat. She gasped into his mouth as he separated her warm, swollen lower lips and plunged a finger inside her.

He ripped his mouth from hers and moved it to her ear. "This is wanting to be with you." He pulled his finger out, then matched it with another and thrust them both inside. "I do want you."

"Oh, yes, Lewis," she breathed.

Hosannas of praise rang through his mind when her hands found his trousers and began to tug the fabric apart. He suckled her earlobe, bit her neck, tongued her throat as she made a hash of his clothes. He heard a button pop off, a seam rip, but then, gloriously, he was free. A hit of cold air shocked him; then her warm palm had him covered. He moved against her hand, not caring to hide his desperation as he circled her pearl with his thumb, trying to match her pleasure to his.

CHAPTER 11

Lewis could hear Victoria breathing hard in his right ear. His mathematical mind calculated that this meant she was not too much shorter than he, tall for a woman. Yes, he could take her against a wall without lifting her. Then he shut down the analysis before he could decide whether loving her again was a good idea or not.

He reached for her right leg and pulled it up along his, then tore his fingers from her cleft. The wet, sucking noise, the smell of her, pushed all further thoughts aside, leaving only want, only sensation.

"Don't," she whispered.

"What?"

"Don't stop. I need you, inside."

His cock found her swollen lips, already slick with her juices. He slid home, gasping at the precision of her fit. His hand was shocked by cold when it made contact with the window behind her head, but he tempered that icy sensation by warming his lips against her open, heated mouth.

She broke the kiss, whispering in a broken voice, "Lewis, how I've missed you."

"Yes," he said in return. "I know."

His hips pistoned against her yielding body. He felt her fingers slide shyly around his buttocks, then grip harder with each thrust. Though he wished he could tell her to lose all inhibition, he realized there was little more he could ask for up against a wall in an open corridor. Her hand on his bum, her teeth raking the edge of his jaw, her little moans every time he seated himself fully, were all he needed to stay in the moment. The way her honey dripped around his cock, signifying her pleasure at his intimate touch. The grip of her body, that tensing and releasing of intimate muscles, undid him.

God, he was coming now. He felt his palm slick under her thigh, sweat on his lower back. Her fingers slipped, then gripped him again, more intimately, closer to the cleft of his buttocks, pulling him apart slightly. The air snaked cold against the back of his thighs, making him twitch and enter her again. Her head thudded against the window, just as her body clenched around him with heavenly pressure, pulling him with her into shuddering, mindless, release.

When he had control of his limbs again, he cradled her head in one hand and let go of her thigh. Still inside her, he reached for a chair and lowered himself onto it, until he was shrouded in hair and shawl and evening gown. Bending his head, he kissed the tops of her breasts, licking into the deep shadow between them. How he wanted to take her back to his room and do this all over again, but Eddy mustn't know. He couldn't betray Victoria's privacy even with his own apprentice.

"This was so naughty," she murmured, her lips sliding slickly along his ear. "I thought marriage would be like this, at least I longed to have it be so."

"I am sorry your wishes went unfulfilled."

"Me, too, but I shall remember this forever. You have such power over my body. I never knew I could feel so much, just that I had to surrender. It is a woman's lot."

"You think it is only the woman who must? I do not agree. You have more power than you know."

"My father has more power over me than I have over one hair on your head." Her fingers tangled with the curls behind his ear. He needed a barber, and badly, but the ecstatic pleasure he felt along his scalp from her gentle tugs had him rethinking that.

"Don't give him your power," Lewis said, trying to focus on her words. He understood she was saying something important. "You are a widow. I do not believe your husband was poor."

"No, but other than his funds, there was nothing. All the property was entailed. I never had a home aside from my father's house."

"Why not set up an establishment of your own? In London. That is where you want to be, correct?"

"There is a duty I owe my father. I am his only child."

"Don't you think he will adopt Penelope? Her parents do not seem to be able to care for her."

"More that my uncle does not want to," she said slowly. "I have yet to entirely understand the situation."

"I think you can obtain more independence, if you are willing to fight for it. Especially with there being another young blood relative."

"I can't sacrifice Penelope to my desires."

He felt himself slip out of her as she pulled away. Her petticoats would be stained, but she didn't seem to mind. And they had forgotten her rubbers. "I do not suggest sacrifice, merely that the family business is not only in your hands. Besides, Penelope might want to remain in Liverpool."

Victoria laughed. The husky sound rumbled through his chest, luscious and feminine, though her voice was pitched low for a woman.

His cock stirred, and all he could think to say was, "Hmmm."

"Be still," she whispered. "I think someone is coming, but we are safe here in the shadows."

He pulled her head against his throat, tucking her face against him. But her dark hair was a better camouflage than his pale hands, so he slid his arms under her shawl and listened to her breathe.

After a moment, he heard the same faint footsteps as she did, but then a door opened. Probably Adela Dickondell and Maud Wilson, who shared the room next to Victoria's. After a couple of minutes, all sound had been swallowed into the dark.

"I should go," Victoria said.

"Should you?" He didn't want to let her go.

"It would be foolish to risk further exposure. There are other rooms along this corridor."

"I wish I could bring you back to my room, sleep with you in my arms."

He felt the whisper of air when she shook her head. "I don't think you do, not really. You'll want to wake early, go to the stables, fix your submarine."

"You don't think I would lie abed, waiting for you to wake so we could take this pleasure for ourselves again?"

She smiled against his jaw. "I think you prefer more limited interludes, but I will not complain."

"I hope you underestimate me." But he suspected she was right.

"You aren't sure." She kissed him, just where the stubble of his beard met the smooth curve of his cheek.

Honesty was not useful here. "Thank you for making love with me."

She sighed. "Thank you for helping me with my tale." As she rose, her skirts rustled, then paper rattled and she was away, back down the hall, leaving him alone with his thoughts. They were not pleasant ones either. Would he, just as he was, ever be able to make a woman happy? Why did he only want complicated women?

In the morning, Victoria found her father in the corridor outside her room. She had been thinking about declining breakfast, since she had indulged quite heavily in pudding the night before. While she had danced, then dueled intimately with Lewis, she was convinced her corset could not be laced quite as tightly as it needed to be this morning.

"Here to escort me downstairs?" she asked him.

He looked startled, as if he hadn't considered spending time with her, even though he'd been lurking.

"Weren't you here to speak with me?"

He coughed. "Of course, my dear. Where is your cousin?"

"Already gone to the nursery for breakfast."

"Are you going to breakfast?"

"I thought I would walk around the lake."

He hesitated, glancing down the corridor. She wondered if he'd had an assignation . . . but no, this was her father. Authoritarian he might be, but he certainly was not licentious.

"You do not have to attend me," she said. "I am happy to be alone."

"No, no, I could stretch my legs. Are you dressed warmly enough?"

She nodded. They stopped in his room so he could outfit himself to face the late December chill. Wind rattled the windows of the house as they exited from the ground floor, but down by the lake the air died to the level of breeze. She took a deep breath of the marine air and relaxed. Her father, however, did not have relaxation in mind.

"Where do you stand with your suitors?" he asked.

"Taking care of Penelope has made it a difficult process," she said.

"Nonsense." He took her arm to lead her around a muddy spot. "It is good for men to see you caring for a child."

She lifted her eyebrows. "When men are courting, I don't think that is what they want to see."

"When they are courting you, they had better. You are not some young miss just out of the schoolroom, but a widow."

"I'm still young," she protested. A gull cawed, startling her as it came from somewhere behind and flew across the lake.

"Who do you prefer? Parker-Bale or Dandy-Willow?"

"Neither. They are a matched pair of buffoons."

"The Baron of Alix, then? I've seen you speaking."

They reached the first turn. The Fort was out of sight now. She breathed in the unadulterated landscape, the browns and greens of winter. But her father would not let her commune with the nature spirits. "He is Scottish, father. If you will not let me live in London, surely you won't want me in Edinburgh."

"If you can win over the Earl of Bullen, you can live anywhere you like," he said. "I'll hire managers for the business."

She chuckled. "I haven't seen him so much as look at a woman, unless it is to glare at one of his female relatives."

"He has a mistress, you know. In Pevensey."

"Really?" she said tartly. "I wonder when he has time to see her."

Her father sighed and pulled her out of the way of a puddle. "I am attempting to make you understand that it is possible for him to be tempted, crude though I'm being. But you are a woman of the world now. You must know these things."

"Of course, Father. As your only child, it is natural I have more exposure to reality than a similar lady would. I do not mind. But I think the earl is out of the question for the remainder of this house party, at least. He is obsessed with the submarine."

"It would be easier to have his attention in London, but I'm not sure he spends any time there."

"So that is all the suitors, then?" She wished he would mention Lewis.

"I want you to consider Samuel Dickondell."

"He's twenty, a mere stripling."

"Not so much younger than you. A country education, but rumored to be intelligent enough."

"I much prefer Lewis Noble," she snapped.

"Intelligent, for certain," her father agreed. "With all the improvements he made to the Redcake factories, he would be an asset to our enterprises. But will he go to Liverpool? I don't believe so."

"No, but couldn't you hire the managers you just mentioned? I'm sure we could spend some time there; that is, if he was willing to marry me."

Her father narrowed his eyes. "I won't sacrifice the business to hired managers for anything less than a title. I will concede that Mr. Noble has distant ties to fashionable society, but that is all."

"What about my happiness?"

"Why?" Her father's tone became sarcastic. "Pray do not tell me you have allowed yourself to be so foolish as to fall in love with an inventor."

She stared at the gray, lumpy surface of the lake, the waving ferns at the edges. A sense of despair came over her, an unfamiliar sensation. Had she fallen in love with Lewis? Or was it merely her introduction to passion that had her so entranced by him? "Of course not, Father," she replied, doubting the truth of her answer.

"I understand what you are telling me, however. You want a mature man, a man of intelligence."

"I'm surprised you haven't suggested the eldest Dickondell," she said with a sourness that matched the feeling in her stomach. She needed a cup of tea, heavily laced with cream, to settle it.

"He is spoken for, whether he knows it or not."

"To his cousin?"

"No, she has nothing to offer. The Dickondells are going to do very well for themselves in this generation."

"If you say so."

"The earl and the baron are of an age. Late twenties. If we cannot have the earl, I suggest we concentrate on the baron. Edinburgh is not so very far away."

She heard the slight crack in her father's voice and squeezed his arm. "If I leave you, Father, you could take Penelope in. She's a clever little thing. Why not hire a governess for her and have her live with you? She will be as much company as I ever was."

"She's an angry child," her father said.

"Give her a chance. Or you could remarry."

"As difficult as marriage has been for you, the idea does not come highly recommended."

"You would do well with the ladies if you exerted yourself. Lady Florence, for instance, would be an excellent choice." Or a horror, Victoria's conscience argued, but at least she was appropriate, and titled.

Her father's eyes widened. "Do you wish to kill me, daughter?"

Victoria laughed and rested her head on her father's shoulder for a moment. "Not Lady Florence, then. What about Lady Barbara? She is my friend. You might be able to persuade her, especially now."

Her father made a noise but didn't respond. She saw men coming around the next bend of the lake. A couple of the Dickondells, the baron.

"Working up an appetite before breakfast, eh, Courtnay?" Clement asked, brandishing his walking stick.

"Nothing like a brisk morning," her father said. "Would you be so kind as to walk my daughter back to the house? I have an appointment."

Clement looked confused but agreed. Victoria smiled at the baron, who offered her his arm. Her father nodded his approval and took off on a side path that she thought led into town. How odd he was being, but at least he'd smiled slightly at the baron's gesture.

As she walked along, the men all solicitous of her boots on the muddy path, she wondered how she could possibly make love to the baron while mooning over her late-night lover. She wanted no touch but his.

When they were out of earshot of her father, Clement turned to her with a slight smile. "I do apologize, Lady Allen-Hill, but we are going to ride this morning."

"I am capable of reaching the house myself," she said icily, not liking his supercilious gaze. Clement thought too highly of himself. Did he imagine a woman with a title would find him such a good catch? Not one with money, certainly. While he had something to offer, she was not so desperate as to settle on a man with relatively young parents and a large family all living in a big house on a farm. Really, she found his attitude irritating.

"Ye must not," said the baron, sounding acutely Scottish in the presence of all these southerners. "I will happily forego my ride for the pleasure of accompanying ye."

She bowed her head in agreement, as he really did sound pleased. "I would like that, sir."

He held out his arm for her again. "Mind the mud, my lady; ye have done well so far and I would not like tae take worse care of ye than your father has."

They shared a smile, but still she sank inwardly. If not for Lewis, she might come to appreciate the Scotsman more fully, but she could not see herself with anyone other than the inventor. She had cast herself into the fires of bodily passion and so she would burn.

Lewis thought he might see Victoria in the dining room that morning. He'd gone down to the stables early, but instead of his usual bread and cheese he'd made the trek back, even changing his shoes so that he wouldn't be too disreputable. No one seemed to know where she was, however. He ate a plate of kippers and eggs, then attempted to chat with the countess while he finished his tea, ignoring the leers of Lady Florence. The woman was impossible. Eventually, he ran out of anything to say, once the weather and yesterday's sermon had been discussed. They both avoided the subject of the submarine, a sore point with the countess. She thought her son could be making more of the house party, but Lewis realized the most eligible candidate here was Victoria, and if she was destined for Liverpool, she could no more marry Nicholas than she could marry him. Still, he wondered how this trysting of theirs would end. Probably abruptly. And painfully soon.

He nodded to the countess and her sister, then left the dining room to head back to the mudroom and his boots. Servants still scurried through the hallway, bringing pitchers of hot water to the rooms of late risers. They huddled against the walls as he passed, a guest walking through servant corridors. This lifestyle might be Victoria's, but it wasn't his. While he knew that, he would miss her when she departed the south. At some point he would return home as well, but probably not as soon.

As he traded his shoes for sturdy boots, he thought of a romance that had turned out more happily than his situation was likely to. His cousin, Sir Gawain Redcake, had managed to romance a northern woman, then persuade her to move to Battersea. But Lewis knew himself to be happy as a bachelor, working odd hours, whether due to orders or because inspiration struck him. A wife would want order, cleanliness, predictability, children. And Eddy drove him half batty as it was. Did he desire little ones? Did he want to persuade Victoria and her father to change their minds about her future residence?

Once, he'd thought he wanted that domestic happiness. His lost love, Alys's children. His boots on, Lewis meant to rise from the hard wood bench to his feet, but memories struck him hard. His brain had trundled down these well-worn tracks for years, but now, in consideration of his nascent feelings for the toothsome, sensual Victoria, stray memories began to form into a picture different from the story he often told himself. Were his memories nothing but a fairy tale? As he began to recall the incidents of 1886, he remembered his proposal to Alys had been a manufactured thing, built out of the fear that her father would marry her off to someone utterly unsuitable. He'd offered for her in order to let her have some semblance of the life she'd wanted in London. He had loved her though, right? Why had he carried that torch for so long if he hadn't?

But she had been more of a sister to him than a romantic figure for so long before those final months. His offer had been practical, for all he'd tried to cloak it in romance, with the damnable mechanical bird that had been broken so soon after he'd finished the laborious effort of crafting it. Alys had not protected his invention or his heart, but she had made the right decision. She and her marquess were two of the happiest people he knew, and the marquess delighted in his family. No second thoughts there, for all that the wedding had been a rushed affair.

To think, he'd never even kissed Alys, when he knew the secret chambers and pulses of Victoria's body. He wanted to know more. That breathy moan she'd gifted to him when he first entered her would surely be different if he slid into her slowly, or thrust with brutal efficiency. Or perhaps from a different angle; that might change the cadence of her breath. How could he not learn these things? He sighed, closing his eyes as he felt his cock surge to life from the sheer jolt of his imaginings. He leaned his head against the wall as he fought for control, but a cough returned him to reality. Opening his eyes, he saw a lad of about twelve pressed against the wall, likely the boot boy.

After stammering an apology to the young servant, who probably wanted to get at the coats dangling above his head, he stood, shaking his head to put himself out of his reverie. Victoria had to be outside; he couldn't imagine her hiding in her room or in the nursery. The reality would be better than any daydream. Besides, the sooner he put her out of his mind, the better he would do at his work.

He needed to see her. After grabbing his own waxed cotton coat, he tossed a coin to the lad and went out the mudroom door, which led down the hill to the stables. He ignored Nicholas's wave from the stable door and kept walking, bent on the path around the lake. The reeds and other vegetation, along with the trees on the other side of the path, cast reflections on the water, as if an entire natural city grew on the surface, adding color to the water. The Fort played no part in the image; it was too far away. He was struck with a desire to see his own face, to add a human element to the mirror. For all humanity had done to change the landscape, so much of it was still untouched.

These thoughts made no sense to him. But some things mattered, in his insignificant viewpoint at least. Like Victoria. Far off in the distance, he could hear male voices. A company of men must be heading to, or returning from, the village. A dog barked, too, perhaps spotting some errant beast it could chase.

And then he saw a female form. A long coat, covering her almost to the hem of her black gown, sturdy boots, a graceful, hip-swinging walk. A low-slung top hat covered her forehead to her eyebrows, and a scarf protected her throat. He'd have liked to see more of Victoria, but the real trouble was that she was holding the Baron of Alix's arm, chatting with easy familiarity. As he watched, she smiled at the tall Scotsman. Lewis's stomach lurched, preparing to eject his morning kippers.

Was this not the woman who had come apart in his arms the night before? While he did not expect their relationship to continue indefinitely, surely she could have been exclusive to him until the end of the house party? Was she so desperate for attention?

Victoria's head turned away from the baron, as if to check her footing on the muddy path. When her gaze moved, she caught sight of Lewis. Their eyes met. The smile vanished from her face. The hollows under her cheekbones deepened and her expression became shadowed, as if she suddenly felt as sick as he did.

This evidence made him feel no better. Was she playing a game with him, with the baron, with Dickondell? What was Victoria after? She did not comport herself as a flirt. While she had a ready laugh, she seemed more serious than that. She would never age into a Lady Florence.

The baron waved to him in easy familiarity. "Hello, Noble. Taking a break from the submarine today?"

Lewis shook his head. Before he could counsel his own words to caution, he said, "No, I came looking for Victoria."

The baron's eyes widened at Lewis's use of the lady's first name. He had been entirely inappropriate. Victoria's lips tightened into a thin line. She swallowed hard before speaking.

"How can I assist you, Mr. Noble?" she said in clear tones.

He had never heard her voice sound so cultured, so society. Cut to the bone, ashamed of his behavior, he lied, "Lady Barbara asked me to find you. I apologize for speaking so familiarly on her behalf." He nodded to the baron and turned away, taking rapid steps toward the stables.

Murmurs floated on the breeze behind him, the baron and Victoria speaking. He closed his ears to the sounds and stalked back to his work. It was where he belonged, not chasing after ladies, even if this one was his midnight lover.

Victoria's feet seemed to take flight as she separated from the baron. She ran up the steps to the back of the Fort, not sure what she was escaping from. Her shame, perhaps. She'd seen the crushed look in Lewis's eyes. First at the Punch and Judy show, and now this. But she felt angry as much as ashamed. What did he expect? Didn't everyone know her father meant her to find another husband? It would be different if she'd had a child from her brief marriage, but she hadn't. A lady in her position had to try again. Her life's purpose hadn't been fulfilled, no matter how unsuited she was for it, given her failure to take the unruliness out of Penelope. A marriage and children, running a house; that was her training, her goal, her expectation.

Feeling the heat of tears, she wiped under her eyes, then tore off her coat and sat on the bench in the mudroom to replace her boots with slippers. Her skirt was dotted with mud, but Lady Barbara wouldn't care about that, not if she stayed away from the upholstery.

She went directly to her friend's room and found her there, staring into the mirror at her dressing table.

"My, but you look bemused," Victoria said.

Barbara smiled wanly at her through the mirror.

She crossed to her friend and put a hand on her shoulder. "Has something happened? Lewis—Mr. Noble—said you had asked for me."

Lady Barbara's head turned slowly on the thin stalk of her neck. "No, I came directly here from the parlor after my mother spoke to me. Perhaps she asked Lewis to find you."

"What's wrong?"

"Nothing," Lady Barbara said. "You must be patient, my dear. All will be revealed soon. I hope you will not find me too weak for friendship after this."

"I don't understand." Victoria met her eyes in the mirror.

Her friend sighed. "My mother was determined to make this house party work for both Rowena and me. Now that Rowena has made her choice, I must be settled immediately. It is not even eleven o'clock but it has been a very long day already."

"I agree." Victoria perched on the edge of the bench in front of the dressing table. Her skirt was a windblown, wrinkled disaster compared to Lady Barbara's neatly pressed silk. What did the countess have planned? Her friend seemed to like Lewis best, but she doubted even Queen Victoria could persuade the inventor to marry where he didn't want to. "I need to change before luncheon."

Lady Barbara didn't even glance over. "The post came."

"Anything of interest?"

"I heard from a friend of mine in Brighton. She shed some light on the mysteries of your uncle's separation from your Aunt Clarissa."

"Oh?" Victoria's thoughts changed direction instantly.

"Yes. Her housekeeper knows your aunt's minder."

Victoria frowned. "She has a *minder*?"

"I'm afraid so. My friend said the gossip is that your aunt hears voices. She claims Saint Catherine of the Wheel is speaking to her."

"Like she's having visions?" Victoria put her hand to her forehead.

"Yes. Apparently, your aunt feels a great affinity for Saint Catherine, and Joan of Arc is said to have counseled her, too."

"That doesn't sound good," Victoria whispered.

Lady Barbara shook her head. "Do you think Penelope knows?"

"I know she doesn't." But the thought of the little girl's mysterious rages made her nervous. Could Penelope have the same disease as her mother?

She heard footsteps in the hall and realized Lady Barbara's door was open. Standing swiftly, she shut it without looking to see who was in the corridor.

CHAPTER 12

Lewis saw no surprise on Victoria's face at dinner that night when the earl announced a toast. He was seated across from her. The table was wide, but a silver salver topped with clove-studded oranges between them did not block his view. He leaned back in his chair and accepted the glass of champagne the butler handed him.

"I am happy to announce the engagement of my sister Barbara to Mr. Clement Dickondell," the earl said, raising his glass. "In 1890 we will celebrate a double wedding here at Pevensey-Sur-Mer Fort. In February, I believe. I hope you will all rejoin us for the festivities."

"Here, here," someone called from the bottom of the table. Probably Samuel Dickondell. The entire family, including the parents, along with the Shield relatives, had come for dinner that night.

Lewis had found himself faced with Alys yet again. His heart had given the usual extra kick when he saw her shining red hair and her beautiful face, but he took no joy in it. He had no physical hunger for Alys as he did for Victoria. With yet another engagement being announced, the crowd should be busy surrounding the daughters of the house. No one would miss Victoria or him, not even the earl, who would not be able to escape to his submarine that evening.

Still, the thought of taking Victoria carnally while Alys was present gave him pause. Victoria caught him staring at her and stopped drinking in midsip. With a troubled smile, she lifted her glass and toasted him silently. He nodded back, unable to break their shared gaze.

Cousin Rose poked him in the ribs. He jerked to the side and turned to her. "What?"

She regarded him with a smirk. "I must have found a sensitive spot."

"You are too old for tickling," he reproved.

"I was merely trying to capture your attention." Rose sighed. "Isn't all of this wedding business romantic? The countess must be so pleased by the success of her house party."

"I do not see why. She is marrying her daughters to local farmers. All of this expense to marry off the ladies to local denizens."

"She needed the party to make them come up to snuff." Rose covered her mouth with her napkin and coughed. "It had the intended effect."

"Is that how it works? Positively Machiavellian."

"Matchmaking mamas have their ways. The countess likely only approved Ernest's suit because Clement was willing to propose as well. Clement, being the heir, is a much better catch. My mama, of course, does not think like that."

"She did not have much to do with either Alys or Sir Gawain's marriages," Lewis agreed.

"No." Rose pursed her lips. "I should take her to task for that, but it would do no good."

"Is there anything I can do on your behalf?" Lewis inquired. "I sense you wish your mother would do something."

She gave him a quick nod, then spoke into his ear. "Rupert Courtnay."

Lewis squinted instinctively, as if to limit the impact her request made on him. What would Rose want with Victoria's father? Was it a game? Was she warning him that she knew about his involvement with Victoria? He turned to face her full on and saw she was twisting her snowy white napkin into a limp rag. "You are serious?" he asked, sotto voce.

She nodded, a jerky movement of her head.

"Are you love with him?"

She licked her lower lip, then the upper. He waited, but she didn't speak.

"Don't settle, Rose," he warned. "You are only twenty-one. There is time. Another three years, at least, before you must worry about your prospects."

"I'm locked away in the country for my health," Rose said, a spot of sharp color appearing on each cheek. "I'm not recovering. I need to act before it is too late."

"Liverpool?" he asked under his breath. "You understand what marrying him would mean. All those factories. And constant rain."

"Rain keeps the air cleaner."

"The dampness won't be good for you." He didn't want her to sacrifice her life to a marriage.

"I'm told the countryside outside the city is lovely. Maybe I could spend much of my time there. Or in Southport, especially in the summer."

"It sounds as if you have it all planned out."

"But I have no one to speak for me." She pressed her hand to his arm. "Is there anything you can do on my behalf? I do think he likes me, but I'm not sure if he is looking for a wife."

He glanced at Victoria, who was regarding them curiously. She met his gaze, then turned to the Baron of Alix, who was on her right, to answer some question of his.

Lewis gritted his teeth, feeling an insult even when Victoria could have done nothing but respond to a direct question from a dinner partner. The wheels and cogs of a plan turned in his head.

"I will see what I can do," he said, though he was unsure if any man should marry a woman the age of his daughter. "Are you and Lady Allen-Hill close?"

Rose smiled. "I like her more each time we meet. She has a fertile imagination and is better with her cousin than she believes. My maid tells me the child is positively ungovernable, with wild rages over the smallest things, yet Victoria keeps her calm. Penelope is no trouble at all when Victoria is present."

"Her gift is instinctive?"

"Yes, or she simply understands the girl at some deep level."

"I like her very much," Lewis said.

"Who? The lady or the child?"

Lewis tilted his champagne glass to his lips and drained it, feeling the bubbles pop against the back of his tongue. "The lady, of course. I've scarcely met the child."

"I wonder if I should have to raise her if I marry Mr. Courtnay," Rose mused. "I should endeavor to spend time with her."

Lewis grinned. "You might not be up for the challenge."

"She would spend most of her time with a governess," Rose mused. "Her custodial relative would only have to see her an hour or so a day, but one does not like to think of any child of the house terrorizing the servants."

"I used to terrify my old nurse," Lewis said. "She stayed on well past the point I should have been turned over to tutors because my mother had a soft heart. I was so curious."

"I remember hearing stories of you nearly burning your house down."

"And exploding things." Lewis chuckled. "I initially developed a taste for chemistry."

"You had turned to mechanics by the time you came to live with us. I still remember your birds. It's a pity you turned to engines."

"They are better business," Lewis said, hoping his flat tone would close that particular subject.

"Thank you for agreeing to help me," Rose said softly.

Lewis nodded, but he had yet to decide how much help to provide. He had hardly spoken to Rupert Courtnay. How much help could he be? But he did have an idea for fixing his situation with Victoria and simultaneously quashing her budding romance with the Baron of Alix.

He chided himself for calling it that. What did it matter to him if she was attractive to other men? The baron offered Victoria his arm when dinner was over, escorting her to the drawing room instead of staying behind for private conversation among the gentlemen. He knew the baron did not like cigars, but still, the gesture smacked of overfamiliarity.

In fact, he monopolized the rest of Victoria's evening. The two stayed at the piano, inexpertly interpreting holiday carols. Rose cast glances at Lewis from her seat at the far end of the room, imploring him to speak to Courtnay. But he knew he'd have to choose his time carefully. He wasn't the head of Rose's family; therefore his approach must be indirect. His cousin hadn't been compromised in any way. Or so he thought. Had the pair kissed?

He regarded the imposing figure standing by the fireplace with the earl. They had come in together, smelling of whiskey, speaking about machinery, something that normally would have fascinated him, but tonight he couldn't find that place in his brain. No, his eyes kept returning to the curve of Victoria's back as she bent over the keyboard, the sensual indentation of her waist, the flare of her hips. He remembered touching that round bottom, recalled the noises he made, the moistness between her thighs.

Torture, sheer torture. Eventually, he left the room and went to the stable, hoping to fine-tune the instruments in the conning tower.

Lewis spent most of the night with the submarine, losing the hours until the first hint of watery gray winter sky peeping over the lake forced him to realize dawn had come. He went back to his rooms then, sleeping until the noon hour.

When he went downstairs, after Eddy had all but kicked him awake, he found Victoria, Rose, and Penelope all seated in the morning parlor. The baron was nowhere to be seen, and Victoria looked at him with great interest.

He wondered if she had come looking for him during the night. Eddy hadn't indicated that was the case, but he wouldn't necessarily have known. He hoped to God she hadn't spent it with the baron. His cousin lifted her eyebrows to him, and he wondered if she had been campaigning to enter the affections of Rupert Courtnay's family, in anticipation of him speaking to the man on her behalf.

"Do you have one of your horseless carriages here, Lewis?" Rose asked.

"Why, did you want to close out the year with a drive?" He sat down, crumpling the back of his jacket in the process.

"Victoria would like to go to Brighton today, if possible."

"This is not the season," he said, confused. "I don't think the weather will please you."

"I wish to take Penelope to see her mother," Victoria said.

Her cheeks did not have the rosy hue he had become accustomed to seeing, he now noticed. "Is she ill?"

"Perhaps."

"I want to see Mummy," Penelope interjected. "Daddy had her sent away."

The child did seem genuinely distressed. Where Victoria had lost color, she had gained it. A red flush colored her face and she looked hot, disagreeable. He recalled she'd been ill earlier in the week.

"This may not be the best time," he said as gently as he knew how. "You have not been feeling well, Miss Courtnay, and perhaps it is the same for your mother."

"That's not what Lady Barbara said," the child complained. "She said Mummy ought to be locked away."

Victoria closed her eyes. "My cousin overheard part—an unfortunate part—of a conversation. She is insisting on seeing her mother, and with my father gone and unable to provide counsel, I do not know what to do other than go to Brighton and see for myself."

"Your father is gone?" Lewis traded glances with Rose.

"He went to the village and hasn't returned yet."

"You mean since yesterday?"

She nodded.

Lewis scrubbed his face with his hands. He hadn't even had a cup of coffee or tea yet this morning. Err, afternoon. "Could he have gone to Brighton?"

"I do not know, Mr. Noble."

Penelope jumped up from the sofa and collapsed into a kneeling position at his feet. "Please take us? I must see Mummy. I have so much to tell her."

"It might make things worse," he said over the girl's head, but he could see Victoria didn't know what to do. As for Rose, she simply wanted to please her prospective suitor's daughter. She would be of no use.

"Is knowing the truth ever really a bad thing?" Victoria asked.

Lewis thought about that. "Sometimes illusion can be splendid."

Victoria's eyes went to the girl at his feet. "I think we are past that point."

"You may be right. There is a motorized carriage in the stable. It is an earlier version, open to the weather; just a cart with seats, really."

"It isn't snowing. If we bring furs and hot bricks, it should be fine."

He nodded and stood, careful to maneuver around the girl. "I will see if I can start it up. But I'm not willing to take Rose. She is too delicate for the trip under these circumstances."

His cousin glared at him but nodded. She might dislike her limitations, but at least she had learned to accept them over the past few years. Or, at least, when marriage wasn't involved.

An hour later, he'd managed to construct an awning over the front bench of the carriage with the help of one of his men. He'd gotten the machinery started and was reasonably certain he could take them safely to the outskirts of Brighton. If not, he could rent a horse somewhere along the way and harness it to the carriage. It still had the necessary hardware.

He saw Victoria and her cousin walking down from the Fort, followed by two servants, their arms heaped high with comfort items for the chilly drive.

Twenty minutes later, they were off, chugging along the muddy path around the lake, to pick up the road to the village. Thick white smoke trailed behind them, but at least it was a pure color, with no tinge of gray, which might indicate problems. He wished he could be alone with Victoria on a pleasure trip, but her cousin kept up a steady stream of commentary from the rear seat of the cart, pointing out every small specimen of wildlife crossing their path and proving they were far from private.

"Mood swings," he muttered.

"Can you blame her?" Victoria asked softly. "All of the uncertainty she's faced. And me with no idea what to do with her."

"She adores you."

She glared at him. "That is not the point. You can adore people who are perfectly terrible. It is all a matter of perspective."

"Am I perfectly terrible?" he asked.

"That is assuming I adore you," she said, pointing her nose in the air.

He had never noticed the slope of her nose before, only the flatness of the bridge, the way her nostrils made perfect half-moons around the sides. But from this angle, he saw it had a certain downward geometry. Her profile gave the impression of an inward-facing young woman, rather than the gregarious soul he found her to be. She had spent a lot of time alone. He wondered what her thoughts were, what her dreams and fears might be, apart from what her father wanted from her.

Had he ever thought to ask? She would not tell him the truth now, with a child-sized conduit straight to her father sitting in the backseat.

"I do not assume your adoration, only your gratitude for my conveying you to Brighton."

She laughed heartily at that, turning her head so that he saw only her public face again, and not the more secret side of her. "A gentleman should be pleased to do any favor for a lady."

"But I am promised to the earl," he said. "I am disappointing my patron."

"Oh." She dismissed the thought. "You are too successful to be so beholden. I have heard all about you from Rose. A man who can command any fee he wishes for his work is not a man in thrall to anyone."

He wondered if she really saw him that way. People were now offering him a level of respect he'd never received before, especially from his uncle, Sir Bartley Redcake, who had treated him almost as a nuisance even while he proceeded to transform the man's businesses with his innovative, time-saving inventions. He still found it hard to behave as a success. Arrogance did not seem to be part of his nature. But, perhaps more importantly, he did as he pleased most of the time, and three years earlier that had not really been the case. By that alone he knew he'd come a long way.

He'd also been able to build his own workspace. A house, a couple of servants to keep him fed and dressed, the financial responsibility of Eddy and some other employees, all of them had been easy to afford. He could hold his head high and do what he liked with the majority of his day.

"As you say," he told Victoria. Would she respond better to assurance than naked need? If he thought only about the next night, the next gift of sex, would that carry him through?

By early afternoon, they had reached the outskirts of Brighton. Small cottages dotted the landscape, surrounded by trees and the bare winter plots of summer vegetable gardens.

Victoria kept an anxious eye on landmarks. "That must be the church, and there is the vicarage with the bronze weather vane."

Lewis nodded and drove into the field next to the cottage where Clarissa Courtnay lived. When the engine was off, he asked, "Should I go in first and see if the situation is suitable for Penelope?"

"Certainly not," Victoria said. "We must all know the truth."

"Victoria," Lewis said in a soft voice, "I cannot agree with you."

Her lips tightened and she glanced into the rear, where Penelope was curled up on the bench, asleep. "Very well."

Lewis hopped down and walked up the shell-strewn path to the front door of the cottage. He used the knocker and was rewarded a few minutes later by the appearance of a sober-looking woman dressed in an old-fashioned black dress with a wide skirt.

"My name is Lewis Noble. I have brought Mrs. Courtnay's daughter and niece for a visit if she is receiving," he told the woman.

She registered no surprise, as he might have expected, but the hour was such that visitors might be likely to call. "I will ask her to come into the sitting room."

He tried to smile, but the emotion died before it reached his lips. She was so stoic. Did she need that level of control to live in the midst of madness?

When he reached the cart, he found Penelope awake and in the front seat with Victoria.

"Can I see Mother now?" the child asked.

"Yes." He shrugged at Victoria.

"Did she come to the door?" she asked.

"No, there was a servant." He held out his hand and Victoria took it. The press of one glove against another held little intimacy, and he wished he could cup her cheek, kiss her brow, in support of what was likely to be a difficult meeting. Either her aunt would be mad or not, and that meant either disappointing Penelope or causing Victoria to lose faith in her father and uncle.

She looked tense as she helped her cousin exit the carriage in turn. Lewis pulled a tarp from the back and spread it over the seats so they would remain dry, then followed them to the front door. The servant gestured them in without further speech, and they were directed to a plain sitting room, far too large for the limited furnishings. Victoria and Penelope sat in straight-backed wooden chairs that had been only roughly finished.

The family had plenty of money, so why the poor surroundings? Had no one checked on the situation? Lewis began to think for the first time that Victoria had been right to demand to come. He stood next to the unlit fireplace and wondered where the household sat during the day. While the temperature was above freezing, it had surely been that low overnight and was scarcely temperate now. He left his gloves on, and only unwound his muffler. The servant had not offered to take any of their coats.

Impatient, he began to search for a coal scuttle. Penelope shivered and Victoria wrapped her arm around the girl.

"I thought we would come inside to warm up," she said. "But it isn't much warmer."

"We're out of the rain at least," Lewis said. "This household might need some reordering."

Victoria nodded. "I am not pleased. At least it is clean, though."

After a few more moments of waiting, the servant returned, followed by a very thin woman with watery blue eyes and Penelope's wide mouth.

The girl sat up straight when she saw her mother, but Lewis was surprised to see she didn't run into her arms, or even attempt to do so. Instinctively, she knew that was a bad idea.

Clarissa Courtnay did not speak, merely regarded her daughter and niece impassively. He wondered if she'd been dosed with opiates.

Victoria forced a smile and rose. "Aunt Clarissa." She stepped forward and gave her aunt a hug.

The woman did not pull away, but she didn't respond either.

"I brought Penelope for a visit." Victoria chattered on about their reason for being in the area, Penelope's cold, the other children visiting the nursery, the masquerade ball.

Penelope talked a little about the fairy tale Victoria had been telling her but stayed huddled on her chair. The servant stood in the corner, ever watchful but offering nothing.

After a few minutes, the women had seated themselves. Victoria continued to chatter brightly, but her gaze roamed the room.

"I know you hate me," Clarissa Courtnay said suddenly.

Penelope's mouth drooped as Victoria protested.

"Of course not, Aunt Clarissa. We've missed you and love you dearly," Victoria said.

"I know it," Mrs. Courtnay insisted.

"It's time for a rest," said the servant, stepping forward. She held out her hand to her charge, and Mrs. Courtnay stood obediently.

Penelope rose from her chair so suddenly that it teetered on three legs. She flew at her mother, grabbing her around the waist. "When are you coming home? I want to go home!"

Mrs. Courtnay stared off into the distance as her daughter sobbed against her bodice. He saw Victoria blink hard, a sheen of tears in her eyes.

"The lady says I must remain here," Mrs. Courtnay said.

"What lady?" asked Victoria.

The woman seemed not to hear her. "I'm to be here to greet the king when he returns."

"There hasn't been a king for over fifty years," Victoria said. She clasped her hands together in front of her. Lewis could see the tension in her rounded shoulders, the way her arms were held stiffly against her body.

"Well, now," said the servant, "Mrs. Courtnay is ready for a lie-down. I will return to escort you out."

Lewis helped Victoria pull the sobbing Penelope away from her mother, who never lifted a hand one way or another. Victoria held Penelope tightly as the two women exited the room.

"You're shivering," he said. He quickly took off his greatcoat and wrapped it around her shoulders, then tucked the outer edges around Penelope.

The trio stood silently for a moment.

Victoria broke the silence eventually. "I have never known Aunt Clarissa not to offer tea. Not ever. She was always so polite."

"I think she's taking medicine," Lewis said.

She nodded. "I saw her pupils. I hate to think how bad she is without it, if she can say such things while so heavily medicated."

"She doesn't know what she is saying," Lewis said.

"I'm never going home," Penelope said, breathing heavily between each word. "Mother is never going to be well."

"We do not know that," Victoria said. "But it is best to be realistic. At least she is calm, and clean."

Though not particularly well cared for. "Do you think there are fires in other parts of the house?"

"I would assume the kitchen is warm, at least. This room is not very welcoming. There might be another parlor."

Judging from the circumference of the outer walls, Lewis doubted it. Mrs. Courtnay might spend much of her day locked in her bedchamber, for instance. "We'll check the chimneys when we go," he said. "Make sure there is smoke coming out of some of them. I half-expected to meet your father here, since he has been away."

Victoria sighed. "I have no idea where he went. He doesn't like to say."

A mistress? Likely. Lewis wondered again if the man was any kind of suitable match for Rose, though her choices were limited. He remembered hearing how the Dickondell men had surrounded her like bees around a flower when she had first moved into the area a few years ago, but they had scarcely noticed her at the house party. Clearly she had been declared unsuitable for them, and now that two of them had snagged the earl's sisters they were above Rose's touch. Her ill health was all too evident.

Penelope had calmed by the time the servant returned ten minutes later. Victoria's expression hardened when she saw the woman.

"Do you have enough money to run this household sufficiently?" she demanded.

"Yes, ma'am."

"Then why is my aunt so thin? Why is there no fire? Why didn't you ask my aunt if she wanted to serve tea?"

The servant's expression remained utterly impassive. "You will not wish to discuss this in front of the child."

"I'll take Penelope," Lewis said. He helped Victoria unravel the child from around her waist and walked her back toward the kitchen. While it was a stunning breach of etiquette, she needed to warm up before they left.

While the fireplace was cold in the kitchen as well, the stove was hot and the room was at least twenty degrees warmer. He took a cloth and poured steaming water from the kettle into a cup.

"Put your hands around that," he told Penelope. "Drink it when it cools."

"Thank you," she said, sitting in the chair closest to the stove.

He poked around a bit, and decided the kitchen was well enough stocked for him to take a bit of bread and cheese for the child. He cut off slices of both and warmed them in the oven until the cheese was melted, then served her.

Penelope ate slowly, her solemn expression telling him without words how utterly bereft she was. When her food and water were gone, she put one hand to her forehead, the picture of childish despair.

"Will she ever be better?"

"It can happen," Lewis said. "But I do not know what the chance of it is. I know so little of what has transpired."

"Will I go mad?" Penelope said in a tiny voice.

"I do not know that either," he admitted. "But you cannot spend your life worrying about it. You have to be strong and take what pleasure you can in each day unfolding after the next."

"I feel quite desperate sometimes." She gulped air, her small chest heaving.

"Your mother was perfectly well for a very long time, correct?" he asked.

"I suppose."

"She must be in her thirties," he ventured. Of course, now that he was in his thirties, it did not seem like such a long time to hang on to sanity.

Penelope nodded.

"Don't worry," he said, trying not to show any anxiety. "I'm certain you will be fine."

"You are?"

"You are also your father's daughter, and you have a strong character, Miss Penelope Courtnay. Very like your cousin. I don't see an ounce of surrender in you."

"No?" Her lips curved into a tiny smile.

He shook his head. "I believe you will fight hard against anything, though I would attempt to moderate your temper."

"People say such mean things," she muttered.

"I'm sure they do, but it is a reflection upon them, not you. Say a prayer for them instead of giving in to heated emotions."

"Mr. Noble?"

He heard Victoria's muffled voice on the other side of the green baize door. The door opened and she appeared.

"Are you ready to depart?" She looked pale but composed.

For himself, he could not wait to leave. They would be pushing daylight on their return and he didn't like the idea of driving on the mucky path around the lake after dark.

He took Penelope's cup and poured another few ounces of steaming water into it. "Here, drink this before we leave."

Victoria took the cup gratefully.

"I am sorry I did not offer refreshments," the servant said, entering silently. "I explained why. Would you like me to serve you now?"

"I understand," Victoria said, inhaling the steam from the cup. "And no, we must be on our way."

"I took some bread and cheese for the child," Lewis said.

The woman nodded, unperturbed.

Five minutes later, they were back in the carriage. While the motor warmed, Lewis checked the chimneys. Only one had smoke rising. "They are going to freeze."

"It is better than burning," Victoria said. "I will explain later, but for now, let us return to Pevensey."

He nodded and drove out of the field. Penelope huddled under her furs and wrapped the tarp into a kind of a tent around her, even though they had the awning to protect them from the occasional drizzle. Victoria pressed herself tightly against Lewis, her head drooping against his shoulder at times.

He felt intense gratitude that she found comfort with him, instead of holding herself stiffly apart in her grief. They did have a real, alchemical connection. He would go to her in his grief, too; he knew that. But what good did that do them, when she planned to spend her life in Liverpool? His cousin Rose had more likelihood of spending time with Victoria than he did.

CHAPTER 13

Victoria had intended to go downstairs for the New Year's Eve ball. She had an elegant white-and-black dress that perfectly complemented an ebony feathered headpiece, and she suspected tonight would be the final main event of the house party. This would likely be the last night to meet local society. Also, Lady Florence's maid had said her father had returned, and she desperately wanted to speak to him. He had not turned up for afternoon tea in the parlor, or come to her room after she dressed.

But Penelope refused to go up to the nursery. And so Victoria found herself in an armchair at the end of the corridor near her room after dinner, in the very alcove where she and Lewis had explored sensual delights in such a naughty and discoverable manner. She shifted uncomfortably in the armchair, the mere thought of his flesh pounding into hers making her moist between the soft skin of her thighs.

"Why are you sighing? Are you sad?" Penelope asked, her tone plaintive as she wriggled on the opposite chair.

Victoria stared at the three-tiered stand of marzipan fruits between them. Pure marzipan was too sweet for her tastes now, after so much effort to reduce, but she thought she might indulge in one of the dates, which was stuffed with marzipan, topped with an almond, then dusted with sparkling colored sugar. "I am deciding if I am hungry enough for one of these treats. You really shouldn't have brought so many."

"I thought they might cheer me." Penelope chose a tiny blueberry-colored marzipan treat and popped it into her mouth. "They are terribly pretty."

"Jings, but that's a lot o' marzipan," said the Baron of Alix.

Victoria hadn't even noticed him in the corridor, which was a sign of her sorry state. Had he been coming to see her? His room wasn't nearby. "Hello, John."

He smiled warmly at her, and she knew he was pleased she had remembered to use his first name, as he'd requested when they'd agreed to be friends. "May I escort you to the ball, Victoria?"

Before she could explain Penelope's wish to keep her nearby, she heard the sound of a door opening farther down on the corridor. Quick steps loped toward them and two people appeared. Victoria inhaled sharply at the sight of Lewis, lean and dangerous, his eyes shadowed by the brim of an American cowboy hat. The planes of his face were made sharp by the tilted hat, and his studied sneer thinned and lengthened his sensual lips. The rest of his clothing was conventional evening wear. Eddy wore nice clothing as well, though one side of his collar was askew. She glanced at John and realized the baron had a sailor's cap sloping back on his head, which she hadn't even noticed. Her headdress was still back in her room, too heavy to wear for no purpose.

Penelope swallowed her unchewed blueberry treat and began coughing when Eddy winked at her. Victoria patted her on the back until she stopped.

"Is that marzipan for anyone?" Eddy asked.

Penelope nodded her assent, though she still couldn't speak. Lewis narrowed his eyes in the baron's direction and pulled a chair away from the wall. She hadn't realized there were more chairs hiding along the stone walls and shivered at the idea that people could have observed them when they coupled without her ever seeing them. The shadows were deep and consumed the stone.

John took a seat, too, and the four of them each chose a marzipan creation. Eddy grabbed an entire stem of grapes, though the men were more abstemious, each taking a banana. Victoria sighed and surrendered to one of the date confections.

Lewis stared hard at her. "Have you shared your solution to the five coins riddle with Penelope?"

She smiled, amused that he remembered her fairy tale. She hoped to ease the tension she felt emanating from him. Did he think she had planned to meet John here? "Yes, when I was sitting in the back of the carriage with her yesterday. To be honest, Penelope, Lewis imagined the juggling ice creature, not me. He's very creative."

He nodded. "I couldn't hear you with the wind in my ears. What comes next?"

"The jars. Four jars unopened," Penelope said somewhat indistinctly around a marzipan pear.

The baron shook his head and grinned. The sailor's hat must be pinned because it did not budge from its precarious position. "I look forward tae hearing the entire story."

Victoria glanced at the cowboy hat again, amazed at how it toughened Lewis's features. She wished they were alone so she could kiss him, to see if she could soften those hard lips. "I need to write it down so I don't forget."

"You can share it with your children someday." John's expression warmed.

It made Victoria acutely uncomfortable, sitting here with such a nice man . . . and her lover, who was not looking so nice at that moment. No, Lewis was disgruntled, but he had no power over her, not when he had not proposed. She did not expect him to put her father's wishes for her over his own business, but he could be more circumspect.

She shifted uneasily in her seat. Lewis's gaze went from her armchair to Penelope's, then back again. His eyes drifted to her décolletage. She felt her skin grow hot.

"Er." She cleared her throat. "And so to the jars. Princess Everilda remembered a tale of the jars that might be relevant. The four jars carried purity, humility, stewardship, and Christian charity. The female virtues."

Lewis lifted a brow and she glared at him.

"My story is set long ago," she pointed out.

"Go on," he said through gritted teeth. John, in contrast, smiled pleasantly.

"Of course, the princess had no idea how the legend of the jars would play into her quest to free Prince Hugh from his stepmama's trap. She decided to go for a quiet walk and pulled a thick fur mantle around her shoulders. Like today, there was only a little ground before the lake, and she was soon at the edge, where she found four jars bobbing among the reeds."

"Was Moses there in a basket, too?" John asked, mischief dancing in his eyes.

"My story is not set that far back in time," she reproved. "No, it was the cusp of the New Year, though a little earlier in the day, so there was still light."

"The jars?" Penelope prompted.

"Yes. They were clear, and a strange kind of light emanated from them. Princess Everilda wondered if they were safe to touch. Luckily, she found a discarded shepherd's crook on the ground."

"How fortuitous," Lewis murmured.

Victoria was tempted to throw a marzipan apple at him. "She used it to pull the first jar out of the reeds. When she had it on the ground next to her, she knelt on the muddy bank and leaned close. It emitted a hum.

"She counseled herself to be brave and, after drawing her dagger from her belt for security, unstoppered the first jar. The ray of light rose into the air, and Prince Hugh's face appeared, positively angelic in the crystalline nimbus. 'Are you true?' he asked.

" 'Of course,' she cried, and his image vanished. Desperate now to see her beloved's face again, she pulled the second jar to her and unstoppered it.

"His face appeared again. 'Are you proud?' he asked. She responded resoundingly, 'No!' He vanished yet again.

"This time, she waded into the lake herself and grabbed both of the remaining jars. When she opened the third jar, the prince showed himself. 'Is the castle secure?' She did not know how to answer, for the malevolent designs of the dead queen had surely invaded her realm, yet no human foe was causing a problem.

" 'I don't know,' she answered, as honestly as she dared. Then she opened the last jar.

" 'Are the people fed?' asked Prince Hugh.

" 'Of course,' she said, surprised. 'There is no hunger among the castle folk.'

"The jars flared again, and Prince Hugh appeared above them. 'Take a basket of bread to the bell tower of the church at midnight and feed the birds.' She held out her hands to him in despair, but he vanished." Victoria popped the rest of her date into her mouth, satisfied by her story.

"Three bells unrung is the next clue," Penelope said.

"Fascinating," John exclaimed. He brushed one hand against another, then pulled gloves from his pocket. "May I escort ye to find your headpiece, Victoria?"

She saw Lewis's jaw work when he heard her name. Did he think she had offered her body to the baron as well? She lifted her chin. "Penelope would like me to stay with her."

"Ye canna," John said. "She's meant tae go tae the children's party in the nursery. Come, Miss Penelope, ye do not want to miss that. I understand the vicar's children are here and are expecting ye."

Victoria watched, bemused, as he jollied her cousin into taking his hand and walking down the corridor. She expected Lewis to pause outside her door, but he followed John and was trailed by Eddy. They all vanished up the staircase and down the corridor, leaving her alone. She went into her room and attempted to place her headpiece, but she couldn't balance it alone. The maid had disappeared. She gave up after fifteen minutes and plucked a plume from the headdress, affixing it to the back of her head, then tied a scarf around her forehead so she looked like an Indian princess. *Cowboys and Indians.* She'd keep Lewis connected to her one way or another. Just seeing him in that hat had made her knees weak. She would do better to ignore him at the ball and let her father see her doing as he asked.

By the time Lewis had asked Victoria for a dance, her card was full. She hadn't seemed very sorry to refuse him. He'd heard her breath catch earlier that night and knew she felt something, but perhaps it was only lust. While he'd been raised not to ascribe such coarse feelings to a lady, he knew Victoria, at least, was an exception to the rule.

Some part of him was not surprised when he ventured back down his corridor a little after midnight, when the champagne had been drunk and good wishes bestowed all around, and found Victoria there. At least this time she was alone. No children, no Scottish baron, not even the marzipan. She had what looked like a beauty mark on her cheek, but when she turned into the flickering light of the candle that burned on the windowsill, he suspected it was a dot of frosting from the enormous, multiple-tiered cake that had been served, brought down from Redcake's in London.

He lifted his finger to her cheek and wiped the sugary substance away. Buttercream. He'd know that smell anywhere after years of designing, installing, and maintaining equipment in the bakeries.

"What?" she asked, putting her ungloved fingers to the place he'd touched.

He pulled out a handkerchief and wiped the substance away. "You must have been into the cake."

"Just one bite, to see if it tasted as good as I remembered."

"Did it?"

"No," she said softly. "Everything is too sweet now. Cake, marzipan, chocolate drinks."

"Why did you do it? All that self-denial?"

"You don't think I deny myself much, do you," she said with a wry twist of her lips.

"I know you do," he said. "Food, at least."

Her voice was all but swallowed up by the shadows. "Why are you so cross with me?"

He considered his response for a moment, then chose honesty. "I was jealous when I heard the baron call you by your Christian name."

"We agreed to be friends."

He silently saluted the baron for his underhanded tactic with the most eligible heiress present at the house party. "He's not a suitor, then?"

She sighed. "I must marry someone someday, Lewis. My father has softened his requirements somewhat. The baron would suit him."

"But not me." He knew he shouldn't feel irritation, but he did.

"I am sure he would be delighted to have you join the family in Liverpool, if you cared for me more than you care for your work. But I know you well enough to understand the truth."

"You do?"

"Of course. We shall only have this." She stepped toward him, wrapping her arms around his waist. "I find myself unable to say no to you, for the little time we have left."

"I have not asked anything of you," Lewis said. He knew he had been foolish the moment he opened his mouth. Her arms released him and she stepped back. The single candle only offered him the odd glimpse of her face.

"No?"

"No. I did not know I would find you here. But now that I have, I should wish you a very happy New Year. Best wishes to you, Lady Allen-Hill." He bowed stiffly, feeling like some old-fashioned courtier in a play, and went to his room.

She came after him, her footfalls light on the carpet. "Lewis! Please." Her hand closed on his biceps.

"Will you allow me inside you tonight?" he asked harshly. "Moan your pleasure, clutch at my back, call my name, then simper and make love to the baron with your eyes at breakfast?"

"Why are you being so cruel? Take off that hat so I can see you." She lifted her hands to his face.

He tore it off, threw it to the stone floor, then ran his fingers through his matted hair. "What else? Shall I take off my jacket, my trousers? Do you want me to expose myself to you right here, where anyone can walk by? Do you want to be compromised, Victoria? Force your father to see your wanton ways so that he will let you do what you want?"

She drew breath sharply. "I want him to be happy, to know his life's work is secure in good hands. I've never been a disappointment to him."

"Then why do you pursue me? Why do you risk yourself?"

"I want you to want me more than anything!" She coughed.

He knew her ire had exceeded her ability to breathe in her tight stays. How often had he heard Alys complain about the restrictions of gowns. Victoria's gown was laced so tightly that her cleavage fairly popped from the top, a delectable bounty that he ached to sample, even as it lessened her ability to argue.

"I don't want you more than anything. More than most things, I imagine, but less than my pride, less than my self-worth. It was very difficult for me to make my uncle see that I was more than his lackey, that I had value. I will never subordinate myself to another man. I have too much talent." He bent down and picked up his hat, then placed it over his heart.

"And too much success," she said slowly. "There is no benefit to you. Mr. Lewis Noble is too successful to apprentice under Mr. Rupert Courtnay. No, I would need one of those popinjays who were sent away for that. But me, I still want a real man."

"Find someone your own age. I'd have been an excellent candidate when I was, what, twenty-one like you?"

She nodded. "Precisely. But then I wouldn't know what I was getting, and isn't that important, too?"

"You picked unwisely." He could tell she was close to tears, though of sorrow or rage he couldn't be sure. "Your father has chosen his desires over you. You must understand that. As you are not beholden to him financially, I am not sure why you let him dictate to you still."

"It is just the two of us. I have no mother, no sisters or brothers."

"Then does he not owe you your happiness? I disliked how my uncle treated my cousins, and I dislike how your father treats you."

"If you do not respect him, once again, that is reason enough not to want to work with him."

"Under him," Lewis corrected, feeling weary. "Never with him. That's not what your father wants. Go to bed, Victoria, and dream of what your future holds. I hope it is something good."

He pushed his door open, not looking back as he closed it behind him. Then he leaned against it, his back cold against the unforgiving wood, and wondered what the hell was wrong with him that he couldn't just take the pleasure she offered, her future be damned and obviously not his problem.

He felt rather than heard the initial raps on the door. For a second he stood still, confused, then realized the knob was turning. He moved away and the door opened. Victoria stood there, and as he looked at her, she stamped her foot quite deliberately.

"Why won't you be my real man?" she demanded.

"What in God's name is that supposed to mean?" He leaned one arm against the lintel and stared at her. Not for one moment had he thought she would come after him. What spirit she displayed, however misplaced her passion was.

"What haven't I offered you, Lewis? Give me something, anything, to dream about, some kind of future. Ask me to deny my father, ask me to run away with you, tell me you love me, something." She paused, staring at him with those huge gray eyes. "Please?"

He couldn't bring himself to bridge the gap between them, that space of a doorway. "You worked hard for that title of yours, hard to please your father. Why throw it all away now?"

She tugged the cowboy hat away from his chest and put it to her own heart. "Because I love you."

Her claim made him want to snarl. She was trying to trap him. "You only think you do because you never experienced pleasure between a man and woman before."

"How easily you say that." Her gaze drifted down his body, stopping at the obvious erection belling the fabric of his trousers. "Maybe it is even true."

"Victoria," he said, trying to gain a moment's peace so he could think. Nobility meant nothing to this girl. She didn't want him to do the right thing, to say the right thing. She wanted some barbarian, some Viking to sweep her over his shoulder and carry her off to a fur-lined cave. And then submit to her father in the end, as she did.

She tossed out her arm, her hand sweeping an arc in the direction of his crotch. "You can want me like that yet not make a move. I thought I understood men, but I don't. I'm not some rarified creature just because I married into a title. I'm flesh and blood, and I like it that way. I came here for exactly what you've offered me: sweat and the scent of passion and physical love. Now I think it was all an accident, some mistake. It's like a dream, those times I've been with you." She shook her head, folded her arms over the cowboy hat, crushing it to her, and stalked off.

"Victoria," he called. "Turn around."

"No. I'm going to bed."

He watched her traverse the hall, open her door, then slam it shut.

After a minute, he wondered if she was leaning against the inner side of her door in the moony fashion he had, but thought not. He was a creature of thought and she was a creature of action. And he had to think. Because if he went after her, which would lead to the need for a proposal, he might lose everything, end up under her father's thumb, and all for what? He'd been willing to do exactly that for Alys, but he'd changed so much since then. He wasn't a romantic anymore, right? He'd left his twenties behind, was a mature man. There was no need to give in to a young woman's sense of drama just because he liked fucking her. So he stayed in his room alone. And yet ... and yet ... he spent most of the night awake in his lonely bed, unable to banish her from his traitorous thoughts.

When he climbed out of bed, bleary-eyed and unsettled on the dawn of the new year, he resolved to take some action that had him spending time with Victoria in unimpeachable circumstances. Even a married couple didn't spend all their time in carnal pursuits. He needed to know if he even liked her, if there was more than an obsession. If he didn't, there was no point in even addressing her again, much less attempting to seduce her. As for marriage, he'd all but hardened himself against that. Except for that one tiny thing she'd said, about defying her father. Would she do that for the sake of love? It went against any natural feeling of a daughter for a father, the duty she owed him. But he thought passionate Victoria might do exactly that, if she loved enough.

Yes, he needed to know if he had any hope of feeling the same, given his craving for her touch. He remained in his room, sketching a change to one of the submarine's instruments, drinking the coffee and eating the buns Eddy had procured for him, until late morning. Then he went downstairs and found the countess in a small parlor, conferring with the housekeeper.

He waited until she had dismissed the woman, then cleared his throat.

The countess, a somewhat faded and too-thin woman who nonetheless resembled her daughters, nodded to him. "Mr. Noble? What can I do for you today?"

"I have a request."

"Some provisions for the stables?" Her tone was derisive. She didn't share her son's lust for his project.

"No, a dinner seating."

"Whatever do you mean?"

"I would like to be seated next to Lady Allen-Hill at dinners from now on. She had been next to her suitors from Liverpool, but since I understand they've departed, I would like to move to one of those seats."

"Mr. Noble, I'm afraid I cannot make that change."

"Why not?"

"Her father sent me a note yesterday, requesting that Lady Allen-Hill be seated between himself and the Baron of Alix for the remainder of the festivities. I agreed."

Lewis put his hands on his hips and looked down, attempting to contain his ire. Victoria's father was one step ahead of him, procuring for the baron. He'd obviously settled on the man or he wouldn't have placed himself on her other side.

"I believe a proposal is forthcoming," the countess said meaningfully.

"I was told they were merely friends," Lewis said.

"Perhaps my daughters' happy news has inspired other young lovers. Friendship is a lovely basis for a future together."

"So you say," he muttered, thinking of himself thrusting between the soft thighs of the friend of the baron. He cleared his throat. "Thank you for your time, my lady."

"Mr. Noble, I could seat you next to Adela Dickondell. She's out now and quite pretty. I'm sure my son would be pleased to have you form a connection in the neighborhood. You've been so useful to him."

"I imagine you've seated my cousin Rose next to Mr. Courtnay?"

She lifted her eyebrows. "Yes, as before."

"Put me on my cousin's other side, if you don't mind," he said. "I think that is for the best."

As the countess lifted her eyebrows, he turned and stalked out of the room. He didn't stop moving until he'd reached the barn. Mud caked up the sides of his good shoes. He kicked them off, banishing them to a heap of straw in the corner, and reached for a pair of boots and a satchel of tools.

"I'm going to work on the barometer," he told the earl.

"I was going to load the submarine into the water again," Nicholas said. "To make sure the leak is fixed."

"That's fine. I can work on the instrument inside the submarine."

Nicholas lifted his eyebrows. Lewis was struck by the fact that he and his mother had the same pure, blue-gray eyes. The earl shrugged. "Fine with me. Bang hard if it starts to leak."

"You'll know." Lewis joked, "It will sink to the bottom of the lake."

"That won't happen fast enough for there to be any danger."

"Fair enough." Lewis tossed his satchel into the submarine. "Let's get her down to the water."

"The sooner the better," Nicholas agreed. "The temperature is dropping. I wouldn't be surprised if we had more snow, and if there's too much ice, we won't be able to do any testing."

"Possibly you chose the wrong time of year to adequately enjoy your obsession."

"A bit snappish today, old man," Nicholas said. "Something troubling you?"

"Really? You want to chat over tea like a couple of old women?" He thrust his feet into boots so cold they made crackling noises.

"No," Nicholas said. "Let's get to work."

Victoria hadn't woken as angry as she remembered feeling when she'd fallen asleep. Penelope slumbered beside her, her face soft and childish. Victoria tucked a stray curl behind the girl's ear, out of her eyes, and she murmured in her sleep, turning away. Then Victoria remembered what she'd said to Lewis. She'd told him she *loved* him.

Words thrown out in the heat of the moment. Her blood had been hot, her thighs damp, her breath coming fast. She'd said it to him, then insulted him, then run away. No wonder he didn't want her. She was a ninny who barely knew her own mind. He was a decade older than her and, God bless him, he wanted an equal, not a child. She had to stop flouncing away and playing word games. They needed to talk, in daylight and alone. See each other's eyes when they were thinking clearly, before the champagne flowed at endless parties. His cowboy hat was on her bedside table, mocking her. She touched it with one finger, then pulled away, irritated by her object worship.

She went through the regimen of breakfast and morning chatter with the ladies, but as soon as she could, she broke away, saying she needed air.

"Snow is coming," Lady Rowena said, hunched over a fine pillowcase she was embroidering for her trousseau.

"I won't be gone long," Victoria said. "I just need to get some color in my cheeks."

"Color in your cheeks is all very well, but if your lips become wind stung, no gentleman is going to want to kiss you," Lady Rowena said with a knowing smirk.

"Rowena!" her sister protested. "Don't be indelicate."

"Everyone knows Lady Allen-Hill has set her cap at the baron," Lady Rowena said. "She might even get him, too. But she has to act fast."

"What have you heard?" Victoria asked.

"My mother and your father spoke about it," said the girl.

"I had no idea," Victoria admitted.

"Really? Is your father making arrangements without telling you? I would have thought a widow had more autonomy."

"I'm a young widow," Victoria said absently. "I expect it would have been different if I'd had children."

"By next year's house party, we might all have babies in our arms," Lady Barbara said dreamily. "You should marry him, Victoria. And come back next Christmas."

"If I marry him, I'll probably be in Edinburgh, staring out at the endless rainy gray skies, instead of here, where it is bright."

"But cold. If you are going to live in Edinburgh, toughening up would be wise," Lady Rowena said. "Are you sure you don't want Samuel? We could be sisters."

"He's younger than I am," Victoria said. "Surely that is reason enough to dislike the notion." She stood and took her leave, then bundled herself warmly and begged a couple of cream scones from a kitchen maid. She wrapped them in a napkin and tucked them into a pocket, hoping to use them as an excuse to get Lewis's attention.

The brisk air blew her down the hill toward the stables, making her grateful for her sensible boots and warm coat. The wind carried sound toward the lake, but it seemed as she drew closer that she heard shouts.

The stable was deserted when she reached it. She frowned, and realized the submarine wasn't inside. Had they towed it to the lake again? She pushed through the rear doors of the stable and saw men running down the dock. Some were already in the water, pounding on the metal hull of the submarine, which seemed rather low in the water, though she could still see most of the top. She craned her neck in every direction as she walked, hoping to see Lewis and find out what was going on.

No one paid any attention to her as she stepped onto the slippery surface of the dock. "What's happening?" she shouted, becoming alarmed by the strain on the men's faces, the way they were frantically checking the rope harness around the submarine, which allowed them to tow it back up to the dock.

"Pull!" she heard, and recognized the earl's voice. "Damn it! We have to get him out!"

Victoria's hands went icy cold in her gloves. She raced forward, reaching for the end of one of the ropes, joining the crew of men who were trying to tow it in.

"Closer!" a man said over his shoulder.

She stepped closer and took up a position a hand's width behind him, then started to pull.

"Get off the submarine!" the earl shouted at a man who was on top of the hull, attempting to pry open the hatch. "We need to stop it from taking on water."

"Where is Lewis?" Victoria asked, tugging as hard as she could.

"Inside the craft," said a grim-faced man, a groundskeeper, who was pulling at the rope so hard that his face was red.

CHAPTER 14

"No," Victoria whispered.

The deck shuddered as the tip of the submarine touched the water-logged ramp. She welcomed the reverberations, grateful for their progress. How were they going to lift it from the lake?

"The water it took on is making it extra heavy. Can we get it on a cart?" one of the more senior men asked.

"We don't have time. Lewis hasn't responded," the earl said. "There are no sounds from inside."

Victoria could see the tendons in his neck bunch in tight relief as he pulled. She felt skin tearing on her palms, despite her gloves, but she didn't stop pulling. More men joined them, grabbing the rope behind her. She could smell male sweat and her own fear, fighting the rope as she painstakingly stepped backward with the men.

Inch by inch, the submarine came out of the lake, green with scummy slickness. Men groaned and pulled, breathing hard, but it seemed to come faster as it broke free of the water. The earl winced as the metal scraped.

"I don't see any damage," he said, frustrated. "Where is the leak coming from? Why didn't Lewis do anything?"

The two men in front of her traded glances, looking somber. Did they think her lover was dead? Her stomach clutched, but she ignored the cramp with iron control, and kept at the rope. She wouldn't think of anything but the physical effort of saving him. They pulled until it seemed her arms were all but dropping out of their sockets. Finally, the earl called a halt. By then, the submarine was on the part of the dock that didn't slope down to the water.

"Get some blankets and hot water bottles!" he shouted at an under-gardener. The man ran off while employees began to work on the hatch.

Victoria heard a cry behind her as Eddy came hurtling down from the stable, his face contorted with fear. Dropping the rope, she grabbed for the youth when he flew past her, afraid he'd knock some of the men into the water. Now she could see the ice that had formed along the reeds. It had not been a good day for an experiment.

"Got it!" the assistant at the hatch called. "Who's going in?"

The earl used his arms to leverage himself onto the slippery metal surface and crawled to the hatch, then peered into the inky darkness. Victoria hugged Eddy, allowing them to creep closer. She didn't want to add any complications, but she must know if Lewis was all right. She couldn't tell whether the lad was crying or gasping for air.

The muffled sound of the earl's voice was barely audible, but she couldn't make out any of his words. Then his head popped up and he pulled his feet to the hatch, dropping down. A moment later, she heard retching, and more indistinguishable words.

Eddy grabbed her coat sleeve. "What's happening? Where is he?"

The assistant waved his arm, ordering more men forward. Victoria barely kept her balance on the dock as three burly men approached. She let Eddy go and pulled off her coat as she saw Lewis's head appear over the hatch. His hair was plastered so darkly to his skull with water that she'd never have known the original color was blond. Arms reached for him. She saw him weakly push them away, his grin wry as he was unable to fight off the men so willing to carry him. Her stomach contracted when she realized he was alive.

"Place him here," she ordered, tossing her coat onto the dock and bundling her scarves into a pillow.

Eddy, next to her, was crying freely now, forgetting all manly composure.

As carefully as they could, they laid Lewis down on her coat. She tried to wrap it around him, but he was too broad for that. The earl stripped off his own coat, as did Eddy, and laid their outerwear over him.

"We need to pick him up again, get him to the house," the earl said.

"I'll be fine," Lewis said, then coughed hard.

"Get him onto his side," Victoria cried.

The men turned him just in time, before more of the water he'd inhaled came out of his mouth.

"Found the leak," Lewis said, gasping. "Bleeding thing opened right over me, showered my face. Couldn't breathe. Would have drowned standing up, but then it rocked, knocked me over, out of the spray."

"Doesn't matter now. We need to get you warm," the earl said. "Heave ho, men."

The four burliest men took Lewis by the arms and legs. The earl gave orders, marching them rapidly up the dock. Eddy ran alongside, one of Lewis's cold, pale hands in his. Victoria wished she'd thought to do the same but instead picked up her sopping coat and scarves, then trotted to the rear. The men moved slowly as they went up the hill, then faster through the curtain wall and into the courtyard. The boot boy stood aside, confusion furrowing his young brow, as they pushed past him into the mudroom.

"Can you get him up the stairs?" the earl asked.

"Just tell us where to go. 'E's an 'eavy one, milord," the man who had Lewis's left shoulder puffed.

"Take him up the servants' stairs," Victoria called. "It's closer."

They went down the long hallway to the left of the mudroom. Eddy ran ahead to open the door. Lewis gave the order to be let down, insisting he could walk.

"No. Let us do this fast," the earl demanded. "We need to get you out of those clothes."

"A couple of shoulders under my arms and I'll do fine. No room to carry me," Lewis insisted.

"Do as he says," Victoria interjected. "It will be faster than arguing with him."

A goofy, unfocused smile broke over Lewis's face when he saw her. The men who were holding his legs slowly let them drop to the floor. Lewis's knees buckled, but then he found his footing, and the two men who had held his shoulders tucked themselves under his armpits instead. Victoria could see the water from Lewis's clothes dripping down their bodies.

She shook her head at him, but the infuriating man just grinned and slowly turned away. "I'm going to nurse him," she told the earl. "I'm a widow."

The earl shrugged. "I'm not going to stop you. I have a leak to repair."

She shook her head in disgust. "Was it worth a man's life to find it?"

"He didn't die. You're going to dry him out, right?" The earl smirked at her, then held out his arm to her.

He actually had the gall to apply levity to the situation. How were gentlemen trained that they could joke about nearly dying? Perhaps they couldn't go to war without such a mentality, or risk their lives in other ways.

When they reached the top of the stairs, the men insisted that Lewis be carried again, but two of them formed a chair with their arms and staggered to his room in that fashion. Eddy opened the door and Victoria was able to reach the coverlet and pull it down before her lover was deposited on the mattress.

"Get his clothes off quickly, before he soaks the bed," she urged.

The men looked at her strangely, as if they'd decided their work was done as soon as Lewis had made it inside.

She grimaced. "Eddy?"

"Right. Got to get the boots off, milady. You work on his jacket and I'll tackle the laces."

She nodded and pulled the sodden coats off Lewis's front, which had all but been glued to him with the water. Then she began to work on the buttons of his jacket, wincing as her torn palms touched the icy fabric.

Lewis could do nothing but cough and she feared for his lungs. While the workmen left, the earl ordered tea. A footman arrived carrying more blankets and hot water bottles. Victoria ordered that they be tucked around his pillows for now and kept working. After a couple of minutes of tapping his foot and looking irritated, the earl began to worry at a boot lace as well.

"You have disgusting feet, pale as a dead jellyfish," the earl said when he'd achieved the removal of the sock on his side.

Eddy almost fell over as the boot on his side finally popped off, releasing a stream of water over the foot of the bed.

"I'm going to need you to roll out of your jacket," Victoria told Lewis.

He attempted to comply but began coughing again and lay back.

"Give me your arm." When he did as told, she crossed it over his belly and pulled him over, panting at the exertion. Eddy ran to grab the jacket and waistcoat from under his back.

"Milady, your hands," the boy said. "You need those doctored."

"What did you do?" Lewis asked, twisting to grab at her hand.

"Doesn't matter," she said briskly, pulling them away.

A maid appeared at the door with a teapot and cups on a tray.

Victoria nodded. "Good, let's get this into Mr. Noble. Can you fetch some beef tea, please? That would be better. Very strengthening."

The maid set the tray on the bedside table and went to get the broth. Victoria began to work on Lewis's shirt.

"Both socks off now, milady. Should we work on his trousers?" Eddy asked.

"Certainly not," Lewis said, sounding stronger, as if in response to the effrontery of the question. "I will do it myself."

Victoria glared at him. "You will lie back and do as you're told."

"You are not taking off my trousers, Lady Allen-Hill." He said her name with great emphasis.

She realized he didn't want her to reveal her overfamiliarity with his person. "I am a widow, sir. You have nothing I have not seen."

"Nursed your husband, did you?" Eddy asked.

Actually, she had not been involved in the intimate details of caring for Sir Humphrey's body. She'd been such a new bride that his valet had taken on most of the nursing duties, although she had done her best. She made a noncommittal noise as she pushed Lewis's suspenders down his arms. Coughing all the while, Lewis rolled out of his shirt. The earl found a nightshirt and they got it over Lewis's torso after Victoria wiped him dry as best she could with a towel. By the time that had been done, a footman had assisted Eddy with the lower half of Lewis's garments.

"He should have the thickest wool socks you can find on his feet," Victoria told Eddy. The boy went to look for some in the bureau.

They tucked Lewis in, adding hot water bottles, and spooned beef tea into him. His skin still felt icy after an hour, though he had stopped coughing. Victoria stared at his pale face, wishing she could curl up against him and offer him warmth. A wife could do that, but not a lover. She'd offered a bath, but he refused it, pleading exhaustion.

"I think he just needs to rest," the earl said, coming back to the bed after stirring up the fire. "It's blazing hot in here now."

"You should see to your own attire," Victoria said. "You have been in those damp clothes for too long, Lord Bullen."

"I'll keep watch over him, milord," Eddy said. His eyes were still reddened by emotion. "You've missed luncheon, Lady Allen-Hill. And you are damp, too, if you don't mind me saying."

"The same goes for you," she told the boy. "I'll send someone up with hot, nourishing food and ensure you are checked on every fifteen minutes or so."

"He'll be right as rain by tomorrow," the boy promised. "He wasn't in that long."

"I know," Victoria said.

Lewis smiled at her and took her hand. "You've done everything for me you could. Let nature take its course now."

She nodded, her throat suddenly parched. "I shall check on you later." Head held high, she left the room. Tears came when she had the door shut behind her. How close had she come to losing him? It was best not to consider what had not happened. He would be fine, since he was so young and strong. Strange that she had not understood quite how large and muscular he was when she was in his arms. But just now, she'd felt quite overwhelmed by his size.

When she reached her room, she ordered a bath, thinking they perhaps should have insisted on that for Lewis, but it was too late now. When she was safely in the steaming water behind the screen, she finally gave in to emotion and sobbed.

When she climbed out, every muscle still ached. She clumsily doctored her hands but fell asleep before she had wrapped them properly. She woke up within half an hour, her body too sore for proper rest. An hour later, she had just finished dressing herself in a simple wool gown when Penelope appeared, trailed by a nursery maid.

"Did you know there is a wishing well on the property?" the girl asked. "We should make a wish for the new year!"

I could wish for Lewis to suffer no ill effects from his experience. "Yes, that sounds like an excellent notion after we check on Mr. Noble." She felt quite warm, especially since she'd slept before the fire.

"Do you think the wishing well was here in Princess Everilda's day?" Penelope asked as the maid went to retrieve their outerwear.

Had the girl decided her story was real? Victoria smiled at the notion. She supposed her cousin had to find something to believe in after yesterday's troubling revelations about her mother. "It probably was," she said cautiously.

"Do you think it will be important to the story?"

"I have no idea," Victoria said. "When last we left the princess, she was waiting until midnight to go to the bell tower." The maid handed her a coat. It wasn't her fur-trimmed winter coat, and it took her a moment to remember that that was still on the floor of Lewis's room somewhere. "I wonder if you might have someone retrieve my coat, and Eddy Jackson's as well, from Mr. Noble's floor and have them brushed and dried?"

"Yes, milady," the maid promised, handing her a pair of gloves. "I couldn't find a muffler for you."

"Also on the floor," Victoria said.

"We heard what happened at luncheon. Poor Mr. Noble. Will he take sick?"

"I hope not."

"What happened?" Penelope demanded.

"He was trapped in the submarine when it sprang a leak," Victoria explained. "But the earl got him out."

"He's a hero, like Prince Hugh."

"Prince Hugh hasn't done anything except get himself captured," Victoria said. "The princess is the heroine."

"There has to be a hero." Penelope screwed up her face. "Is he going to do something marvelous at the end? Like kill a dragon?"

"Or his stepmother," Victoria muttered.

"She's already dead. I think you should have a dragon."

"Why can't the princess be the brave one? Girls can do all sorts of things."

"Boys are always the heroes of adventure stories." Penelope stuck her hat on her head.

"They shouldn't be," Victoria said, putting on her gloves. "Come, let's go before the snow starts." They scratched at Lewis's door, but Eddy said he was sound asleep, so she decided to return later.

She had made no attempt to be smart. Her old winter coat, a warm bonnet that covered her ears, thick wool gloves. At least it kept out the worst of the wind as they dashed out of the front gate and across the drawbridge that reached across the stream that meandered past the front of the Fort. Here, Victoria could more clearly see the ancient architecture, which was what had inspired her to spin her fairy tale. Off in the distance, she could see hints of a town, the tall spire of a church.

Once, there had probably been additional defensive structures, but they were all gone now. Penelope took her hand and led her through a frosty meadow. Peals of laughter greeted them as they walked across the slippery, dormant grass. Several children, accompanied by nursemaids and Lady Rowena, passed them on their way back to the Fort. The earl's sister even smiled at them, apparently pleased by her wish.

"Happy New Year!" Penelope cried, her words dancing on the breeze.

Victoria pulled her bonnet more tightly over her ears. Her cheeks were already icy and she could see clouds, dark with snow, gathering above them. They ran to the wishing well, exclaiming over the quaintness of the multicolored stones that made up the base, the shiny copper bucket that was clearly maintained by the servants. In the distance, they could see people walking up from the town in their Sunday best.

"This must be a local tradition," Victoria commented. She took her cousin's hand and placed a shiny new shilling in it, then pulled one out of her pocket for herself.

"The maid told me you have to put your coin in the basket, then lower it down and tip it out as you say your wish," Penelope reported. She tossed her coin in and began to turn the handle to lower the basket, her lips moving.

When the basket reached the calm, reflective surface of the water, she waggled the rope until the bucket rocked and turned on its side. As the bucket righted itself, Penelope pulled it back up. "Now you have to drink a sip of the water."

A wooden ladle was attached to one of the well's posts with a rope. She dipped the ladle in and took a sip, then shuddered. "Freezing!"

Victoria glanced up as two birds flapped their wings overhead, seeming to come out of nowhere descending onto the cross post where the copper basket's rope was hung. "White storks?" She recognized the long red beaks and the sharp black feathers at the end of each wing. "Shouldn't they be wintering somewhere warm?"

"Magic birds," Penelope breathed, her face breaking into the first contented smile Victoria had seen from her this holiday. For once, she looked like a child instead of a miniature, cross adult. "They're beautiful. Now I know my wish will come true!"

The birds clicked, their beaks moving rapidly. Then, without warning, they lifted their wings and flew off.

Victoria had to admit the effect of the birds had been magical, especially since they were so evidently out of season. "I hope your wish does come true."

"It's your turn." Penelope hopped up and down on one foot.

She didn't have much time before the townspeople made it up the hill, so Victoria quickly dropped her coin into the bucket and lowered it, until it was far beneath the water. But she didn't know what to wish for. Some generic hope for a new husband who would smooth out the edges of her life and give her children? A specific wish that Lewis would decide he wanted her despite the cost? No, neither of those; they were both selfish. Instead, she spoke under her breath: "I wish that everyone will be healthy and all the loving relationships that have been formed at this house party are deepened and strengthened in the coming year."

She pulled the bucket out, hoping the well had accepted the coin. The bucket was indeed empty of anything but water. She followed Penelope's lead and drank a sip of the icy water, then let the dipper drop back against the rocks. After a hopeful glance at the empty, leaden winter sky, she knew the birds wouldn't be coming for her wish, but at least they'd given her an idea.

She and her cousin stepped away from the well and exchanged holiday greetings with the townsfolk. As they walked down the hill on their way back to the Fort, she saw the first fluffy snowflake. Penelope darted ahead, trying to catch flakes on her tongue. Acting like a child again, with no worries beyond the immediate, just as she should be.

Despite her fears for Lewis's lungs, Victoria felt entirely uplifted by the sight. She smiled to herself as she approached the Fort. The tall stone walls seemed to reflect the gray of the sky, stern and imposing. Yet the stream and the bridge softened the medieval sight somehow, made it look almost homely. A place of refuge.

"Let's go peek in on Mr. Noble," she suggested.

"I can bring him some peppermint sticks. I know where the housekeeper keeps them."

"He might like that," she agreed. "Maybe we can bring him a hot cup of chocolate with one."

Penelope struggled out of her coat in the front hall, handed it to a footman, and ran down the long passageway toward the housekeeper's office to comply.

Victoria took off her own coat and tossed everything in her room, then fixed her hair while she waited for Penelope. She still ached, but her wish had buoyed her spirits. Twenty minutes later, her cousin arrived, trailed by a maid carrying a tray with a pot of chocolate and a handful of peppermint sticks. They went down the hall and she scratched at Lewis's door. A footman opened it and gestured them in.

Eddy bounced up from beside the bed when they entered. Penelope did a little side-to-side hop when she saw him. He was a favorite of the girl's.

Considering that this might be a good way to get some time alone with Lewis, she said, "Why don't you tell Eddy about the wishing well, Penelope? He might like to go, too."

As Penelope chattered happily about their experience, Victoria went to the bed. The outside light had faded due to the snow, so oil lamps had been lit and the candle sconces in the wall were ablaze, along with the fire.

"Quite a contrast from outside," Victoria said, placing a hand on Lewis's forehead to check for fever.

His eyes had been closed, but he opened them at her touch. "Eddy said it was snowing."

"Yes. Penelope caught snowflakes on her tongue. Lovely to see her scampering about."

Lewis raised himself on an elbow. She could see a dusting of fine blond hairs in the open placket of his shirt. The sight of the strong column of his neck, the shadowed base of his throat, all made her want to lick, taste, even smell. To think he might have died today. Her breath caught in her throat and she swallowed hard.

Forgetting about the chocolate, Penelope asked if she could take Eddy to the wishing well. At Victoria's nod, the girl ran to retrieve her coat.

"You sure it's safe for me to go, guv?" Eddy said, coming back to Lewis's side.

"I'm perfectly well," Lewis said. "Her ladyship will keep an eye on me."

"I'll be back inside of an hour," Eddy promised, then frowned. "I don't have a coat."

"Take one of mine," Lewis offered. "It will be close to fitting."

As the door slammed behind Eddy two minutes later, she smiled. "I think a whirlwind came and went through here."

"Felt that way to me," Lewis said. He pushed himself into a sitting position.

Victoria tucked pillows behind him to help.

He nodded his thanks. "What's on the tray?"

She walked over to it and poured him a cup of the still-steaming liquid, then placed a peppermint stick and a piece of shortbread shaped like a tree on the saucer.

"Very festive," he commented as she placed the cup and saucer in his hand. "You have the look of a woman with a question."

"Do I?" She tilted her head.

"Oh, yes. You've opened your mouth half a dozen times since you came in here, but nothing of substance has come out yet."

"Oh, Lewis," she sighed. "It was the most magical surprise. Really, I almost believe in the wishing well." Especially after the near fatal disaster.

His lips quirked with amusement. She noted they were still rather pale, as were his cheeks, but his speech seemed fine. No wheezing or difficulty.

"Don't forget, I am a scientist. What happened?"

She told him about the white storks.

He nodded thoughtfully and chewed on his shortbread. "Maybe they were angels, come to reassure her. My mother used to claim angels came from Heaven in the shape of birds."

"I've never heard that before."

"No? Well, we aren't from the same part of the country. Maybe it was some local superstition my mother picked up."

"You used to make mechanical birds," Victoria ventured. "Don't you think it would be lovely for Penelope to have a white stork? Such beautiful birds. Would you allow me to commission one? Or even two, since that is what we saw?"

"No," Lewis said, setting down his cup with a china-upon-china clink. "I don't make birds anymore."

"I'll pay exceedingly well," Victoria said. "I know they aren't as lucrative as your horseless carriages, but I'll make up the cost. It would mean so much to her, I really do believe that. All of a sudden she was a child again. I want her to keep that feeling."

"I understand that, but I still won't do it. I made them in a chapter of my life that has closed." His voice went raspy. He picked up his peppermint stick and bit off the end.

"Not even for me?" she wheedled.

He shook his head. "Not even for you, Victoria."

"This can't be your final word on the subject."

He coughed. "It can, believe me."

She stared at him, feeling mulish. "You aren't feeling well. Perhaps you shall reconsider in the morning."

"If I am not amenable to a request made by a woman who has just plied me with sweets, and has been involved in saving my life, I can assure you I will not be reconsidering in the morning."

"Stubborn," she muttered.

He smiled. "Very. Now why don't you come sit next to me and share those chocolate-scented lips? I've nearly come back from the dead, you know, and I could use a little human comfort."

"Eddy will be back."

"I'll just lift up your skirts," he suggested. "You can ride me."

"Lewis!"

"Victoria." He arched a brow.

"My stays wouldn't allow for that," she said, her cheeks pinkening with the knowledge that she genuinely regretted saying no to him. "Besides, it might make you wheeze. You shouldn't exert yourself."

He ran his tongue over his lower lip, then touched the tip to the corner of his mouth. Victoria stopped breathing, overwhelmed by the sensuality of his gesture.

"You'd have to help me undress, then undress again. They won't be gone that long."

"Lock the door," he commanded.

"Very well," she agreed, unable to think of a reason not to.

CHAPTER 15

Victoria's skirts swished around her legs as she went to lock the door. Lewis watched her full hips sway sensuously and wondered if she felt every movement against the weight of the fabric, the way her stays pressed into her breasts, still gloriously plump and heavy despite her efforts to reduce.

He loved those breasts; her hips, too. The rest of her might be slim and athletic, but she was round in all the right places. He knew he'd feel as excited by her body even if she lost the delicate shape she had now. It didn't matter, as long as she never lost her innate sensuousness.

Even though he'd rejected a future with her, she still was eager to play. After his brush with death, he didn't seem to be able to stay away from her. He needed her, needed that warm, soft flesh underneath him, needed to be inside her heated depths.

She turned around, her back against the door, and began to unbutton her dress. At least it was not so ornate that she could not remove it herself. The placket down the front opened and she let the soft, green-trimmed black wool drift down her shoulders almost dreamily until the garment pooled at her feet.

He pulled himself to the edge of the bed and gestured for her to come to him. In a long nightshirt and socks, he felt silly, exposed, but the way she looked at him, that naked hunger, made him not care.

With an engineer's precision, he worked her out of her corset cover and stays, staring into her eyes every moment he could. She took a deep breath when she was free of the confining device, then smiled.

"Now I can bend."

He reached under her petticoats and picked up one of her knees, placing her foot between his legs. She breathed steadily as he undid the laces, then pulled off her shoe. He captured her gaze as he repeated the maneuver with her other leg. His fingers roamed up her stocking until he found the garter. She exhaled as he pulled down the warm winter wool.

"I'm going to take you wearing all of these petticoats." He grinned. "They will bell around us and keep us warm. Even if someone unlocked the door and came in, they wouldn't be able to see what was happening underneath."

"Don't you want to touch me?" She blinked.

He pulled down the second stocking. "Oh, my hands will be under your skirts, holding your hips tightly while I thrust deep inside your honey."

Her lips parted. "Oh."

He untied the ribbon on her chemise. The linen fell down her shoulders, exposing the tops of her breasts. "I can't wait. I have to have you on top of me."

They slid over the covers until he had his back against the head of the bed again. Her scent surrounded him, a mix of snow and coconut-scented hair. He pulled her over his lap until he was nestled between her legs, then pressed one hand between her thighs while he nuzzled her breasts. Her soft dark curls tickling his forehead added to the sensation of being surrounded by the perfume of her body. She was warm, swollen, and damp against his fingers.

"Move your hips," he said.

Her gaze was soft and unfocused as she complied. She slid against him, growing hotter, wetter. Then her eyes closed. "Lewis," she said, his name a low keen that made his cock throb.

He pulled up her skirts and looked at her hips moving against his fingers, her glistening hair and sweetly pink flesh. She gasped as he put two fingers inside her.

"Too rough; sorry," he apologized.

"No, more," she begged. "I need more. Oh, Lewis. It feels so good."

"I can make it even better." He pulled her chin to him, parted her lips in a deep kiss, then grabbed her bottom and positioned her over his cock.

Meaning to help her stretch to accommodate his throbbing length, he settled her gently. But she had other ideas and pushed down hard, sheathing him in one fluid motion.

He groaned, nearly losing control. "What you do to me, woman."

He felt her smile against his mouth. "The same you do to me, sweetheart."

She rocked against him, her hands never stopping as they roamed over his shoulders, pectorals, chest, and arms. He kept his hands on her bottom, urging her into every thrust, taking her mouth with hot, openmouthed kisses. All too soon, he felt himself losing control. Her tight sheath, the silky damp inside of it, was more than he could resist.

He came hard, his forehead falling to her shoulder. She shuddered and called out his name, then her body relaxed limply against his. He'd given her the same pleasure she'd given him. The thought made him smile, but mostly he wanted to sleep.

He turned on his side, still inside her, and lay back on the bed. The pillows had shifted enough to cradle their heads.

She blew hair out of her eyes and smiled sleepily at him. "I shouldn't fall asleep here or you'll be forced to make a declaration to my father."

Alarm gave him the strength to lift his head. "You should go."

"What?" Confusion darkened her features.

His heart rate, which had slowed a little, picked up speed again. "I'm not going to spend my life under your father's thumb, Victoria. I've worked too hard for my independence."

"We made love again. Surely that means something to you." Her lower lip trembled.

"House-party antics," he said dismissively, hating himself for it.

But she could not have expectations of him, not while she insisted on following her father's plan for her life. "I appreciate our lovemaking very much. You've brightened my holidays tremendously."

She pushed against his shoulder painfully, using him as an anchor as she sat up. "I don't believe you're this cold, Lewis. I can't believe the man I'm in love with could be like this."

"Believe what you will, but the future your father envisions for you will not include me." He coughed spasmodically.

"Oh, for the love of God," she muttered, reaching for a cold pot of tea and pouring him a few ounces.

He was so surprised at her blasphemy that he found it hard to swallow. "Look," he rasped after a first sip of much-too-strong, very cold tea. "My cousin Rose has asked me to speak to your father on her behalf. I will do that."

"What does that have to do with me?"

"Rose is young." He lay back against the pillow, feeling utterly exhausted by the day. "She might give your father a son. It would dilute your inheritance, but—"

"I don't want for anything. My husband left me decently provided for," she muttered. "And she's not that young. We're the same age."

"Good. Then it shouldn't matter to you if my conversation has some effect."

"You are talking about things that might happen in the future, far from now. My father wants his business succession settled. I want to be with you, Lewis!"

"You knew how I felt. Do not make me responsible for your expectations."

She sniffed and looked away. "He is not a bad man."

"Obviously I would not consider him for my cousin, who is as close to me as a sister, if I thought he was. But a man treats a wife differently than a son by marriage. I like my independence too well."

"Better than anything."

They stared at each other. She broke the gaze first and ground her teeth together until he could hear the clicking.

"You need to help me redress."

"Of course," he said, hating that she'd lost that relaxed, sleepy look she'd had after they made love. But she was correct; he did like his independence more than anything else. It was too hard won. "I will find you a towel first."

She glared at him. "I can find my own." Somewhat unsteadily, she made her way to the dressing room. Water and towels had been left on top of a cabinet there.

By the time she returned, he had her corset ready. She had already retied the ribbon around the neck of her chemise and straightened her two petticoats. He made quick work of the corset, then helped her with the rest of her garments.

"You should go back to sleep. I will get your fire going again."

"I'm quite warm now." He smiled at her, but she didn't return it. For all her wantonness with him and her seeking after other men who might marry her, he wondered if she was not as secure in her sensuality as she seemed. "Would your father be kind to Rose, do you think?"

"I'm sure he'll treat her like a queen, especially if she bears him a son," Victoria said with an edge of sourness he'd never heard from her before.

"I am sorry you do not think that would satisfy him."

"I'm in no hurry to remarry, but he wants me settled. I've already lost time starting my own family."

"Are you so eager to be a mother? I admire how kind you've been to Penelope." He was disgusted with himself as he realized admiring a woman's maternal qualities was all but an announcement that he thought her worthy of being his partner in marriage.

"I think I finally understand her. I was unsure of my abilities to manage her when I first came to Pevensey-Sur-Mer. If nothing else, I feel more confident." She sighed. "I must, as her mother will be no help."

"I expect she'll be sent to school."

"I won't let that happen. It's not a good place for a girl like her, to be in a stern environment away from anyone who loves her."

"I expect you are correct about that." He felt the back of his throat tickle again and knew he should rest.

She waited for a moment, but when he didn't speak again, she seemed to come to some decision. "Good-bye, Lewis. I look forward to finding out how your conversation with my father goes."

Before he could find words, she was gone. He leaned wearily against the pillows, wishing he had the strength to think through every possible outcome of the decisions he might make about her, and his cousin, but he fell asleep before he'd satisfied himself with even one hypothesis. Except this: If Rose married Rupert Courtnay, he would never be entirely free of Victoria. He would see her on holidays, with her husband, the children she would have. Would he be jealous of that husband? The answer, unfortunately, was yes. Yet that could change nothing.

Victoria was sorting through her wardrobe with the aid of Lady Florence's maid late the next morning when a knock came at the door. She felt tired and out of sorts. Thoughts of Lewis and the difficult choices she faced had kept her up late, especially as she had left his bed in the late afternoon and found herself seated next to John at dinner. He had been affectionate and charming. She liked him too much not to respond, even though she felt only friendship for him.

She nodded to the maid, who went to open the door. A moment later, the woman returned, followed by Rose, who held a basket covered in a snowy white cloth. Rose had a shy, somewhat downcast smile on her pale, pretty face. She offered the basket to Victoria.

"Thank you," Victoria said, surprised by the gift. "Have you been to see Lewis?"

"Not yet, but we received word from the earl about what happened. How dreadful." Rose crossed her arms and hugged herself. "I can't imagine what it must have been like for you to witness."

"Terrifying," Victoria admitted. "I looked in on him this morning. He was still abed, but he has more color in his face and he only coughed once." She left out the rest of the story.

"My entire family is praying that his lungs remain unaffected," Rose said. "I brought you a bit of sunshine in thanks for your help yesterday."

"Sunshine?" Victoria pulled back the cloth, embroidered with a large gold *R*, and found a selection of jars. She pulled out one, then another, to see a colorful assortment of jams.

"Our housekeeper is a wizard with fruit. I've never tasted better. I thought you could take them back to Liverpool with you when you return home."

"Thank you." They stared at each other. Rose seemed to be balancing on the balls of her feet, ready to flee or leap, depending on what she said.

Victoria cleared her throat. "I understand you have expressed some interest in my father. I'm sure Lewis will attempt to play matchmaker when he is well again."

"What is your opinion?" Rose folded her hands together. Her shoulders were high, her neck sinewy and tense.

"I don't know," Victoria said. "I haven't thought about it very much."

Rose stepped closer. "I know it is bold of me to ask, but has your father ever mentioned me?"

"He keeps close counsel. It is difficult to know what he is thinking. Just because he has not spoken of you to me . . . well, it does not mean anything." She set the heavy basket on the floor.

"I see." Rose swallowed hard. "I will leave you to your project. Enjoy the jams."

Victoria realized she was being rude for no other reason than her pain over Lewis. "Thank you, but you needn't go. I'm simply checking my gowns for any damage. My hems get so muddy, and then I can't see what needs repair."

"I have excellent eyesight," Rose ventured. "I can help."

"That would be lovely, thank you." She handed Rose a dress, and they worked in near silence for a time, checking for frayed hems.

Eventually, Rose asked, "Are you enjoying the house party? Has it worked out the way you planned?"

"In some ways," Victoria said, though she wasn't about to explain that her main goal in coming here had been to lose her virginity. "It has given me some measure of clarity about my life moving forward."

"I understand you've learned the truth about your aunt," Rose said sympathetically.

Victoria nodded. "At least I understand now. I hope Penelope can face the truth and still thrive."

"You're very good with her," Rose said. "And then there's my cousin. You seem to have become close."

"Not close enough." Victoria held a cloak up to the light to see if a stain she thought she had observed was real.

"Can't you bring him up to snuff?" Rose ran her fingers along the inside of a hem, looking for broken stitches.

"He claims he will never work for anyone again and believes my father would attempt to put him directly under his thumb."

"He had some dreadful rows with my father, who has a choleric temperament, to say the least. Lewis is very mild, but even he had his fur ruffled."

"I expect it was painful to be refused your sister's hand in marriage." She said the words casually, but she was desperate to learn more about the gossip.

Rose shook her head. "That never would have happened. He was only trying to help Alys stay in London. They were no closer than any of us."

Victoria wasn't sure Rose was correct, but it was fascinating to hear another perspective. "I believe he cares for me a little, but not enough."

"If you want to remarry soon, you'll have to work fast. The house party is almost over," Rose said.

"As you are attempting to do?"

They shared a conspiratorial smile. "Exactly. Do you have other prospects?"

"The Baron of Alix," Victoria said. "But I was not looking to remarry as quickly as my father might wish."

Rose let the hem drop and began to examine the cuffs. "You'll need to redo these." She paused. "Do you like the baron? He's very handsome."

"I agree. And pleasant."

"If he proposed, would you say yes?"

Victoria took the dress and decided she agreed about the cuffs. She'd give the mourning gown to the maid to do with as she wished. "He suits my father. A title or a man to run the factories: That is what I am tasked with on the marriage market."

"He wants to protect his interests, one way or another. But you want to marry for love."

"If a man isn't willing to do anything for you, is it really love?"

"Don't you want a man who is strong?" Rose asked. "I'd rather have a man know what he wants—to be ruthless, even—in pursuing his interests. It shows character."

"I am my father's daughter. I suppose I want to be the ruthless one, accomplishing what I want." She dropped the cloak with a sigh. It did have a soot stain. "This will need a vinegar wash." The maid took it and placed it on the bed with the other washables.

"Lewis is quite strong-willed for a relatively quiet person." Rose tossed a yellowing chemise into the same pile of clothing.

"I have noticed," she admitted. "I will have to bring the baron up to snuff if my father insists."

"If you love Lewis, you shouldn't marry someone else," Rose ventured.

"He loves someone else," Victoria said. "Alys."

Rose wrinkled her nose. "He doesn't; he's just been romantic about her, to protect his heart. And keep himself free of entanglements, I expect. Men are like that, you know, when they aren't ready. They swing between indifference and ruthlessness."

"Perhaps you are right. My relationship with my late husband was almost tepid in comparison to what I feel for Lewis."

"You think your husband was indifferent to you?" Rose shook her head.

Victoria winced. "He died so easily. I suppose it wasn't his fault, but I did wonder, you know, if I wasn't worth living for."

"That's a terrible thought," Rose said. She put an unblemished velvet gown aside. "I admit I've wondered myself if any man would ever really love me. I know I wasn't even worthy of it in the past. I was a bad sister."

"You mustn't be so hard on yourself," Victoria exclaimed.

"No, it's true. My foolishness led to my older sister's ruin. All of our lives changed. None of us could take advantage of being related to a marquess because of our sinful behavior. He never really took my sister, and therefore any of us, into fashionable society."

"How do you see my father? As a consolation prize?" How would her proud father deal with that?

"Not at all." Rose leaned forward and took her hand. "I like him very much. Oh, I know he's older, and not exactly good society, but I love his stern, mysterious air, his decisiveness. And yet he doesn't seem to have a temper."

"He's too good at getting his own way to resort to temper," Victoria said.

"I like that, because I do have one," Rose said. Her smile revealed a dimple in one cheek. "I want a man who isn't afraid to know what he wants. It makes me . . . well, fluttery, I suppose."

"My father gives you the flutters? That's something." Victoria contemplated Rose. "That is what Lewis gives me." *At the very least.*

Rose squeezed her hand. "Let us help each other, then. If your father marries me, maybe you can have Lewis on his terms instead of your father's. I'll do what I can to keep you in front of him. I'll blackmail him into attending parties. You just have to be patient. If I marry your father, you could be engaged to Lewis in a year or so, don't you think?"

Victoria forced herself to nod, while quaking at the mere thought of that word. *A year.* "What if he meets someone else first?"

"He wouldn't even be at this house party if it wasn't for that dratted submarine. He doesn't see himself the way women see him. He's being paid to be here by the earl and doesn't realize he's as much a prime marital candidate as anyone else. You knew that, didn't you?"

Victoria took her hand from Rose and twisted her fingers together. "I suppose I did."

"I don't imagine he meets very many respectable ladies. Not with his head always buried in an engine."

"Does he meet unrespectable ones?" Victoria squeaked.

"How would I know?" Rose asked. "No one would tell me, and there is nothing to overhear down here. If I lived in Battersea, it might be different."

Victoria looked at the clock. "It is past time to dress for dinner."

"I will let you dress, then." Rose patted her hand again. "I will wait downstairs in the drawing room. Some of the family might be down there by now."

* * *

Victoria was seated between her father and the Baron of Alix at dinner again. Rose sat on her father's other side, which meant Victoria only had to speak to the baron; her father had no interest in conversing.

She kept half an ear on Rose's conversation, curious to see how she would behave. She spoke well on a variety of general topics without being overly silly. Could Rose, at twenty-one, manage to hold her father's attention? Surprisingly, yes. Victoria herself sometimes thought she was boring him. But then, she'd had little stimulation since Sir Humphrey's death, and before that she'd only been interested in wedding plans. Perhaps she'd been as dull as the expression on her father's face warranted. She'd learned a great deal from listening to conversations with his business associates over dinner, however.

She sighed and glanced across the table, where Lewis often sat. Tonight, though, he had taken a tray in his room.

"You are rather quiet," the baron said. The candlelight reflected in his warm brown eyes, making them glow. He had fine looks. Thick, dark hair, a narrow face, a very patrician nose. A good figure, too, though rather on the lean side. She hadn't known she liked well-developed muscles until she'd seen Lewis without a shirt on. Still, John had an appearance that would please any woman. His mouth tilted slightly when he spoke, and a full lower lip gave him a sensual air. She sighed. Perhaps she simply preferred blond men.

She fluttered her eyelashes at him. "Simply taking in the sight of you in that magnificent tie."

He self-consciously touched the gleaming black silk dotted with a diamond pin. "I am fancy tonight, eh?"

"You look magnificent," she assured him.

They continued in a similar flirtatious vein throughout dinner. During her brief exchanges with her father, he seemed approving. When they finished their meal, John offered her his arm and escorted her to the drawing room, then went back to join the men for their cigars.

She expected to end the evening with further flirtation with John and was very surprised to see Lewis, dressed more casually than the other men in a black suit and a green and red tartan vest, in the doorway, with the earl at his side.

* * *

Lewis found his eyes going directly to Victoria as the men entered the drawing room. He had joined them in the hallway because he wanted a word with the earl. His legs were rubbery, but he thought he could do well enough if the coughing stayed at a minimum.

They found seats in a loose circle and began to talk about the submarine disaster. Out of the corner of his eye, he saw Victoria sit down on the sofa next to his chair. The baron joined her. She wasn't wasting time. The man was clearly besotted with her, and he wondered if she realized that.

What would happen if the baron proposed? Not his problem. Victoria had to make her own decisions. Then he noticed another interesting pairing: Rupert Courtnay had actually gone to join his cousin Rose at the piano.

The sound of metal ringing against glass caught his attention, and he turned to see Frederick Dickondell, the patriarch of the clan, with the countess. He bowed slightly to the crowd as conversation diminished.

Lewis winced.

"Not another engagement," Victoria muttered. "Is there a prize for house parties with the most romantic couplings?"

The baron was smiling at Victoria. Lewis wanted to punch him in the face. Smarmy bastard. Did he think she was giving out hints? If so, it was more likely to be to him, seated on the other side. Did the baron ever wonder why she'd started to pay attention to him so suddenly?

Frederick Dickondell began to speak again. "Come forward, my dear son Samuel and Maud. I would like to announce the felicitous occasion of their engagement."

The crowed clapped politely, with a few weak "hear, hears," but it was obvious no one really cared. The third Dickondell engagement could not hold their attention, particularly when the young man in question was marrying his own second cousin, who had lived with the family for years.

Lewis could not help remembering the lack of excitement at his proposal to his cousin when he had lived with the family for some time. He understood why no one would care. Nothing to gossip about, really. No desperate secrets to uncover. Why had Samuel allowed this at such a young age? He supposed Maud was the same age. Perhaps they had loved each other from the cradle.

When he glanced back at Victoria, she had her head quite close to the baron's, who was speaking intently to her. Lewis's stomach churned at the thought of the man proposing. Could it all be a trick? Could she have enticed the baron to propose to make him come up to snuff?

No, he didn't really think that. She didn't bother with hidden motivations. The truth of her infatuation, or even love, was written on her expressive face. Good God, he couldn't stand to sit next to the simpering pair of them any longer. He stood, careful not to look at the sofa, and ignored the earl's next question. After straightening his jacket, he walked to the piano and leaned against it.

Rose was playing a Mozart piece somewhat ineptly. Rupert Courtnay didn't wince when her timing was off. Either he had a tin ear or he was enraptured by the girl. Lewis hoped for rapture.

Rose blushed when she finished the piece. "I am a better singer, I am afraid."

"I'm certain you have a delightful voice, my dear, but I quite enjoyed the piece. One of my favorites," Courtnay said smoothly.

Lewis waited to see if the enigmatic older man would smile, but he did not quite go to such an extreme.

Rose cleared her throat delicately.

"Do you require a glass of punch?" Lewis inquired.

"Oh, tea, I think." She smiled at him.

"Here is champagne coming, courtesy of the latest engagement," Lewis said.

Courtnay frowned. "Yet another one? Wasn't paying attention."

"I think that's all the male Dickondells paired off now," Lewis told him.

Courtnay lifted his bushy, gray-threaded eyebrows. "No dealings with them. The family must want to keep wedding costs low by combining ceremonies."

Lewis nodded. "Local farming family. Connected to the Shields. Nice people, really."

"Nice will get you nothing in this world."

"Interesting point. Rose, why don't you see if you can flag down a tray of that champagne?" He meant for her to go away.

"A gentleman might offer to do that for a lady," she demurred.

He glared at her behind Courtnay's back.

"But then," she continued, "you were nearly killed so recently. You are probably all but too weak to stand."

"So thoughtful, our Rose." Lewis directed the remark to Courtnay as she walked away.

"Thoroughly nice girl," the man rumbled.

"Speaking of this excessive number of engagements recently, are you considering matrimony yourself?" Lewis inquired.

CHAPTER 16

"I've been married," Courtnay said with no display of emotion. "But she's long gone now; my wife, I mean."

"Yes, of course," Lewis said. "I meant remarriage. A second bride?"

Courtnay, normally a rather still man, tapped the heel of his shoe on the floor. "Might get a bit lonely when Victoria remarries. I expect her to soon, you know."

Lewis winced. "This has been the most engagement-filled house party in the history of house parties." He covered the piano keys, noticing his hands were shaking slightly.

"All those Dickondells. I can't understand why my daughter didn't snatch one up."

Because she is in love with me. But Lewis didn't want to reveal that to this man. No, he saw Courtnay's hard, secretive edge. He'd never let anyone completely in, even his successor. Rose, having learned a harsh lesson about being a gossip, might make a good wife for such a tight-lipped man. "There are still more potential brides available, sir."

"Are you looking for a wife?" The man's sharp eyes regarded him.

He cocked his head. "No, no, but my cousin has her eye on a gentleman."

"Rose?"

"Yes, sir."

"Lives down here with her family?"

"Willing to move. She's from Bristol originally, then lived in London before Polegate."

Courtnay's nostrils flared, as if scenting prey. "Been to Liverpool?"

"Not that I'm aware of, but a girl will do anything for the right man."

His bushy brows pulled together. "Why would I be the right man, Noble?"

Lewis shook his head. "She likes you, might love you, even. You'd have to answer as to why."

"Old enough to be her father. She's Victoria's age." His eyes squinted as he pondered Lewis's words.

"She likes Victoria," Lewis told him. "I doubt they would clash. She's been kind to Penelope."

"Wish my brother would pull his head out of his cups long enough to deal with that situation," Courtnay rumbled. "Bloody mess, family."

"Sometimes. Wouldn't it be lovely to have a wife to deal with those domestic concerns?"

Courtnay's gaze drifted up to the ceiling. "I shall have to consider that." He clapped Lewis on the shoulder, exhibiting the iron strength of a younger man. "My thanks for making me aware of the situation."

Lewis nodded as Courtnay turned away. Victoria was standing at the window now, her soft gaze on the handsome baron, right next to her, his head tilted in her direction. As he watched, the baron put his hand on her cheek and brushed a stray curl behind her ear. He clenched his fists. Why was the Scotsman daring to touch his woman?

"Trouble in paradise?" Courtnay asked.

Lewis stared at the man. Could he have some idea of what had transpired?

"Are you in love with Victoria?" Courtnay continued.

"She is not for me," Lewis said stiffly. "I have too much keeping me in the London area."

"If you aren't willing to fight for her, then you are quite correct," Courtnay said.

I'm willing to fight to have her in my bed, but not to give her my name. "Are you saying that you don't really expect her to marry a successor for your business? That this has been some kind of a game to you?"

"I don't imagine she has entirely explained the situation to you, Noble. I trust my daughter to do what is best for herself and the businesses she will someday inherit."

Lewis stared at Courtnay. What a load of rubbish. Victoria did not see any way out of the situation her father had put her in. What game was this? It made him ever more certain that he would not want to be in business with Rupert Courtnay, much less under his thumb. "I trust her to do the same for herself, and for Penelope. She's headstrong but a good woman."

Courtnay nodded. "I agree. She does her duty."

Lewis took his leave of the man and went upstairs without another glance at Victoria and her Scotsman. It seemed she had made her decision, to flirt so openly with the man in front of her lover.

He did wonder, though. Wasn't it always said that women had a type of man they found attractive? He was blond, muscular, an inventor with oil crusted under his nails and in the lines of his palms. The baron was dark and lithe, a nobleman who spent his time managing family interests. How could Victoria find them equally striking?

Victoria had seen Penelope off to the nursery that morning with a promise to meet her an hour before luncheon for puzzles and more of the fairy tale. She'd thought of an interesting twist to the part about the unrung bells. But when she entered the puzzle room, Penelope wasn't there. Lady Rowena sat at the large puzzle of Pevensey-Sur-Mer Fort with her new fiancé, Ernest Dickondell. Victoria suspected the girl had done the puzzle of her own home so many times that she knew the pieces by heart, could tell from which of them had been dotted by tea, or treacle tart, or bits of marzipan, what corner they belonged in. It was an excellent way to keep touching Ernest. She managed to slide her hand against his repeatedly as she somehow ended up with pieces that needed to be placed just by Ernest's.

Victoria toyed with the pieces of the Hampton Court puzzle for half an hour, but when Penelope still didn't appear, she became nervous. She left with a wave at the lovebirds and went up to the nursery, where the maid said she had wandered off after breakfast.

"That was hours ago!"

The maid sighed. "I'm sorry, milady. The countess has a cousin visiting who left their three children under our care without any extra help. Two of them are ill."

Victoria made a face when she heard the sound of sneezing somewhere off to the left, behind a rocking horse. "I'll let you return to your work. Thank you."

She went down to their room, but no one was there. Penelope's coat, muffler, and mittens were also not present. Should she go to luncheon without her cousin or look for the girl? Maybe she'd gone back to the wishing well. Victoria went to the window and pulled back the lace curtains underneath the heavy velvet drapes. The remains of snow had desiccated, turning to ice, but the sky was clear and the sun was out. It wouldn't be too bad of a walk. She put on her coat and went outside, regretting the loss of a meal.

Outside, the sun offered plenty of light but little warmth. She hunched her shoulders and wondered if she should have told someone where she was going. Would the baron be concerned if she didn't turn up? Had Lewis left his sickbed for good? If so, he was more likely to eat sandwiches in the stables than have a proper meal with the house-party guests.

Maybe she wanted to avoid both of them. She set out across the moat, hoping someone watched her from a window and wished they were spending time with her. Funny to make such a specific wish now, when she'd been so careful to wish generally on the proper wishing well day. The truth was that she had no idea who she really wanted to be thinking of her.

The handsome inventor crept into her thoughts, ruinously, as she walked through crunchy grass. Remnants of brown and gold leaves that had fallen a couple of months before still dotted the landscape. An impenetrable collection of brush and holly bushes were off to the left, alongside her, as if pointing the way up the hill to the wishing well.

She squinted into the sun, wondering if she could see Penelope from here, but the well was still too far away. Of course, she could be wrong. The girl could have gone anywhere, but it wasn't like her to make plans to meet her cousin and then not follow through. She liked Victoria's company, even when Victoria didn't quite know how to manage her moods.

Her exhalations puffed white tendrils into the air by the time she crested the hill. She stared out at the landscape, the town laid out in one direction, the long trail of bushes in another, water on a third side, the hill on the last. But she didn't see Penelope. Had she any pocket money? Would she have gone to town to buy candy or such? Maybe she was following Eddy Jackson around the stables. Or even visiting Lewis.

The thought of that man inevitably moved him to the forefront of her thoughts again. Why was he stuck there? Instead, the baron's blue eyes should come to mind, the skin around his eyes crinkling charmingly when he smiled. And he smiled often, a happier soul than his rival. For that reason alone, he should be first.

Could he make her feel the passion Lewis did? Would he even try? She'd discovered Sir Humphrey had a mistress, an actress who went weeping to his grave monument nearly every day for two months until she'd found a new protector. London friends had told her about the infamous wailing of the woman, catty with their enjoyment of the tale. No wonder she'd wanted to experience lovemaking, to understand why it could drive a sane woman to such outbursts when it was lost.

She knew now that nothing could take the place of it. Touching Lewis, feeling him inside her, his kisses on her cheek, her neck, her mouth, her breasts; no, nothing could compare. If John was an undemanding lover, careful and modest, she might go as mad as her Aunt Clarissa.

She shied away from the thought of what might have driven Aunt Clarissa mad in truth. Her uncle was no figure of fantasy but bald as an egg and round as a Christmas pudding. Had he ever inspired lust?

She reached the well and stared down into its depths. The copper bucket had been removed. Were you only allowed to wish one day a year? Penelope had brought her the tale and she hadn't inquired further into its mysteries.

As she stared into the well, images that reflected in the choppy water began to resolve. She saw more tall, wild holly bushes groaning with berries, the church spire, some kind of old building. Turning around, she looked in the direction of the building, wondering if she was near an interesting ruin. The hill sloped up a few yards, and on top she saw a crumbling stone bench. On top of that bench was a figure, and that figure was her missing cousin.

What was Penelope doing? Feeling a hot rush of fear, Victoria scrambled up the hill, grabbing at a scraggly tree at the halfway point to maintain her balance. "You'll catch your death up here," she called as the wind whipped around her.

Penelope didn't turn around. Victoria couldn't see her arms, and she wondered if the girl was hugging herself. Despite her reducing, she was breathing as hard as she could, wishing she didn't have to wear her stays so fashionably tight. She coughed once or twice before she regained her breath and made it up the last few feet.

"Penelope!" The girl still hadn't turned around, but Victoria saw her head tilt. Bending into the wind, she went to sit on the crumbled end of the bench next to her.

"I was watching for the storks," Penelope said after a moment. Her lips were wind chapped, her cheeks bright red.

"You have been here for a while." Victoria pulled a handkerchief from her pocket and opened it to reveal two large squares of shortbread, studded with currants and orange zest. She hadn't planned to eat them except in a case of extreme emergency, but she and Penelope had both missed the midday meal.

The girl snatched one of the treats and took an enormous bite. She bent over it as if it were her last meal, her eyes closed to savor the taste.

Victoria broke an edge off hers and let it melt in her mouth, resigned that the fate of most of her treat would also be eaten by her hungry cousin. When Penelope finished the first cookie, she handed the second one over, then waited for her to finish it before speaking again.

"I don't like that you left the Fort without telling anyone," she said.

"The countess saw me going out when she was greeting her cousin," Penelope said in a sulky tone.

"That was hours and hours ago! Have you been here all morning?"

"Yes." Penelope pulled off one glove and picked crumbs out of the nubby wool with pale, bloodless fingers.

Victoria took the girl's hand and put it to her cheek. "Penelope! How can you stand to be this cold?"

"I can hardly feel my fingers anymore," she said.

Victoria squeezed her eyes shut. Penelope was not behaving like a normal child. Could she get through to the girl, or was she destined to repeat her mother's madness? "Let us go back. Perhaps we should return to London a few days early. Would you like to see the sights instead of staying here?"

Penelope pressed her lips together. They were the same color as the rest of her skin. "No."

"I know the air is better here, but why are you outside? At the very least, you could be cozy in the stable, pestering Eddy."

"He told me to leave him alone," Penelope said in a low voice.

"He did?" She found that hard to believe. Eddy was a thoroughly nice young fellow, and so patient.

"He said he was busy."

"That might have been true, you know."

Penelope sniffed, then coughed. First Lewis had risked his health and now her cousin. What was wrong with everyone? How had a simple house party become so complicated? Both of them were all but suicidal. Penelope needed to know she was loved, and Lewis needed some project other than that blasted submarine. She knew she had to talk him into making Penelope a stork. A symbol of hope would be so helpful.

She took Penelope's hand and drew her from the bench. "We must get you warm, dear. Come now."

Penelope stumbled a little as they began to walk down the hill in a zigzag fashion, attempting to keep away from the little pebbles that skittered under their shoes, throwing them off balance. Victoria heaved a sigh of relief when they reached the base and found the path back to the Fort.

An hour later, she had Penelope tucked into bed with a nursemaid hovering over her. The girl's cheeks, pale with cold, did not look much better, but color had returned to her lips. She sipped chocolate and nibbled on a biscuit while Victoria changed her gown. Her hems had been damp and muddy by the time they had returned.

She buttoned up the front of her simple wool dress and pinched her cheeks. They still felt wind-chapped and chilly, but Lewis's room would likely be kept very warm still, so she would not feel cold for long. She couldn't resist checking on him. A nurse's pride, she told herself.

After blowing a kiss to Penelope, she went to Lewis's room. While he might be in the stables, she hoped, only two days after his ordeal and especially because it was pouring rain, that he'd had the sense to remain indoors. Indeed, Eddy opened the door when she knocked and ushered her inside.

Lewis had his hands on his hips, pushing his red velvet smoking jacket away from his body. He stood staring at his bed, which was covered with drawings, a frown creasing the skin between his eyebrows. As she watched, he poked at one of the drawings with a fingernail and muttered something under his breath.

"He's trying to decide if a design flaw caused the leak, or if it's an execution issue," Eddy reported.

"Are you speaking Greek?" Victoria asked.

Eddy grinned. "No, milady. I hates book learnin'."

"I was never very fond of it myself. Many a time I was supposed to be learning mathematics and read novels instead. My father couldn't make an accountant of me."

"Hence his insistence on marrying you off to some fop or nobleman?" Lewis interjected in an acid tone.

"He wants to marry me off to someone with intelligence or position. If the man has position, then he will know the best managers to hire to run things."

Lewis turned to her and snorted. "Do you have any idea how many noblemen are idiots? Inbred, you know. The ones who inherit titles hire their less-fortunate siblings to manage their estates and such, or gamble them away, or make other poor decisions."

"They aren't all like that."

He sniffed. "No, I'm sure your late husband was a paragon."

Frustration overtook common sense. "Lewis, can't you let this submarine project go? It's already nearly killed you once."

"I'll figure it out." He narrowed his eyes at her.

"Couldn't you take a break? Penelope is so broken right now. I really do think it would give her so much pleasure to receive one of your famous birds. I would love a white stork for obvious reasons, but really, anything would work. Especially now because she's gotten herself so cold. I'm afraid she's going to have to stay in bed for the rest of the house party." She put her hands together, imploring him.

"What did she do?" Eddy demanded.

"She went back to the wishing well, alone, early this morning, then climbed that hill nearby and sat on the bench in the wind for hours."

"Why'd she do that?" the boy asked.

"She was hoping the birds would return."

"In the dead of winter?"

Victoria nodded. "I'm afraid so."

"She must be as mad as a hatter," Eddy gasped.

"Do not." Victoria squeezed her eyes shut. "She's just a little girl."

"I mean no offense, milady. I'm sorry. Should I go see her?"

"Not until you can be much more sensitive with your language."

Eddy's smile faded. "Of course, milady. I am sorry." He whirled around and pulled open the door, then vanished into the hallway.

Victoria sighed. "It has been a trying morning."

When she turned, she caught Lewis staring at her. His intense gaze burnished her skin, licking heat up her legs and down her breasts. She swallowed hard and put her hand to her chest. Had she laced her stays too tightly when she'd changed? How hot was it in here?

"There won't be any birds," Lewis said, his voice gravelly.

The rough tone seemed to work on her like stone, abrading her senses. Her nipples peaked and she felt moisture between her thighs. What was he doing to her? She couldn't think of anything but him, and the longing she felt to be back in his arms.

"Please," she implored, forgetting what she wanted from him.

He moved away from the bed and passed her. She smelled rich leather and sharp bay on his skin, plus a faint touch of wood smoke. He went to the door and locked it. The snick of the key had an air of finality.

"Come here." He reached out his hand behind him, not glancing back.

Fingers trembling, in his thrall, she obeyed, ignoring the shock of pain on her abraded palm when it met his. His rough fingers slid along the soft flesh of her arm and he pulled her to him until she was up against the door. He sank to his knees and gathered her skirt, then her petticoats, and disappeared beneath them.

"I have to taste you," he said on a low moan.

She felt his arms pushing her legs apart. Her body shook hard. Struggling to remain upright, she tipped her head back against the door. Pins dug into her scalp as the skin of her throat tightened.

He had her legs spread now, his fingers ripping up the slit in her drawers, opening them, exposing her to his dark desires. She shuddered when she felt his breath against her newly exposed thigh, then on the wiry curls over her womanhood.

His blunt, clever fingers spread her completely open to him. Despite all her clothing, she could smell the sweet musk of her own arousal. When he licked—long, raspy, and wet—all along her most private place, her knees all but buckled. She keened, gasped, implored, then grasped her skirts in her arms and held them against her chest so he could use those clever hands for something else.

And oh, but he did, his fingers whispering along her thighs as he licked her from one round of pleasure to the next, thrusting his tongue into her channel, swirling it around her pearl, sucking, blowing, biting. She remembered he had planned to experiment on her. That conversation seemed an age ago.

She breathed so hard, she could hear a gale in her ears. Wanting to see him, she opened her eyes, was caught by the image of a ghostly woman in a mirror across the room. A man was between her legs, his head bobbing. The woman had her mouth open. Her eyes were dark pools of lust. She panted, her chest moving rapidly with every motion of the man. She could see his darker hands against her pale thighs, the red jacket against her white drawers.

He sucked her pearl hard, thrusting fingers inside her, and she fell apart. Her eyelids drooped, her fulfillment giving a light show as she cried out, her entire body quivering through a maelstrom of pleasure.

When her legs could hold her no more, she sagged to the floor, her skirts falling around her waist.

Lewis brought his mouth, that clever mouth, to her ear and suckled her soft lobe. She could smell herself on his skin, his breath, his fingers when he pulled them from her channel and put them to her lips.

"That's the taste I can never forget, Victoria. Your sweet honey. I will remember it every day of my life."

She blinked, almost overcome by the tenderness in his voice. But he didn't want her, not really. He, at least, realized this was only lust. She was a fool to love him. Sniffing hard couldn't prevent tears from welling up in her eyes, dripping down her cheeks.

"I've made a mistake." She struggled to her feet, dropping her skirts. Somehow her knee hit Lewis and he overbalanced, landing on his backside, staring up at her with surprise.

She pointed her finger at him, as if to scold, but her entire body still shook from the force of her climax.

"Victoria."

"We have to stop this."

"You came to me," he said quietly.

She wanted him inside her. "For a bird, Lewis. A bird. I wanted Penelope to have a bird. That was all." She waved her hands over her midsection, then wiped her face. "Not this."

"You were a willing participant while it lasted."

"Oh, and do you expect reciprocity now?" she shouted. "Do you want me on my knees?"

"I'm surprised a gently reared lady would think of such a thing," he said in a stiff voice, before pushing himself into a standing position.

"My passion for you has tormented me with every naughty thought that can be imagined. Every way to touch your body, every way you might touch mine." She waved her hands again. "Oh, I might not know quite what to do, what might be most pleasing, but I assure you, sir, I've had at least rudimentary thoughts on every brand of pleasure possible."

He didn't speak.

"All I want is a bird for my cousin. You know what she's suffered. If you won't marry me and enjoy my body for the rest of our lives, the least you can do is spend a day crafting her a bloody bird, instead of killing yourself in that damnable submarine!" She turned the key in the lock and opened the door. After stamping out, she slammed it closed, then stalked back down the corridor to her room.

With her hand on the knob, she stopped. She couldn't go inside, not so disheveled and smelling of sexual pleasure. Not with Penelope in bed. Cursing herself for every kind of fool, she went to Lady Rowena's quarters. At least the girl wasn't naïve, not after catching herself Ernest Dickondell.

Lewis went to the stables on Saturday, resolved to return to the submarine project. He shared his insights concerning the leak, leaning over his blueprints with the earl, and they went to work, fixing the design of metal plating on the hull, only eating cold sandwiches for lunch. By two P.M., thanks to the inadequate food and damp conditions, Lewis's cough had returned and the earl insisted he return to the Fort.

He felt a tremor under his feet as he went up the hill to the mudroom. Earthquakes did occur sometimes in this area, and he wondered if that was what he had experienced, slight though the sensation had been. It was no stronger than the reverberations from a heavy cart as it rolled by. Of course, no cart was nearby.

"Did you feel an earthquake?" he asked the boot boy in the mudroom, but the boy just shook his head.

He asked the first maid he saw the same question, but she hadn't felt it either. Maybe the old fort was too stable for a small quake to be felt. "Is tea being served anywhere presently?"

"Lady Rowena and Miss Courtnay had a tray sent into the puzzle room less than ten minutes ago, sir," the maid said.

He nodded and decided to go there. Gloves weren't practical in the stable and his hands felt like blocks of ice. He walked down the corridors, stamping his feet to get feeling back into his toes.

Just as he had his hand on the doorknob of the puzzle room, he heard boots pounding through the hall. Eddy appeared, hair flopping over his eyes as he raced, waving something at him. Lewis opened the door and Eddy flew through, not stopping until he banged into a table with a half-finished puzzle on it. The pieces flew into the air with all the force of a hurricane behind them.

Thankfully, Lady Rowena and Penelope were at a different table, the tea tray behind them. Fires blazed under both chimneys. The air smelled temptingly of the evergreen boughs that decorated the mantels. While the modern lighting was quite good, beeswax tapers also scented the air delightfully, their flames dancing above three-pronged candelabras set on tables along one wall.

"Good heavens," the young lady cried. "I thought we were being invaded."

"My apologies," Lewis said. "This young jackanapes could not figure out how to put the brakes on in time to avoid discomfiting you."

"I am sorry," Eddy said. "Can I speak to you, sir?" He pointed back to the corridor.

Lewis nodded his head and regretfully followed his apprentice back to the chilly hallway. "Where have you been? I haven't seen you this afternoon."

Eddy shoved a grubby handkerchief at him.

"What's this?" Lewis asked, taking it.

"It's a bird," Eddy said, working his jaw until it protruded. "I knew you wouldn't make one for the girl, so I did it."

CHAPTER 17

Lewis frowned at the lad, feeling as if Eddy had reprimanded him. "I made the decision to leave mechanical birds in my past. An inventor has the right to move on to the next project."

"You might be able to fix the submarine if you worked on a bird," Eddy insisted. "You know what you're doing with them things, and maybe you could design the feathers to work like the hull plating. Solve your design problem."

"I believe I already fixed that yesterday," Lewis said, crossing his arms over his chest and tucking his chilled fingers into his armpits.

"I don't think you did," Eddy insisted. "You were muttering about it last night, and that's always a sign your mind's still workin'."

Lewis chuckled. "Think you know everything, don't you, boy?"

"I've been wi' you a long time now, sir. I bet if you worked on the right kind of bird you'd get it sorted out. The movement of the wings could simulate the submarine hull."

He sighed. "I shall take your suggestion under advisement. What did you make? It seems to me you've already met Lady Allen-Hill's requirement."

Eddy bowed his head, his bravado leaving him. "It's just a carving. I painted it a little, to look like the stork she saw."

Lewis realized the blotches on the handkerchief were black paint. "Might have needed to let it dry a bit longer."

"It's dry enough," he muttered.

Lewis opened the splotchy cloth to uncover a hand-size rendition of a white stork, complete with a long, skinny red beak. No attempt had been made to define the feathers, but Eddy had done a perfect job with the overall shape and distinctive coloring of the bird. "It's a lovely job, Eddy. I'm sure she will adore it."

"Will you give it to her?"

Lewis smiled and handed it back to him. "I won't take credit for your work, lad. You should have the honor."

Eddy blushed and ducked his head. "I'm too coarse for the likes of Miss Penelope. I shouldn't even speak to her."

"She's not some fine lady but the niece of a manufacturer. Wealthy, to be sure, but not a blue blood."

"But what am I, Lewis? Just some Cockney who never even knew his own father."

"You're a self-made lad," Lewis said, putting his hand on Eddy's shoulder. "You're going to do fine things with your life, be a man to be proud of. That's more important than family, in my book. You go and give her the bird."

"I knocked over that puzzle," Eddy said, staring down at the floor with his jaw outthrust. Lewis noticed a hint of fuzz on the boy's upper lip that hadn't been there before the house party.

"We'll pick it up together," Lewis promised, giving the boy a little shove. "Now go, and no bashfulness."

The sight of fourteen-year-old Eddy, blushing and stammering, his hands shaking as he handed his creation to the small girl, warmed Lewis's heart like nothing else could. The girl's gasp of pleasure, the way she flung herself artlessly against Eddy until he was forced to hug her back, made him almost contemplate a design for those black-feathered wings. Was Eddy right? Could the project help him with a better design for the submarine?

He rubbed his cold fingers over his forehead, feeling his innards stiffen at the mere idea of making a bird again, of revisiting that unhappy time in his life when he was unappreciated and under his uncle's thumb.

When his best friend and cousin, Sir Gawain, was a grumpy, bitter, wounded ex-soldier being forced to learn accounting. When Sir Gawain's twin, Alys, fought against the family's urge to become country gentry with every bit of her strength and still lost the battle against her father. When Rose and Matilda, the younger girls, were selfish and grasping. Now, Sir Gawain and Alys were happily married with children, and Rose had grown into a lovely and sensitive young woman. Matilda was fulfilling her potential as the new heir to the Redcake's businesses, handling her father better than anyone in the family ever had. Had everyone moved on but Lewis? Why was a silly mechanical bird the symbol for everything that had been wrong three years before?

"Why are you so unable to supervise your cousin properly? She's going to have to go away to school if you can't manage her," Victoria's father growled.

He stood in front of the large fireplace in the drawing room before dinner. Victoria wanted to tell him to move away, that his coat might get singed, but her father was in a foul mood.

"What were you thinking, allowing her to go out of sight and leave the Fort for a full morning?"

Victoria's lips tightened, leaving her unable to speak any kind of defense. Was his criticism just? She was supposed to be concentrating on husband-hunting per his orders, not watching her cousin every moment.

"And fawning over that Lewis Noble in his sickbed. You want a healthy specimen, Victoria."

She found her voice. "He nearly drowned, Father. It is not as if he came down with some random illness."

He snorted. "Nonetheless, it is a poor showing for someone who works outdoors as he does."

"We are having an uncommonly cold and damp winter for these parts," she protested. "Besides, the issue at hand is my competence to manage a nine-year-old girl."

"A highly emotional one at that," her father muttered.

"She has every reason to be."

"Why in God's name did you find it necessary to take her to see her mother? Your lack of judgment makes me wonder."

Victoria pressed her lips tightly together again. Tears welled up in her eyes. "I love Penelope, Father. I am not, perhaps, the most natural mother, but I am trying. She is not the average child."

"No, she's a Courtnay." Her father sniffed and drew himself up, placing his hand in his pocket, a dandified gesture that seemed uncharacteristic.

Victoria turned and saw Rose enter the room. When she turned back, she saw color had come into his cheeks. She also realized he'd taken pains with his hair, taming his graying locks with pomade. The shiny result was not displeasing, at least not to Rose, who gave him a warm smile.

Her father smiled in an almost sickening fashion as well.

"I can see I'm losing your interest, Father, and indeed I am happy to see you so glad to see Rose Redcake. But please, give me another chance. Don't send Penelope to boarding school. We will do very well together in Liverpool, she and I. I promise."

"How are you going to find a husband there?" he asked. "You've rejected every eligible man in our circle."

"I will do my best to resolve the matter quickly, before we leave," she said, though the notion made her queasy.

He raised an eyebrow. "How do you plan to manage that?"

Rose's gaze turned away as the door opened. Three men entered: Lewis, the Baron of Alix, and the Earl of Bullen.

"Don't trouble yourself, Father. I'll bring someone up to snuff." Hopefully, she could look forward to a long engagement at least, a time when her father would be pleased with her and she would still have some freedom of movement. Time for Rose to enact her plan with Lewis.

"If you are engaged by Twelfth Night, I won't send Penelope to Miss Treadgold's Academy," her father said. "Mind you, she's already been entered there, so it is the work of a moment to put her on the train to Birmingham."

His words hit her with the power of a physical blow. "You'd send her so far away? I had no idea you'd taken such steps." Victoria pressed her hand to her stomach. Why on earth would her father threaten such a thing? He did look a bit wild-eyed, as if he hadn't been sleeping.

"I have no time or inclination to be less than practical," her father said. He puffed out his cheeks, then blew, as if discarding the conversation. "Keep your promise to me and we'll have no need to discuss the matter further."

He stomped away, heading toward the liquor decanters along one wall, under a portrait of the first Earl of Bullen, dating back to the seventeenth century. The long-dead nobleman glared eternally at his descendants, probably missing the Scottish lands from which he'd come so long ago. Victoria wondered what had happened to the original family who'd held the Fort.

That thought, that dynastic thought, could only hold her attention for a moment. Today was January 4. She didn't have much time to become engaged. Tomorrow was her deadline. Staring at the knot of men in the doorway, she considered.

Would the Earl of Bullen agree to a false engagement to keep him off the marriage mart? Considering how little he seemed to notice the ladies crowded around him, thanks to his absentminded inventor's air, probably not.

So that left John, the Scottish baron. She liked him, but she'd have to live in Scotland if they truly went through with a marriage, give up everything she knew. Penelope would be forced to live far away from either of her parents if she went with her, but allowing her to start over might be the kindest thing Victoria could do for her.

Would John be willing to take Penelope on? Victoria knew she would have to find out, and soon. She took a few steps toward the trio and smiled tentatively. John immediately caught sight of her and stepped away from the other men. When he reached her side, she moved toward the piano and sat. He sat next to her as she fingered a German dance piece by Shubert.

"Are ye going to play?" he asked.

"The dinner gong will be soon."

"Ye wanted tae speak to me alone, then?"

She turned to him, determined, saw the open, friendly expression on his face "We agreed to be merely friends, once."

"My position in life does not allow me tae manage English factories," John said carefully.

"My father has lifted that stricture in your case."

"In mine?" His eyebrows drew together. "Have ye spoken of me?"

She nodded. The right side of his mouth lifted into an engagingly lopsided smile. She couldn't quite imagine kissing that mouth, but once she was away from Lewis, surely his sensual power over her would recede, and she had Penelope to think about. Miss Treadgold's Academy was notoriously cold and unloving. Only the naughtiest girls were sent there, girls with parents who wanted them out of the way because they were an embarrassment. They'd be fed properly, and educated a little, but nothing else. It was not a good place for this high-strung child.

John cleared his throat. "Should I speak to your father?"

"Is that what you want to do?" Victoria forced herself to stop fiddling with the sheet music and folded her hands into her lap.

"I like you, Lady Allen-Hill. I think we should suit."

"My cousin Penelope would have to live with me. You must be aware of that." She glanced sideways at him. "I don't want her sent away from me."

He seemed unperturbed. "I don't see that she presents a problem. Does Edinburgh?"

"It might be an improvement over Liverpool."

He chuckled. "I thought ye had your heart set on London. And Lewis Noble."

"Come, John, you can't imagine my father would accept him for me."

"No man would be happy tae have his daughter lose a title, once gained." John ran his index finger over her knuckles in a quick gesture of affection. "I cannot blame him for that."

"You would have to hire managers for all the businesses someday."

"I will educate myself on the issues and the men, just as I do for my Scottish properties. I'm a hard worker, Victoria. I won't lose your fortune. I'll be generous tae ye."

"I believe you. May I ask you a question?"

"Of course." He spread his fingers on his thighs. "Anything."

"Why did you come to this house party? Were you looking for a wife?"

"I was meant tae take a look at the Gill girls," John said. "I was at Oxford with Nicholas. He thought I might want to marry one of his sisters."

"You went to school with the earl? I had no idea."

John nodded. "Ye see, it isn't so unusual after all. Honestly, I am a better catch than those Dickondells, but one has the sense the Gills are happy to stay down here, near their ancestral lands."

"I was just remembering they were Scottish originally."

"Long ago. They came south with James I. The Gills are a bonnie lot, but I'll be happier with ye, I think. And it's time I marry."

She knew he didn't love her, but with her deadline looming, this engagement would be quite good enough. In fact, she liked him better than she had Sir Humphrey. It was only the passion she'd experienced with Lewis that made her sorry. But John was handsome, fit, and amiable. He would not be unpleasant to look at or speak to over the breakfast table. Assuming she had to go so far as to actually marry him.

"Please do speak to my father, if you have resolved that you would like to do so," she said, staring at the stark black and white keys. "I have no objections."

His hand went over hers, his palm pressing the back of her hand. Her skin was cold underneath his.

"It makes sense that'd ye'd be nervous and shy," he said in a low voice. "Your first experience was brief and rather painful, with your sudden loss and plunge into widowhood at an age when ye should have been attending parties and enjoying yourself. I am glad I found ye here, before you went to London and were swept back into fashionable society."

She forced herself to smile at him. He didn't seem to realize her father had meant to keep her in Liverpool with him, not flit around London. But the deeper she moved into her commitment to him, the more she wanted to turn and implore Lewis with her eyes, to stop this before it was too late. She didn't want to ruin John's life.

"As soon as it is all settled, we should leave the Fort," she said. "Go right away. There is so much to do, and I need to hire a governess for Penelope. She has been running wild."

"Of course," John said. "We will go to London on Tuesday. Ye won't want to miss the Twelfth Night bonfire party."

"They have a bonfire that night?" She'd never heard of such a tradition.

John nodded. "Commemorates some battle in ancient times."

"I see. Well, plenty of those around here."

"Are you going to end that fairy tale with a big battle?" His eyes crinkled with humor.

"I shouldn't think so. It's a child's tale, after all."

The butler came in with the gong and waited expectantly for the crowd to hush.

John patted her hand one last time. "I'll speak to your father this evening, or at least make an appointment with him. Ye might be sorting out my bachelor household by summer."

She forced a smile. *Summer.* "You are so very good to me, John."

The sound reverberated through the room, and they stood. She took John's offered arm and went to their place in the procession. The rest of her life had begun. She told herself not to be selfish and regret any of it.

John sat next to Victoria at the church services the next morning. He asked her to walk back with him instead of riding in the carriage. Penelope had stayed home because of her cough, so Victoria was free to acquiesce.

Their breath puffed out clouds of winter white as they walked back from the village. She was astounded when John took her to the wishing well.

"Did you come here on New Year's Day?" he asked.

"Yes." She didn't want to explain that she'd come again due to her desire not to expose Penelope's wildness.

"Did your wish involve me?" he asked with a teasing grin.

"In a way," she said. "I made a general wish, to be honest."

"Very noble of ye. It is obvious to me that ye always think of others, Victoria." He took both of her hands in his. They both wore gloves, but somehow the intimacy was there, even more so than all the times she had stood or sat next to him. They were face to face. She could see every bit of the faint shadow, already present from his heavy beard despite the time of day, a sharp, short scar above his left eyebrow, his adorably lopsided upper lip. She would soon know this face as well as her own.

"I spoke to your father, Victoria, and he has agreed to the match. Indeed, I believe he welcomes it, despite the fact that ye will be leaving Liverpool."

She nodded, though her heart had begun to pound. When Sir Humphrey had proposed, she'd been calm, cool. But this proposal felt very different.

"We will love each other in time, my dear, I know it. We have too much affection for it tae be otherwise. A half-year engagement, I think, long enough for us to become true intimates."

Unable to speak, she nodded again.

"What do ye say? Despite your knowledge that I was tae speak to Mr. Courtnay, I still want ye to have a voice. Will ye do me the honor of becoming my baroness, Victoria?"

She swallowed hard and tried to will moisture to her parched mouth. But before she could speak, she was knocked off balance by a sudden jolting under her feet. The sound of stone cracking came from her left. John rocked from side to side, an expression of surprise on his face that surely matched her own. She dropped to one knee when the ground jolted again. John fell over her, whether from losing his balance himself or in an attempt to protect her, she didn't know.

They stared into each other's eyes, and she thought he must be planning to kiss her, but he didn't.

After several moments, when nothing else happened, he spoke. "Divine providence has spoken, my dear. Ye will give me your answer another time? I'm sure ye will want to check on your young cousin."

"Of course," she stammered. Then the wishing well seemed to vibrate next to her hip. *Danger.* The ground rumbled again.

John lifted himself off her and pushed her away from the well. She rolled over, her face picking up prickling stabs of pebbles as she rotated. He dragged her to her feet and they stumbled down the slope as the well crumbled into itself, the multicolored stones collapsing. Within seconds, the wooden beams clattered across the top of what was now nothing but a two-foot-high circular wall. The sounds of the destruction reverberated, along with a fuzziness in her eardrums from the sheer shock of what had transpired.

"Holy Mother," Victoria whispered. "Will the Fort be spared?" Was Penelope all right? Lewis? Her father?

"Let us hope we were at the center of the damage right here," John said, a grim cast overtaking his normally sunny face. He lifted his hand to his eyes and looked toward the village. "I can still see the church spire."

"That's a good sign. It's an old building, like the Fort." He took her arm and they trotted toward the Fort as fast as she could move in her constricting skirts.

They made it halfway down before seeing anyone else. Figures appeared at the base of the low hill they were atop and ran toward them with the agility of youth.

"Any word on the town?" a man she recognized as an undergardener called.

"The church spire still stands," John said. "What is the news at the Fort?"

"Still standing, though I expect they lost a lot of china and such," the man said.

"There are ruins in the lake," shouted the boot boy. "Just appeared in the water, they did! Pushed up from under the earth."

"How strange," John said. "We saw the wishing well collapse in the oddest manner."

The third man, one of the Fort's footmen, shook his head. "Nothing natural about earthquakes. The countess said to check on the village. Good luck to you."

John and Victoria stepped off the path to let them pass, then continued on their journey, excitedly discussing the ruins now that they knew the Fort had held. The ground under their feet rattled a couple of times, but nothing like the previous violent movements transpired.

She balked when they reached the drawbridge. "Do you think it is safe to go across?"

"The moat isn't that deep, only up to our knees, so I wouldn't worry," John said.

She nodded and they stepped slowly across the damp, creaking wood and through to the house in the courtyard. Inside was a scene of disarray. Maids were clearing away glass and china from vases that had been in the hall. Paintings had fallen, their frames on the marble floor, partially shattered. The grand staircase looked intact. She could see a long crack across the ceiling, though, and pointed it out to John.

"Just the plaster, I think," he said, squinting. "I should probably find the earl and see where I can be of assistance."

"I'm going to check on Penelope, then find my father."

He nodded, all business, not even smiling, and headed toward the earl's study. His mien reminded her rather painfully that neither of them thought of this as a love match, not for now at least. If he loved her, she'd have had a kiss, a hug, a longing glance, *something*, before he parted with her after a trying experience. But still, that meant the engagement might be easier to break if she could find a way to manage it later.

She forced herself up the stairs to check on Penelope, finding more ceiling cracks as she went. Paintings were on the ground in the hallway upstairs as well. She could see the chairs in the nook at the end of the hall all on their sides, as if a naughty child had upended them.

Her door was closed, but the frame hadn't been warped, and she opened it easily. Penelope was in bed, red-faced and sniffling. When she saw Victoria, her expression changed to one of wonder, and she pushed the covers back and launched herself at her cousin.

Victoria wrapped her arms around Penelope as the girl sobbed. "Has no one checked on you?"

The girl sniffed and shook her head.

"I'm so sorry. I came right here."

"First?"

"Yes." Victoria set the girl at arm's length and retied the ribbon holding her long brunette curls out of her face. "You came first, as if you were my own child."

"You aren't old enough to be my mother." Penelope's lower lip protruded.

"No, but I love you that much," Victoria assured her. "Don't doubt that."

"Uncle Rupert is going to send me to that horrible school. My father told me so in a letter."

"Why hasn't your father come to you?" Victoria asked. "Do you know why?"

"I'm not supposed to know these things, but he had a doxy. I heard my mother shouting at him all the time. I think he's gone to live with the doxy. What's a doxy?"

Victoria blinked. "I expect your parents' marriage was so painful, he found himself a lady friend."

"That's very naughty of him."

Victoria nodded, then shook out her skirts briskly. "You aren't going to that school. I've arranged it with Father. You are going to live with me, always, until you marry someday."

"I am?" The girl's pout became a look of wonder.

"Yes. Now, do you want to get dressed? I understand there are ruins poking out of the lake and I'm terribly curious to see them."

"Yes," Penelope said. "I promise I won't even cough."

Victoria regarded her critically. "Wrap a muffler around your mouth and nose to keep the air warm. That should help. But this shouldn't be missed."

Penelope dug through her trunk and Victoria helped her dress. They were ready to leave in ten minutes. So far, they hadn't felt any additional tremors.

They went out the back of the Fort and started down the hill, but something seemed wrong. Victoria realized what it was after a moment: the stables had collapsed. The structure that had been at the base of the hill for who knew how long had quite disintegrated. Victoria put her hand to her mouth, utterly shocked by the ruin of everything Lewis, the earl, and all of his men had been working on. Splintered boards were everywhere, and nothing stood above Penelope's height. Bales of hay were scattered and broken across the landscape, and she could smell noxious odors that must be chemicals that had poured out of broken containers.

"Oh my goodness." Penelope's eyes were huge above her muffler. "Do you think anyone was killed?"

Victoria wondered uneasily if it was safe to be anywhere nearby. Was there a risk of fire? But she didn't want to frighten the girl. She changed their path to take them far away from the remains. "Don't be gruesome, darling. I'm sure we'd have been told. The countess sent some of the men who worked here to the village, so I'm positive no one was even injured. Look at all the men combing through the wreckage. Surely that's about as many men who were working there."

She recognized the earl, taller than the others, pointing to a lump on one end. Was that the submarine? Had it survived? Lewis was nowhere to be seen. She couldn't resist the sharp pang of fear that stabbed her heart. But no, she was correct in what she'd told Penelope. They'd spoken to those men by the well and had passed several maids. Someone would have reported fatalities.

They gave the destruction a wide berth as they headed to the lake. She couldn't see anything in the chilly gray waters at first, but they followed the path around until she saw a knot of people standing in the muddy reeds.

They waded into the muck to join them. She saw a shock of blond curls and recognized Lewis instantly. The stabbing pain in her chest suddenly vanished. Next to him stood Rose, dressed for the outdoors in fashionable attire. She didn't see her father in the small crowd and wondered where he'd gotten to.

Rose saw her and waved. Victoria stepped nearer.

"Have you seen my father?"

"He's inspecting some of the outbuildings with one of the Dickondells," Rose said. "The earl gave everyone who asked a task."

"What is your task?"

"We're to document the ruins in case the earth swallows them again." Rose held up a sketchbook. "See? A photographer isn't available, though I think someone was sent to the village for the local man."

Victoria glanced at Rose's charcoal sketch, then out to the water, where the spiky original stone ruins were on display. "Is this what the earl wanted to find with his submarine?"

"There is an old legend," Rose said. "Lewis, you know the story, don't you?"

He nodded absently. "I believe it goes something like, 'Once upon a time . . .'"

CHAPTER 18

Victoria smiled despite herself. Was she really about to say good-bye to this man forever so she could marry John? How could he tell an old legend so calmly, as if she wasn't about to throw away the love she felt for him? Didn't he sense the end of their romance? Couldn't he feel her torment? Her heart hardened as she resolved to focus on Penelope's needs rather than her desire for this infuriatingly independent man. She couldn't see the future, know if she'd ever even see Lewis again. "Once upon a time?"

"Not all of us can be the original storyteller you are," Lewis said, tightening his nubby green muffler around his throat. "Now, if you look at the top of the ruin, you'll see it is a bell tower, yes?"

Penelope clutched Victoria's sleeve. "Like in your story? With the three bells unrung?"

Lewis looked at her with surprise. "That is exactly how the legend goes. When the Normans came, the priest was supposed to ring the bells to warn the Fort and the villagers so they could take refuge. But the bells were new, and the first time he attempted to ring them, they all cracked."

Victoria peered across the lake, trying to ignore the way her pulse pounded. She could see black spots in front of her eyes. "Is one of the bells still there?"

"I can't imagine how," Rose said. "They'd be more than eight hundred years old."

"Depends on what they were made of," Lewis said. "The bell tower was probably stone, but the bell would be metal. What would be gone would be what held it in place. Probably a wooden beam, which would likely disintegrate when exposed to air."

"I swear there is a bell," Victoria said. "Truly." She pointed. Or was it only a spot in her vision?

"It's just a legend," Rose said. "I mean, I've drawn it, so I can see what you mean, but there is no evidence it even is a church."

"I probably have the idea in my mind because of the fairy tale," Victoria admitted.

"It doesn't have a happy ending," Lewis told them. "The bell maker leapt from the tower in despair and the priest died in the Norman attack."

"Gruesome," Penelope said. "Why would Prince Hugh have told Princess Everilda to go to the tower that night if all that was going to happen?"

"So she could see the Normans coming," Victoria said. "And go back to the castle to warn everyone. Otherwise they wouldn't have known."

Lewis squinted. "I think you are right about the bell, though, oddly enough. A pity all the men are checking outbuildings and the village right now. We ought to paddle out there and get a closer look."

"Shouldn't you be helping at the stables?" Victoria asked, irritated by his casual attitude.

"I did as the earl asked," he said. "Hmmm; I wonder if there is a rowboat still tied to the dock. Did anyone notice if the dock survived?"

Lady Barbara shook her head. "I'm quite sure it didn't. We went down there to see if anyone had fallen into the water."

"This quake has given and taken away, it seems," Lewis mused. He canted onto his left hip and shaded his eyes with his hand. "Let us hope we have a chance to study the old church before another earthquake sends it below again."

"So you've lost your submarine but gained a new project?" Victoria asked, not hiding her sarcasm.

"The submarine idea is going to be overhauled," Lewis said, rubbing his hands together. "Our current prototype is worthless, so the only thing of worth that we lost is the building. The earl will rebuild and we'll be back to work in a couple of weeks." He gave her a calm smile.

"The house party will be over soon," she said, irritated that her mood didn't seem to affect him.

He nodded. "I'm sure the countess will put everyone to work repairing the Fort after the guests leave."

"Then she'll have weddings to plan," Lady Barbara said with a soft smile.

"I'll keep the earl out of the way for you," Lewis said. "He's going to come up to Battersea with me for a couple of weeks to fabricate the new submarine."

"How wonderful," Lady Barbara said. "We don't need him wandering the Fort moaning about the expense."

How utterly focused on work Lewis was. He didn't seem to care that they might never see each other again after a couple of days. She might be moving to Edinburgh, though, of course, he didn't know that yet.

"I believe there is a small boathouse on the far end of the lake," Victoria said, ready to end the conversation.

"You are correct," said Lady Barbara. "It's only used in summer, but there might be a rowboat."

"Why don't we walk over to check?" Victoria said to Lewis, already stepping away. "Rose, will you let Penelope sketch with you?"

Rose smiled knowingly. "Of course. I have extra charcoal."

Lewis joined Victoria on the path. They hopped numerous mud puddles as they made their way toward the boathouse. She couldn't help thinking of how much fun it would be to hold hands with someone while taking this path. It would feel like dancing, all of this maneuvering and hopping. But Lewis had his hands in his greatcoat pockets, and rightfully so, since any number of people might be about.

"Did you feel the earth move?" he asked.

"Yes. I was near the wishing well when it collapsed."

"Had Penelope gone there again?"

"No, I went there with John." She gave the name careful emphasis.

"You seem quite fond of him."

"He's a lovely man."

"Rather dark."

For the first time, emotion had colored his words. "I don't take your meaning."

"I didn't think you found dark men attractive."

"I don't think we ever discussed my ideal of male beauty," she snapped.

His cheek tensed, but he didn't respond. Just then, she spotted a squat building past the part of the path that turned to go alongside the far end of the Fort and on to the village.

"That must be the boathouse there."

He nodded. "I believe you are correct, Victoria."

"Lewis," she said, stopping on the path, her fingers icy under her gloves. "We're going to be very busy from now on. I have to keep a close eye on Penelope, and we'll be packing for our return. Then to-morrow night is the bonfire celebration. So I'd like to say good-bye to you now, in case there isn't another opportunity."

His eyebrows drew together. "What is your point?"

"You'll be busy with the earl," she said impatiently. "Discussing your submarine. I'll be busy with Penelope, and . . . well, other things. So good-bye, good journey, and good life to you." She held out her hand.

"I don't believe that is necessary," Lewis said, glancing at the boathouse. "Really, Victoria, we'll see each other again. We might even wind up on the same train north. So don't be dramatic."

Little did he know how hard she was trying not to be exactly that. Didn't he know that even now, he still had the power to change every-thing for her? "Good-bye anyway, Lewis, just in case."

He nodded absently. "Don't you want to go in the boat with me and row out to the ruins? How often will you have the opportunity to see a thing like that?"

"It wouldn't be proper."

"Come now." His lips curved faintly. "When has that ever trou-bled you?"

"Daylight," she said. "It's daylight. I'm only bad in the dark."

"The Fort will be all but empty during the bonfires," Lewis said. "We can say our good-byes then."

She pressed her lips together, wishing she could scream. He wanted to make love to her again? Men were so obstinate, so focused on themselves. Perhaps it was better she didn't love her husband. Love didn't bring happiness, only pain. "Enjoy your boat trip. I'll tell the others what you are doing so they can keep an eye out."

"Afraid I'm going to drown? You should at least watch out for me yourself, so you can shriek for help if I capsize."

"Fine," she said. "I'll stay right here and watch."

She did just that, wiping away tears as he went into the building. She heard doors creaking, wood sliding, and then a splash as oars hit the water. Lewis soon appeared, rowing out of the boathouse toward the ruins with powerful strokes. He never looked back, never checked to see if she'd done as he asked. Her heart was breaking over him and he didn't care.

Victoria next saw John at tea. It was a shoddier affair than usual; so much crockery had been damaged that they ate their sandwiches on silver salvers cadged from the butler's pantry. She suspected the countess was overjoyed that the house party would be ending soon.

Her father was sitting on a sofa, talking to Rose. She went up to him just as John stood from his place next to Samuel Dickondell and moved purposefully toward the piano. Was that a signal to her?

"Papa, should we leave?" she asked. "Because of the earthquake?"

"Oh, you must not," Rose said. "The countess could be ruined socially if her guests ran off after nothing more than a little earthquake."

"The family needs to make repairs."

"It can wait for another few days," her father said. "We don't want to look as if we are fleeing, and I believe you have business to transact."

"How romantic," Victoria said, feeling her mouth twist. "Really, Papa."

"Whatever do you mean?" Rose asked.

"Congratulate me, Miss Redcake. I am about to acquire a new son," her father said.

Rose turned to Victoria, her gaze somber. "Oh?"

"The baron has spoken to Papa," Victoria confirmed.

"How charming," Rose said, though not in a tone of congratulations.

Her feelings were hurt, Victoria realized. "I had better go see what he wants. The piano is our special place, you see."

"Go on," her father said jovially. "I'd wish you luck, but you don't need it."

Victoria nodded and walked through the room, feeling the stares of every inhabitant stabbing her in the back. Her cucumber sandwich had formed an uneasy knot in her stomach. At least Lewis wasn't there to witness the end of her freedom, of her passionate explorations. No, she was to become a wife again. That happiest of occasions in a woman's life, the fulfillment of all her dreams, tasted like ashes.

As she reached the piano and John stood to welcome her, she noticed he wore a fine black evening suit she'd never seen before, with a new silk necktie. His thick black hair had been slicked back and tamed. He looked younger than his twenty-seven years, and surprisingly anxious, given that he'd already proposed once and had her father's permission.

"How are ye this evening, Victoria?" He forced a smile.

"Very well, thank you. And you?" Her palms itched underneath her gloves and the skin of her arms felt very cold.

"I will know better in a moment." He cleared his throat. "I know it has been a trying day, not at all the one I might have planned for ye."

"You cannot control the earth's movement."

"No, nor the stability of structures." He smiled for a moment. "I hope ye came through your ordeal unscathed?"

She had a few bumps and bruises, but it would be unladylike to mention them. "I am happy to be so."

"Have ye given any thought to my question?"

She realized they were both still standing. As more people came into the room, the clatter of teacups against silver salvers became all but intolerable. She wondered why the cups had survived when the plates had not.

"Victoria?" He put his finger on the sliver of bare skin between her sleeve and her glove.

The skin-to-skin contact made her shiver. "I'm sorry. The air feels very close."

"Probably debris in the air from everything that fell and broke. Did ye notice the artwork in this room has changed? I believe they consolidated the paintings with unbroken frames in the most public rooms."

"I noticed the greenery is gone. I suppose it all fell down."

"The earthquake cleared away the holiday decorations a day early."

"My goodness," she murmured. "It is a lot of work to run an establishment of this size."

"I have two homes, my ancestral pile and a house outside Edinburgh. Nothing so overwhelming as this."

She forced a smile. "Then I shall have little to do with my time."

His eyebrows lifted. "Does that mean ye will say yes?"

"Yes, John." As if she had a choice. She wanted to clutch his hands, to find an anchor somehow. An engagement should feel like finding port, not sailing out into a stormy sea, but it didn't this time. It simply didn't feel right.

She glanced around, wondering if anyone had noticed their private conversation, and found herself staring right into Lewis's eyes. He had a blank expression, rather than his usual concentrated one. Had he seen John caress her wrist? She tossed her head defiantly. What if he had? They were engaged now. John was entitled to a few liberties. It was not as if anyone expected her to be a blushing virgin bride.

"May I make an announcement?" John asked.

She couldn't bear it, not with Lewis watching her. "What about waiting until the bonfire? Even though tonight is Twelfth Night, the countess delayed it a day due to the earthquake," she said. "That seems like such a romantic way to end the celebration here, and the house party."

"Of course." He grinned at her, then touched his hair self-consciously. "We'll keep our delicious secret for tonight and announce it tomorrow."

She nodded and glanced away again. Lewis had vanished. What had he seen in her face? Triumph, relief, fear? "Also, I must say I heard the champagne supplies were destroyed in the earthquake. We need to give the butler some time to find replacement bottles."

He laughed. "Very well. We wouldn't want to toast to our future with tankards of ale."

Victoria woke the next morning to find Penelope sitting up in bed, staring at her. She blinked and wiped the sleep from her eyes. "What?"

"It's January sixth," Penelope said.

"And?"

"I've always received presents today." Penelope bounced on the bed. "Do I get presents?"

Victoria yawned. "Your present is that I've agreed to marry John and you're going to live in Edinburgh with us. No boarding school."

Penelope threw her arms around her cousin, overbalancing them until they fell back on their pillows. She giggled and rested her head on Victoria's shoulder. "Thank you."

"You are very welcome."

"You'll be happy with him, won't you? Like Princess Everilda will be with Prince Hugh?"

"We don't even know how that story ends."

"Will you finish it? There isn't much left. Just two croaking ravens and saving the merman from the sea, which is obviously Prince Hugh." Penelope pulled the carved bird Eddy had made her from under her pillow and set it on her knee.

"Then you already know how the story ends. The two ravens are like your white storks, ready to make wishes come true. Of course, the princess wanted to wish for her prince to come. But the Normans were attacking and she couldn't make a selfish wish."

"No, she's a princess," Penelope agreed. "So what does she wish for?"

"That her people will be safe."

"That priest died."

"He died of shock when he saw the ships approaching shore. It wasn't in the actual attack. As the princess cradled his dying body, the two ravens settled above them on the bells. She knew they were magical creatures and begged them to hide her people from the Normans."

"Did they?"

"A thick fog swirled into the village, obscuring all the buildings. Then the earth moved, just like it did yesterday. Waves as high as the bell tower lashed at the ships and threw them off course. The Normans never landed at Everilda's castle. She ran down from the tower toward the sea, stopping on a cliff to look into the white-capped waves."

"What did she see?" Penelope asked, bouncing on the bed until her small bird tumbled to the sheet.

"A head bobbing, of course. Was it a man? Everilda saw a tail, though. What could it be? She'd heard of such things, of course, living so near the water. She ran to the secret path that went to the shore from the cliff. Few knew which of the spindly trees could hold a person's weight as they climbed down, but she knew each one, and even in the fog she was sure-footed. When she reached the shore, the merman washed in on a huge wave. Though he could have dragged her out to sea forever, she charged forward, grabbing the merman by the shoulders and pulling him to safety.

"When she had him past the rock line, she turned him over, because he had been facedown in the waves. His face was blue and his hair was made of green seaweed. A soaking-wet shirt of white lawn covered his chest, but below that a long black tail stretched down where his legs should have been, until they became a wide broom of black fin. Despite the odd coloring and frightening tail, she recognized her true love."

"It was Prince Hugh?"

"Oh, yes, under an enchantment. She had risked her life to save him from the sea's clutches. But now he was a fish. Could he even breathe on land? She knew what she had to do."

"She needed to give him a true-love kiss?" Penelope's eyes were wide.

Victoria nodded. "Exactly. She bent down, put her warm lips to his cold ones, and breathed humanity back into him. She could feel his skin warm under her mouth. Soon, he was kissing her back enthusiastically. When she lifted her head, she saw his hair had gone back to his normal blond curls and his face had lost the strange blue tinge."

"Was he wearing clothes?" Penelope put her hand to her mouth. Her cheeks were bright red.

Victoria laughed. "It didn't matter to the princess. She and the prince ran hand in hand to the village, still worried about the Normans. But when they reached the top of the cliff, they could see all was well and the ships were gone. They went to the church to kneel down and thank God that they had been spared. And who should come in? A man in a shiny, supple black cassock. It was the priest, who had been resurrected by those magical crows. He married them immediately."

"Did they ever see the evil queen again?"

"Of course they did, but that is another story." Victoria grinned at the child, quite pleased with herself.

Penelope nodded. "I guess that is a good ending, all things considered. I'm glad the priest didn't die."

"Me, too. I know it's probably just porridge for breakfast, thanks to the condition of the kitchens, but I find myself starving this morning."

"No maid came with a tray."

Victoria nodded. "Everything is still at sixes and sevens, I expect."

"I'll help you dress," Penelope said. "Even if it is only porridge, we should go down. It is our last day and I don't want to miss anything."

Victoria thought Penelope should be going to the nursery, not downstairs, but on this last day, what did it really matter?

They used what was left of the previous day's water to wash up. She glanced at her face in the mirror. Did she look any different now that she was an engaged lady again, soon to be a Scottish baroness? No. Something troubled her, though, as she stared at her dark braid. Shouldn't Prince Hugh have had black hair instead of blond curls? For her future's sake—for John's sake—she needed to banish Lewis from her every thought. She had to be honest with herself. Lewis didn't care enough to offer for her, even if Rose schemed successfully and in time to stop her wedding to John.

After breakfast, they wandered through the public rooms. Penelope chattered away about the damage they found: cracked ceilings, broken moldings, shattered vases. Victoria remembered moments where she'd spoken to one of her suitors or shared pieces of her fairy tale in every one.

When they entered the mirrored gallery, Victoria expected to find cascades of shattered glass, but instead, the miniature Versailles was completely intact. The room was in the oldest part of the Fort. Perhaps this section had been spared. She hoped the beautiful rococo ballroom had been safe from damage as well.

As they walked down the ornately decorated gallery, they heard whispers in a corner near the carved wood fireplace at the end. Victoria put a finger to her lips and turned to leave, but Penelope grabbed her hand.

"It's Uncle Rupert!"

Victoria peered into the gloom. Her father was kneeling in front of Rose. As she watched, her father took Rose's delicate fingers in his bearlike paws and kissed the tips, then spoke in a low voice. She stood, entranced, as Rose's lips trembled. Her father said something else and Rose responded; just one word it seemed, but the right one, for her father kissed Rose's fingers again, then pulled the young woman onto his lap and kissed her soundly.

Penelope hopped and started clapping. "Huzzah! Many happy returns!"

Victoria hissed, "Shhh," and grabbed for her, but the romantic spell had been broken. Both Rose and her father turned, blushing.

"I'm sorry, but Penelope is beside herself. Such a romantic proposal. I'm so pleased for you both!"

Her father lifted Rose back to her chair, a demonstration that despite his years, he still had the strength she had so admired as a child. Rose put her hands to her mouth, and Victoria could see how she trembled. Her friend must feel so much relief at finally finding a husband after years of loneliness, ill health, and despair.

She and Penelope came forward, offering congratulations.

"We could have a double wedding," Rose said, smiling.

"I'm sure you want your own special day," Victoria demurred. "My wedding will be a very restrained affair, since it is my second marriage."

Rose nodded. "Will you have a short engagement? I must say, I do not want to wait very long!"

"Until spring at least, so you can have the best flowers," Victoria said.

Rose shook her head. "It is better now."

She didn't say it, but Victoria guessed that flowers made Rose sneeze. "Then perhaps you will marry before I do."

Rose squeezed her hands. "I cannot believe I'm going to be your stepmama, and Penelope's aunt."

Penelope jumped up on the bench and gave Rose a hug. Victoria turned and hugged her father, who was uncharacteristically shy.

"Congratulations, Papa," she whispered.

The mirrors all around them reflected nothing but happy faces, but she knew what lay beneath. Why hadn't her father done this a day earlier? If Rose had a child, her own responsibilities might be less onerous. Her father might be happy enough with his new fiancée to commute Penelope's sentence to Miss Treadgold's Academy. And Victoria might have had Lewis instead of John.

It was too late now. She had said yes. The weddings would proceed. She would be happy. That would be the best revenge on the Fates.

CHAPTER 19

The earl had decided to hold the delayed bonfire near the site of the destroyed stable in order to easily burn some of the unusable wood. The enormous fire lit up the lake and the ruins, bathing the ancient stone structure in light and smoke.

Lewis held a cup of hot spiced punch and ignored the crowd gathered together for the last night of the house party. Twelfth Night had been the night before, but the festivities had been all but obliterated by the earthquake. Now the wine, punch, and spirits flowed freely and everyone was in the mood to celebrate. The temperature had warmed to something approaching normal. Many of the guests had even abandoned their extra layers of clothing and mufflers and shawls, despite the cloying damp.

The air had a putrid scent, partially from the paint that was burning on the coated wood but also from the muck at the bottom of the lake, which had been churned up by the earth's movement. Who knew what else had been there, along with the ruins of the putative church? He wondered if the lake had once been an inlet connected to the sea. Had the church been on an island?

This house party seemed to have been adrift in legend and folklore from the first, between the stories the workmen told during the long days in the stable, Victoria's fairy tale, and Rose's legends. And meeting Victoria herself. He'd never thought he, Lewis Noble, would be an aristocrat's lover. This Christmas season had been a dream, and never more so than now, when he regarded his lover bathed by the flickering bonfire, next to another man.

He watched with a curious sense of detachment as the earl called the assembled guests to attention with a small gong and announced the arrival of champagne.

Footmen wandered through the crowd with trays of the beverage served in an assortment of containers. Flutes, wineglasses, even teacups—whatever they had undamaged in the Fort—until everyone had champagne.

Then the Baron of Alix announced his engagement to Lady Allen-Hill. Lewis heard Victoria's name with a sense of unreality, as if it was part of a tale and not his actual life. He understood her reasons. After all, he had given her nothing and her father had made his position clear. So the lady wasn't strong enough to fight Rupert Courtnay. He hadn't wanted to spend the next twenty years or so battling him either, so he understood.

But then he lost all comprehension of her action. Rupert Courtnay himself took a position in front of the leaping flames and, instead of restating the baron's words, announced his own engagement. Cousin Rose came to stand with him, blushing furiously as the guests pressed forward, offering congratulations to the foursome.

The countess laughed and held her son's arm when the local vicar made a joke about this being the most successful house party in the history of house parties and that he hoped to have the honor of marrying every one of the newly engaged couples. Bullen merely looked bored.

Lewis turned away, his ears tuning the noise down to nothing but the furious buzzing of bees. Victoria had accepted the baron when she might have been released from her father's demands. Why hadn't she waited to marry, at least for a year or two? Rose might not be strong, but she was young. They would know soon enough if she could bear a child.

Betrayal. Victoria had betrayed what they had felt for each other. If she could have slipped out from under her father's thumb, they could have been together.

He turned away from the festivities in disgust. A footman had left a tray on a tree stump and he placed his teacup of champagne there, untouched. The cup of punch, however, he drained in one long gulp; then he went to the refreshed bowl of steaming brew and ladled more into his cup. He had no need to stay sober in anticipation of pleasing a lover tonight.

He had resolved to take a long walk in the firelight, just him and his punch, when Penelope skipped up to him. Her light step indicated a different girl than the moody nine-year-old of days gone by.

"Why are you so happy?" he growled when she stopped in front of him.

She did a little dance. "I'm to live with Victoria forever."

"How is that any different than before?"

Her eyes grew wide. "My uncle was going to send me to Manchester, to a dreadful school where the students often die, it is said."

He snorted. "I don't believe you."

"It's true. One of the maids said she overheard Uncle Rupert telling Victoria that if she didn't become engaged by today, I was going to the school. That's not exactly what Victoria told me, of course, but I don't think the maid was lying."

What could have prompted Courtnay to be so cruel? Lewis squeezed the handle of his cup until it broke in his hand. The bowl of the cup fell, his steaming punch swallowed by the thirsty earth.

Surely the man knew he was about to propose; why put his daughter in such a position? It defied logic. But he had done it, and the baron had announced the engagement, and either way, Lewis's happiness had been destroyed. Rupert Courtnay now had himself another titled son-in-law.

At least he now understood why Victoria had made her decision, and this knowledge made him even more certain that he had done the right thing in refusing her. Being under Rupert Courtnay's thumb would be intolerable.

"I need another cup," he muttered and stalked back toward the punch bowl. Penelope's mouth dropped open. Surely she didn't think he was going to congratulate her on her good fortune? He was happy she was spared the apparently dreadful school, but he'd lost something precious in the bargain. Enough lovers littered his past for him to know how rare Victoria's passion had been, how sweet. Even if he hadn't fallen in love with her.

If he even had. How could he love her when he'd never stopped loving Alys? Either way, his love seemed doomed to only bring him unhappiness.

He heard a sniff behind him and turned to see Penelope, her good mood quite gone, sniffling back tears. Swearing to himself, he moved back to her just as she bent to pick up his broken cup.

"Don't touch that; you'll cut yourself," he barked. He took her arm to pull her away from the shards.

A footman rushed up and cleared the mess away with an apology.

"I didn't want someone to step in it." The girl sniffled again.

"It isn't your problem," Lewis said.

"Have you been to Edinburgh?" she asked tremulously. "Is it nice?"

"I believe it is rainy."

"And everyone talks with a different accent. What if I don't understand them?" Penelope's voice rose, and Lewis was suddenly chilled with the knowledge that she was going to fly into one of her rages.

He glanced toward the bonfire, toward Victoria, who could calm the girl like no one else. Penelope broke into loud, ringing sobs and tucked her eyes into her sleeve. At least they seemed desperately loud to him, but no one in the crowd around the bonfire even looked away. He patted Penelope's shoulder, trying to soothe her.

"Come, Penelope. Change is always hard, but it isn't as if you aren't far better off than you might have been. You need to look forward with hope, not fear."

She rubbed her nose and did a nervous jig. "What if she has a baby and forgets about me? She might send me to the school after all."

"I'm sure she wouldn't send you to that school," Lewis said. "Don't waste your time worrying about the distant future. Just think about now. A jolly time planning weddings, then moving to an exciting new city. New friends, new adventures."

"Why didn't you propose to my cousin? I thought you liked her." Penelope's tears stopped and she looked at him sharply.

Too sharply for a nine-year-old. What had she seen? They had never been as careful as they should have been. "I wasn't for her, Penelope. It's as simple as that."

"Do you like the baron?"

"I do. He's a good man. He will treat your cousin well."

She frowned. "I'd rather it was you."

He wanted to tell her that he felt the same way, but that would have been childish, and he was anything but a child. "Your uncle is marrying my cousin, so I'm sure we'll see each other again someday. Until then, I wish you the very best."

She stared at him, her lower lip pursed into a pout.

"Give me your hand," he said.

She held one tiny mittened hand out to him and he took it in his own, then kissed the back of it. "Fare-thee-well, Miss Courtnay, and happy travels. You are a strong girl and you are going to be fine." He smiled at her, then added, "Go back to your family now."

She turned away obediently. The momentary urge to get very drunk had passed. Instead, Lewis decided to pack. He was leaving very early the next morning, well before breakfast. It was best to be gone before anyone else was awake. He didn't want to see Victoria again.

It seemed they were the last to leave the next afternoon. All the horses had been engaged in transporting the house party to various way stations, homes, and train stations in the area, and they had managed to be just a little too behind to catch any of them.

When Victoria entered a sitting room to wait for a footman to appear with news that a carriage was available, she was surprised to find John sitting near the fire with a letter. Having not seen him at all that morning, she'd thought he had already departed. Which would have been odd, of course, now that she had time to reflect. Although Rose had returned to Redcake Manor, her family seat, for the time being. But she was planning a trip to London soon to purchase her trousseau, and they had made plans to shop together. Her father was in the library, discussing something with the earl, who was leaving for London in a couple of days, after he'd helped his mother order the rest of the repairs that were needed at the Fort.

"You look very serious," she said to John as she unraveled her muffler.

"It's just luck that this letter reached me," he said. "I had thought we'd be gone by now."

"I couldn't find my favorite boots. The boot boy had left them somewhere. The entire day has gone like that."

"Ah." His eyes flashed back to the paper.

"We're just waiting for a carriage now."

He nodded, not looking up. "Ye will not mind if I stay here until tomorrow?"

She tilted her head. Something about his demeanor had changed since the previous night. She tried to peek at the letter, but by accident or design, he had his hand over the majority of the writing. Still, she thought it was female handwriting. "Of course not, John. If you have business . . ." Her voice trailed off, and she hoped he would explain.

He scratched his chin. "Thank ye, my dear. Your father will be going with ye, so ye ladies will not have tae travel alone."

"We would be fine alone. We came down here ourselves. Though Rose was with us, but that was a mere accident."

He nodded again, even more absently. A footman poked his head into the doorway.

"The carriage is here, Lady Allen-Hill."

Victoria wondered how long it would be until she was referred to as Baroness Alix. Or if it would even happen, given John's sudden change in behavior. However, the engagement had been announced, and if he cried off, there would be a scandal, at least in this corner of Sussex.

"Well." She forced a smile. "We will see you in London in a few days."

"Of course, my dear." John stood and kissed her cheek, a dutiful peck that felt as dry as sawdust.

She sighed. "Good-bye for now." She followed the footman out the door, leaving John to his letter.

Lewis left the Fort on horseback, a mode of transportation that had become highly unusual for him. Eddy, a former London newsboy, had ridden even less, but he exulted in the experience, riding his horse so recklessly that Lewis was afraid the lad would provoke his horse into rearing.

He urged his horse into a canter and flew down the muddy lane after the boy. Eddy crowed that reckless laugh of youth, and Lewis, getting into the spirit of things, whooped as they raced. It felt good to have the wind in his face and blowing in his ears. For a time, all through their ride to Heathfield, he didn't have a care in the world. He could have been a boy again, back before his parents died, when his Grandmother Noble still lived in the country and kept horses. How long ago it had been, and how thoroughly everything had changed.

They did manage to make Hatbrook Farm in one piece. By the time Lewis left his horse at the stable, he was quite sober again: the inventor, the thinker, the loner. He sent Eddy on ahead, wanting to take a quick look around to make sure the earthquake hadn't done any damage to his tool shed on the property.

He had agreed to take dinner with the Shield family before going to Battersea in the morning. The marquess had some business to discuss with him regarding improvements to his winery. After Lewis checked his equipment, he drove the marquess's horseless carriage to the vineyard outbuildings and acquainted himself with the layout, so that Hatbrook wouldn't have to explain the basics. He spent an hour with the manager, grateful he'd cleared his head with the ride so that he could focus on business and put Victoria behind him.

By the time he'd driven back to the carriage house, he felt his usual self. Lewis Noble, inventor and satellite member of the Marquess of Hatbrook's family, had returned. He'd left his dream world behind along with Christmas.

Lewis changed in the room Hatbrook had told him to call his own, feeling melancholy. He left off the frivolous waistcoats and ties in the tartans, rubies, and greens of the holiday season and dressed soberly in black. Why had he even packed such items when he'd gone to the Fort mostly to work? He supposed he'd felt some need to get use out of the clothing, handmade gifts from his cousins the year before.

Until he had left the Fort today, there had been a slight sensation of magic buzzing in the back of his brain, some sense of life not being lived quite normally. It had begun on the side of the road, when he had seen Victoria before Christmas, and had stayed ever since. Would he forget her now, in an effortless fashion born of lack of proximity? Could he throw himself back into his inventions, his over-abundance of work? He had his horseless carriage business, the sub-marine, the winery project. Work was always available with the Redcake factories and bakeries. He had no time to ruminate over the lover he'd lost to the Baron of Alix.

No doubt his thoughts would drift back into their usual channels, the occasional melancholy thought of Alys, lost to him forever, fol-lowed by a gradual increase in sexual thoughts, which would be laid to rest by some casual encounter among his acquaintances, usually some widow as lonely as he.

Eddy came in without knocking, his hair dripping, smelling of soap. "I like the smell of oil better than horse," he complained, wrin-kling his nose.

"We'll drive up to London tomorrow. No need to ride again. I want to check the gears on Hatbrook's new vehicle."

"It's ready?"

"It will be. I'm going to work on it tonight. I drove it today for a while and pinpointed what wasn't operating properly." Lewis knotted his tie and peered at himself in the mirror. Should he have bathed, too? He didn't smell of horse, but then, he'd learned to block odors, working in the conditions he did. He checked his watch and undid his tie. Coming to Alys's table smelling of horse would not be a good start to this brief visit.

An hour later, he was bathed and redressed. Downstairs in the drawing room, the resident adult family members had assembled. When he arrived in the doorway, he steadied himself, awaiting the usual heart pangs that occurred whenever he saw Alys for the first time after a few days. When he didn't spot her, he wandered through the drawing room, accepting a glass of port from a footman and say-ing hello to Hatbrook's Aunt Mary, who had never married after her fiancé died and still lived in the same rooms she had inhabited all her life.

She wore a curious, old-fashioned cap with a black ribbon that was intricately folded and pinned just above the lacy edging. The folds reminded him of the wings of the birds that so fascinated Penelope, and he thought of Eddy's suggestion that he use a bird design project to work on the submarine's outer casing. While he'd designed bird automatons in the past, he'd never thought much about the reason birds had feathers.

"Do you know much about birds, Aunt Mary?"

"I'm no scientist, boy," the old lady said with a grimace, exposing her aged teeth.

"I was wondering how they stay dry."

"And you a scientist? They rub oil over their feathers, you see, something they make with their own bodies. Even I know that." Her gaze sharpened. "Hatbrook has some books somewhere. His grandfather fancied himself a naturalist."

A woman in his peripheral vision turned, and he realized with a jolt that it was Alys. She'd been standing not two feet from him all along, and he hadn't even noticed her. No heart pangs, not even recognition. What was wrong with him?

Aunt Mary caught his startled expression and smirked. "Just cannot find a way to move on, can you, Lewis? Don't be like me, with your heart forever promised to someone who doesn't want it."

"I'd always heard you told your fiancé on his deathbed you'd never marry."

She shrugged, "As if he would care once he'd gone to heaven. But back then, you know, so many men had died in the wars. I never met another man worth having."

He knew that wasn't the case for him. He had indeed met another woman worth having. Her father had been what stopped him, not her. "You know?" he said. "I have moved on. I even think I fell in love. It wasn't meant to be, but I did feel something new."

"Then why did you stare at Alys?"

He patted her arm. "Because it didn't hurt, and that surprised me."

She nodded slowly. "Who is the lucky lady? I understand Alys's sister Rose has found a husband at last. Are you engaged? I don't hear too well anymore, unless the speaker is close to me. I might have missed the news."

"No, I'm not engaged. Her father wants her to marry someone he can groom to run his businesses, and I'm not about to do that."

"Ah, the lady isn't worth it? That's a paltry love. You spend a few hours a day with the father, then your nights with the lady." She smiled again. "Her charms must not be excessive."

He remembered those lush, generous curves, her thighs spread wide to receive him, the way her mouth felt against his. "Her charms are . . . well, everything."

"Clearly they are not," Lady Mary enunciated, "or the father would not trouble you."

"Perhaps you are correct. I have been unhappy for so long, I don't know how to permit myself to indulge in happiness."

"At least you have time to remedy things."

He grimaced. "No. She accepted another proposal of marriage."

Lady Mary lifted her scant eyebrows. "That is a pity, but if she is still unwed, you might be able to persuade her."

"That wouldn't be honorable." He drained his glass, wishing the port had been something stronger.

"Honor versus happiness," she mused. "At least you have your work. That is a consolation."

"It does keep me busy." But his thoughts went to that sad little girl, and what Victoria had sacrificed to keep her out of that horrible school. Could he not sacrifice his time to build her a bird? "Do you have any feathers, Lady Mary? I'd like to take a look at some."

"I know my great-niece left headdresses here," she said. "There were feathers in some of them. Her rooms are vacant."

Lady Elizabeth had no need for headdresses now, since she had married the Baron of Alix's younger brother, a man with an actual career as a private inquiry agent, and had gone to live in Edinburgh. How odd to think of his Victoria as a close family connection to Alys. Lady Elizabeth was Alys's sister-in-law, and now she would be Victoria's as well.

The thought made his stomach turn. The port sloshed around. "I believe I will forgo dinner and have a look at those feathers."

"Why?"

He shook his head. "It is the final commission the lady I lost asked of me, one I turned down. But out of love, I should make a bird for her cousin, don't you think? It is the only thing she asked of me. And she gave me everything."

Lady Mary narrowed her eyes. "I thought you were to spend the evening in conference with Hatbrook, discussing winery issues."

"He will wait." Lewis patted her arm. "Make my apologies, will you? I'm going to steal the feathers and then spend the evening in my toolshed."

"Inventors." Lady Mary sighed. "Go on, boy. I will make your apologies, if you promise me this."

"What?"

"That you deliver this bird you are going to make in person, to the lady you lost. Give her a chance to see you. If she loves you, not the other man, you owe her that."

"I'm still not willing to marry her and take on the position of her father's apprentice," he countered.

"Ruminate on what the lady is worth to you while you make the bird," she said. "If you think this was a mere passing affair, then move on to the next lady. But if you see her and still feel that sweet pain in your heart, then pray reconsider, for the sake of all my long, lonely years."

He stared at the lined face, the look of sorrow in her gaze, and knew that someday Alys and Rose's children might look at him with that sensation of pity for the loneliness of his life. "At least we had love."

"You don't have to lose it." She patted his arm. "Think hard, Lewis."

He nodded. "Thank you, Lady Mary. You have been a great help."

Without a backward glance at Alys—or, indeed, any of her happy family circle—he went up the stairs and found the abandoned rooms of the former Lady Elizabeth Shield, now Beth Alexander. A small dressing room was behind one of the doors in the bedroom. Still stuffed with clothing, the wardrobes daunted him at first, but he found an array of plumage poking out of an old Chinese vase to the side of the wardrobe containing woolens. He blew dust off the feathers and examined them closely, not sure what such inanimate objects could tell him that he didn't already know. But he wanted the bird to be as perfect as possible. It would be the last one he'd ever make.

After a few minutes, he took the feathers and went to the first floor of the Farm, where the library was located, and looked for the section on natural history. Soon, he was ensconced in an armchair, reading about feathers. Since he would need a microscope to see some of the features described, in this case a book was of more value than a feather itself. He read about the shingling effect of feathers, and about the tiny barbs that helped keep feathers together. Also inspiring was the idea of a shaft down the middle with more flexible material on the outside. When he'd exhausted the information about feathers, he found a watercolor reproduction of a white stork in one of the books and tucked it under his arm.

While Penelope might care more about appearance than function, he might as well work to both their benefits. He knew he wouldn't sleep tonight, but in the end, when he handed Penelope the bird, he wanted to be able to make peace with the fact that he'd lost his Victoria. He didn't want to spend the next three years mourning her, as he had Alys.

CHAPTER 20

It took Lewis a solid twenty-four hours to complete the white stork for Penelope, even with Eddy's help. By Wednesday evening, dazed with exhaustion, he didn't argue when Eddy insisted he go to bed. The next morning, when he checked in his shed, the paint had dried on the nonmetallic parts of the bird and it looked ready for delivery.

Dressed in a warm but scratchy wool suit against the cold, he regarded the bird critically. What would a little girl find to love about the thing? He had captured the delicacy of the stork, the beautiful neck and slender orange-red beak and legs. Would it give her hope as she settled into her new life in Edinburgh?

"I wonder if I should make another one and give it to Lady Allen-Hill as a wedding present."

"That seems exceedingly foolish to me," said a voice behind him.

Lewis glanced over his shoulder. He didn't need to see the man to recognize Hatbrook's voice, however. "Why?"

"Talk her out of the engagement," Hatbrook advised, folding his arms over his broad chest as he leaned against the inner door.

Lewis turned. What did Hatbrook know of his business? "Why do you say that?"

"Aunt Mary gave me an earful." A smile crinkled the corners of

Hatbrook's eyes. "Your Twelve Nights of Christmas were eventful, it sounds like. Either that or she'd dipped deep into the sherry."

To think he assumed he could trust an old woman with his secrets. More fool he. "I didn't think of her as a gossip."

Hatbrook grinned and rubbed the back of his neck. "The old girl continually surprises me. What if you gave the lady a child, Lewis, have you thought of that? Do you want the baron raising your offspring?"

"He might not go through with it." Lewis smiled.

"I know Lady Allen-Hill only slightly, and I'd hate to think she'd take the man to bed just to make sure he wouldn't be critical of her child's birth date, but it's something you have to consider. For a man of science, you are surprisingly obtuse at times."

"What do you suggest I do? Follow her to London and skulk around her house until I can bribe her maid into telling me if she's had her courses?"

Hatbrook tilted his head. "I'd be direct with the lady, but of course she might lie. You need to tell her she has no business getting engaged until she knows if she's carrying your child."

"It's too late for that," Lewis protested.

"As long as the engagement hasn't been reported in the London papers, there is still time. The only ones who've heard about the engagement are a few people at an obscure house party."

"The Earl of Bullen's house party," Lewis said. "That's hardly obscure."

"I'm throwing you a bone, Lewis. Grasp it. Pack up that damnable bird you made and get yourself to London before it's too late." Hatbrook picked up a screwdriver and tossed it into an open drawer.

"She did it for her young cousin, you know. I wouldn't marry her, and Courtnay threatened to send the child away to school if she didn't find a fiancé in something like forty-eight hours." Lewis put his favorite wrench into his traveling tool kit.

"Then make sure the child is in your pocket," Hatbrook said. "Use her."

"I don't want to live under Courtnay's thumb. I had enough of that with Sir Bartley." He gritted his teeth as he put the rest of his wrenches into another drawer. Unfortunate that the man would use a child as his pawn. He would not suffer similarly.

"Be a man. Refuse. Once you've married the lady, you can do what you want. Obeying Courtnay isn't exactly part of your marriage vows." Hatbrook tossed paint-spotted rags into a refuse barrel.

"He might take Penelope away." Lewis stared at the bird again.

Hatbrook shrugged. "I don't see the problem. You have lawyers. Make sure you have legal guardianship of the child before you make your refusal to go to Liverpool obvious."

"I don't think legal guardianship is on offer," Lewis said. "She has parents; they are just a combination of unwilling and inept."

Hatbrook hung two hammers on the pegboard. "Speak to Rose. She can work on Courtnay. She's marrying the man, after all."

"I expect you'll be happy to see her gone north," Lewis said, remembering the old anger Hatbrook had against Rose for gossiping about Alys's premarital lovemaking.

"Not especially. She's matured. One of those rare people who learn a lesson and change for the better. Unlike her sister Matilda." Hatbrook shook his head as he wiped the worktable clean of metal shavings, then tossed that rag into the barrel.

Lewis grinned. The man kept a tidy property. "Now there is a beacon for misadventure." He glanced at the bird, which seemed to be staring at him critically. "Some minor adjustments to the face, I think. It doesn't look peaceful enough to give to a child."

"Do something about the eyes," Hatbrook said. "But don't tarry too long. Once the announcement hits the papers, you're sunk."

Lewis opened a paint can and found a clean brush. "I have to hope they are too busy settling back in after a long trip away to have managed it."

"I'd have said that I hoped she was regretting her decision to marry the baron, myself."

"That too, but she'll make the best of it, for Penelope's sake. Besides, I don't want Victoria to be unhappy. That would be a cruel wish to have for the woman I love." He dipped his brush into the white paint.

Hatbrook's smile faded. "That is true." He held out his hand.

Surprised, Lewis lifted his grimy hand to Hatbrook's and the men shook.

"I'm glad you've moved on," Hatbrook said in a low voice, wincing as he said the words.

At that moment, Lewis realized that Hatbrook had known of the torch he'd carried for Alys all these years. "I have been difficult to be around, haven't I?" he said.

Hatbrook's eyes rose to the heavens for a moment before returning to him. "We wish you all the best. Fix that bird's gaze and send it home."

"Yes." Lewis regarded the bird again. "As swiftly as possible."

Lewis called at Rupert Courtnay's London mansion on Friday afternoon and asked to see Penelope. The footman who answered the door looked askance at the large, sheet-wrapped bundle under his arm, not to mention the fact that he'd asked for a child, but allowed him in after he'd presented his card.

Lewis had waited an extra day in Heathfield, allowing the bird time to dry while he caught up on his sleep. Every dream he'd had was of Victoria: their past, their unlikely future. The staff had done their best to remove the paint and metal shavings from his attire. He'd been so enthusiastic about his project that he hadn't changed into work clothing when he'd started on the bird, who he had nicknamed Welly, since he'd come into their lives at the destroyed wishing well. The suit he'd worn when he started the project would never be the same again, and his most sober waistcoat had been ruined, so he was back in an unfortunate green and ruby tartan today. It was either that or wait another day to visit so he could return home and retrieve more clothing. But he knew that would cause him distraction on any number of fronts, and every day he delayed was another day Victoria or the baron, or Rupert Courtnay, could write an engagement notice for the papers.

When he was shown into a small sitting room, he unwrapped Welly, concerned that the paint might have smudged, but the white stork looked fine, kindly even, after all the work Lewis had done to perfect his face. Eddy had helped resculpt the eye sockets as well, which added to the bird's appeal. The boy might have had a future as an artist if he wasn't so mechanically minded. Lewis rewrapped the bird and pulled a red ribbon from his pocket. He tied a bow around the neck to make his offering more festive. When he was done, he stepped back and regarded it. The bird was still a cloth-covered lump with a sloppy bow around its neck, but at least it appeared he was trying.

After five minutes, a maid opened the door and Penelope ran in, followed, as he had hoped, by Victoria. Penelope's white dress was smudged at the hem, possibly from kneeling too close to a fireplace, but Victoria looked slim, cool, and perfect in lavender silk. Her dark hair was coiled into an elaborate coif, making her appear even more remote, like a woman ready to be immortalized in oil. Her gray eyes regarded him expectantly, though she said nothing.

The moment he'd seen her, his palms started to tingle, dampen. His collar felt too tight and the fire must have been freshly fed with coal because it felt like a firing kiln in the room. Sweat broke out at the small of his back. He checked the door behind her, wondering if Courtnay would arrive, too, but thankfully no one else entered. And there were no other afternoon callers, at least not in this room. Perhaps the family wasn't officially at home yet. Or were merely stopping for a few days before returning to Liverpool.

Why was no one speaking? His throat felt tight. He desperately wished for a tea tray, but nothing had been offered yet. He attempted to squeeze out a few words. "I am glad to see you looking so well. I never said good-bye in Pevensey."

"Why wouldn't we look well?" Victoria asked.

"Yes, of course. Such a happy time for you," Lewis managed. Didn't she regret how things had ended at all? "Is the baron here?"

"He hasn't left the Fort yet, as far as I know. I thought you had come asking for Penelope, not John."

Had her hands, already clasped together, twisted very slightly? How still she was, the imaginative, impulsive young lady he knew turned into this cool goddess. Something had gone wrong with the baron; he just knew it. She was holding herself in check, as if in fear of pain.

Penelope took his hand, forcing his attention to her. "It is lovely to see you again, Mr. Noble."

He grinned at her, his tension dissolving at her artless greeting.

"So formal, Miss Courtnay? And here I thought we had become friends when you tended me after I nearly drowned."

She nodded happily. "I thought so, too."

"Then you must think of me as Lewis, even if we don't see each other very often anymore."

Her forehead creased, as if she didn't quite understand.

"I brought you a present," he told her.

"A present? It's not my birthday," the girl said.

"I know, but it's sort of a memory, from the wishing well. I thought you might like it."

Victoria's chin went up. Her gaze went to his. They shared a long moment of silent communication. He could almost hear her question, her silent *well done*. Nodding slightly, he took the child's hand and walked her to the table in between two chairs, where he'd set his creation.

Penelope tilted her head, regarding the ribbon intently as Victoria moved behind her. "It's rather a large present. I find large presents are the best. They are often toys."

"What is the best gift you've ever received?" he asked.

She clapped her hands together. "A dollhouse. From Cousin Victoria and Uncle Rupert, three years ago. I played with it for hours and hours. I'm too grown-up now, of course."

"You can use it to practice your decorating and sewing skills," Victoria said. "There are plenty of uses for a dollhouse."

Penelope wrinkled her nose. "I want to see the new toy."

Lewis cleared his throat. "It's not exactly a toy. More of a friend."

"If it was a pet, I'm sure it would have moved by now," she said.

"Perhaps it is stuffed," Victoria suggested.

Lewis shook his head. "Unwrap it, Penelope. Eddy and I made our best effort for you."

"Eddy worked on it?" Penelope smiled as she gently untied the ribbon, then wrapped it around her wrist and held it up to Victoria so she could tie a bow. "There, now I'm a present, too."

Victoria ruffled her hair. "Must you make such a ceremony of the unwrapping? I want to see what's inside."

Lewis held back his grin. Victoria was an impatient woman, always.

Penelope gently unwrapped the top of the sheet, gasping as the face of the bird was revealed. Her hands moved faster, unraveling the linen, until the white stork stood exposed.

Lewis had sculpted, with Eddy's help, the head from wood. The feathers were all metal, though, cut and painted to look like the real thing. "The beast's balance is imperfect," he warned. "You'll need to be gentle."

"Is it an automaton?" Victoria asked.

He'd wanted a different reaction from her than this temperate question. "No. I didn't want to take the time. It would have delayed the delivery, and I didn't know how long you would be in London."

"She's beautiful," Penelope breathed, touching a feather.

"Be careful; they are probably sharp," Victoria warned.

"It's not a toy," Lewis agreed. "But a friendly art piece."

"I love her," Penelope said. "Can't I hug her, just a little?"

She turned to Victoria, who nodded. When Penelope put her arms gently around the bird and touched her cheek to the side of its beak, Victoria turned to him.

He wanted to see her smile. She made his soul levitate when she looked at him with laughter in her eyes. He stepped closer and she drew away from Penelope, who had started whispering to the bird.

Victoria put her index finger on his chin, her thumb just beneath. Her fingers were cold, her gaze remote. Almost close enough for a kiss, she blew out a breath instead of pulling his mouth toward her. Her mouth against his would be perfection, but he needed her smiles even more, especially now. He waited, staring down at her, a captive to her touch, wondering what she might do next.

"Why have you come?" she asked, any hint of a polite social smile disappearing.

She didn't release him. Her fingers stroked fluidly along his jaw as he spoke, reminding him of the way she moved with him when they made love. "To bring the bird, of course. You did ask me more than once to make it."

Her fingers tightened slightly, denting his skin. "You did a lot of work to please a little girl who is no connection to you. Work you'd refused."

He put his hand on her face, tracing her left cheekbone. His fingers tingled and he wondered if she felt the same bond with him still. "I needed to show you that I understood. If you could sacrifice yourself to marriage to protect her, I could unbend enough to make her the bird you said would help her cope."

Before Victoria could respond, Penelope lifted the bird, holding the ungainly creature just under the wings. "I want to show it to Nanny." She didn't look at them, so engrossed was she in the bird.

"Be very careful going up the stairs," Victoria said, dropping her fingers from his face.

His jaw felt cold and she turned her head so that his fingers fell away from her, too. He wondered if she'd ever allow him to touch her again.

Penelope nodded happily and carried the bird out of the room.

"Thank you," Victoria said, turning back to him. "She is pleased. I hope she remembers the feeling she had at the wishing well every time she looks at it."

"I'm sorry it isn't an automaton, but there wasn't time."

"It might have frightened her if it was." Her hand went to the nape of her neck, as if she was testing her coiffure for a stray pin. "I'll expect your invoice."

What was she thinking? How was he going to turn this goddess back into a flesh-and-blood woman? He needed a strategy. Perhaps all he could do, now that it was all but too late, was be honest.

He went to the door that Penelope had just walked through and turned the lock. Her fingers bent at the sound, and when she pulled her hand away, pins clattered to the floor and a thick ringlet slithered along her neck and curled around the neckline of her dress.

He smiled. The goddess transformed.

"There is no charge. You know, it took losing you for me to realize I loved you." He watched as a hint of color came into her cheeks. "I wish I had understood that as soon as you knew you loved me."

She inhaled so sharply that he could hear the squeak of her breath when he knelt at her feet. He picked up a pin and she reached for it, but instead, he poked one end into her palm and slid it up her wrist until it touched the lacy sleeve of her dress.

"I can't breathe," she whispered.

Slowly, he ran the pin along her inner arm. So close he could feel her breath on his hair, he stood back up, her breath moving down his temple, to his cheek, to his throat. The pin rested at the tip of her arm socket. He moved it across her shoulder as she shuddered, then up her neck, and rested it finally on the slight indentation in the center of her plump lower lip. "You still want me, and I'm not going to let another man take what's mine."

"I've agreed to marry him."

"I don't care." He took the loose ringlet in between his fingers and curled it around his hand until her chin was forced up and her face was only an inch from his. "You gave yourself to me. You can't take yourself back."

"I didn't want to." She swallowed, her gaze intent on his. "You threw my love away."

"I didn't know I wanted it." He pressed his lips together and blinked hard. He couldn't lose her again.

Her eyes glistened. "I don't think John wants me either. He received a letter. I think there is someone else. A mistress? A fiancée? I don't know."

"You should be both to me. Forget him," Lewis said, tightening his grip on her curl until her lips rested on the corner of his mouth. "He's not relevant. Only me. We're done with this mess, done with your father dictating your future or mine."

"We're done?" she whispered.

"Yes. You are of age and I can afford to support you. We'll live on our own terms. Your father isn't really going to send Penelope somewhere as dreadful as that school. I don't believe it, but we'll go to her father if necessary."

"I can't just walk away from my engagement. John has expectations. It's been announced."

She said the words, but her tone was hopeful. "It was a mistake. If he is having second thoughts as well, he'll be grateful to you for backing out. No notice has gone to the papers, correct?"

"No, I insisted we wait until he arrived in London." She smiled tentatively.

Lewis spotted a writing table against the wall and pointed to it. "Sit down, Victoria."

She took the pin from his hand and opened it.

"No, leave the curl down. You'll start a new fashion."

She shook her head ruefully and went to the table, seating herself in the straight-backed chair. "Who am I writing to?"

"The baron, of course. Terminate the engagement, or at least tell him you need to see him right away."

She looked at him, humor in her gaze. "Why don't I use the telephone? They have one at the Fort. You of all people should think to use the latest inventions."

"A letter is more permanent," he said.

"But a telephone call would be faster."

He could not help but be pleased by her eagerness. "Where is the instrument?"

"In the butler's pantry. I will see if I can make the call." She stood so quickly that the chair rocked. He grabbed the back to keep it from falling over.

When he moved to follow her, she put up her hand. "I need to have this conversation privately. I owe him that much."

"Very well." He watched her walk out the door, then said, "Stop."

"What?"

He pushed her gently against the back of the door, then knelt at her feet.

"What?" she whispered again.

"Marry me."

She set both hands on his head. "I would love to."

They stared at each other, and he knew they shared the same sense of unreality, the same feeling that Christmas had returned to their hearts.

When she was gone, he stood against the fireplace, his arms crossed over his chest, head bowed, praying that the baron would not have some weapon of argument that won her back.

A few minutes later, the door opened. He looked up, assuming her attempt to make the call had failed, but it was Penelope.

She grinned at him. "Nanny likes the bird."

He forced himself to focus on the girl. "His name is Welly. Did I tell you that?"

"Wishy," she corrected. "I named him Wishy."

"Very well." He pushed his hands into his pockets. "Listen, Penelope, I've asked your Cousin Victoria to marry me."

"But she is marrying the baron."

"I've asked her to reconsider," he stated. "Are you willing to live with me in Battersea instead of in Edinburgh?"

Penelope considered. "Doesn't Eddy live with you?"

"Not in my house. He has a room on the property, however, above the machine shop, and takes his meals with me. Very independent-minded, that lad." Now he was collecting another stray child.

"Will you marry soon, so I don't have to go away to school?"

"As soon as I can manage," he said. "I promise."

She nodded slowly. "You are nice enough, but you do silly things. Will you promise to be more careful in the future and not attempt to drown yourself?"

He chuckled at the prim cast of her mouth. "I promise. Your cousin would have my head if I did something so stupid again. After all, she's already lost one husband. It wouldn't do to repeat the experience."

"No, it certainly would not," Penelope said, sounding much older than nine. "We are agreed, then."

He held out his hand and she gave it a small, businesslike shake. Then, she tossed her head and flew into his arms, her head pushing into his chest as she flung her arms around his midsection. He dug his heels into the carpet to keep from falling back a few steps as her weight collided with his.

The door opened again and Victoria stood in the doorway, wiping at the corner of her eye with a finger. He lifted an inquiring eye at her, and she nodded.

"It's over. I told him I'd made a mistake, and he said he had, too." She blinked.

The room seemed to warm again as he gestured at her. She lifted her skirts and ran to him, a smile breaking out across her lovely face. Colliding into his side, she wrapped one arm around him and the other around Penelope, then tucked her face against his collarbone.

"I've been alone a long time," he said, squeezing her tighter with his free arm. "But no more. We'll be married as soon as we can, so soon that we'll be a scandal, but no one will mind when they see how in love we are."

"Exactly." She tilted her face up to meet his. "We'll make them all understand that this is the way it is meant to be."

"I love you, Victoria, my Christmas angel." He took her chin in his hand just as she had done to him, but his fingers were warm, and her mouth under his was as fiery as pepper when he kissed her. His goddess resolved into a human woman again. "My wife."

By the time he lifted his head, Penelope had long since vanished. Victoria took his hand in both of hers, her flesh blood-warm now, and tugged slightly.

"Come upstairs," she whispered. "I have an engagement gift for you."

He knew what she meant by the hot look in her eyes alone. They had both made the right decision in the end, and as he followed her out of the room, her ringlet bouncing against her shoulder, he crunched hairpins under his boot heel without even noticing.

About the Author

Heather Hiestand was born in Illinois, but her family migrated west before she started school. Since then she has claimed Washington State as home, except for a few years in California. She wrote her first story at age seven and went on to major in creative writing at the University of Washington. Her first published fiction was a mystery short story, but since then it has been all about the many flavors of romance. Heather's first published romance short story was set in the Victorian period and she continues to return, fascinated by the rapid changes of the nineteenth century. The author of many novels, novellas, and short stories, she is a bestseller at both Amazon and Barnes & Noble. With her husband and son, she makes her home in a small town and supposedly works out of her tiny office, though she mostly writes in her easy chair in the living room.

For more information, visit Heather's website at www.heather hiestand.com. Heather loves to hear from readers! Her email is heather@heatherhiestand.com.

Don't miss the rest of the Redcakes series, already available where eBooks are sold!

The Marquess of Cake
One Taste of Scandal
His Wicked Smile
The Kidnapped Bride (novella)

Some cravings
must be indulged...

The Marquess of Cake

THE REDCAKES

HEATHER HIESTAND

His craving could be her undoing…

One Taste of Scandal

THE REDCAKES

HEATHER HIESTAND

First comes seduction...

His Wicked Smile

THE REDCAKES

HEATHER HIESTAND

Desire is a
most delicious
pursuit...

The Kidnapped Bride

THE REDCAKES

HEATHER HIESTAND